HELL FOR
BREAKFAST

HELL FOR BREAKFAST

A SLASH AND PECOS WESTERN

WILLIAM W. JOHNSTONE

AND J.A. JOHNSTONE

P

PINNACLE BOOKS
Kensington Publishing Corp.
www.kensingtonbooks.com

PINNACLE BOOKS are published by

Kensington Publishing Corp.
119 West 40th Street
New York, NY 10018

All Kensington titles, imprints, and distributed lines are available at special quantity discounts for bulk purchases for sales promotion, premiums, fund-raising, educational, or institutional use.

Special book excerpts or customized printings can also be created to fit specific needs. For details, write or phone the office of the Kensington Sales Manager: Attn.: Sales Department. Kensington Publishing Corp., 119 West 40th Street, New York, NY 10018. Phone: 1-800-221-2647.

First Kensington Books Hardcover Printing: August 2021
First Pinnacle Books Mass-Market Paperback Printing: November 2021
ISBN-13: 978-0-7860-4382-8
ISBN-13: 978-0-7860-4383-5 (eBook)

10 9 8 7 6 5 4 3 2 1

Printed in the United States of America

Chapter 1

Danny O'Neil wasn't sure what made him turn back around to face the depot platform. An unshakable premonition of sudden violence?

He'd never felt any such thing before. The sudden stiffening of his shoulders made him turn around and, holding the mail for the post office in the canvas sack over his right shoulder, he cast his gaze back at the train that had thundered in from Ogallala only a few minutes ago.

As he did, a tall man with a saddle on one shoulder and saddlebags draped over his other shoulder, and with a glistening Henry rifle in his right hand, stepped down off the rear platform of one of the combination's two passenger coaches. He was obscured by steam and coal smoke wafting back from the locomotive panting on the tracks ahead of the tender car. Still, squinting, Danny could see another man, and then one more man, similarly burdened with saddle, saddlebags, and rifle, step down from the passenger coach behind the first man.

The three men stood talking among themselves, in the snakes of steam mixed with the fetid coal smoke, until one of them, a tall strawberry-blond man with a red-blond mustache, set his saddle down at his feet, then scratched a match to life on the heel of his silver-tipped boot. The blond man, wearing a red shirt and leather pants, lifted the flame to the slender cheroot dangling from one corner of his wide mouth.

As he did, his gaze half met Danny's, flicked away, then returned to Danny, and held.

He stood holding the flaming match a few inches from the cheroot, staring back at the twelve-year-old boy through the haze of steam and smoke billowing around him. The man had a strange face. There was something not quite human about it. It was like a snake's face. Or maybe the face of a snake if that snake was half human. Or the face of a man if he was half snake.

Danny knew those thoughts were preposterous. Still, they flitted through his mind while his guts curled in on themselves and a cold dread oozed up his back from the base of his spine.

Still holding the match, the blond man stared back at Danny. A breeze blew the match out. Still, he stood holding the smoking match until a slit-eyed smile slowly took shape on his face. It wasn't really a smile. At least, there was nothing warm or amused about the expression. The man dropped the dead match he'd been holding, then slowly extended his index finger and raised his thumb like a gun hammer, extending the "gun" straight out from his shoulder and canting his head slightly toward his arm, narrowing those devilish eyes as though aiming down the barrel of the gun at Danny.

Danny felt a cold spot on his forehead, where the man was drawing an imaginary bead on him.

The man mouthed the word "bang," and jerked the gun's barrel up.

He lowered the gun, smiling.

Danny's heart thumped in his chest. Then it raced. His feet turned cold in his boots as he wheeled and hurried off the train platform and on to the town of Harveyville's main street, which was Patterson Avenue. He swung right to head north along the broad avenue's east side. He'd been told by the postmaster, Mr. Wilkes, to "not lollygag or moon about" with the mail but to hustle it back to the post office pronto, so Wilkes could get it sorted and into the right cubbyholes before lunch.

Mr. Wilkes always had a big beer with an egg in it for lunch, right at high noon, and he became surly when something or someone made him late for it. Maybe he was surly about the lunch, or maybe he was surly about being late for the girl he always took upstairs at the Wildcat Saloon after he'd finished his beer. Danny wasn't supposed to know such things about Mr. Wilkes or anyone else, of course. But Danny was a curious and observant boy. A boy who had extra time on his hands, and a boy who made use of it. There was a lot a fella could see through gauzy window curtains or through cracks in the brick walls of the Wildcat Saloon.

Wilkes might be late for his lunch and his girl today; however, it wouldn't be Danny's fault. His grandfather, Kentucky O'Neil, knowing Danny spent a lot of time at the train station even when he wasn't fetching the mail for Mr. Wilkes, had told Danny to let him know if he ever saw any "suspicious characters" get off the train here in Harveyville. There was something about the infrequent trains and the rails that always seemed to be stretching in from some exotic place far from Harveyville, only to stretch off again to another exotic place in the opposite direction—that Danny found endlessly romantic and fascinating.

Someday, he might climb aboard one of those trains and find out just where those rails led. He'd never been anywhere but here.

For the time being, he had to see Gramps, for Danny couldn't imagine any more suspicious characters than the ones he'd just seen step off the train here in dusty and boring old Harveyville. They had to be trouble. They sure *looked* like trouble!

As Danny strode along the boardwalk, he kept his intense, all-business gaze locked straight ahead, pinned to the little mud-brick marshal's office crouched between a leather goods store and a small café roughly one block ahead.

"Mornin', Danny," a voice on his right called out to the boy. Not halting his stride one iota, Danny only said, "Mornin'," as he continued walking.

"Hey, Danny," Melvin Dunham said as he swept the step fronting his barbershop. "You want to make a quick dime? I need to get Pearl's lunch over to her—"

"Not now, Mr. Dunham," Danny said, making a beeline past the man, whom he did not even glance at, keeping his eyes grave and proud with purpose beneath the brim of his brown felt hat.

"Hello there, handsome," said another voice, this one a female voice, as Danny strode passed Madam Delacroix's pink-and-purple hurdy-gurdy house. "Say, you're gettin' taller every day. Look at those shoulders. Carryin' that mailbag is givin' you muscles!"

Danny smelled sweet perfume mixed with peppery Mexican tobacco smoke.

"Mornin', Miss Wynona," Danny said, glimpsing the scantily clad young woman lounging on a boardwalk chair to his right, trying not to blush.

"Where you off to in such a rush . . . hey, Danny!" the girl called, but Danny was long past her now, and her last words were muffled by the thuds of his boots on the boardwalk and the clatter of ranch wagons passing on the street to his left.

Danny swung toward the door of his grandfather's office. Not bothering to knock—the door wasn't latched, anyway—he pushed the door open just as the leather goods man, George Henshaw, delivered the punchline to a joke he was telling Danny's grandfather, Town Marshal Kentucky O'Neil: "She screamed, 'My husband's home! My husband's home!'"

Mr. Henshaw swiped one hand across the palm of his other hand and bellowed, "The way Melvin told it, the reverend skinned out that window faster'n a coon with a coyote chewin' its tail, an' avoided a full load of buckshot by *that* much!"

Gramps and Mr. Henshaw leaned forward to convulse with red-faced laughter. When Gramps saw Danny, he tried to compose himself, quickly dropping his boots down from his desk and making his chair squawk. Looking a little guilty, his leathery face still sunset red around his snow-white soup-strainer mustache, he indicated Danny with a jerk of his hand, glanced at the floor, cleared his throat, brushed a fist across his nose, and said a little too loudly, "Oh, hello there, young man. Look there, George—

it's my favorite grandson. What you got goin' this fine Nebraska mornin', Danny?"

Mr. Henshaw turned to Danny, tears of humor still shining in his eyes. "You haven't let them girls over to Madam Delacroix's lure you into their cribs yet, have you, Danny boy?" He was still laughing a little from the story he'd been telling, his thick shoulders jerking.

"No, no, no," Gramps said. "He just cuts wood for Madam Delacroix, is all. His mother don't know about that, but what Nancy don't know won't hurt her—right, Danny?"

Gramps winked at the boy.

"Sure, sure," Mr. Henshaw said, dabbing at his eyes with a red cambric hanky. "First they got him cuttin' wood and then he's—"

"So, Danny-boy—what's up?" Gramps broke in quickly, leaning forward, elbows resting on his bony knees. He chuckled once more, the image of the preacher skinning out that window apparently still flashing in his mind.

Danny took three long strides into the office and stopped in front of his grandfather's desk. He drew a breath, trying to slow his racing heart. "You told me to tell you if I seen any suspicious characters get off the train. Well, believe-you-me when I tell you I just seen three of the gnarliest lookin' curly wolves you'll ever wanna meet get off the train not ten minutes ago, Gramps!"

Gramps arched his brows that were the same snowy shade as his mustache. "You don't say!"

He cut a glance at Mr. Henshaw, who smiled a little and said, "Well, I'll leave you two *lawmen* to confer in private about these *curly wolves.* I best get back over to my shop before Irma cuts out my coffee breaks altogether." Judging by the flat brown bottle on Gramps's desk, near his stone coffee mug, the two men had been enjoying a little more than coffee. "All right—see ya, George," Gramps said before returning his gaze to Danny and lacing his hands together between his knees. "Now, suppose you tell me what these *curly wolves* look like and why you think they're trouble."

"One's a tall blond fella, almost red-headed, with crazy-lookin' eyes carryin' one fancy-ass . . . er, I mean . . . a real *nice-lookin'* Henry rifle."

George Henshaw had just started to pull the office door closed behind him when he stopped and frowned back through the opening at Marshal Kentucky O'Neil. O'Neil returned the man's vaguely incredulous gaze then, frowning now with interest at his grandson. Not nearly as much of the customary adult patronization in his eyes as before, he said, "What'd the other two look like?"

"One was nearly as tall as the blond guy with the Henry. He was dark-haired with a dark mustache—one o' them that drop straight down both corners of his mouth. He wore a dark suit with a cream duster over it. The blond fella must fancy himself a greaser . . . you know—a bean-eater or some such?" Danny gave a caustic chuckle, feeling adult enough suddenly to use the parlance used in reference to people of Hispanic heritage he often overheard at Madam Delacroix's. "He sure was dressed like one—a red shirt with fancy stitching and brown leather pants with conchos down the sides. Silver-tipped boots. Yessir, he sure fancies himself a chili-chomper, all right!"

"And the third fella?" the lawman prodded the boy.

"He was short but thick. You know, like one o' them bareknuckle boxers that fight on Saturday nights out at Votts' barn? Cauliflower ears, both of 'em. He wore a suit and a wide red necktie. Had a fancy vest like a gambler."

"Full beard?" Henshaw asked, poking his head through the front door.

Danny turned to him, nodded, and brushed an index finger across his cheek. "He wore a coupla tiny little braids down in front of his ears. I never seen the like. Wore two pistols, too. All three wore two pistols in fancy rigs. *Tied down.* The holsters were waxed, just like Bob Wade waxes his holsters."

Bob Wade was a gunslinger who pulled through the country from time to time, usually when one of the local ranchers wanted a man—usually a rival stockman or a nester—killed. Kentucky never worried about Wade. Wade usually did his killing in the country. Kentucky's jurisdiction stopped at the town's limits unless he was pulling part-time duty as a deputy sheriff, which he had done from time to time in the past.

He should probably have notified the county sheriff about Wade, but the county seat was a long ways away and he had no proof that Bob Wade was up to no good. Aside from what everybody knew about Wade, that is. And maybe a long-outstanding warrant or two. Notifying the sheriff all the way in Ogallala and possibly getting the sheriff killed wouldn't be worth taking a bullet from an ambush himself, by one of the ranchers he'd piss-burned by tattling to the sheriff.

He was too damn close to retirement and a twenty-dollar-a-month pension for that kind of nonsense.

"The big fella wore a knife in his boot," Danny continued.

"How do you know that?" Gramps asked. His attention was fully on his grandson now. There was no lingering laughter in his eyes anymore from the story about Reverend Stillwell skinning out Mrs. Doolittle's window. The old laughter was all gone. Now Gramps leaned forward, riveted to every word out of Danny's mouth.

"'Cause I seen the handle stickin' up out of the boot well."

From the doorway, Henshaw said in a low voice, "The knife . . . did it have a . . ."

"One o' them fancy-carved ivory handles." Danny felt a smile raise his mouth corners and the warm blood of a blush rise in his cheeks. "In the curvy form of a naked woman."

He traced the curvy shape in the air with his hands, then dropped his hands to his sides, instantly wishing he hadn't gone that far. But neither of these men chastised him for his indiscretion. They were staring at each other. Neither said anything. Neither really had much of an expression on his face except . . .

Well, they looked scared.

Chapter 2

When Kentucky had ushered his grandson out of his office, assuring the boy that, yes, he would vouch for him to Postmaster Wilkes, about why he was late, O'Neil walked up to one of the only two windows in the small building, the one between his desk and the gun rack holding a couple of repeating rifles.

He slid the flour sack curtain back and peered along the street to his left, in the direction of the train station.

George Henshaw walked up beside him, nervously smoothing his green apron over his considerable paunch with his large, red hands. Henshaw was bald and gray-bearded, with a big walrus mustache even more ostentatious than the marshal's soup-strainer. He also wore round, steel-framed spectacles, which winked now in the light angling through the dust-streaked window.

"You think it's them, Kentucky?" Henshaw asked, keeping his voice low though the boy was gone and none of the four jail cells lined up against the building's rear wall held a prisoner. He and Kentucky were alone in the room.

"Hell, yes, I think it's them," the lawman said, gazing

through the dust kicked up by several ranch supply wagons heading toward the train depot. "Don't you?"

"I don't know. I guess . . . I was hoping . . ."

"We knew they'd be back. Someday. We knew it very well."

"Yes, I suppose, but what are we . . . ?"

Henshaw let his voice trail off when he saw his old friend Kentucky narrow his eyes as he continued to gaze toward the depot. The man's leathery red cheeks turned darker from a sudden rush of blood. Henshaw thought he could feel an increase in the heat coming off the pot-bellied lawman's bandy-legged body.

"What is it?" Henshaw said, his heart quickening. He stepped around behind O'Neil and gazed out over the man's left shoulder through the window and down the street to the south.

Kentucky didn't respond. His gaze was riveted on the three men just then stepping off the depot platform and into the street. They were carrying saddles, saddlebags, and rifles. Sure enough—two tall, lean men and one short, stocky one. Not just stocky. Laden with muscle that threatened to split the seams of Kinch Wheeler's checked, brown wool coat. Sure enough, he had a knife poking up from his lace-up boot with fancy deer-hide gaiters. He'd always been a natty dresser. Wheeler must have walked straight out of the prison gates and over to the nearest tailor's shop. Turning big rocks into small rocks for twelve years had added to Wheeler's considerable girth.

Henshaw slid his gaze to the blond man in the Mexican-style red shirt and flared leather pants down the outside legs of which silver conchos glinted. He lowered his hand from his face, wincing as his guts writhed around in his belly with cold, dark dread.

"Christ," Henshaw said over Kentucky's shoulder. "Those twelve years really screamed past."

"They sure did."

"What do you think they came back for?"

O'Neil gave a caustic snort. Henshaw knew what they were doing back in Harveyville as well as Kentucky himself did.

Henshaw nodded slowly in bleak understanding.

O'Neil turned away from the window, retrieved his Smith & Wesson New Model Number 3 from the blotter atop his desk, and returned to the window. Again, he peered out, tracking the three as they slowly moved up the street toward the office. "Oh, Christ," he said, hating the bald fear he heard in his voice. "They're coming here."

"They are?" Henshaw jerked his head back toward the window and drew a sharp breath.

"Of course they are!"

The three men moved up the middle of the street as though they owned the town. Horseback riders and wagons had to swerve wide around them. One horsebacker rode toward them with his head down as though checking a supply list. He raised his head suddenly, saw the three men heading right toward him, and jerked his horse sharply to the left. He turned his horse broadside and yelled angrily at the three men as they passed. The horsebacker's face was creased with exasperation.

While Kentucky hadn't heard the words, he'd heard the anger in the man's tone.

"Easy, now, Ed," he muttered to the man—Ed Simms from the Crosshatch Ranch out on Porcupine Creek. Noreen must have sent him to town to fill the larder. "Just keep movin', Ed. Just keep movin'"

Ed hadn't been in the country twelve years ago, so he

didn't know about the Old Trouble. Hell, a good two-thirds of the people in Harveyville and on the ranches surrounding it hadn't been in the country back then. They wouldn't know about it, either.

But Kentucky knew. He knew all too well. He knew well enough that beads of sweat were rolling down his cheeks and into his white mustache and his knees felt like warm mud.

He was going to die today, he thought as he watched them come. They formed a wedge of sorts, the tall, blond Calico out front, leading the way, like the prow of a ship cleaving the waters with supreme, sublime arrogance. O'Neil didn't know why Calico's return had taken him by such surprise. He'd known this day had been coming for the past ten years.

Hadn't he? Or, like Henshaw, had he lied to himself, telling himself that, no, in spite of what had happened, in spite of O'Neil himself organizing a small posse and taking Calico's trio into custody while they'd been dead drunk in a parlor house—and in spite of what they'd left in the ground nearby when they'd been hauled off to federal court in Denver—they wouldn't return to Harveyville.

Well, they had as, deep down, Kentucky knew they would. The three men, as mismatched a three as Kentucky had ever seen—the tall, blond, dead-eyed Calico flanked by the thick-set punisher, Wheeler, and the dark-haired and mustached Chase Stockton, who'd once been known as "the West Texas Hellion"—kept coming. As they did, Kentucky looked down at the big, heavy pistol in his hands.

He broke it open and filled the chamber he usually kept empty beneath the hammer. When he clicked the Russian closed and looked up again, the three outlaws had veered left and were heading toward the opposite side of the street from the marshal's office.

"Look at that," Henshaw said softly, under his breath. "They're going into the Copper Nickel! You got a reprieve, Kentucky. They're gonna wet their whistles before they come over here and kill you!" He chuckled and hurried to the door. "With that, I bid you adieu!" He stopped at the door and turned back to his old friend, saying with an ominous wince, "Good luck!"

Kentucky raked a thumbnail down his cheek. "Why in the hell are they . . ." The light of understanding shimmered in his eyes. Then his eyes turned dark, remembering. "Oh, no."

Norman Rivers set a bottle of the good stuff on a high shelf behind the bar in the Copper Nickel Saloon. He had to rise up on the toes of his brogans to do so, stretching his arm high and peeling his lips back from his teeth with the effort. As he did, his sixteen-year-old daughter, Mary Kate, ripped out a sudden shriek from where she swept the stairs running up the room's north wall, on Rivers's right.

Rivers jerked with a start, inadvertently dislodging the bottle of the good stuff from the shelf. It tumbled toward him, bashing him in the temple before he managed to grab it and hold it against his chest, or it would have shattered on the floor at his feet—four-and-a-half dollars gone, just like that!

"Gallblastit, Mary Kate—look what you did!" Rivers scolded, turning toward the girl as he held a hand against his throbbing temple. "What's got into you, anyway?"

"That damn rat is back! Scared me!"

"Hold your tongue, damn you! You almost made me break a bottle of the mayor's good stuff!"

"Why do you put it up so high, anyway?" the girl shot back at him from halfway up the stairs. She was a pretty girl, really filling out her simple day frocks nicely, and she knew it and was too often high-headed about it. Her beauty gave her a confidence she otherwise did not deserve. She was sweeping barefoot when if Rivers had told her once, he'd told her a thousand times not to come down here without shoes on.

She didn't used to be this disobedient or mouthy. It had something to do with her mother dying two years ago, and her body filling out.

Rivers held the bottle up, pointing it like a pistol at the insolent child. "I have to put it up so high so you don't mistake it for a bottle of the rotgut and serve it to the raggedy-assed saddle tramps and no-account drifters who stop by here to flirt with you because they know you'll flirt back!"

Color lifted into Mary Kate's ivory cheeks, and she felt her pretty mouth shape a prideful half grin. She shook a lock of her curly blond hair back from her cheek and resumed sweeping the steps. "I can't help it if they think I'm pretty."

"I can't help it if they think I'm purty!" Rivers mocked the girl. "He pointed the bottle at her again and barked, "You shouldn't be makin' time with such trash. You oughta at least *try* to act like a lady!"

"You mean like the high-and-mighty Carolyn?" Mary Kate said in a scornful singsong as she angrily swept the broom back and forth across the step beneath her, kicking up a roiling cloud of dust. "Look what it got her!"

"Married to a good man!"

The banker's son, no less.

"Hah!" Mary Kate laughed caustically. "Everbody knows prissy Richard leaves her alone at home every night, to tend those three screaming brats, while he—"

"That's enough, Mary Kate! I told you I never wanted to hear those nasty rumors again. And what did I just tell you? *Get some shoes on!*"

Mary Kate stopped at the second step up from the bottom, thrusting the broom back and forth across the first one and shaking her head slowly, hardening her jaws. "Boy, when I'm old enough and have made enough money to flee this backwater cesspool, I'm gonna—"

She looked up when boots thumped on the stoop fronting the Copper Nickel and three men filed into the saloon—two tall men, one blond and quite colorful in his Spanish-style dress. Mary Kate's father, Rivers, had just seen the trio in the backbar mirror and jerked with such a start that the bottle he'd nearly placed, finally, on the high shelf, tilted forward, slammed into his head—the opposite temple from before—and shattered on the floor at his feet.

Mary Kate looked at her father, who held his head, cursing. Then she turned to the tall, red-blond drink of water standing just inside the batwings. The blond man grinned and winked at her.

Mary Kate brought a hand to her mouth and laughed.

Rivers glared at her, then turned his head slowly to regard the three newcomers. He felt a tightness in his chest, as though someone had punched a fist through his ribs and was squeezing all the blood out of his heart. All three men had their heads turned toward Mary Kate. The blond man was smiling at her. She was smiling back at him, still covering her mouth with her hand.

Rivers did not like the expression on the blond man's

face. Nor on Mary Kate's. At the moment, however, he felt powerless to speak, let alone do anything to break the trance the blond man—Ned Calico?!—seemed to be holding his daughter in.

Finally, the shortest of the three, but also the heaviest and all of that weight appearing to be muscle, which the man's gaudy checked brown suit could barely contain, removed his bowler hat from his head and tossed it onto a table. "I don't know about you fellas," he said in a heavy Scottish accent, "but this feller could use somethin' to cut the trail dust!"

He kicked out a chair and glanced at Rivers, who still held a hand to his freshly injured temple. "Barkeep, we'll take a bottle of the good stuff."

That made Mary Kate snicker through her nose.

The tall, blond man in the Spanish-style duds broadened his smile, slitting his flat blue eyes and curling his upper lip, revealing a chipped, crooked front tooth that took nothing away from his gambler-like handsomeness. He switched his gaze to Rivers and said, "What's the matter, apron? Did you hear my friend here? A bottle of the good stuff!"

He stepped forward and kicked out a chair from the table the big man—what was his name? Wheeler? Yeah, that was it. Kinch Wheeler. The third man was Stockton, a laconic, cold-blooded, gimlet-eyed, dark-haired Texan. Rivers hadn't thought of them, he suddenly realized, in a good many years. But for several years after "the Old Trouble," as everyone in town back then had called it, he hadn't been able to get their names . . . as well as their faces . . . out of his head. For years, he'd slept with a loaded shotgun under his bed. Now, just when he'd forgotten them—or hadn't been remembering them, anyway, and having nightmares about them, and when his shotgun was clear over at the other end of the bar—here they were.

One of them, Ned Calico, making eyes at his daughter the same way he'd made eyes at another girl so long ago . . .

And there wasn't a damn thing Rivers could do about it.

"The good stuff—pronto!" barked Stockton, as he stepped up to the table and plopped his crisp black bowler down beside Ned Calico's and Kinch Wheeler's. He scowled across the room at Rivers. His face was broad, dark, and savage, his hair long and oily. Time had passed. Twelve years. There was some gray in the Texan's hair, and his face, just like the faces of the other two men, wore the dissolution of age and prison time. But here they were, looking really no worse for the wear.

For the prison wear.

And now, sure as rats around a privy, all hell was about to break loose.

"That man there," said Ned Calico, leaning against his elbow and pointing an accusing finger at the barman, "is either deaf as a post or dumber'n a boot!"

"I got it, I got it," Mary Kate said, walking toward the bar with her broom and scowling bewilderedly at her father, who was just staring in slack-jawed shock at his customers.

"No," Rivers said, finally finding his tongue. "No, I, uh . . . I got it."

Mary Kate stopped near the bar, scowling at him, baffled by his demeanor.

"No," said Ned Calico. "Let her do it." He looked at Mary Kate again and smiled his devil's smile. "I like her. She's got a way about her, I can tell. Besides that, she's barefoot an' she's pretty."

Mary Kate blushed. She turned to the bar, casting her

father a mocking, insouciant smile, and stretched her open hand across the mahogany. "You heard the gentlemen, Pa. A bottle of the good stuff."

Rivers stared at the three spectre-like men lounging in their chairs, smiling at him coldly, savagely, three wolves glowering through the wavering, murky mists of time.

"Mister Rivers, I remember you," Ned Calico said, throwing his head back and laughing. "Did you miss us, you old devil? Wasn't you one o' the townsmen that old lawman roped into helpin' him take us down when we was drunk as Irish gandy dancers on a Saturday night in Wichita? Why, sure it was!"

He laughed and shook his head, though his eyes had now grown cold with admonishing.

"I hope you got a few more bottles of the good stuff 'cause we're gonna be here awhile and it's gonna be a party!"

He looked at Mary Kate. He looked her over really well and blinked those devil's eyes slowly. Again, the girl flushed.

Calico returned his gaze to the barman and said, "Don't that make you happy?"

The three wolves watched Rivers's pale jowls mottle red, and laughed.

Chapter 3

"Come on, Slash—wake up. We're gonna be late to the church. It's your weddin' day!"

"Leave me alone, damn you, Pecos."

"Slash, dammit, haul your ass out of bed!"

"Go 'way—I'm still sleepin'."

"Come on, Slash! You're about to git hitched!"

The words were a cold bucket of water dumped over Jimmy "Slash" Braddock's head. They were a giant, rock-hard fist to his mouth. Instantly wide-awake, Slash found himself sitting up in bed, his stag-gripped Colt .44 in his right hand, the barrel snugged up taut against the underside of Melvin Baker's, aka the "Pecos River Kid's," whiskered chin.

"What the hell did you just say?" Slash raked out through gritted teeth.

Sitting on the edge of Slash's bed in the shared living quarters of their freighting business in Fort Collins, Colorado, the Pecos Kid stared into his partner and former cutthroat's dark brown eyes, and grinned. Very softly, gently, knowing that Slash was coiled up tighter than a diamondback about to strike even in his best moods, but most of all when he was awakened from a dead sleep with the news that he was about to be married . . . and that the hammer of his .44 was ratcheted back to full cock, Pecos said, "Say, now . . . say, now . . . it's all right, Slash. You're gonna hitch your star to the wagon of one Jaycee Breckenridge, the purtiest woman in the Rocky Mountains if not the whole Western frontier. Easy, now . . . easy . . . it ain't so bad. Everything's gonna be all right, Slash. It's *Jay-cee*."

He was glad to see the light of understanding wash into Slash's hard-eyed gaze. It was followed quickly by a flush of embarrassment in Slash's somewhat severely carved, deeply tanned, handsome face. He was even gladder to hear the benign click of Slash easing the hammer of his Colt down against the cylinder, and to see him lower the pistol to the bed beside him.

"Oh my," Slash said, raking a hand down his face. "Oh my, oh my, oh my." He looked up again at Pecos with a slightly confused furl of his dark brown brows that were touched very lightly with the gray of his fifty-some-odd years. "I'm, uh . . . I'm gettin' hitched today. I'm gettin' m-married."

It was sort of a statement and a question rolled up into one.

"Why, sure ya are." Pecos kept his voice calm and gentle, though he could still feel the cold indentation where Slash had ground the barrel of his pistol into his chin. He felt as though he were trying to comfort a half-wild dog, one who might leap on him at any second or suddenly wheel and run away, howling. "This is what you've wanted, Slash. Jaycee Breckenridge. Imagine that, you lucky old cuss! You're about to marry . . ."

"Okay, okay, okay," Slash said, tossing the single wool blanket back from his lean and still-hard body clad in wash-worn red longjohns. "You don't have to rub it in." He climbed to his feet, and Pecos sat on the cot, watching him stomp a little stiffly over to the washstand, pour water into the cracked porcelain bowl from the pitcher, and lower his face to the cold water, swishing it around while loudly blowing bubbles.

Slash kept his face in the water for nearly a minute. When he finally lifted his head and reached for a towel, Pecos rose with the two cups of steaming black coffee he had in his hands, walked over, and offered one to Slash. "Here ya go. Have you a few swallows of that. It'll clear the fog."

Slash glanced at him skeptically. "Any panther juice in it?"

Pecos grinned. "What do you think?"

"All right," Slash said, and took the cup.

He blew on the black surface then took a couple of quick, thirsty sips before staring through the steam rising from the rim at his partner, who stood four inches taller than Slash's even six feet. While Slash was dark-haired and dark-eyed, and lean but stocky, Pecos was tall and long-limbed, with long, gray-blond hair, a gray-blond mustache and goatee, and soft, pale-blue eyes. Those eyes always seemed to betray the tenderness inside the man, even when he was gambling and trying to maintain a poker face, or when he was angry about something, which didn't happen all that often.

Pecos was hard to rile.

Slash, on the other hand, could climb a hump at the drop of a hat.

"It's really happening, isn't it?" he asked Pecos.

"It's really happening, pard." Pecos sipped from his own cup. "Don't worry about it. You made the right decision.

You've been head over heels in love with Jaycee for years now. Hell, you were in love with her even back when Pete was still alive."

Pistol Pete Johnson had been one of the founding members, along with Slash and Pecos, of their former bank- and train-robbing gang, the Snake River Marauders. Pistol Pete and Jay hadn't been married. Not in the legal sense of the word, anyway. They'd been married in every other way for nearly ten years, living together between holdups in a small cabin hidden deep in southern Colorado's San Juan Mountains before Pete had been killed by a posse's bullet roughly six years ago now.

It was true that Slash had tumbled for Jaycee long ago. Maybe even back when Pete had first introduced her to him and Pecos and the rest of the gang, almost twenty years ago. Of course, Slash had never announced his feelings until recently. That was the thing about Slash. He often didn't know what he was feeling at any given time— if it wasn't anger, that was. Expressing those feelings— aside from anger, of course—was not easy for him. In fact, it was damn near impossible.

That's why his marrying Jay had been so long in coming, and he'd hemmed and hawed for so long over finally asking for her hand—scared to death of committing himself to someone for the rest of his life. Maybe even more scared of *loving* someone, even a woman as kind and warm and beautiful as Jay, because when you loved someone you were as vulnerable as a deer in the sights of a Sharps Big Fifty buffalo rifle. It wasn't easy for Slash to feel vulnerable.

He'd been an outlaw too long. He'd been hunted for too long. Leaving himself vulnerable meant the possibility of taking a bullet or of serving a long stretch in a federal pen. Or, worse, of getting his heart broken and feeling miserable.

Pecos, on the other hand, wore his heart on his sleeve. He'd been in and out of love so many times, he'd forgotten all their names. That's why it was ironic that of the two of them, the laconic and temperamental Slash was the one who was finally walking down the aisle this day.

At least, Pecos hoped he was. Pecos wouldn't rest easy, sure that Slash wasn't going to cut and run, until Pecos had carted him over to the church and made sure he'd slipped his mother's wedding ring on Jaycee's finger. Pecos wouldn't relax until he'd held Slash's trembling hand—hell, held his whole trembling body down against the floor, if he had to!—while Jay slipped her ring on his finger. Only then would he breathe easier, secure in his knowledge that his old partner, who was really more like a very close brother to him than a friend, was safely in the arms of the woman he needed as much or more than Jaycee needed him.

They needed each other. And neither was getting any younger.

"Yeah, I reckon I have been in, uh . . ."

"Love with her."

"Right."

"Go ahead," Pecos prodded him. "You can say it. It ain't gonna kill you, Slash. It's just a word."

Slash took another couple of sips of his whiskey-laced coffee. "I, uh . . . I love her." He took another, deeper sip from his cup.

"See?" Pecos said, gently patting his old friend's shoulder. "You said it and you're still kickin'." He chuckled as he turned to the door of their bedroom, which opened onto the living area and kitchen area of their crude wood-frame cabin. "Come on out here, now. I whipped us up a big breakfast. We gotta stuff it down quick, though, 'cause we only have us an hour. Hell, I think Jay and Mira already done headed over to the church."

Mira was the pretty young woman whom Slash and Pecos had rescued from a life of crime similar to the one they themselves had led. Mira worked here at their Front Range Freighting Company. Hell, she not only worked here, she ran the place. The only thing she didn't do was haul the freight.

She did everything that supported the hauling of the freight, including securing and drawing up contracts, keeping the books, and supervising the wranglers and blacksmith who tended the mules and repaired the wagons. Not only that, but she kept house, cooked for Slash and Pecos and the hired hands, and generally held down the fort when they were out skinning mules on freight trails webbing the Front Range of the Rocky Mountains, which they did when they were not on some lawdog mission for Chief Marshal Luther T. "Bleed-'Em-So" Bledsoe.

The two former outlaws worked unofficially for the chief marshal stationed in Denver's Federal Building when Bledsoe needed a certain, usually "sensitive" job done off the federal books by a couple of unofficial deputy U.S. marshals. The unofficial status covered the old federal's behind. If things didn't go according to plan, and Slash and Pecos got caught doing something illegally sanctioned by him in his unofficial capacity, or they were killed, he could play dumb about having hired them.

In other words, they usually took the jobs Bledsoe didn't want anyone to know about, which meant they were usually of a particularly dangerous or legally murky quality. Old Bleed-'Em-So had signed them on for such nefarious and usually highly dangerous doings in exchange for granting them both clemency for their criminal pasts and for keeping them from stretching hemp in the main yard at the federal pen. He'd chosen them because they themselves had been particularly cunning and slippery.

Who better to send after particularly cunning and slippery outlaws than a pair of particularly cunning and slippery outlaws?

Bleed-'Em-So had gotten them both in some tight situations over the past couple of years. Some so tight they'd often thought they'd have been better off dancing the midair twostep wearing a hemp necktie. Still, in exchange for their freedom, they remained on unofficial retainer to the old devil, who they knew was partly exacting slow revenge on them for their having eluded him for years. And, of course, because it had been one of Slash's bullets, albeit an inadvertent one, that had pierced Bledsoe's spine and confined him to a pushchair.

"I'll be right behind you," Slash told Pecos as he stepped into a pair of ragged denim trousers. He pulled on a wool shirt but didn't button it. He ran fingers through his longish, salt-and-pepper hair, which he wore down over his ears and collar, then shoved one of his Colts down behind the waistband of his trousers. Having been a target for as many years as Slash had been, he didn't go anywhere—not even out to the kitchen—without at least one loaded gun on his person. His credo had always been that unexpected things *always* happened when you were least prepared for them.

Slash Braddock might have been many things—including scared right down to his boots about what was about to happen to him later this morning—but being unprepared was not one of those things.

He strode stocking-footed out to the kitchen, where

Pecos was just then piling hotcakes onto a platter on Slash's side of their eating table. Slash stopped beside a ceiling support post from which tack and a hurricane lantern hung and watched his partner pile a big helping of fried potatoes and onions onto the platter, as well. The potatoes and onions were nicely browned; Slash could smell the butter wafting up with the charred smell of the cooked potatoes and the onions.

He watched Pecos lay six long, thick slabs of bacon over the potatoes and then add a couple big spoonfuls of scrambled eggs beside the potatoes and the bacon. Finally, Pecos poured from a small tin kettle he'd heated on the stove a thick, smoking, dark brown pool of maple syrup over the pancakes onto which two big dollops of butter were melting.

Under normal circumstances, Slash would have fairly flung himself into his chair, rolled up his sleeves, took up fork and knife, and buried his snout until the trough was empty. But these weren't normal circumstances.

He was about to go to church.

To be married.

"Good Lord—what's the matter?" Pecos asked, glancing at his partner over his shoulder.

Slowly, he straightened from the table and turned around to face Slash, frowning in dark fascination. "I'll be hanged if you don't look about as white as I ever seen a man look. Why, you're as white as a fresh-laundered sheet. You're whiter'n a Canadian after a long northern winter!"

Slash gulped, swallowed. Wheeling, covering his mouth with his forearm, he ran to the shack's back door, making choking and strangling sounds. "Go ahead and eat, Pecos— I'll be right back!"

Chapter 4

"You sure he's all right?" Isaiah Hawkins asked Pecos. "I never seen a man that white. Not even a white man as white as Slash."

Isaiah himself was Black. A big, beefy blacksmith. He rode in the back of the buckboard wagon with the two hostlers, Kelsey Shimmer and his cousin Harley Shimmer. Both Shimmers were tall and lean and in their twenties—uncommonly shy, sly, and quiet men good with mules.

Isaiah held a big fistful of yellow and lavender wildflowers as he rode with his back against the buckboard's side panel, the elbow of that fist resting on the top of the panel. He wore his usual work shirt and bib-front blue overalls but with a too-tight, black, age-coppered coat that made him fit for a wedding. He scrutinized Slash carefully, up where the soon-to-be-hitched cutthroat rode beside Pecos, who was driving.

Pecos glanced at Slash. "He's all right. Just a little off his feed is all." He elbowed Slash then glanced, grinning, at the three men riding behind him. "You just wait till tonight. After he's done moved into Jaycee's fancy digs at the Thousand Delights . . . and she turns the lamps down low . . . and lets all that copper-red hair flow down over her shoulders."

He glanced at Slash again, and winked. "He'll be back on his feed again in no time."

Jaycee was owner of the Thousand Delights Saloon and Gambling Parlor, the nattiest such institution in Colorado's northern Front Range. Jaycee's food, liquor, gambling, and girls attracted money-eyed men not only from Denver but from as far away as Kansas City and St. Louis, as well. She'd used the stake that Pistol Pete had left her to buy the place after Slash and Pecos had bought the freighting business in Fort Collins. They were all friends. Close friends, they chose to live close. Over the past couple of years, Slash and Jaycee had grown ever closer.

Thus, here Slash was with Pecos and big Isaiah and the Shimmer cousins, following the trail along the shimmering Poudre River on a golden summer morning, heading up Poudre Canyon to get hitched at the Cache de la Poudre Lutheran Church, which sat in a jade meadow in a horseshoe curve of the picturesque stream, ringed by tall pines and aspens.

Slash cast a cockeyed glance at Pecos and said, "Anybody ever tell you you talk too gall-blamed much?"

"Well, you." Pecos grinned and winked again at his owly partner. "All the time. But it's never stopped me, has it?"

When Slash only turned his head forward to stare over the bobbing head of the horse in the traces, Pecos reached into his suit coat, which he'd had tailored for the occasion, and produced a silver traveling flask. He nudged Slash's shoulder with the flask, flipped open the cap with his thumb. "Here. Take a shot. It'll put some color back in your cheeks."

Slash shook his head and scrubbed the back of his hand across his mouth. "Nah, I gotta do this sober. I owe her that much. Since she's doomed to put up with my wretched ass for the next ten, twenty years. I should at least marry her sober." He glanced at Pecos with one brow arched and a faint smile on his lips. "Don't you think so, pard?"

Pecos's smile broadened. "You know what I think, pard?"

"What's that?" Slash asked.

"I think I see some color returning to your cheeks. What's more, I think you two are going to have a very long and happy life together."

Slash's own smile broadened if only a bit, and then he turned his head forward again.

From back in the box, Kelsey Shimmer said, haltingly, "I, uh . . . I'd take a pull of that whiskey, Pecos . . ."

Returning the flask to his pocket, Pecos cast a look of mock castigation over his shoulder at the hawk-faced Shimmer cousin and said, "Now, Kelsey, what did I tell you boys about imbibin' during the day? Shame on you!" He glanced at Slash, winked, then pulled the flask out of his pocket and handed it back into the box. "Well, since it's a special occasion and all. But go easy on that stuff. I don't want you fellas noddin' off during the service!"

As they rounded a bend in the sunlit trail, Slash saw the white-painted church sitting off in a green, sun-washed clearing on the trail's south side. He was surprised by how many buggies, carriages, wagons, and saddle horses sat in the gravel lot in front of the church and even in the grass to the side of it and clear to the rear, near where tables and chairs had been set up for the picnic following the wedding.

On the other hand, he wasn't surprised. While his only

real friend here in Fort Collins was his old partner, Pecos, and Mira Thompson and the three men in the wagon behind him, of course, Jay knew practically everyone in town. It was always said that Jay never met a stranger, and it was as true here in her relatively new hometown as it had been anywhere else. Of course, one could say she mixed well for business reasons, to keep customers coming back to the Thousand Delights, but that would be a cynical point of view.

Slash held many cynical points of view, but none about Jay. The reason Jay had so many friends here and around Fort Collins was because she was genuinely warm and friendly, and people liked her instantly. It helped, of course, that even in her mid-forties, she was still a beautiful woman, with warm, amused jade eyes and all those delicious tresses of flowing red hair. Her body was still at once slender and voluptuous, and she had a hale and hearty way about her that just made people—women as well as men—naturally attracted to her.

Slash knew a thing or two about that himself. He could be a taciturn old coot at times. No, most times. But never around Jay. Her free spirit and ardent charm, and even her talkativeness infected even him. When he was around her, he felt like a whole different person than the mopey, cynical, scornful, and sarcastic lout he normally considered himself to be. Around her, he himself became warmer, more optimistic, and even at least a little more chatty than usual.

Thinking about their differences now, he wondered what she saw in him. What could he give her that could equal what she'd given him and would no doubt continue to give him in the years ahead—namely, a richer life? How could such a curmudgeon as himself make her life richer in return?

"Stop thinkin'," Pecos said as he drew the buckboard around behind the church, wending his way around hobbled or tied horses and parked wagons.

Slash glanced at him. "Huh?"

"Stop thinkin'." Pecos pulled the wagon to a stop before the church's back door. "You're gonna do just fine."

"Oh, I'll survive the service. That's not what I'm worried about."

"I know what you're worried about. You're worried that you don't deserve her."

"Yeah," Slash said, drawing a deep breath. "That's about the size of it."

"Well, you don't."

Slash whipped his shocked gaze back to his old friend. "What?"

"You don't deserve her, you crotchety old fool." Pecos climbed down from the driver's seat and walked around in front of the horse, beckoning to Slash. "But for some crazy damn reason, she's decided to marry you anyway. So let's get you on in there and say 'I do' before she wises up and changes her mind!"

Slash hardened his jaws. "Why, you . . ." He climbed down from the seat, and as Kelsey Shimmer climbed up to take the reins and park the wagon, Slash stepped up beside Pecos before swinging toward him sharply and burying his right fist in the taller man's belly.

"*Ouff!*" Pecos cried as the air exploded from his lungs. He dropped to one knee, his face turning as red as a Colorado sunset. "You black-hearted cuss! Whoever heard of the groom assaulting his best man before a wedding?"

"You just did. You got the ring?"

Groaning, Pecos touched his coat pocket. "Yeah, it's there."

"Slash!"

He whipped around to see Mira Thompson come flying out the church's back door, an angry scowl on her otherwise pretty, fine-boned face framed by a rich mass of brown curls.

"What?" Slash said, absently admiring the natty-looking bridesmaid's gown the comely girl wore. Just because he was marrying Jay didn't mean he couldn't still appreciate the wares of other women, did it? If so, he might as well call off the whole thing right now.

"What do you mean—*what?*" Mira stomped past Slash in her dainty, high-heeled shoes and crouched to help Pecos up from the ground. "I saw what you just did to Pecos!"

"He had it comin', darlin'—I swear!"

"He's your best man!"

"Believe me—I looked around but no one else would do it."

"Never mind him, honey," Pecos said, climbing heavily to his feet with Mira's assistance. "He's just all het up about tyin' the knot. He always takes to violence when he's nervous. We should warn Jaycee before it's too late!"

"Warn Jaycee about what?"

Again, Slash turned to the door. This time, a hot stone dropped in his belly. His lower jaw loosened and his knees turned to putty. Jaycee Breckenridge stood before him. It was either she or some red-headed angel sent from heaven in the cream silk-satin wedding dress that Jay had had tailored especially for today—all pleats and folds and curlicues of creamy white lace accentuating the curvaceousness of Jay's long-legged, slender-waisted, proud-bosomed figure. A misty cream veil obscured her cameo-pin face to beguiling effect, accentuating the rich reds of her hair curling across her shoulders, sausage curls jouncing against her pale, lightly freckled cheeks.

Jaycee looked from Slash to the red-faced Pecos then back to Slash. "You boys haven't been roughhousing out here, have you?"

Neither Slash nor Pecos seemed to be able to find their voices. They both gazed at the heavenly spectacle before them in slack-jawed silence. Mira looked from Slash to Pecos, then laughed and rushed forward, taking Jay's arms.

"Good Lord, Jay—don't you know it's bad luck for the groom to see his bride before the wedding?"

Jay cast her gaze back to Slash once more and, turning under Mira's guidance, said, "See you soon, Slash."

Then she and Mira were tucked safely back inside the church and Slash had to reach down and pick his jaw up off the ground. Or it felt that way, anyway.

Pecos stepped up beside him and offered the flask again. "Sure you don't want a bracer?"

"I don't want one, but I need one. Give me that!"

Slash popped the cap and took a hearty pull. He gave the flask back to Pecos. "Thanks."

"Don't mention it. Now, suppose you pull your horns in long enough for us to get you hitched? I can't wait to get you the hell out of my shack and over to Jaycee's suite of rooms at the Thousand Delights!"

"*Your* shack?" Slash said as they walked into the church together. "That's *our* shack. We went even-steven on it!"

"*My* shack now. I wonder how long it's gonna take me to get your stench aired out of it."

* * *

The next half hour passed in sort of a waking dream for Slash Braddock.

He felt mildly intoxicated though he couldn't be, for he'd taken only a single pull from Pecos's flask. In the waking dream, he entered the main worship area of the church through a side door, and, only half aware of the crowd filling the pews to his left, he, with Pecos by his side—oh, Lord, what would he do without his old former cutthroat pard at a time like this?—he stepped up to the rail separating the pulpit from the nave. The preacher waited at the pulpit wearing a tender if slightly skeptical smile as well as his flowing white robes, a long purple stole with gold tassels, a gold cross hanging down his chest. Slash stood there before the pulpit and beside Pecos, sweating and self-conscious—he'd never been the center of attention, aside from a posse's attention, in his entire life—for what seemed a good half hour but was probably only a couple of minutes.

A low roar of hushed conversation, occasional echoing foot thuds and scrapes, and shifting of bodies rose from the pews. Slash could smell the musky-cherry aroma of Jay's perfume mixing with the smell of pew varnish, hair tonic, sweat, chewing tobacco, and cigar smoke. He hoped like hell that all those aromas wafting toward him, along with the heat—the church was like a furnace!—didn't send him dashing to the outhouse again.

Suddenly, just before Slash thought he would have to cut and run to the privy and make a damn fool of himself, the organist in the choir loft began playing the "Bridal Chorus."

Pecos elbowed Slash, who turned to see Jaycee come walking slowly down the aisle, her arm hooked through that of the town mayor, Charlie Reagan. Mira Thompson walked behind her, smiling dreamily, flowers in her hair and in her gloved hands. Charlie had stuffed himself into a fashionable wool suit that could hardly contain his short, portly body. Slash couldn't help smiling at that. Of course, Jay would have the mayor lead her down the aisle. Jay had friends in all the right places.

What in hell did she see in the former cutthroat, Slash Braddock, anyway?

Hell, she could have had Charlie—if Charlie hadn't been married, that is—or any other of the twenty or so well-attired, moneyed men filling the pews, switching their vaguely incredulous, not so vaguely envious gazes from Jay to Slash and back again. There was the rancher Tom Early of the Double-Cross spread north of town. His wife had died two years ago. There was the newspaper publisher Norton Kinghorn—around Jay's age and also single as well as worth a small fortune, and educated, to boot. There was Tom Childress from Denver—a might old, but he'd never been married and his holdings in several gold mines up around Leadville had made him richer than some Eastern railroad magnates. Known as a cutthroat businessman, whenever he was around Jay, he glowed and preened like a schoolboy with a hard crush.

Some of those unmarried men, including the red-faced and gray-bearded Childress, sat with Jay's garishly appointed girls, who'd had their hair elaborately fixed and faces carefully painted. They wore outlandish, ostrich-plumed picture hats as they sat beaming lovingly and admiringly toward their madam walking slowly past them, waving and fluttering and cooing to each other like delighted little birds.

Slash's only three friends in the place—aside from Pecos, that is—sat in a far rear corner, snickering and passing a bottle. *Damn them—where in the hell had they found a bottle?*

Jay fairly floated down the central aisle of the nave, in all that satin and lace, her face beguilingly veiled. Her deep-red hair shone like molten gold in the sunlight angling through the tall stained-glass windows on either side of her. Slash watched her walk toward him.

No.

Yeah, she walked toward him. Not toward Kinghorn or Early or Childress or anyone else. She walked toward *him*—former train-robbing cutthroat, current unofficial troubleshooter for a lunatic lawman, and part-owner of a moderately lucrative freighting company.

Not only did she walk toward him, she stopped *before* him. Not six inches away from him, she smiled up at him through her veil. She took the flowers she was holding in one white-gloved hand. With her other hand, she swept the veil up away from her face, rose onto the toes of her little satin slippers, and planted a reassuring kiss on his cheek.

Her lips were full and warm. They shot bayonets of raw pleasure into Slash's middle-aged loins.

She slid her lips to his ear and said very softly and a little throatily, "I love you, you old cutthroat."

Mira smiled over her shoulder at Slash. The girl's upper lip fluttered with emotion, and she blinked tears of happiness from her eyes.

The next thing Slash knew, James and Jaycee Braddock were husband and wife and striding up the aisle arm in arm, in a rain of rice, to the hoots and catcalls of the well-wishers.

When Jay tossed her flowers, big Isaiah dropped his bottle, shattering it, and caught them.

Chapter 5

The next morning, Slash woke with a wail, sitting straight up in bed.

"Slash!" The familiar, sleep-husky woman's voice had come from his right. Familiar, yet . . . he couldn't quite place it. Nor his surroundings—a room far better appointed, *stylishly* appointed—than his and Pecos's rustic frame cabin crouched in the dusty freight yard. "Slash, honey—are you all right?"

He was vaguely aware of the rumble of rain and the sporadic claps of rolling thunder. Of the air spiced with the freshness of a western storm.

His heart was still thudding heavily.

A soft hand closed over his right arm and then she was sitting up beside him, with one hand holding the bedcovers over her bosoms, her red hair hanging in sleep-tangles across her shoulders and down her long, pale, freckled arms. Slash turned to Jaycee Breckenridge. No, Jaycee Braddock. Mrs. Slash Braddock. He blinked slowly, frowning, as his billiard balls settled into their rightful pockets, and he got himself oriented here in his new home, with his new gal.

His new wife.

"A dream, Slash?" she asked, sliding a lock of his salt-and-pepper hair back from his left eye. "Were you dreaming?"

Slash nodded, still breathing hard. He cleared his throat. "I reckon. Cra—crazy damn dream, too."

"Tell me."

"Catch party was after me. Posse." Slash drew a breath, shook his head.

"Here." Jay grabbed a bottle off the small table on her side of the bed, and handed it to him. "Have a little hair of the dog. Calm you down."

"Thanks." Slash took a pull from the bottle, then one more. He gave the bottle back to Jay. "Yeah . . . that's better . . ."

Jay took a small sip from the bottle, then set it back on the table beside the bed. He and she had sat up late after the previous day's festivities—after the previous day's *all-day* festivities—that had included, following the wedding, a long, leisurely picnic along the river behind the church . . . then a short siesta in town before supper here in the dining room of Jay's own Thousand Delights Saloon and Gambling Parlor . . . then a night of toasts and dancing and gambling and singing and more dancing . . . and then off to Jay's suite here on the saloon's third floor.

Off to *her and Slash*'s suite here on the saloon's third floor.

Where they'd made love a little awkwardly at first, not unlike a young, inexperienced couple, shy with one another though this couple had known each other for going on twenty years now. They'd settled down by laughing it off and sharing the bottle and whispering sweet, drunken nothings in each other's ears, then trying it again . . . again . . . then one more time, until they'd wrestled that wildcat down and tamed it till they had it purring in the corner . . . and the bed singing in rhythmic key . . . and they went to sleep chuckling and kissing and nibbling each other's ears, eager for the next day when they could start it all again—their new life together.

Despite all the busthead he'd consumed, Slash had slept well . . . until the dream.

"Catch party?" Jay said, tenderly smoothing his hair back, rubbing his back. Her body was warm beside his. And she smelled sweet. Not like Pecos at all.

Slash nodded. He swallowed, hesitating, having a hard time finding the words to express the dream—the old dream he'd had so often.

"Tell me, Slash," Jay prodded, frowning at him curiously. "Tell me about the catch party. Did they have you trapped?"

Slash blinked, stared back at her. He felt blood warm his cheeks, and he was suddenly self-conscious. He turned away from her, smacked his lips, chuckled. "Never, uh . . . never mind. It was just a stupid dream. Same one I been having for . . ."

"Tell me," Jay encouraged him, squeezing his arm.

"Nah, no . . . it's just a crazy damn dream. You'll laugh."

"I will not laugh."

"Yeah, you will."

"No, I won't!"

Slash shifted around uncomfortably. "Oh, hell . . ."

"Slash, have you ever told your dream to anyone?"

"Ah, well . . . once . . . a long time ago I told it to . . . well, you know . . . I told it to . . ."

"Pecos?"

Slash shrugged. "Who else would I have told it to? The

only reason I told it to him was because I was drunk, sittin' around a campfire one night. Can't even remember where now."

"Did he laugh?"

"Oh, yeah," Slash said, chuckling. "Of course he laughed. He laughed an' called me a sissy and threw a stick of firewood at me, an' went to sleep. It's a silly damn dream. Stupid. I don't know why I keep havin' it!"

"Tell it to me, Slash."

"Nah, nah, nah. I shouldn't have said anything." Slash threw his covers back. "Damn, I'm hungry. Why don't we go downstairs and get us a big, old break—"

He tried to get up but she gave his arm a hard tug with both hands, pulling him back down on the bed. "Not until you tell me your dream."

"Ah, Jay, come on, now. It's just a silly old—"

She placed one hand on his chest, holding him down, and crouched over him, the ends of her hair feeling like silk dangling against his face and shoulders. "Slash," she admonished him, one brow arched. Her face was a foot away from his. "I promise I will not laugh. If there's a naked woman in it I might give you a thrashing, but I won't laugh."

She grinned and pinched his nose. "Come on. I'm your wife. You have to tell me everything. I want to know everything inside your head. Fair's fair. You'll soon know everything that's inside of mine whether you want to or not." She laughed.

Slash chuckled. "Well . . . all right."

Jay laid her cheek against his chest and caressed his arms with her hands. "Tell."

He wrapped his arms around her and stared at the

ceiling. "It goes like this. Remember, you said you wouldn't laugh."

She poked him hard in the belly. "Slash Braddock, if you don't tell me the damn dream . . . !"

"All right, here goes. In the dream, I'm out riding hard. It's a cold, dark night. I'm ridin' with Pecos and Pete and all the rest—Billy Ray and Johnny and Ben Carlson—you know, before those two drunk gamblers shot him out of the privy in Flagstaff. Anyways, we're out ridin' hard. We got a catch party doggin' our trail. We're riding hell for leather and then we're suddenly in a woods and I look around me and suddenly Pecos ain't there. Pete's not there, either. None of 'em are there! All the Snake River Marauders are gone. Vanished. Vamoosed!"

"Oh, dear," Jay said, glancing up at him with concern.

"It's just me, ridin' all alone. I call out for 'em, but they're not there. Vanished. So I keep ridin' . . . and ridin' . . . and ridin' . . . till I realize I been ridin' in frantic circles. All the while, the posse's behind me . . . all round me . . . closin' in on me. I hear 'em whoopin' an' howlin' like wolves on the blood scent. I keep ridin' faster an' faster, duckin' low in the saddle to keep tree boughs from scrapin' me off my hoss. I call for Pecos an' Pete . . . and Ben . . . and Tex Lamb . . . an' there's nothing but the posse closin' ever tighter."

He paused and gestured for the bottle. Jay grabbed it off the night table and handed it to him. He took a big gulp then gave it back to Jay, who took a small sip before returning the bottle to the table. She snuggled against him again, resting her cheek against his chest.

"Go ahead. What happens next?"

"This is the real crazy part."

"Go ahead."

"I ride along until I see a woman stretched out on a fallen tree. I stare down at her, and it's my mother."

"Your mother?"

"My mother! I climb down from my horse and I walk over to her. Her eyes are closed. Must be asleep. I nudge her and I say, 'Hey, Mamma, it's . . .'" His voice cracked with emotion. He cleared his throat, swallowed. "I said, 'Mama, it's me, Jimmy. I thought you was dead!'"

He sucked a sharp breath, shook his head, brushed a tear from his cheek. "She opens her eyes then, an' she frowns up at me, sort of perplexed-like, and she says, 'Jimmy, where on earth have you been? I've been right here, waiting for you all this time. Don't you realize that wolves are right behind you?'

"I reach for her, thinkin' suddenly I'll be saved at last. I'll go with her an' I'll be safe. But I can't feel anything. It's like she's not really there at all. Only air. And then I realize the posse has caught up to me. They're all around me. Only, there are no men there. No men and horses. Sure enough, Mama was right. All around me are the glowing red eyes of wolves about to make the final leap." He glanced down at Jay, who gazed up at him now, her own eyes shimmering with tears. "That's when I wake up."

"Oh, Slash!"

"It's a terrible damn dream." Again, self-consciously, he brushed a tear from his cheek. A strangled sob worked its way out of his throat. "An' old outlaw . . . his name was Frank Harlan . . . an old, old man when I ran into him in Miles City up in Montana. He had a pet crow named Lucifer." Slash chuckled. "Anyway, he told me once that dreams mean things about our lives. That they are God's way of tellin' us about ourselves while we sleep, in ways we won't listen to, let alone understand, while we are awake."

Slash shook his head, puzzled. "But I for the life of me can't figure out what he's trying to tell me. Makes no sense to me. My mother . . . the catch party . . . wolves . . . ?"

"Oh, Slash." Jay sat up, smiling while she sobbed, and sandwiched his craggily handsome face in her hands, sliding her face up to within inches of his. "It just means that you lost your mother way too young. When we lose our mothers so young—as I did, too—those damn wolves always seem close." She kissed his nose. "Way too damn close. And it seems like we have to face them all alone. But you don't have to face them alone anymore. Now, you have me."

Slash considered that, nodding slowly. "That makes sense." He smiled at her, feeling great relief. Also feeling a renewed appreciation for this wise, beautiful woman he'd married. "Thank you very kindly. Damn, I wish I would have married you a long time ago. I wish I'd told you the dream, years back . . . instead of Pecos."

"I need to take Pecos over my knee and whip his ass for him, for calling you a sissy!" Jay said in mock fury but also laughing. "Are you still hungry?"

"I'm hungry, all right." Slash wrapped his arms around her, gave her a lusty grin. "But not for food."

Jay chuckled as he rolled her onto her back and closed his lips over hers.

They both jerked with a start when someone pounded loudly on the hall door. Automatically, Slash thrust his right hand toward one of his two pistols hanging off a bedpost but forestalled the movement when Pecos yelled, "Slash! Sorry to wake you so early after just gettin' hitched.

I'm sure you'd like to, uh, *sleep in*, but you're gonna have to get up and haul ass, I'm afraid."

Slash glared at the door. "What the hell are you talkin' about? I'm on my honeymoon!"

"We're on our honeymoon," Jay yelled at the door. "Go away, Pecos, you lout!"

"Yeah, go away, you lout," Slash said. "You hurt my feelin's. A boy misses his mother. Even a middle-aged one. Don't mean I'm a sissy!"

"Wait," Pecos said from the other side of the door. *"What?"*

Slash cursed and pecked Jay's cheek. "Sorry, honey. I'll be right back."

Jay only chuckled as he crawled off the bed and stumbled naked to the door. He opened the door and stood staring up at the big, long-haired galoot before him.

"You hurt my feelin's—you know that?"

"What the hell has gotten—wait, wait, wait, now!" Pecos raised his arm chin-high to block his view of his partner's nether regions. "You need to get some pants on before you start cryin' about me hurtin' your feelin's. Good Lord, man—look at yourself. Are you still *drunk?*"

He peered around Slash at Jay sitting up on the bed, holding the bedcovers up to her neck, laughing hysterically. "Is he still drunk?" Pecos asked her.

Jay shook her head. "No, he's not drunk. We just had a heart-to-heart, Slash and I did. He told me his dream."

"Dream? What dream?"

"The one about my mother an' the wolves," Slash said. "I got drunk an' told it to you, an' you called me a sissy. Not only that, you threw a stick at me!"

"Ah, hell!" Pecos said. "I was just joshin'. I know you ain't no sissy, Slash. Hell, you're tougher'n whang leather.

I was just climbin' your hump. Hell, I'm the one who cries himself to sleep at night after I shoot a deer. Especially a doe. I get all choked up over does."

"Jay said the dream meant I missed my mother. And there ain't nothin' wrong with that." He glanced over his shoulder at his wife. "Is there, honey?"

"None whatsoever," she said, smiling tenderly and then with amusement at her husband's naked backside. "But you better get some pants on, Slash, before you catch your death of cold. Chilly in here, with the storm."

"I figure if I stand here nekkid long enough," Slash said, still scowling up at his hulking partner, "this miscreant will leave. How come you ain't gone yet, Pecos?"

Pecos hung his head. "Ah, hell."

"What is it?" Slash said. He didn't like his partner's tone. He knew Pecos's tones inside and out, and he didn't like this one at all.

Pecos drew a breath, then looked from Jay to Slash over the top of his still-raised arm. "Bleed-'Em-So's men rousted me out of bed a half hour ago. Hell, I'd just gotten to bed two hours before that. Me an' big Isaiah an' the Shimmer cousins sat up all night in the freight yard, toastin' you and Jay."

"I thought you looked a might green around the gills. Tell Bledsoe to go to hell."

"You tell him. We got forty-five minutes to meet him at the usual place. I already packed your gear and saddled your horse. Be waitin' in the street for you." Pecos peered over his shoulder at Jay again, and winced when he saw her glaring at him. "I'm awful sorry, Jay. It ain't my fault. I know you an' Slash was gonna take the train up to Cheyenne for your honeymoon an' all, but . . . aw, hell."

He lowered his arm, turned, and lumbered off down the hall, hang-headed.

Slash stood staring into the hall, fists tightly balled at his sides.

Bledsoe.

He slammed the door and turned to Jay.

Jay had her arms crossed on her chest. "I am going to kill that man," she fumed.

"Not if I get a second shot at him first."

Chapter 6

The old freight trail between Fort Collins and the moldering town of Cedar City was practically a red clay river of mud.

As the rain came down—not hard but enough to make the morning good and wet and chilly and downright uncomfortable—mud splashed up from the horses' hooves. It splattered across Slash's and Pecos's high-topped boots and stained their black wool trouser legs clear to their knees despite the cream-colored rain ponchos each man wore.

As they rode at spanking trots, following the old, now defunct trail that meandered between rocks and patches of sage and prickly pear, Slash said, "I'm gonna jerk that little cottonheaded squirrel up out of his pushchair, and I'm gonna slap him till his dentures fall out!"

"I don't blame you a bit, partner, but remember the paper he holds on us."

"I don't care about no paper. Diddle the amnesty! I just got married, an' me an' Jay was about to . . . well, you know . . . until you came hammering away on that damn door!"

"On account of him, not me, I feel the need to point out."

"On account of him, but it still almost got you shot." Slash couldn't help chuckling at that.

Pecos cast a scowl at him from beneath the broad brim of his high-crowned Stetson. He had his twelve-gauge, double-barrel Richards coach gun hanging from its wide leather lanyard down his back. Even the barn blaster's rear stock was taking some of the mud kicked up by Pecos's buckskin's rear hooves.

"Dreary damn cold day to be out," Pecos grumbled, hunkering down inside the slicker as the rain kept coming and thunder rumbled. Clouds hung down, gray as tattered washrags, over the surrounding buttes and shelving dikes. The air smelled pretty but that was about all you could say for a midsummer storm. It spiced up right nice. Still, Pecos preferred the sunshine. He didn't like mud. He didn't like cold and rain unless he had a pretty woman to snuggle under the sheets with, near a popping fire and with a jug of whiskey nearby.

That reminded him of something that made him smile. He turned to Slash and said, "So, uh . . . how'd it go?"

Slash glanced at him. "Huh?"

"Last night."

"What do you mean?"

"I mean *last night*."

"Oh." Slash chuckled and rode on for a time, holding his reins up high in his gloved hands. "Well, you know, it ain't like layin' with a whore, Pecos."

"Was that your first time? I mean, with a woman who wasn't a whore?"

Slash looked around, frowning in deep thought. "I'll be damned if it wasn't!" He chuckled in pensive bemusement. "Sure enough. I've never lain with a gal that wasn't a whore. Came close a coupla times but never managed to close the deal. I never knew how to talk to a gal who wasn't a whore. Like I said, it ain't the same thing. It ain't as easy."

"No, you gotta talk. I 'spect that didn't come easy for you at all."

"You know, you're not gonna believe this," Slash said, turning to his partner again as the trail narrowed between two close sandstone outcroppings stippled with dripping cedars, "but it did."

"No! Really?"

"Yeah."

"Imagine that. Talkin' with a woman comin' easy for Slash Braddock." Pecos scowled straight ahead at the misty gray horizon and gave his head a single, befuddled wag. "Imagine that."

"Talkin' with Jay came easy for me."

Slash chewed on that for a time, and his smile grew. "And I didn't just want to get 'er done an' over with, neither, so I could get back downstairs to the boys and another round of farrow or high five. No, no. I wanted to stay right there . . . and look at her . . . and *talk* to her, by damn . . . Listen to what she had to say."

"*Listen to what she had to say?*" Pecos stared at his partner in hang-jawed exasperation. "Oh, this is just too damn much!"

They rode on along the banks of the Poudre River, and Slash thought of Jay lying all warm and soft in those silk sheets on her nice, big bed with its feather mattress—all red-haired and smooth and freckled and long-legged and naked under the quilts—and a fresh wave of anger rolled over him. "Damn that nasty old weasel! We was just startin' to have fun, Jay an' me!" He punched his saddle horn, making his Appaloosa flinch and glance back at him skeptically.

"Ah, well," Pecos said. "You got all the rest of your lives to have fun." He couldn't help feeling a twinge of jealousy. More than a twinge, if the truth be known.

The thing was, he wasn't sure which one he was more jealous of—Slash or Jay.

Ahead, spread out in the sage at the base of a low ridge, Cedar City came into misty view. Chief Marshal couldn't have picked a more out-of-the-way place to meet his two covert troubleshooters. Bleed-'Em-So thought it prudent that he and the two former cutthroats keep their arrangement as secret as possible. The marshal didn't think it would reflect well on the federal government if folks knew it had amnestied two career criminals in return for their service, i.e., running down owlhoots every bit as bad as Slash and Pecos once were—and worse—and killing them.

The Eastern newspapers would have an ink-fest if they found out that Uncle Sam had turned loose two criminals and turned them into paid assassins.

Apparently, Bledsoe and even the president of the United States thought it made sense, though, given the nasty cut of outlaw who currently ran off their leashes on the still relatively lawless Western frontier. Who but two cutthroats would be better qualified for running down and bringing to justice—or flat-out killing—their own?

Bledsoe's sending Jack Penny and a whole pack of nasty bounty hunters to kill them, and then Slash and Pecos killing the bounty hunters instead, with Penny now included, had been a pretty good test of their abilities. Even at their advanced ages, though neither Slash nor Pecos saw their midfifties as being all that advanced. Of course, Bledsoe hadn't intended Penny's ambush to be a test. He'd genuinely wanted Slash and Pecos dead.

Who could blame the man?

Slash himself had crippled Bledsoe many years ago. He hadn't intended to, but the lawman—a deputy U.S. marshal at the time—had caught one of Slash's ricochets. It had shattered Bledsoe's spine, confining him to a pushchair.

Slash knew that, given their history, Bledsoe wasn't going to pull any punches when handing out job assignments to the two former cutthroats. Slash and Pecos were always going to be going after the worst of the worst and on the most secretive missions.

Until their tickets were punched.

Luther T. "Bleed-'Em-So" Bledsoe would not shed any tears at their funerals. If they received funerals. Which they almost certainly wouldn't.

Bledsoe kept an office of sorts here in the little near-ghost-town of Cedar City, which sat amongst rocks and cedars in a broad horseshoe of the Poudre River. The town had never been a city, despite its obvious aspirations, and had ceased even to be a town when the army pulled out of Camp Collins, which was the original name for Fort Collins. Now it wasn't even a fort anymore, and all that remained of Cedar City were a few abandoned mud-brick dwellings, an abandoned livery barn and stock corral, and a single saloon, the Cormorant, which mostly served the rare drifter and local cowpuncher and gave a home to the old gentleman who owned the place—a stove-up former Texas Ranger, Tex Willey.

Tex and the chief marshal had been friends for a couple of generations, having worked together in chasing curly wolves in their heydays.

These days, Bledsoe came out here to get work done when he found himself drowning in red tape in his bona fide digs in the Federal Building in Denver. It was a handy location, given its close proximity to the railroad line. An old freighting trail, still in good repair, offered access from the rail line to Cedar City.

Now as Slash and Pecos rode into the ghost town from the west, they saw the old Concord mud wagon that Bledsoe had had customized for himself, nattied up a bit with brass fittings and gas lamps, softer seats, velvet drapes offering privacy, and brackets on the side for housing his pushchair. The horses milling in the corral flanking the mud wagon were likely the two that had pulled Bledsoe out here from the train. They sheltered from the rain beneath the brush ramada.

The other two would be those of the two deputies who always escorted and ran interference against possible assassins.

The wily old reprobate had locked up his share of owlhoots over his long years of service to Uncle Sam, and he had a poisonous personality to boot. There were plenty of gunslingers who would love to add the crippled old devil's notch to their pistol grips.

The two deputies sat on the main building's roofed front stoop, to the right of the door, smoking. Slash couldn't see them well in the stormy murk—they appeared as watercolor figures as he and Pecos approached the stoop in the rain, but he could see the badges pinned to their coats and the coals of their cigarettes when they took drags, the gray smoke wafting like gray mist around their high-crowned, broad-brimmed Stetsons.

The two former cutthroats tossed their reins over the rail worn down to a mere stick in places by the reins of many a soldier's horse, then negotiated the untrustworthy three steps to the porch. The two federals regarded them blandly but with sneers in their eyes. The older of the two, with considerable gray in his hair and mustache, leaned back in his hide-bottom chair, the chair's front legs lifted several inches off the floor, his black, hand-tooled leather boots crossed on the rail before him.

He turned to the younger man beside him, winked, and said, "Heard you got hitched, Slash."

Slash and Pecos stopped. Slash glanced at Pecos then at the older of the two deputy U.S. marshals. "How in the hell . . . ?"

"Word gets around. The chief likes to keep tabs on you, don't ya know. He don't like no surprises, though that, even he'd have to admit, was a surprise!"

"*Married?*" exclaimed the younger federal. He appeared all of red-cheeked sixteen to Slash, but Slash had lost his judge of a man's age somewhere back when he himself was around forty. He supposed this man was around twenty-six or -seven. "Who would marry this old scalawag?" The young federal looked up at Slash, stretching his mustached upper lip back from his teeth in speculation. "Whore?"

Again, Slash and Pecos shared a glance. Turning back to the brash young federal in his officious black wool suit and five-dollar haircut, he said, "Your sis wanted to, but I was too much man for her. Ain't you noticed her walkin' funny?"

The kid was out of the chair like the devil from a jack-in-the-box. He strode toward Slash, eyes glazing, jaws hard. "You want to say that one more time, cutthroat? Huh? Just one more time so there's no doubt why—"

"Hey, hey, hey—rein in the acolyte!" Pecos said, throwing out his right hand, palm out.

The older federal laughed, then leaned out to grab the kid by the tails of his Prince Albert coat and dragged him straight back toward him. The kid's red cheeks turned redder, with a white patch across his forehead, as he kept his enraged eyes on Slash, who grinned back at him, slit-eyed.

There was nothing Slash enjoyed more than ruffling the feathers then filing the horns of bureaucratic popinjays.

The road ranch's front door opened, and an old man with snow-white hair hanging down his back in a tight braid, and a crow's dark-eyed face with a sun-seasoned, liver-spotted beak of a nose, stood in the opening. Tex Willey's pet badger stood on his shoulder, glowering at the newcomers, as did Tex himself. Tex wore a soiled apron and greasy undershirt, an even dirtier towel draped over his other shoulder.

The old Texas Ranger and roadhouse manager didn't say anything. He just dropped his chin and hooked his thumb over his shoulder, then stepped to one side.

"Aw, ain't he cuter'n a speckled pup," Pecos said to the badger as he stepped past Willey and entered the road-house.

"Don't pet him," Tex warned, "or you'll leave here without a hand."

"Why do you keep him, then?" Slash asked as he too stepped into the roadhouse.

"Why does a man get married?"

"Fair point."

Slash followed Pecos to the rear of the dark, broad, low-ceilinged room. There were no customers yet, so all the chairs were still overturned on the tables. There never would be many customers—maybe a few raggedy-heeled cow nurses from area ranches or a market hunter or two. Willey still ran a hog ranch out here when he could find the women—usually destitute soldiers' widows from Fort Collins—desperate enough to turn tricks this far out in the tall and uncut, but mostly it was a sad, dirty, windblown, and tumbleweed-infested little place the prairie was fast reclaiming.

Mostly, Tex sat out here and drank and played solitaire and smoked and sawed on his fiddle for his badger, and waited for the forces of nature to reclaim him, as well.

Slash rapped his knuckles on the door of the old storeroom that Bledsoe now used as a part-time office.

The knock was answered by a raspy man's voice saying, "If you're anyone but my two raggedy-heeled, over-the-hill cutthroats, stay out. I got work to do!"

Slash curled his upper lip at Pecos, then tripped the door's latch and stepped into the roomy office that owned the molasses aroma of cured meat, liquor, meal, and malty ale. "I just found out from Lassiter you knew I got married yesterday!" he accused as he strode toward Bledsoe's messy desk behind which the old, gray-headed marshal sat in the pushchair that Slash's bullet had confined him to.

"That's all right—no need to apologize."

"What?" Slash gave an exasperated laugh. "Why in hell would I apologize to you for gettin' hitched?"

"You didn't ask my permission."

Pecos walked up to stand beside Slash, chuckling. "Why in hell would either one of us need your permission to get hitched?"

"Because I own your asses. Both of 'em. Bought and paid for 'em. You want to see the receipt?"

Slash drew a tight, deep breath and glanced again at Pecos. Pecos kept his own angry gaze on the little cotton-headed, bespectacled lawman sitting there in his breakfast-stained, outdated, ill-fitting suit. "The clemency."

"Damn right, the clemency," Bledsoe said in his infuriatingly matter-of-fact tone. "You two should have hanged. You should be in some unmarked grave in a prison cemetery—dust, dust, dust! But you're not. That makes you mine." He patted the egg-stained lapel of his coat with the withered hand holding the cold cigar. "So the next time either one of you finds a woman desperate enough to hitch her sad star to your wagon, you come visit me with your hat in your hands, and I'll think about it."

"Desperate woman?" Slash snarled, glaring down at the old man. "*Sad star?* You can go to hell, you warty old mossyhorn! I only came out here to tell you in person I quit. I'm heading back to town and then my bride and I— who I made one very happy woman last night, I ain't too proud to boast—are heading to Cheyenne for our honeymoon!"

Bledsoe sat back in his chair, grinning like the cat that ate the canary. He ran his bone-white, long-fingered hands through the cottony down of his unkempt hair and thumbed the smudged spectacles up his long, lumpy nose. He turned his head to his left and said, "Miss Langdon, please bring that certificate of amnesty over here, will you?" He held up his cigar and smiled up over his desk at Slash and Pecos. "I need something to light my cigar with."

Chapter 7

Slash saw his tall partner's head swing toward where Bledsoe's comely female assistant, Miss Abigail Langdon, sat at a second desk in the former storage room. This desk abutted the wall to the right of the chief marshal. Her desk was every bit as large as Bledsoe's, and just as cluttered. A tall, stylish, pink lamp burned, illuminating her cool, remote, severely Nordic beauty in the flickering light's shifting planes and shadows.

Miss Langdon flipped a heavy, curling lock of red-gold hair back behind her shoulder, revealing her wide cheekbones that tapered severely down to a fine chin and regal jaw. Her crystalline eyes, long and slanted like a cat's eyes, lingered on Pecos's tall, broad-shouldered frame, raking him up and down. A dark cloak was pulled around her shoulders, over the purple velvet gown she wore so well. She reached for a shot glass on the desk before her, amidst the clutter of open files and dossiers and bound books on federal law, and sipped.

All eyes were on her, watching her. Even Bledsoe's.

The chief marshal worked with Miss Langdon every day. Still, her mystery was obviously not lost on the wasted old scoundrel in the pushchair. Whenever Slash saw them, they each always had a drink. He'd swear they must work and drink together all day long. Bledsoe probably needed the tanglelegs to calm his heart, working so closely with such a delectable, inscrutable creature—straight out of a boy's Viking fantasy.

She probably needed the hooch to distract her from the tedium.

Now she plucked an envelope up off the desk and rose from her chair.

As she did, rising to her full Amazon height, keeping her cool, crystalline eyes on Pecos, Slash heard his raw-boned partner draw a deep intake of air, felt the body heat rise in the taller man's frame.

Pecos quickly doffed his hat, cleared his throat, shifted his weight, and licked his lips. "Uh . . . hello there, M-Miss Langdon. Didn't notice you over there. Kinda hidden by the shadows this rainy day."

Slash didn't believe that a bit. Pecos would have known she'd be here. She went everywhere that Bledsoe did, being his personal assistant as well as his official government secretary. Pecos would have been anticipating seeing her here, and his eyes would have found her in the room first thing. His heart had probably turned a somersault in his big, broad chest, then ping-panged as Slash could have sworn he heard it doing now as she moved lithely and without sound. Through the shadowy tentacles of the storm flashing in the window toward her boss's desk, the pleats of her gown billowed lovingly around her long, curvy legs.

She didn't say anything to Pecos. But she kept her eyes on his, long enough to acknowledge his greeting with a silent but unmistakable one of her own. A very faint flush rose in those high, chiseled, alabaster cheeks as she turned toward Bledsoe, extending the envelope in her long-fingered hand. Her eyes stayed on Pecos as she said, almost too quietly to be heard above the small fire crackling in the small sheet-iron stove flanking her boss, "Here you are, Chief Marshal. As requested . . ."

Slash squelched a chuckle. Pecos had reacted to the remote beauty, whom Slash judged to be in her middle twenties, though with a decidedly more mature air about herself, the first time they'd met. Abigail Langdon had reacted similarly to Pecos. It was almost as though the two were giving off invisible sparks of attraction—a primitive reach for each other.

Bledsoe saw it now, too. Leaning forward in his chair, he studied the two with an amused half smile, then set down his cigar and took the envelope from the young woman's hand. He switched his gaze to Slash. Holding the envelope, across the front of which had been typed CERTIFICATE OF AMNESTY—BRADDOCK AND BAKER, he plucked a lucifer match from a silver tray and scratched it to life on the scarred surface of his desk.

As disinterested as though her boss was merely picking his teeth, Miss Langdon returned coolly to her own desk, smoothed her dress down against her nicely shaped behind, and sat down in her chair. She shook her hair back, the thick red-gold locks tumbling bewitchingly down the back of the cape. She picked up her ink pen, dipped it in a bottle of indigo ink, crouched over the open folder of papers before her, and resumed scribbling.

She was beyond caring about something as tedious as a clemency, or what it would mean for the two men standing in the room before her boss's desk if Bledsoe should use it to light his cigar.

Slash looked at Bledsoe smiling up at him with open challenge. The flame of the man's match was two inches from a corner of the envelope holding the key to the two former cutthroats' freedom. All three men knew that if that certificate was destroyed, Slash and Pecos would be wanted men again. They would be hunted men again. They would no doubt be caught and made to dance the midair two-step with fresh hemp coiled around their necks.

Slowly, Bledsoe moved the envelope closer to the smoking flame.

Pecos stared at the envelope and the flame, nervously rubbing his big hands on the still-wet and muddy front of his rain slicker. "Uh, Slash . . ."

Slash stared at the flame. He looked at Bledsoe grinning up at him, very slowly moving the envelope closer to the match. Slash thought of Jay, the beautiful bride he'd left in her warm bed back in Fort Collins. He cursed, leaned forward, placed his hands on the edge of the desk, and blew out the match.

He straightened, glaring down at his slow executioner. For that's what old Bleed-'Em-So was, all right. An executioner. He was just taking his time killing them, sending them on his most dangerous jobs, his most secret shenanigans, knowing full well that sooner or later he'd send them into a box canyon of trouble they'd not be able to shoot their way out of.

In the meantime, he would use them to his own benefit.

Still grinning, Bledsoe dropped the match into the ashtray. He dropped the envelope onto the blotter, picked up his cigar and a fresh match, and sagged back in his chair. Flaring the match to life on the edge of his desk, he poked the cigar into his mouth and said around it, "Mm-hmm. Wise decision. Very wise, Slash. I'm glad you still got the good sense you were born with, though the previous fifty-odd years of your life have proven poor evidence of that."

"Just tell us what lion's den you're sending us into this time, so we can get after it," Slash snarled at him. "I'm getting sick of the stench in here."

Pecos gave him a hard look of reprimand, then turned to Bledsoe's pretty assistant and said, "No offense, Miss Langdon. He didn't mean you. He meant your boss's stench!"

She glanced up at him with a faint, preoccupied wrinkle of her brows as she continued scratching at her reports.

Pecos cast Slash another reproving scowl. Slash shrugged.

Bledsoe glanced from the obviously lovelorn Pecos to Miss Langdon and gave a throaty chuckle. When he'd gotten the stogie lit to his satisfaction, he tossed the match into the ashtray, plucked another envelope off his desk, and slid it across toward Slash and Pecos.

Pecos looked down at the envelope, which was addressed to Bledsoe at the Federal Building in Denver, then looked up at Slash and gave a sheepish shrug. He couldn't read. Not that Slash was any valedictorian, but he knew his letters and could write his name.

Slash gave a caustic snort, then picked up the envelope and slipped a single lined sheet out of it, and opened it. Haltingly, he read aloud, having to sound out some of the words while using his right index finger to track them:

Dear Friend Luther,
I could use some Help up here if You can spare a
couple of Men. Discretion is Necessary. Ned
Calico is back. I will explain in full when Your Boys
arrive. Send good men please Luther.

Gun Men.

Your Friend Always,
Kentucky

Slash frowned curiously at Bledsoe, then looked at the front of the envelope and said, "Kentucky O'Neil—Harveyville, Nebraska . . . ?"

"I want you to look into it." Bledsoe tossed yet another envelope across his desk. "There's cash for train tickets and a few necessities. Damn few. As usual, no vouchers, no paper trail. You'll catch the train in Cheyenne this afternoon. Switch to the South Platte & Nebraska Panhandle Line in Ogallala. You'll head straight south to Harveyville. Now get the hell out of here. I and Miss Langdon have a lot of work to do before we return to the infernal hellhole of Denver. Came out here for some peace and quiet and," he added with a sly wink, "to send you two out on a discreet assignment. Operative word here is *discreet*."

"Hold on, hold on, Chief," Pecos said, holding up his hands. "You gotta give us more information than that."

Bledsoe nodded at the letter. "That's all I got."

"Who's Kentucky O'Neil?" Slash asked.

"And who's Ned Calico?" Pecos asked.

"Kentucky's an old friend of mine. We served together in the War of Northern Aggression. We met again out West, a few years later. Kentucky turned outlaw for a while, but I set him straight. He lawdogged around the West for a good many years before settling down in Harveyville to raise his daughter. Never made it big, but he's made an honest living.

"As of the last twelve years, he's been the town marshal of Harveyville—a growing town in prime cattle country along Frenchman Creek. As for Ned Calico, he's an outlaw that Kentucky sent away about twelve years ago with two other curly wolves. Anyway, from that letter from Kentucky himself, sounds like Calico returned to Harveyville after his prison stint. Probably to get even for Kentucky having taken him and his two cohorts down while they'd been passed out in a parlor house. I want you two to go up there and see what kind of trouble he's causing. If it's too much trouble . . ."

He paused and glanced at Miss Langdon. "Miss Langdon, check the door, please."

Miss Langdon set her pen down, rose, walked to the door, opened it, and poked her head into the main drinking hall. She pulled her head back into the office and turned to Bledsoe.

"All quiet, Chief."

Bledsoe puffed the stogie, hooded his eyes against the smoke, grinned, and looked at the two reluctant lackeys standing before him. "If he's causing too much trouble, kill the peckerwood. Give him a coward's funeral."

Slash and Pecos looked at Miss Langdon. As stoic as ever, she simply strode back to her chair, sat down, and resumed her work.

"All right," Slash said, drawing a deep breath and turning to Pecos. "Sounds simple enough. Shoot him and drag him into the nearest ravine."

"Right," Pecos said with a droll chuckle. "Don't get much simpler than that."

"What're you two still doing here?" Bledsoe gave a backhanded wave of dismissal and leaned forward in his chair. "Skedaddle!"

Slash and Pecos turned toward the door. As they did, Slash glanced at Pecos and tossed his head to indicate the Amazonian princess sitting at the desk to his left, scratching the pen across her work, her pretty pink tongue pressed with concentration against the inside corner of her bee-stung mouth.

"What?" Pecos mouthed.

Again, Slash tossed his head to indicate Miss Langdon. "Spark her a little!" he wheezed.

He stepped to the door, opened it, and walked out, drawing it closed behind him but not latching it. Pecos headed for the door, hesitated, then stopped and turned back to Bledsoe. Holding his hat over his chest, he cleared his throat.

Bledsoe looked up from his work, scowling incredulously. "What the hell are you still—?"

"I was wondering if I could have a word with Miss Langdon, Chief? Uh . . . in private."

His heart thudded as he turned to the young woman, who looked up at him, her red-blond brows arched curiously.

Bledsoe glanced from Pecos to his assistant then back to Pecos. He chuckled and shook his head inside the thick wreath of smoke he'd exhaled. "I reckon it's up to Miss Langdon."

Pecos looked at the pretty young woman. Her cheeks were slightly flushed. Still frowning curiously, she set her pen down, rose, and walked slowly, somewhat haltingly toward him. Pecos opened the office door, cleared his throat, and ushered her out into the main drinking hall.

He was glad that Slash had gone outside. He didn't see Tex Willey, either. He and the young woman were alone at long last.

His heart thumped as though it and him were thirteen years old. He sweated inside his boots as he said, "Miss Langdon, I was wondering if you would do me the honor, sometime in the very near future, of joining me for supper in Denver one night."

Inwardly, he winced. There—he'd spoken the words he'd wanted to speak since the first time he'd laid eyes on

Bledsoe's beguiling assistant. He just hoped he'd live to hear her answer. He wasn't sure. He felt as though his poor old/young heart was about to give out with anticipation and downright nervousness.

"Oh," Miss Langdon splayed her fingers over the bodice of her dress in surprise. Her cheeks turned a deeper shade of red, and she looked down at the floor. "Oh . . . I . . . uh. . ."

Oh no, Pecos thought, his heart racing and hiccupping. *I just made one big horse's ass of myself. Oh well. Not the first time.*

He, too, looked down at the floor, sort of cowering under the blows of her hesitation, as she obviously searched for the words with which to let him down as gently as she could without embarrassing him too severely. "Ah, hell . . . I mean, heck . . . never mind, Miss Langdon. I'm way older'n you and—"

She cut him off by placing her hand on his forearm. "Mister Baker, I would be honored."

He looked up at her quickly, expecting to find that she was merely patronizing him. He'd be damned, though, if she didn't look serious. Gravely serious.

Genuine. Honest.

"Y-you . . . would . . . ?"

"I would very much so." Miss Langdon's long green eyes slanted up at their corners and twinkled as she smiled warmly. "I would very much so, indeed. I've . . . I've felt a connection between us. I felt it the very first time we met, in fact."

"You don't say!"

She dipped her chin. "I do say."

"I felt it, too!"

"Well, then . . . supper it is. Why don't you send me a telegram when you return from Nebraska? In care of the office in Denver will be fine." The honey-headed Viking princess turned away slowly, dimpling her tapering alabaster cheeks with yet another warm smile. "I'll be looking forward to it. Now, I'd better get back to work."

"I will do that, Miss Langdon. I will send you a wire."

"Do be careful in Nebraska, Mister Baker."

"Melvin."

"Call me Abigail."

"Nice to know you, Miss Abigail."

"All right, then."

"All right."

She gave a cordial dip of her chin, stepped back into the office, and drew the door gently closed behind her, giving the weak-kneed and young-at-heart Melvin Baker one more parting smile as she did.

"I'll be damned." Pecos stomped his feet and clicked his heels. "I'll be double-dee—*damned!*"

Whistling, he walked across the drinking hall, wending his way through the tables, and stepped up to the batwings. He gazed out over them, beaming. The rain had let up, though a very light mist hung in the cool air. Clouds were parting and shafts of sunlight slanted through the gaps between them. Thunder rumbled distantly over purple buttes.

Slash sat on his horse several feet back from the hitchrack to which Pecos's buckskin was tied. The two deputy U.S. marshals sat where they'd been sitting a few moments ago, both drinking coffee and smoking and talking in desultory tones.

Slash looked at Pecos. "How'd it go?"

"Just fine." Grinning from bright red ear to bright red

ear, Pecos pushed through the batwings. He raised his hands and released each door with a flourish. "Double-dee fine, in fact. Lead pipe cinch. Got 'er in the bag! You ain't the only one of us former cutthroats who has a way with women, Slash!"

"Oh, I ain't—ain't I?"

"No, you sure as hell ain't!" Pecos planted his fists on his hips and thrust his elbows out like a successful-in-love turkey gobbler fanning his feathers. "She felt a *connection*! Said so herself."

"Oh, stop struttin' an' get mounted. We got us a good pull to Cheyenne an' I'd like to get there before that storm swirls back around."

"Hell, I'll race you there!" Pecos ripped his reins from the hitchrack, did a gleeful two-step in the mud beside his horse, spurs chinging, then tipped his head back and gave a wild rebel yell at the parting clouds. He grabbed his saddle horn, hiked up his leg, toed his stirrup, and pulled.

"*Oh, what the . . . ?*" He and the saddle shot down the side of the horse like a bucket falling into a well. He looked up from the muddy ground where he lay in a heap with his saddle on top of him.

The two lawmen guffawed from their porch chairs.

Slash grinned down at his partner and raised his hat. "Race you to Cheyenne, pard!"

He reined his horse around and spurred the mount into an instant gallop, whooping and hollering like a demented coyote.

Pecos glanced at the saddle's cinch, which Slash had obviously slipped while Pecos had been sparking Miss Langdon. It was one of his oldest and dirtiest tricks. Pecos sat up, fuming and shaking his fist. "Come back here an' take your medicine, you chicken-livered coward! When I catch up to you, I'm gonna wring your scrawny neck till your eyes pop out of your *ugly head!*"

Behind him, the two lawmen roared.

Chapter 8

The next day, trundling through southwestern Nebraska in the single passenger coach of the South Platte & Nebraska Panhandle Line's afternoon combination, Pecos leaned forward to tap Slash's knee. Slash woke with a start, lifting his head and blinking as he looked around at the shabby car with its dull brass fittings, hard wooden seats, and soot-streaked windows. "What is it—we there?"

"No, I wanna smoke."

Slash scowled at him. "You woke me up to tell me that? Roll a smoke, then."

He was about to pull his hat back down over his eyes but stopped when Pecos extended his right hand halfway out from his side, stiffly. "Give me your makin's, you black-hearted devil. My shoulder hurts when I raise my arm."

"Well, then, why don't you move your tobacco sack from your shirt pocket to your coat pocket?"

"Give me your damn makin's, Slash," Pecos snarled, nostrils flaring. "You owe me that much after that trick you pulled. Damn lucky I didn't break my arm. Bad enough it separated! What if Miss Langdon had seen?"

Digging his canvas makin's pouch from his shirt pocket,

Slash chuckled and said, "Your arm ain't separated, so stop moanin' and poutin' like a damn sissy, or I'll tell Miss Langdon you're a nancy boy. Here!" He tossed the pouch to Pecos, who reached for it but missed. The sack hit him in the chest and rolled onto the seat between his legs. "That's the last smoke you're gettin' from me, so enjoy it."

"My shoulder is too separated!"

"If you don't shut up and let me sleep, I'm gonna separate your shoulders from your head!"

"Why don't you just try it?"

"Sissy!"

Pecos glanced around. There were only a half dozen other passengers in the rocking car. One of them was a little girl in a white cambric bonnet trimmed with purple lace along the edges, and with purple strings tied in a bow beneath her chin. She was staring at the two former cutthroats, the skin above the bridge of her pug nose slightly creased.

Pecos smiled at the little gal then returned his glare to his partner and said quietly but tautly through gritted teeth, "Stop callin' me that! That little girl's listening."

Slash turned to the girl—a cute little brunette maybe six or seven years old. She held a rag doll that had straw poking out of its split seams. "Don't mind him, honey. He's just a big caterwauling sissy!" He winked.

The girl tucked her upper lip under her bottom lip, blushed, and looked away quickly.

"Galldang you, Slash. Stop embarrassin' me in front of children!"

"Shut up."

"Don't tell me to shut up!"

"I said shut up."

"What the hell you lookin' at?"

Slash had turned his attention to the window on his left, as he rode facing forward. Pecos sat across from him, facing Slash and the rear of the coach. Rather, something *beyond* the window had caught Slash's attention. He leaned forward in his seat to better stare out the window, slowly turning his head from right to left, tracking what had caught his eye as the train continued rocking and rattling south along the rails.

"What you eyeballing out there in this godforsaken country?"

"Not sure." Slash continued staring at what appeared to be a tree. But an oddly shaped tree. The train was trundling over a low pass in high, rocky badlands country. A canyon of sorts opened below, to the east, and on the other side of it, perched alone atop a cone-shaped bluff, he'd spied this odd-looking tree. It appeared to be a cedar, like most of the other trees cropping up among the rocks around this section of rail.

As he stared at the cedar, trying to bring it into clearer focus, a ridge rose up before him and then all he could see were the near rocks and the wind-twisted cedars growing among them.

"Hmmm," Slash said, giving his head a single, puzzled shake.

"What was it?"

"Couldn't see it clear enough. Odd-looking tree, is all, I reckon."

"You're gonna look odd, too, if you keep climbin' my hump in front of children."

"Oh, shut up and roll your smoke, you crybaby. Look there, we'll be pulling into Harveyville soon." Slash dipped his chin to indicate the small settlement coming into view in the bowl-shaped valley opening at the base of the ridge they were now descending.

Building the quirley in his big hands, Pecos leaned forward and turned his head to stare out the window. Sure enough, a settlement was arranging itself below. A neat little town complete with a white, steepled church situated along a tree-lined creek, which angled around the town from the north before jogging off across the blond, rolling valley to the southwest.

It appeared to be a town of considerable size—at least for being this far out in the tall and uncut. Pecos figured there must be a good five, maybe six hundred people living down there in small log cabins as well as tidy little wood-frame houses flanked by the usual privies, small barns or stables, and buggy sheds. A few chicken coops. The main business district took more definite shape as the train continued rumbling down off the grade and onto the sage- and blond-grass-covered flatland on which the town sat.

Yessir, the town looked hale and hearty, with one three-block main street and a good half dozen side streets. The train tooted its horn as it rumbled up to the small redbrick station, which sat on a sun-washed brick platform at the town's western edge. The main street ran relatively straight east from the station, abutted on both sides by boardwalk-fronted business buildings mostly built of wood but with a good many sturdy brick buildings rising amid the mix.

Slash and Pecos grabbed their rifles, saddlebags, and war bags down from the overhead rack. Slash set his war bag down to pull a dime out of the ear of the little girl who'd been eyeballing him and Slash. The girl grinned as she accepted the coin.

"Don't fret, my peach," Slash told the child, jerking his

thumb toward Pecos. "I just like to get this big fella's goat once in a while. Keeps us both from gettin' bored."

He winked at her. The girl smiled again and, staring at the coin in her palm, followed her mother, a sunburned and overworked honyocker's wife, toward the nearest end of the car, a chicken squawking in the wicker cage the woman carried.

"Married only two days," Pecos said, "and you're already wooin' another."

Slash chuckled, shouldered his gear, and walked down off the coach's rear vestibule and onto the platform. Pecos stepped down beside him. Each man held their respective rifles on their shoulders; Pecos's sawed-off twelve-gauge hung down his back from its leather lanyard.

They looked around at the already all-but-deserted platform. The half dozen train passengers had already disbursed. The little girl and the farm woman were climbing into a rickety buckboard in which a bearded, sunburned man in dungarees and an immigrant cap, his wool shirt rolled to his elbows, sat holding the reins of the plow horse in the traces. The man looked naturally contrary, as did men who toiled relentlessly day after day and without much to show for it. Slash decided that the woman and the little girl, his wife and daughter, had visited the woman's parents in Ogallala, and had brought home a laying hen.

As the wagon rumbled away, the little girl sitting expressionlessly between the man and the woman, Slash cast his gaze down the street beyond them.

A couple of wagons rumbled along the rutted, dusty main thoroughfare. Saddle horses were clumped here and there in front of business establishments. A bushy black dog crossed the street at an angle, tongue hanging. It stopped at a stock tank on the street's south side, in front of a small beer brewery. It rose onto his hind legs, placing its front paws on the side of the trough, and lowered its snoot to draw water.

"Looks pretty quiet, if you ask me," Slash said.

"Sure does. I was half expectin' to hear pistol fire, see men shootin' up the town. Women screamin'. Buildings burnin'. That sort of thing."

"Me, too. A town don't get more peaceful than this one. Less'n it's a ghost town."

"What's our first move?"

"Well," Slash said with a sigh, adjusting the gear on his shoulders, "I reckon we fetch our horses then run down this Kentucky O'Neil fella, the town marshal, and have us a palaver. If this Ned Calico character is givin' him trouble, I reckon we find him, shoot him, and head home."

Pecos shrugged. "Sounds simple enough to me. You best get back to Jaycee before she has enough time to reconsider the terrible mistake she's made."

Slash grumbled a curse, then turned to walk north toward the stock car in which they'd boarded their horses earlier that morning in Ogallala. Ten minutes later, they led both mounts down the ramp and saddled them, and Slash slid his rifle into his saddle scabbard, taking another look around.

Now the only person he could see on the platform was a redheaded kid, maybe twelve years old, eyeing them suspiciously as he backed toward the edge of the cobblestones. He held a mail sack over one shoulder.

He backed into the street, still eyeing the two well-heeled newcomers, until Pecos called, "Say, sonny—look out there, you gotta wagon comin'—"

The kid stopped and turned in time to avoid being run over by a ranch supply wagon heading from south to north along the cross street at the mouth of the east-to-west-running main drag. The man driving the wagon cussed the kid and yelled, "Gallblastit, Danny, would you look where you're goin'? That's the third time I almost killed you in the past two weeks!"

"Sorry, Mister Broughton," the boy yelled after the wagon, blinking against the dust being churned up by its steel-shod wheels. "It won't happen again!"

"Make sure it don't," the driver yelled over his shoulder. "I don't wanna be the one to haul your fool, broken carcass over to your ma!"

As the wagon clattered off to the north, the boy glanced over his shoulder at Slash and Pecos once more. His eyes grew wide before he turned his head forward and took off running down the main drag, angling toward the boardwalks along the street's right side.

Slash and Pecos shared an amused glance.

Slash said, "That junior-Bob is on the lookout for trouble. That's a good sign trouble ain't already here."

"Oh? How so?"

"If trouble was already here, he wouldn't be lookin' for more."

"If you say so," Pecos said, climbing heavily into his saddle, chuckling.

"I say so." Slash stepped up into his own saddle, and sighed. "Yeah, I think we'll be heading home on the next train."

From the direction of the main drag, a gun barked twice, sharply. It was followed two winks later by a girl's shrill scream. Then another gun bark and another shout.

Pecos whipped his startled gaze to his partner. "You still think there's no trouble here, Slash?"

"All right," Slash conceded. "I might've made a quick judgment on too little evidence. *Let's go!*" He rammed his spurs into his mount's flanks and galloped across the platform.

Chapter 9

Slash and Pecos thundered onto the main thoroughfare atop their galloping mounts, looking around wildly for the source of the gunfire.

As they did, another blast sounded. Slash whipped his head toward a brick house looking out of place among the more nondescript wood-frame business buildings on the street's right side, roughly halfway between the train station to the west and where the town dwindled off into prairie to the east.

"There!" he yelled, reining his horse toward the house where a sign hanging beneath the porch roof announced simply: MADAM DELACROIX.

The shot and another ensuing girl's scream seemed to be coming from an open window on the second floor. Slash could see a silhouette moving around behind a red curtain billowing in the breeze.

Another gunshot. And another. Again the girl screamed, then pleaded, "Collie, put the gun away! Put the gun away, Collie. Please, don't shoot me!" Her voice broke into sobs.

"Yep, right peaceful," Pecos quipped as he drew his

buckskin up beside Slash's Appy and swung down from the leather.

Slash, lighter and fleeter of foot than his larger partner, had already dropped his reins and mounted the porch steps. He was across the porch in three strides. He opened the door and stepped into a nattily appointed parlor in which three girls and several men cowered behind arm-chairs and fainting couches and, in one case, behind a potted palm. They gazed anxiously up at the ceiling.

A woman stood at the bottom of the carpeted stairs at the rear of the room, one hand on the newel post, shouting, "Collie, you damn fool—you're hallucinatin' again! Put that gun away before you shoot Wynona or one of the other girls!"

She was a big woman in flowing gowns and with a lace shawl draped across her heavy, sloping shoulders. She held a long, black cigarette holder at the end of which a half-smoked cigarette smoldered. She had her hair done up, and her fleshy face—the face of a woman given to drink and gone to seed—was garishly made up, as well. She turned her head and widened her eyes in surprise to see two un-familiar men striding toward her with all-business expres-sions displayed beneath the broad brims of their black and brown Stetsons, respectively.

Slash had one of his .44's in his hand, and Pecos held his double-barreled gut-shredder in both hands across his chest.

"Who on earth . . . ?" the woman cried.

"Just passin' through," Slash said.

"He doesn't normally get this out of hand," she ex-plained, stepping back to make way as Slash started up the stairs, Pecos right behind him.

She angrily pounded the newel post with her fist. "I

warned his father to keep him to home. I told Gyllenwater I would not put up with his crazy boy shootin' up my place ever again, nor pistol-whippin' my girls! The last one he assaulted so savagely she can't even work no more. She's so ugly, *no man will lay with her!*"

The woman—apparently the madam, no doubt "Madam Delacroix" herself—kept on yammering, but now Slash and Pecos were on the whorehouse's second floor and they couldn't hear much of anything except the girl crying and a man shouting and stomping around in the room ahead of them.

"Oh, stop your damn cryin'," the man shouted behind the closed door. "I know what you said about me to Blackie an' Phil. They told me back in the bunkhouse. Had 'em a good laugh. All the boys did. You don't think that sorta thing gets around?"

There was the crack of a bare hand smashing against a cheek.

Again, the girl screamed and bawled. "Please . . . Collie . . . *please* don't hurt me no more! I didn't say nothin' to nobody!"

"Why, I oughta blow your damned head off!"

Slash and Pecos hurried past a partway open door on their left. A girl peered through the six-inch gap between the door and the frame. She was a small little thing, still looking half-asleep, her brown eyes wide with fear. "Don't let him hurt Wynona no more," she begged Slash. "Wynona's my friend. My *only friend!*"

Tears oozed out of her eyes and rolled down her pale, plump cheeks.

"Yessir, I oughta blow your damn head off!" the man bellowed again behind the door.

Slash kicked the door open with one enraged thrust of his right foot.

A tall, rat-faced, gangly man—naked as a jaybird—stood before him, holding a cigar in one hand, a cocked pistol in the other hand. He aimed the cocked pistol at a naked girl cowering on the bed to Slash's left. The room stank of sweat and sex and liquor. Two empty bottles lay on the floor by the bed, near the man's pale, bare feet. Another half-empty bottle stood on a bedside table.

The man—Collie, Slash assumed—had his head canted toward his right arm and was squinting down the barrel of the cocked Colt in that hand. As the door bounced off the wall and came back toward Slash, who caught it with his left boot, Collie jerked his head toward Slash, eyes snapping wide in surprise. Rage flashed. Collie started to slide his gun toward Slash.

Slash already had his Colt raised and cocked.

Pecos had come up to stand beside him, aiming his coach gun straight out from his right hip.

The two former cutthroats triggered their weapons at the same time. Slash's bullet took Collie through the neck. That was a love tap compared to what Pecos's Richards did. Both barrels flashed, roiling smoke and stabbing flames. The double-ought buck tore into Collie's gut and chest, lifting him two feet up off the floor and throwing him straight back through the window behind him.

He was standing there and then he wasn't.

The only indication he'd been in the room were all the bullet holes in the walls and furniture, the girl cowering on the bed in a tight, naked ball, and the broken window.

There was a resolute thud as Collie struck the porch roof beneath the window. There was one more, softer thud as he rolled off the porch roof to land in the dusty street.

Silence followed until a boy's shrill voice yelled, "HOLLEE MACK-A-ROH-NEE!"

Running footsteps sounded in the street below the window. The runner was hidden from Slash and Pecos's view by the porch roof, but the running steps had the quick beat of a very eager child.

Slash and Pecos glanced at each other and shrugged, then turned to the girl on the bed.

"You all right, darlin'?" Pecos asked, going over and placing a hand on her shoulder.

She lowered her hands from her head and looked at Pecos. Her eyes were china blue and very wide. She was a pretty blonde—small and pale. She'd been beaten up pretty good. One eye was swelling, and her lips were bloody. Charcoal bruises shone all down her arms and on her legs. She looked at where Collie had been standing only seconds before. She looked at the window and then up at Pecos again.

Tears dribbled down her cheeks as she started to cry again. "He . . . he was gonna . . . kill me that time *fer sure!*"

"Wynona!" This from the girl Slash had seen peeking out from behind the partway open door in the hall. She ran into the room and leaped onto the bed beside the blond Wynona. "Oh, God, Wynona—are you all right? Oh, Lordy—I thought he was gonna kill you!"

"He *was*, Jackie!" Wynona sobbed, letting Jackie take her in her arms. "He was gonna kill me! He was crazy out of his *mind!*"

Since Wynona was being tended to by her friend, Slash and Pecos left the room and headed back down the hall. They stopped when the whorehouse madam who they both assumed was Madam Delacroix, though neither believed that Madam Delacroix was her real name—she spoke with a none-too-faint Missouri twang—stood about halfway down the hall, nervously puffing her cigarette that was a mere stub now extending from the long, black wooden holder.

"Oh, dear God—is he dead?" the woman asked, dread in her voice. She waved a quivering hand in the air near her face. "Oh, God—tell me you didn't kill him!"

Slash and Pecos shared a disbelieving glance.

Pecos said, "If we hadn't sent him to the smoking gates, ma'am, he'd have drilled my partner a third eye. One more eye isn't gonna improve his looks any. He needs way more than a third eye."

Ignoring the insult—he figured he had that and more coming after the business with the saddle cinch—Slash said, "He was about to kill that poor girl in there. She had about one more second until we kicked in that door, uh . . . *ma'am!*"

Madam Delacroix was swooning, stumbling back against the wall, placing a hand over her heaving bosom. "But . . . it's just that, well . . . Tom Gyllenwater is, well . . . he's . . ."

"Whatever he is, he should have taken that crazy boy of his in hand," Pecos said.

He continued to the stairs. Slash followed him down, saying, "So much for the kind of trouble I was expecting."

Pecos stopped at the bottom of the stairs and turned to Slash, who stopped about two steps up from the bottom, a hand on each rail. "What do you mean?" Pecos asked him.

"You know—what we was sent here for."

Slash glanced at the three scantily clad parlor girls moving tentatively toward him and Pecos. Apparently, the four men who'd been in the room when the two former cutthroats had entered had beat a hasty retreat. Maybe they were married and didn't like the attention. Maybe they were just allergic to trouble. Whatever the case, now there were only the girls who lived here. Looking frightened as well as concerned, they slipped around Slash and Pecos to climb the stairs to check out the damage on the second floor.

As they did, each one cast Slash and Pecos several dubious glances.

Slash smiled and pinched his hat brim to the gals—two of whom were right pretty while the third was a little plainfaced—then turned back to Pecos and said, "Did you already forget about Ned Calico, you damn fool? That man up there wasn't Ned Calico. He was local. We just stumbled into a local affair like two deer chasin' their reflections through a saloon window."

"Oh . . ." Pecos winced and nudged his hat down on his forehead as he scratched the back of his head. "That's right. I reckon we should have thought it through." He chuffed and pointed an accusing finger. "You was the one who was so almighty quick to make that leap, though, Slash. I had a feelin' we should . . ."

"Oh, shut up!"

"Don't tell me to shut up or I'll whip your skinny ass!"

"Shut up!" Slash stepped down into the parlor and crossed it, heading for the open front door.

He stepped out onto the front stoop and stopped.

A middle-aged man with a soup-strainer gray mustache and wearing a town marshal's badge on his plaid wool shirt stood over the naked body grimacing up at him from a pool of blood and broken glass. A boy stood a few feet behind the town marshal. He was the same redheaded youngster with the mail bag who'd been giving Slash and Pecos the wooly eyeball back at the train depot.

The boy's eyes were riveted on the naked dead man, so it took him a minute to rake his gaze toward the porch where Slash stood with Pecos coming up from behind to stand beside him. As he did, the boy's eyes grew even wider.

He raised his arm and jutted an accusing finger at the two strangers, yelling, "There they are, Gramps! There they are! The two polecats from the train station! *Didn't I tell ya they looked like a whole week of trouble spillin' over into Saturday?*"

Chapter 10

The old marshal held his hand up to the boy, palm out.
"Easy now, Danny. Settle down. Why don't you get
that mail back over to Mister Wilkes, then fetch the undertaker for me?"

"Are you gonna arrest 'em, Kentucky? Huh? Are ya,
Gramps?" the boy wanted to know, switching his gaze
from Slash and Pecos to the old marshal then back again.
"Boy, Mister Gyllenwater's gonna be some piss-burn . . .
er, I mean, *madder'n an old wet hen* if ya don't!"

The old man whipped around to face the boy directly,
his craggy cheeks turning bright red around his snowy
mustache. "Danny, dammit—what'd I just tell you?"

"Ah, hell. Er . . . I mean, all right, Gramps." Chagrined
and deeply disappointed, the boy gave Slash and Pecos one
more look of wide-eyed, morbid fascination, then turned,
kicked a horse apple, and scampered across the street,
kicking up dust with his shoes.

The lawman turned to Slash and Pecos. His face wore
a sour expression, like he'd just taken a bite out of a lemon,
chewed it up, and swallowed it. He looked down at the
naked dead man grimacing up at him, clucked his disdain

for the situation, then looked around and clucked once more at the gathering spectators drifting toward him from all directions.

He looked at Slash and Pecos again, and drew a deep, fateful breath. "I take it you two are responsible for this." He pointed down at the dead man, as though there could be any question about what or who he meant.

"That drunken fool is responsible for his own demise," Slash said, stepping forward to stand at the top of the porch steps. "Didn't you hear the ruckus he was making up yonder?" He lifted a finger to indicate the parlor house's second story.

"Yeah, yeah . . . I heard it," the old marshal said, flushing sheepishly. "I was makin' my way over here. Don't get around as fast as I used to. Besides, I . . . well, you see, sometimes you just have to give Collie a chance to settle down. He usually does, given enough time."

"If we'd given this polecat any more time," Slash said, pointing down at the naked dead man glowering up at him through half-shuttered lids, "an innocent girl's brains would be painted all over a crib wall!"

"What're you gonna tell him, Kentucky? Huh?" The portly madam was standing in the parlor house's open doorway, nervously scratching a match to life on the door frame and lighting a fresh, ready-made cigarette. "What're you gonna tell Gyllenwater?"

The lawman scrubbed a hand across his mouth and thick mustache as he scowled down at the dead man. "Don't worry, Birdie, I'll figure somethin' out." He glanced up at Slash and Pecos. "You see, the problem is, Collie here—well, he's Collie Gyllenwater. Son of Tom Gyllenwater. The man owns a ranch south of here . . . and a good half of the town."

"I don't care who he is," Pecos said. "His son was shootin'
up the place. And he was about to kill one of your girls,
ma'am." He'd directed this last, with no little accusing in
his voice, at Madam Delacroix, aka "Birdie," nervously
smoking in the doorway.

"Sometimes," the madam said, taking a quick, shallow
puff off the quirley and exhaling smoke through her mouth
and nostrils as she spoke, "we have to make, um, certain
sacrifices here in town. For old Tom."

Pecos looked at Slash in exasperation. "Can you believe
what you're hearin', Slash? I'm startin' to wonder why in
the hell ol' Bleed-'Em-So sent us here. Why would he
think a town like this, one that's willin' to sacrifice one of
its innocent citizens so a rich man don't get his drawers in
a twist, is worth savin'?"

The eyes of Madam Delacroix, Kentucky O'Neil, and
the dozen or so men and women gathered around to stare
down in shocked fascination at the dead Collie Gyllenwater, all jerked toward the two strangers, and widened.
There was a collective gasp. A feverish murmuring arose.

"What'd you say?" O'Neil said, furling his thick gray
brows at the newcomers. "Who sent you here?"

Slash said, "Why, Luther T.—"

"Wait, wait!" O'Neil turned to the small crowd gathered
around him and the newcomers, and held his hands up,
palms out. "All right, folks. Go about your business, now,
hear? There's nothing more to see here. Please don't spread
this around. I'd like to be the one to break the news to
Mister Gyllenwater myself in a, uh, respectful manner. I
don't want him hearin' it from nobody else first. So please
go about your business and don't talk about any of this,
all right? Don't talk about *anything* you heard here today.
Not one word of it. Please!"

Fat chance of that happening, Slash thought, as the crowd reluctantly dispersed, casting inquisitive, guarded glances at him and Pecos and muttering anxiously between themselves.

Madam Delacroix said from the whorehouse door, "*Who'd* you say sent you two fellas?"

"Never mind, Birdie," Kentucky said, holding his big, arthritic hand up at the madam. "I'll take care of it." To Slash and Pecos he said, "Let's continue this conversation in my office, gentlemen. You can follow me over there. Please, not another word until we're behind a closed door!"

He swung around and strode east in a quick but stiff and aged manner along the broad main avenue.

Slash turned to Pecos. "Damn curious."

Pecos shrugged then walked over to his horse, picked up his dangling reins, and swung up onto the buckskin's back. Slash grabbed his own reins and mounted his Appaloosa. They gigged their mounts into slow walks, gradually catching up to the marshal as the man angled toward the squat adobe building sitting between a small café and a leather-goods store and outside which a hand-painted sign identifying the town marshal's office was displayed.

A portly man in a green apron and appearing easily as old as Kentucky O'Neil, stood outside the leather-goods store, glowering toward the newcomers. He turned his gaze toward the marshal, who gave him a brief, dismissive wave as he strode on into his office.

Slash and Pecos dismounted, tied their mounts, then followed the marshal into the office, Pecos coming in last and closing the door behind him. O'Neil stood in front of his desk, his craggy, mustached face owning a deeply incredulous expression.

"Luther Bledsoe sent you here?"

"That's right," Slash said. "After you personally requested that he do so."

The lawman turned his head to one side and narrowed a skeptical eye. "What're you talkin' about? After I 'personally requested that he do so'?"

Pecos canted his head toward his partner. "Show him, Slash."

Slash reached into his coat pocket for the letter. He'd folded it once. Now he opened the fold and handed the envelope and letter to the old marshal. "There you go. You sent it, didn't you?"

O'Neil stared down at the envelope as though it were a dog turd in his hand. He looked at Slash, then at Pecos, then reached out and plucked the envelope from Slash's hand. He held it up in front of him, squinting at it, showing his upper front teeth, then held it at arm's length. He glanced at the two newcomers again then slipped the single leaf from the envelope, opened it, again adjusted the reading distance, and read it.

He moved his lips a little as he did, sort of sucking air and muttering under his breath.

He stared at the letter for a good minute or so, then lowered the note to his side and looked up at Slash and Pecos, chuckling. "I'll be damned," he said, shaking his head and flushing. "You know, I completely forgot about sending this?" He looked at the note again, shook his head again, and chuckled again. "I'll be damned. Boy, I am getting old!"

He turned and walked around behind his desk and slumped stiffly into the swivel chair flanking it. He tossed the letter onto his blotter then sagged back in his chair and chuckled again, amusedly pensive. "Boy, I tell ya.

They're gonna be puttin' me out to pasture soon. Probably not soon enough!"

Pecos stepped up to the desk and said, "You mean you forgot about sending that letter?"

"Yes, sir. Damn. I reckon it's old-timer's disease."

Slash stepped up to stand beside Pecos. He and Pecos shared a skeptical look, then Slash said, "Well, we're here. Bledsoe sent us to help out. We figured the ruckus over at the hurdy-gurdy house involved the Ned Calico you wrote about in that letter. That's why we hurried over there."

"You did, didja?" O'Neil winced, then glanced somewhat sheepishly down at his desk. He ran two fingers along the edge of it and said, "Nah, nah. That trouble with Calico . . . well, it didn't turn out to be as bad as I thought. Not half as bad. You see, the very next day after I sent that letter, Calico and his boys rode on out of town. They just kicked up some dust for a day or two, an' then"—he shrugged his broad, bony shoulders—"they lit a shuck."

He smiled up at Bledsoe's two troubleshooters. "I'm sorry I called you fellas out here on a wild-goose chase. There's a train headed north to Ogallala in two days. There's usually only one train a week, but one of the ranchers made a big cattle sale, so you can hitch along with the freighter. Hell, I'll even have the depot agent add a passenger coach to the combination. Make you right comfortable. The least I can do for wastin' yours and the chief marshal's time."

Slash and Pecos stared dubiously down at the man.

"Your letter sounded right urgent," Slash said.

O'Neil raised his hands. "I reckon I'm gettin' on in years an' overly anxious, to boot. I shouldn't have been so hasty. I do apologize. Please give my apologies to Luther.

I should have waited another day or two. Instead, I sit here feeling like an old fool."

Slash glanced at Pecos, drew a breath, then lifted his hat and ran a hand back through his hair in consternation. "Well, well, well . . ." he said, letting out the breath.

Pecos said, "You an' the chief marshal go back a ways, eh?"

"A ways, yes," O'Neil said, nodding. "We fought together. Met out West a few years after Appomattox." He gave a sheepish grin. "I was wilder in those days. We both were. I got into some trouble, took up with the wrong bunch. Luther set me straight. I feel bad now for having wasted his time with this Calico situation. Yours, too."

Slash smiled, nodded. "I'm sure he'll understand." He narrowed a skeptical eye. "You're sure you don't need our help? This Ned Calico fella has beat a track out of here, sure enough?"

"Oh, he certainly has. He's long gone."

"Remember—pride's a sin," Pecos pointed out, smiling.

Kentucky O'Neil laughed and rocked back and forth in his chair. "Yes, yes, pride is indeed a sin. And while I have been guilty of pride in the past, I assure you I am not guilty of it here. So long, gentlemen. May I recommend the Bon Ton Café for supper? It's in the Longhorn Hotel. The Longhorn is our only real bona fide hotel. Unless you're looking for female companionship, then, well—"

"You probably wouldn't recommend Madam Delacroix's," Slash said, chuckling ironically.

Pecos chimed in with his own satirical laughter. "No, we probably done wore out our welcome over there!"

O'Neil shook his head darkly and stared down at his desk. "Don't even joke about that. That there is a problem."

"Look, Marshal," Slash said. "Why don't you let me and my partner here give the sad news to Collie's family? We can load the body up in a wagon and—"

"No, no!" O'Neil was having none of it. Just the suggestion seemed to terrify him. He moderated his tone a little then added with some chagrin, "No . . . I know Tom Gyllenwater. I'll give him the news. It should come from someone who knows him."

"You sure?" Pecos said. "We could nip the trouble before it even gets started, Slash an' me."

"I'm positive." O'Neil gave both troubleshooters a stern warning look. "You two just make sure you're on that train day after tomorrow. That's the best way for you to nip any possible trouble before it gets started."

Slash and Pecos shared another conferring glance.

Slash shrugged. "Have it your way, Marshal."

He slapped Pecos's shoulder with the back of his hand. "Come on, partner."

He and Pecos started for the door. As Slash drew it open, O'Neil said, "Who are you two, anyway? You look damned familiar."

Again, Slash and Pecos looked at each other. Pecos smiled as he turned back to the marshal. "All you need to know, Marshal O'Neil, is that Luther Bledsoe sent us."

Slash smiled and winked at the old lawman. "It'd be best if you kept it under your hat, though. We work sorta unofficial-like."

With that, he and Pecos left the office, leaving Kentucky O'Neil staring uncertainly after them.

Chapter 11

Kentucky O'Neil looked down at the letter on his desk. He opened it again and muttered the words as he read it:

"*Dear Friend Luther,*

I could use some Help up here if You can spare a couple of Men. Discretion is Necessary. Ned Calico is back. I will explain in full when Your Boys arrive. Send good men please Luther.

Gun Men.

Your Friend Always, Kentucky"

He'd just recited his own name when a shadow passed across the window to his right and boots thumped on the adobe shack's front porch. There was a single knock and then George Henshaw tripped the latch and poked his balding gray head into the room. "All clear?"

Kentucky sighed. "All clear."

Henshaw stepped into the room, then closed the door

slowly and with needless secretiveness behind him. Turning to the marshal he said, "Who were they?"

"Bledsoe sent 'em."

Henshaw frowned. "Bledsoe . . . Bledsoe . . ."

"Luther Bledsoe. Chief marshal for the Western District in Denver."

Henshaw whistled. "Thought the name sounded familiar, but—"

"You remember it from when Bledsoe and another federal—both deputy U.S. marshals at the time—came to collect Calico and the other two, and hauled them off to Denver to face their federal charges. Federal trumps state."

"Ah." Henshaw frowned again, shaking his head. "I don't get it. Why did he send men now, for godsakes?"

"Someone sent him a letter, asking for help."

"Not from here, surely!"

Kentucky tossed the letter to the other side of his desk. Henshaw scowled down at it before picking it up and reading it. As he read, his thin, gray brows became more and more ridged until he tossed the letter back down on the desk and looked at his old friend in hang-jawed astonishment.

"Obviously," Kentucky said, "I didn't write that letter."

"It certainly looks like your crabbed handwriting! If you didn't, Kentucky, then, by God, *who did?*"

"I don't know. At least, I'm not sure."

"Who do you suspect?"

"Not gonna go into it." Kentucky rose and hitched his gun belt and trousers up higher on his hips, tucking his shirt in over his paunch. "I'm gonna go see a man about a horse. Or, something like that . . ."

He grabbed the letter, which he stuffed into a pocket of his worn dungarees. He stepped around his desk, brushed past the portly Henshaw, and opened his office door wide, stepping back to let his old friend pass first. Henshaw turned toward Kentucky, his eyes grave. "Old friend, is this trouble?"

"I told them to leave on the next train."

"So, they believed whatever story you concocted?"

"I think so. I can be pretty convincing when I need to be."

Henshaw chewed on that for a time, then nodded, reluctantly satisfied. "Let's hope so."

"Don't worry—everything's under control, George." Kentucky tried to offer his old friend a reassuring smile. He wasn't sure if it came off or not. The twist of his lips beneath his mustache felt forced and stiff.

"What about Collie Gyllenwater?"

Kentucky gave a caustic chuff. "One problem at a time—all right, George?"

Henshaw held up his fat hands, palms out.

"Now get out of here, ya old scudder. I told ya—"

"I know, I know," Henshaw said, waddling out the door. "You gotta see a man about a horse."

Kentucky stepped out onto the stoop, drew the door closed behind him, and stood looking around at the street for a time, pondering. Absently, he flicked his thumb against the pocket containing the letter.

He dropped down the single step to the street and headed south. At the first cross street, he tramped north. His house sat on the street's right side, a forlorn-looking, tumbledown shack with a matching picket fence. The shack and the fence needed a coat of paint. Probably a couple of coats. If only Kentucky could find the money to buy the paint and the time to brush it onto the house. The boy could help, but he couldn't do all of it. Nancy was busy tending to Kentucky and the boy and her chickens. Hell, with her chickens and eggs, she brought as much money into the house as Kentucky did on his thirty-a-month salary.

Thirty dollars a month after fifteen years.

He clucked and shook his head as he stepped through the broken fence gate and started walking toward the sagging porch. He'd been hearing whacking sounds issuing from the backyard, and now he heard Danny yelling, "Ow! Oh, Momma, please don't hurt me anymore, Momma!"

Whack!

"Momma, please—it hurts!"

Whack!

"Ow! Oh, Momma, please stop hurting me, Momma!"

Kentucky stopped abruptly and turned to scowl toward the house's right front corner, heart quickening. "Good Lord—what in the hell has gotten into that—"

As he continued hearing the whacks and Danny's cries, Kentucky strode as quickly as he could on his feeble knees and arthritic hips around the front corner of the house and followed the hard-packed trail around to the back. He slowed his pace when he saw Nancy smacking a rug, which she'd thrown over a clothesline, with a long stick. Each time she smacked the rug, dust wafted in the midday sunshine, and Danny, swinging on the wooden swing suspended from a bough of the oak near the clothesline, exclaimed in mock pain, "Ow! Momma, that one really hurt! Stop hurting me, Momma! Oh, please stop hurting me, Momma!"

"Good Lord!" Kentucky exclaimed, walking slowly forward, sliding his relieved gaze between the boy and his mother smacking the rug with the stick. "I thought you were . . ."

Nancy stopped beating the rug and turned to her father, brows arched in surprise at seeing him this time of the day. He didn't usually come home for lunch but stayed in his office and ate the food Nancy packed for him every morning.

"Dad!" she said. "What a surprise." She glanced at Danny grinning devilishly in his tree swing, then returned her gaze to Kentucky. "Oh! Did you think I was finally taking the switch to him? Hah! I couldn't catch him if I wanted to."

She turned to browbeat her son. "Danny, you frightened your grandfather with your shenanigans!"

Kentucky threw his shoulders forward and dropped his chin, chuckling. He should have known the boy was funning. That's what Danny did—he had fun. He could find it at all times, in all places, and in many, many ways. Pure mischief, that grandson of Kentucky's.

Kentucky continued forward, still smiling. "Yeah, I should have known. He's too fast for both of us put together."

Nancy glanced at Danny again and smiled a proud mother's smile. She was a pretty, brown-haired, brown-eyed woman, still relatively youthful at thirty. Youthful despite all the hard years of survival here in this backwater town, tending a falling-down house, an energetic young son, and an aging father. She'd lost her mother early and, while she was a tough young woman—a woman of the Nebraska prairie—the heartbreak of that and all the hard years that had followed, raising Danny without a father, and bearing up under the loneliness and the stigma of being a single mother, had taken their toll.

She looked sad most of the time, even when she was trying hard to smile. The lines in her face, especially around her eyes and her mouth, grew deeper every year. Kentucky hated the life she'd been handed, and he hated himself for being unable to improve things for her. Some things, even a man's child, were beyond his control no matter how hard he tried to control them.

Now she looked at her father probingly, stitching her brows together. "Pa, Danny told me about . . . Collie. Is that . . . is that why you're home?"

The smile dwindled on Kentucky's face as he returned his attention to the letter in his pocket. He glanced at Danny, humming absently now as he swung, raking his boots against the ground, kicking up dirt.

Kentucky said, "Son, go on inside and shave some feather sticks for the range."

Danny turned to him, scowling. "I done already shave—"

"Go shave some more," Kentucky said, unable to suppress a grin. The boy, while often defiant, was basically good-natured.

Nancy turned to the boy. "You heard your grandfather. No back talk or you will get a switch over your backside!" She waved the stick at him.

"Holy cow!" Danny said, leaping out of the swing and striking the ground flat-footed, knees bent. His hat tumbled off his head and he stooped to retrieve it. "A fella can't even sit in his swing without being treated like a low-down dirty dog! Just a low-down dirty dog!"

He jogged up the back step and disappeared into the house.

Kentucky turned to Nancy with an ironic smile. "We treat him like a low-down dirty dog."

"Don't we, though?"

"He's got spirit—I'll give him that."

"A little of the devil, too, I'd say." Nancy smiled but the

smile disappeared almost instantly, and she turned a dark, worried expression toward the house.

"No." Kentucky placed his hand on her arm. "No, Nancy. There's no devil in him. Just boy. Good boy and bad boy, sometimes, but he's just a normal healthy boy. Remember, he's half you."

Nancy returned her gaze to her father and gave a cock-eyed smile. "And at least one-quarter you. I'm still debating if that's good or bad." She reached up and flicked his hat brim with her finger. "So, tell me—why the midday visit? What's wrong? Is it Collie? Are you worried about his father?" The lines at the corners of her eyes deepened as she probed her father with deep speculation.

Kentucky drew his mouth corners down then pulled the envelope from his pocket. He showed it to her.

She gasped, started to raise a hand to her mouth, then let it slowly drop to her side. Her cheeks paled a little and she looked up at Kentucky again, guilt in her eyes now. She didn't say anything.

Kentucky held up the letter, waved it. "You're the only one who could imitate my chicken scratch, the way I put words together."

Nancy lowered her head and let out a long, heavy breath. "I'm sorry, Pa." She looked up at him again. "It was an act of desperation. They'd been here two days. I thought they'd stay . . . that it would happen all over again. The terror . . ."

"You didn't trust me to take care of it."

"Well, you know . . ." Now her eyes were none too vaguely accusing, but she let the sharp words trail off.

"Yes, I know. I didn't do much of a job of taking care of it before. I let it go too far. Too damn far." Kentucky turned his head to stare at the house.

Nancy placed a hand on his jaw and turned his face toward hers. "That was as much my fault as yours."

"No, it wasn't."

"Well, what happened, happened. I just didn't want any other girl to go through what I did. I didn't want the town to go through what it went through. I didn't want you to go through what you went through twelve years ago. Pa, you're twelve years older!"

"Bledsoc, Nancy? Luther Bledsoe?"

"I felt I had no choice. You said he was chief marshal now. I knew he could do something . . . that he'd send someone. After I sent the letter, I regretted it. Sort of forgot about it after . . . after all that happened. I guess I'd hoped it hadn't reached him . . . or that he'd ignored it . . ."

"Well, he didn't ignore it."

"He sent someone?"

Kentucky nodded, nibbled the ends of his mustache. "The men who killed Collie."

Again, Nancy gasped. This time she brought the hand all the way to her mouth and kept it there. "I'm so sorry," she whispered.

Kentucky couldn't keep the harshness, the sharp anger from his voice. "Do you realize what you've done? It could have all been over."

Tears shone in the woman's eyes. She scrunched up her face, dropped her chin, and pressed her clenched fists to her temples. "I was so afraid! I was so afraid that . . . that . . . Danny might find out. Or that Calico . . . would find out that . . ."

"No." Kentucky shook his head slowly, his jaws hard. "I'm not so sure you were afraid. I'm wondering, Nancy, if you weren't jealous."

She looked up at him now, incredulous. "Jealous!"

"You know—of the way he was carryin' on with Mary Kate."

Nancy's own jaws hardened now, and fire flashed in her eyes. She swung her arm back and brought her right hand forward. It happened in a rush of emotion, a blur of uncontrolled motion. The hand crashed with a sharp *crack!* across her father's jaw.

"How dare you!" she raked out, trying with little success to keep her voice down.

The blow had slammed Kentucky's face to one side and set his cheek on fire. He staggered two steps back. She hadn't held back one bit. Not one bit.

He turned back to her now, knowing he'd been right, feeling the horror of that as well as a keen tenderness for his poor, lost daughter who'd grown into a life-hardened but still-lost woman. At least, on the inside. The outside was merely a show.

Sobbing, drawing her hand to her mouth and trembling lips once more, tears washing down her cheeks, Nancy turned and slumped off to the house. She stumbled up onto the low stoop and hurried inside, leaving the door open behind her.

Kentucky stared at the half-open door, which was nudged back and forth a little by the breeze. Feeling eyes on him, he raised his gaze to a second-story window. Danny stood there, peering down at his grandfather, curiosity stitching the boy's brows.

Chapter 12

Mary Kate pushed through the Copper Nickel Saloon batwing doors with aplomb, and said, "Yep, it's Collie Gyllenwater, all right. He's layin' out there in the street deader'n last year's Christmas goose!"

Her father, Norman Rivers, glared at her from behind the bar, where he'd just filled two shot glasses and set them before the two townsmen standing at the bar before him. "Mary Kate, what in hell were you doing out there? I told you to stay upstairs!"

Mary Kate shrugged a shoulder. She still looked pretty despite the black eye she was sporting, though the swelling had gone down over the past several days so that there was now only a little sickly yellow arcing around the outside of it and a little swollen dark patch beneath it. "I heard the shooting and decided to go out and investigate. You never know what trouble's coming to *this* town!"

She flounced on one hip and cast her father a sneering grin. "Mary Kate, get upstairs!"

"You wouldn't think it would, though, would you?" Mary Kate said, ignoring her father's order. "Such a quiet town . . . so far off the beaten path." She'd turned to stare absently out the large window to her left. "Just goes to show, trouble lurks in every nook and cranny . . . anywhere on the map. Even way out here on this canker on the devil's ass . . ."

"Mary Katherine Rivers, get your ass upstairs!"

The two men at the bar, shop owners in shabby business suits, stood smiling at Mary Katherine, each with one elbow on the bar. "Imagine that," the one on the left said to the other, then to Norman Rivers still glaring at his daughter. "Collie Gyllenwater—dead."

The taller of the two shop owners turned to Mary Kate. "Did you see who punched Collie's ticket, Mary Kate?"

"A coupla handsome older fellas," Mary Kate said. She was speaking directly to her father in a none-too-subtle mocking tone. "One's a tall drink of water with long hair. The other's shorter and dark. Both look like serious business, if you're askin' me."

"No one's asking you, Mary Kate! Get upstairs."

Mary Kate had turned to peer out the window in the direction of the town marshal's office. "Oh, look there. I think you fellas are about to get your own introductions to the killers of Collie Gyllenwater, for they appear to be headed right this way!"

She flounced again, smiling at her father and nibbling a thumbnail.

Rivers tossed his towel down on the bar, then, cursing under his breath, walked out from behind the bar and over to where Mary Kate stood in her lacy day dress that clung to her like a second skin, announcing every delightful curve of the maturing girl's splendid form. Her blond-colored hair tumbled in rich curls down her neck and across her shoulders, glistening delightfully in the sunlight angling through the dirty windows.

The two men at the bar were swallowing the girl whole with their eyes, as did every man who came in here. About the only good that came of it, to Norman Rivers's way of looking at it, was that his business had increased three-fold over the past couple of years—since Mary Kate had started becoming a woman. At the moment, however, he didn't want her down here or anywhere any newcomer could see her and possibly talk to her.

"Dammit, she's right," Rivers said to no one in particular as he glanced out the window. "They're headed right this way." He gave Mary Kate a hard shove toward the stairs. "Get your ass upstairs right now, Mary Kate, or so help me—"

"What?" Mary Kate spat in sharp defiance. "You'll blacken my other eye?" She blinked, flared a nostril; her upper lip trembled with barely bridled rage. "Or you'll try what you—"

"Damn you!" Rivers lunged forward, picking a chair up off the floor and thrusting it behind his shoulder, threatening to smash it against the girl's head.

Mary Kate screamed as she threw an arm up as though to defend herself from the chair. Keeping her arm raised, she wheeled and ran to the stairs at the rear of the room. She was halfway there as boots thumped on the boardwalk fronting the batwings.

Slash had heard the girl's scream a second before he'd stepped onto the boardwalk fronting the Copper Nickel Saloon.

He glanced at Pecos, frowning, then pushed slowly through the batwings, his right hand on the .44 holstered for the cross-draw on his left hip. He stopped just inside the doors. The only girl in the room was halfway up the stairs. The pretty blonde stopped and turned, one hand on the rail. She peered down into the saloon at Pecos, who stepped in behind Slash to stand beside him, looking around cautiously.

There were three men in the room, and the girl on the stairs. Her dress was so tight she appeared ready to burst out of the garment with the next deep breath. Someone must have smacked her around a bit, for her right eye still wore the remnants of a nasty bruise.

A fat man with a bullet-shaped head and wearing a red cloth vest over a white shirt as well as a green bartender's apron stood near Slash and Pecos. He turned to the girl, and his jaws hardened and his fleshy cheeks above his handlebar mustache turned red.

The girl looked at Slash and then at Pecos with mute, scowling interest and curiosity, then turned her head forward and continued up the stairs.

The apron turned to Slash and Pecos, working too hard to manufacture an affable, welcoming smile. "Welcome, fellas! Sit down an' take a load off or belly up to the bar! I'm Norman Rivers, owner and operator—at your serv—"

He stopped and lowered the hand he'd extended toward the newcomers as the two men in cheap suits who'd been standing at the bar scrambled past him and the newcomers on their way to the batwings. One was still nervously fumbling with his hat, trying to get it set on his head, as he followed the other man out through the batwings and into the street.

Slash glanced at Pecos, one brow arched. He looked at the owner and operator, Rivers, then lifted one arm to sniff his armpit.

"Oh," Rivers said, chuckling and waving a pudgy hand,

"don't mind those two. It was just time for them to reopen their shops after lunch, is all."

He'd turned to waddle back toward the bar, breathing as though winded.

"And the girl?" Slash asked.

Moving heavily around the end of the bar, Rivers chuckled again and said, "That's my daughter. We had a little fallin' out, you might say. You know—father/daughter kind of stuff."

"And the eye?" Pecos asked. "Was that father/daughter stuff, too?"

Again, the man gave a dismissive little wave. "Don't worry, she deserved it. Every bit of it. She can be a handful, that one."

"I saw that," Slash said as he quartered to his right and kicked a chair out from a table.

Rivers chuckled. "Yeah, she's growin' up, Mary Kate is. Most folks notice. Most men, that is. She's entirely off limits, however. She just works days. I want her to spend her nights concentratin' on her school studies upstairs, where we quarter, her an' me. I keep tellin' her I been bustin' my ass to give her a better life than the one I had, and them tight dresses ain't gonna help her one damn bit. All they're gonna do is get her trapped right here in Harveyville with the rest of us."

Rivers was leaning forward across the bar. Now he slapped it, apparently indicating a change of subject, and said, "So, tell me—what're you fellas drinkin'? Beer goes good with my lunch chili, and I got some left, though I might have to scrape it off the bottom of the pot."

"Sounds good," Slash said, removing his hat and tossing it onto the table before him.

"Yeah, I'll take an ale and the scrapin's," Pecos said,

unslinging his shotgun from his arm and setting it on the table before slacking heavily into a chair and removing his hat. He tossed the hat down onto the gut-shredder.

"We'll start you off with a coupla beers, then." Rivers grabbed a schooner and filled it from a spigot behind the bar. He filled another glass and waddled over to Slash and Pecos's table, and set a frothy, malty ale down before each customer. As he did, he glanced at the sawed-off double barrel beneath Pecos's bullet-crowned Stetson, and gave a nervous smile. "Say there . . . say there . . . that's a nasty-lookin' little popper, for sure!"

"Yeah, if looks could kill." Pecos caressed the rear stock and grinned up at Rivers. "But it ain't that nasty li'l gal's looks that do the killin'." He winked.

Rivers laughed, his face turning red again. His eyes weren't laughing a bit, however, as they lingered on the savage popper reclining along the table's edge, near Pecos's right hand.

Nervously, the barman rubbed his hands on his apron. "What're, uh . . . what're you two fellas doin' in town—if you don't mind me askin', of course?"

"Well," Pecos said, "we're here to look into—"

"Just passin' through," Slash broke in, and sipped his brew. Rivers chuckled nervously and continued to rub his hands on his apron. He glanced out the window, in the direction of Madam Delacroix's place, where Collie Gyllenwater was just then being loaded into the undertaker's wagon, then gave one more nervous chuckle and ambled back around behind his bar and through a curtained doorway flanking it.

Staring after him, Slash said, "Damn peculiar," and sucked more of the froth off the top of his beer.

"What is?"

"How folks are actin'. Odd. Secretive. Like they're hidin' somethin'."

"Well, we did shoot the son of some local mucky-muck. That seems to be what has 'em all nervous."

"Is that it?"

"What do you think it is?"

"We're the ones who shot that little privy snake. We're the ones who should be nervous. Why's Kentucky O'Neil nervous? Why were them two shopkeepers nervous—the two who hightailed it out of here like they thought we was bringin' the plague? Why's the barkeep so nervous?"

Just then, as though on cue, Rivers pushed through the curtained doorway behind the bar. He made his way around the bar with a tray on which two bowls of chili smoked. "Here we go, gentlemen—just what the doctor ordered to fill out the hollow left by a long, hard trail!"

As the man, breathing hard as though he'd run a bare-foot mile in rugged terrain, set the steaming bowls in front of Slash and Pecos and then set a plate of crusty brown bread and a bowl of butter onto the table, as well, Slash looked up at him and said, "Why are you so damn nervous, sir?"

Pecos had just sipped his beer, and now he blew half of it onto the table.

The barman tucked the empty tray under his arm, flushed crimson around his ostentatious mustache, widened his little, lake-blue eyes in their pale, fleshy sockets, and said, "Uh . . . what's that?"

Slash slapped the table in frustration. "Why are you so damn nervous?"

A squeal of female laughter came from the top of the

stairs. Slash and Pecos turned to see the pretty blonde sitting on the top step, one bare foot planted atop the other one, leaning forward over her bare knees, snickering into her hand.

The barman jerked his exasperated gaze at the girl. He thrust an angry finger at her, barking, "Dammit, Mary Kate, you get to your room and stop eavesdropping like a child!"

Still snickering into her hand, the girl climbed to her feet, swung around, and ran off down the second-story hall. The slapping of her bare feet sounded in the ceiling. A door clicked open and slammed closed, making the whole building lurch.

When Slash returned his attention to the barman, Rivers was no longer standing at the table. For a big man, he'd fled like a dog with a pullet in its jaws. The curtain over the door flanking the bar was still jostling from his hasty passage.

"Now you went an' done it," Pecos said, spooning chili onto a scrap of the grainy bread then shoving the bread and chili into his mouth.

"Went an' done what?"

"Made him nervouser," Pecos said, chewing.

Slash took another sip of his beer then dug into his own stew. He ate with a pensive air.

Pecos glanced up at him from his own bowl, which he'd already nearly emptied. "What's the matter?"

"Somethin' ain't right."

"Well, maybe not, but what can we do? The marshal sent a request for help to ol' Bleed-'Em-So, but it turns out, after we get all the way out here, he don't need that help, after all. What're we supposed to do, force help on a man . . . and on a town . . . that don't need it?"

"No, I reckon not," Slash said, dunking a slice of bread in his chili.

Pecos looked up at him again. "What're you lookin' so grim about? We get to go home in two days. Hell, we could start out tomorrow, if'n we wanted to ride up to Ogallala on horseback, catch the train from the east."

"I reckon."

"You'll see that fiery-haired li'l missus of yours again . . . sooner rather than later." Pecos frowned suddenly. "Say now . . . you ain't havin' second thoughts now, are ya?"

"About what? Jay? Hell, no!" Slash swallowed a mouthful of food and said, "I know I was nervous goin' in, but now that it's a done deal, I love the married life. Leastways, what I've sampled so far."

He tried not to remember their first night together, only one night ago, since he wasn't going to get to sample more of it anytime real soon. Just a glimpse of remembrance made him smile inwardly, however. Now, back to the topic at hand.

"I can't wait to get home," he said, scraping the last of his chili from the bottom of his bowl, "but somethin' about Ned Calico . . . an' Collie Gyllenwater . . . don't sit right with me."

"Calico's gone," Pecos said. "The marshal said so himself."

"Yeah, I know." Slash swabbed his bowl with a chunk of bread, stuffed the bread into his mouth, then picked up his beer and sauntered to the front window. He swallowed his chili and bread, washed it down with a couple of deep draws from his beer schooner, then stood looking out, beer in one hand, his other hand on his hip.

He stared for a long time back in the direction of the

town marshal's office. Pecos sat back in his chair, rolling a quirley and watching his partner dubiously. A slow ridge piled up over Slash's left eye. It probably piled up over his right eye, too, but Pecos could see only his partner's left eye from this angle.

Slash kept staring out the window, frowning. "That old marshal just climbed into the undertaker's wagon. Looks like he's gonna haul that dead devil's foul carcass out to his ranch, break the grim news to the family."

"Uh-huh."

Slash turned his scowl on his partner. "That's all you got to say?"

Pecos shrugged and took another drink of his beer. He swallowed, smacked his lips, wiped his mouth with the back of his hand, and said, "I thought 'uh-huh' was a very appropriate response to that bit of information. He said he was gonna do it—didn't he? So, he's gonna do it. Why don't you sit down and have another beer? We got some time to kill."

"You'd just sit here and drink beer and let that old man do our dirty work for us?"

"What do you mean? We did *his* dirty work for *him* when we shot the scoundrel!"

"That's a fair point."

"Thank you for that rare compliment."

Slash stepped closer to the window and continued to stare up the street to his left. "Still, though . . ."

"Still, though, what?" Pecos asked with dread in his voice. Slash was not one to let a thing be. Never had been. And, despite marriage to a good woman, Pecos thought he never would be one to let a thing be.

Slash walked over to the table and grabbed his hat. "I'm gonna join him."

"Slash, he doesn't want us out there," Pecos said with deep impatience.

It was Slash's turn to shrug. "He doesn't have to know I'm joinin' him."

He grinned, winked, then headed for the door. He paused just long enough to say, "Pay for our meals, will ya, partner?"

Then he went out.

Pecos cursed, tossed some coins onto the table, grabbed his hat and shotgun, and followed his partner into the street.

Chapter 13

After Slash and Pecos had left town and brought the old marshal into sight ahead of them, they hung well back and followed slowly, keeping pace with the wagon. The trail angled south and then southeast and then back south again through mostly featureless prairie, save a few low mesas and widely scattered haystack buttes.

They saw no ranch headquarters but plenty of grazing beef—from horizon to horizon, in fact. They rode past several forks in the trail, the tines of the fork marked with the names of ranches—the Circle 7, the Jinglebob, the Norcross Triple 8—burned or painted into signs shaved into pointing arrows. The headquarters of said ranches must lie far and wide, broadly scattered across the vast Nebraska Panhandle, all but lost under that broad, blue sky obscured by only a few pale mares' tails of high, wispy clouds.

Kentucky O'Neil continued south in his clattering wagon.

It wasn't hard for two men on horseback to follow a man in a wagon. Especially out on the open Nebraska prairie. The trick for Slash and Pecos was staying far enough behind the wagon that the old marshal didn't spy them on his back trail. There wasn't much for cover out here aside from a few scattered bur oaks and cedars and occasional cottonwoods in the troughs between the grassy, wavelike swells in the rolling prairie. They lingered in these swells then hurried over the rises, where, if O'Neil glanced behind him, he'd likely see their silhouettes clearly outlined against that lens-clear summer sky.

"I'm still not sure what we're doin' out here, Slash," Pecos said maybe a half hour after they'd left town.

"That makes two of us."

"You're the one who thought it so damn necessary we leave that comfortable saloon. That beer went down real good and a second one woulda gone down even better."

"I did think it necessary we ride out here, and I still do. I just don't know why. Yet."

"Oh? Well, when do you think you will know?"

"I reckon I'll know when I know."

"Will you please tell me when you do?"

Slash grinned. "Sure, pard. You'll be the first to know." He winked.

Pecos cursed.

As they climbed to the top of another low rise, Slash pulled back on his reins, stopping his horse. "Whoa . . . whoa . . ."

Pecos glanced at him, frowning. "What is it?"

Slash gazed straight ahead, beyond the next three prairie swells, toward where four horseback riders were galloping down from a pine-stippled ridge in the southwest. They were angling toward where Kentucky O'Neil was clattering in his wagon along the gently meandering trail. The man and wagon were bug-sized from Slash and Pecos's vantage of several hundred yards to the north. The four horsebackers were ant-sized.

Slash glanced at Pecos. "Come on!"

He reined his horse off the trail's east side and booted him into a gallop, quickly descending the ridge toward the next trough between swells. Pecos followed, grumbling and muttering.

They rode out well wide of the trail, circling around behind a haystack butte that humped up between them and the wagon as well as the four riders angling down the ridge toward the wagon from the southwest. Pecos followed Slash up the butte's east side.

Halfway to the top of the bluff, both men dismounted, dropped their reins, shucked their rifles from their saddle boots, and scrambled to the top of the bluff, where the topsoil had long ago been eroded away by wind and water, leaving a spine-like crust of rock. The rock made good cover. Both men dropped to their knees, doffed their hats, and cast their gazes through gaps in the low rock wall.

Kentucky O'Neil was just halting his wagon about twenty feet up the trail, which angled around the butte's west side. The horseback riders were approaching the wagon from fifty yards away, checking their horses down to trots.

They were cowpunchers. No doubt about that. Three young men, one man maybe a few years younger than Slash and Pecos. But damn few. He was a big man, his once-fit body gone to seed. He had a broad, even-featured face with long, dark sideburns and a dragoon-style mustache. A black Stetson sat on his head; dropping from the hat were thick waves of dark brown hair lightly flecked with gray.

His age and bearing indicated he was the leader of the

three men riding with him, and probably more men back at the ranch. Possibly, foreman.

"Kentucky, what in holy blazes are you doing way out here?" he asked as he reined in his white-socked black quarter horse just off the trail, on the wagon's right side. "I didn't think your arthritic old ass could stand a wagon ride through this rough country."

His words had been harsh but his smile softened it, turned it into friendly ribbing.

"It's not good, Wayne," Kentucky said.

"What's not good?"

One of the younger men had ridden his claybank over to the side of the wagon and peered in. He leaned over the side of the box to pull a saddle blanket back to reveal the body resting inside. He whistled and turned to the man Kentucky had called Wayne, and said, "The old man's right, Mr. Blanchard."

Blanchard scowled at the younger man—a wiry blond with quick, nervous movements and bright, shrewd eyes. Blanchard jerked his head to indicate O'Neil and said, "That old man is Marshal O'Neil to you, you little privy rat. You got that, Kyle? He was taming towns—hard, Western kinda towns, end-of-track kinda towns—before you were even a drunken grin on your poppa's ugly face. Understand?"

Kyle stared at Blanchard in sudden shock. "Sure, sure . . . I understand, Mr. Blanchard. I was just . . ."

"Say it."

"Huh?"

"Say his name."

"He's Marshal O'Neil."

"Say it again, you damn tinhorn!"

"He's Marshal O'Neil!"

The other two cow nurses smirked. One chuckled. Kyle cowed them both with a sharp look.

Blanchard turned to Kentucky. Kentucky gave a weak half-smile. Blanchard scowled, shook his head, then turned back to the blond-headed firebrand, Thorn Willis. "What's he haulin'?"

Kyle glanced into the box again, then at O'Neil and then at Blanchard. "Why, it's . . . it's . . ."

"It's Collie Gyllenwater, Wayne," said Kentucky.

Blanchard's big, rugged face crumpled as his mouth opened wide, though he didn't say anything.

"Yep," said Kentucky with a heavy sigh. "It sure as hell is." Blanchard almost looked ready to cry as he stared at the Harveyville town marshal. "Who? That card sharp out of Omaha? If I told Collie once, I told him—"

"No, it wasn't the gambler. I'd just as soon not go into who it was, Wayne."

Hunkered down atop the haystack butte, Slash and Pecos exchanged curious glances.

"Oh?" Blanchard said with a caustic chuff, leaning forward against his saddle horn. "And why's that?"

O'Neil shook his head. "You know how he is. And you know I . . . not to mention the town . . . don't need any more trouble. I'm tryin' to cut down on trouble, not bring more in. We done had our fill of it—don't you think?"

Blanchard laughed without mirth. "You *know* how that's gonna sit with Old Tom, Kentucky!"

"I know."

"Tell me. Let me weigh it." Blanchard glanced at the three younger punchers and put some commanding steel in his voice. "They won't say anything to anybody. You can be sure of that."

"I'm not sure who they are," Kentucky said. "But they were sent by Luther Bledsoe."

Blanchard's thick brows drifted low over his eyes, bulging. "Bledsoe? You mean that deputy—"

"Chief marshal now for the Western District. In Denver."

"How in the hell . . . ?"

"Someone wrote to him, asking him to send gun help. They told him Calico was back, and . . . well . . . I reckon they figured I needed help." The old marshal had added these last words with some chagrin.

"Who in blue blazes sent for the feds?"

"Can't tell you that, either."

"Kentucky, you and I been friends a long time." Blanchard's face was swollen with exasperation. "You know I can't keep all that from the old man!"

"Just tell him two drifters came through. Tell him Collie got crossways with 'em. They shot him and drifted on."

"How much of that is true?"

"Enough."

"They're still in town—aren't they?" Blanchard asked. "That's why you're out here, holding your hat."

"We don't need any more trouble, Wayne."

"Tell that to whoever sent for the feds!" Blanchard swore and shook his head. "Dammit, Kentucky—why didn't you just drag that kid's worthless ass out in the country and dump him into a ravine? We could have told Gyllenwater he disappeared. The old man would eventually assume the feckless fool had gotten crossways with one of his enemies—that card sharp, say. Or a jealous husband." One of the younger men laughed; Blanchard ignored him. "You know how Collie was. Hell, the kid made an enemy at every turn. He'd have believed that— the old man would!"

Kentucky shook his head. "He was shot in broad daylight. There were witnesses. The whole town knows the what and who of it by now."

"Damn!"

"Yeah, I know."

"Now *he's* gonna want to know the what and who of it, too, Kentucky."

"If anybody can reason with him—you can, Wayne. You've been his foreman for many years. He trusts you, respects you. Convince him it's in his best interest to let it go. It's in the best interest of the Rimfire. He built up a good operation out there. Twice. We both know how he did it the second time."

"All right, all right, Kentucky." Blanchard glanced cautiously and with obvious paranoia at the three younger riders flanking him. "We don't need to rehash ancient history right out here in the open."

Blanchard rode up to the wagon and peered inside. "Good God!" He looked at Kentucky. "Damn near cut him in two!" He pointed at the carcass. "I gotta take that back to the headquarters and throw it at the old man's feet?"

Kentucky didn't say anything. He just looked at the big foreman over his shoulder.

The three younger riders looked at one another, silently conferring. None was laughing now. They'd caught on to the gravity of the situation.

Blanchard heaved a sigh. He stepped down from his saddle and into the wagon box behind Kentucky. He handed the Harveyville lawman the reins of his American, saying, "Take my horse back to town, and I'll take the wagon. If you take that boy back lookin' like he is, he'd likely shoot you. I'll send for my hoss tomorrow."

The two men switched places, Kentucky stepping from

the wagon onto the white-socked black. Kentucky turned to Blanchard, his craggy face grave, his eyes wide and round. "He had it comin', Wayne. Collie. If those two strangers hadn't shot him, he'd have killed a girl. He was crazy drunk and out of his head with meanness."

"Yeah, well, that's gonna be the old man tonight. I can reason with him till I'm blue in the face, but you can bet silver cartwheels to army biscuits he's gonna send his hardtails to town tomorrow!"

Blanchard cursed, then shook the reins over the line-back dun in the traces. The horse lunged forward and the wagon rattled off down the trail. The three younger punchers turned their horses onto the trail and followed the wagon, looking at one another and muttering.

Kentucky sat the handsome black American horse sideways in the trail, staring after Blanchard and the wagon. He sat there staring for a long time before he finally turned the horse and lightly whipped the rein ends against the mount's right wither.

The horse lunged into a spanking trot, heading north toward town.

Atop the haystack butte, Pecos turned to Slash. "Boy, that old marshal sure is doin' his best to keep a lit match from touchin' the fuse of one helluva big powder keg."

"He sure is." Slash lowered his rifle and leaned back against the rock he'd been crouched behind. He produced his makings sack and slowly, thoughtfully began to build a quirley. "I sure would like to know what it's all about, though."

"What what's all about?"

"Yeah," Slash said, nodding then licking the edge of the wheat paper. "Exactly!"

Pecos shook his head, deeply befuddled. "Maybe, since

we rode all the way out here, we should just ride on into the Rimfire headquarters and lay our cards on the table."

"Nah." Slash rolled the wheat paper closed around the tobacco, losing hardly a single fleck. "Old Kentucky is tryin' his level best to keep that powder keg from blowin' up. If we rode into the Rimfire without knowing exactly what we're riding in *to* . . . I got a feelin' we'd blow it up, and . . ."

"And what?"

"O'Neil right along with it."

Pecos held out his hand. "Give me your tobacco."

"Go to hell."

"Give me your tobacco, dammit. My arm still hurts!"

"Go to hell!"

Pecos grabbed the makings sack out of Slash's shirt pocket. Before Slash could grab it back, Pecos held it up and away from his more diminutive partner then settled back against a rock, chuckling jeeringly.

He started work on his own cigarette and said, "Well, I'll tell you one thing for sure, that town sure has secrets."

"Yeah, and they're all centered around Gyllenwater and Ned Calico."

"How do you figure?"

"I got no idea."

"Then, why . . . ?" Pecos skipped it. "Never mind. It's too damn complicated for me." He fired a match on his boot heel, lit the quirley, and sent a wreath of blue tobacco smoke sifting around his head in the still, cool air.

He and Slash sat with their knees up, looking around. The sun was on the wane; shadows grew long. Meadowlarks piped on the prairie surrounding the butte. A hunting hawk gave its shrill cry.

Pecos looked at Slash. "I think we're in trouble, old pard. I think the old man's gonna come down on us hard."

Slash drew on his quirley and shrugged a shoulder. "Sounds about right."

"I wish the day that train pulled out would come sooner rather than later. I'd like to hop that train." Pecos tapped ashes from his quirley. "Maybe we oughtta cut our losses and just head up to Ogallala on horseback. Calico don't seem to be here, so screw it."

Slash scowled at him. "Run?"

"Hell, why not? That's what we do. We run *from* trouble. And I fear we got a whole heap headin' our way."

"We run *from* trouble only after we've *caused* said trouble. You know—like robbin' a train. We run but we don't run *empty-handed*, an' that's what we'd be doin' here."

"You think too damn much, Slash!"

"Yeah, maybe." Slash took another drag off his cigarette. "Besides, I'm too damn curious."

"Yeah, I reckon I am, too." Pecos climbed to his feet. "Come on, partner," he said, starting back down the slope toward their horses, taking mincing steps to avoid falling on his middle-aged behind. "We'd best get back to Harveyville and lay in a good supply of ammo. I gotta feelin' it's gonna be a bang-up day tomorrow!"

Chapter 14

Wayne Blanchard drove the undertaker's wagon into the headquarters of the Rimfire Ranch and rolled it up in front of the big main house sitting on its patch of sparse grass, with a lone cottonwood offering shade. The three younger punchers who'd been riding with him branched off to the bunkhouse.

Blanchard knew word would spread fast around the headquarters about who he was hauling inside the undertaker's wagon. He didn't look around, but he could see heads of the men working around the yard turning toward him by ones and twos and threes and fours. Was it his imagination, or did a hush fall over the dusty, sun-washed yard?

As he set the brake, a pretty young woman with dark brown skin and a heart-shaped face framed by long, dark brown curls, stepped through a door and onto the second-floor balcony over the house's roofed porch. She was dressed like a boy but there was nothing boyish about Clara Gyllenwater. Her curly hair fell enticingly beneath her shoulders, and her man's cream work shirt and black vest sported a woman's curves, as did the Spanish-cut black denims she always wore.

All woman—half Mexican with the dusky complexion and eyes to go with it—as well as a saucy manner about her even when she wasn't trying to be saucy, though the best way for a woman to get what she wanted on a ranch that was otherwise populated by all men was to act impudent. She'd known that since she was five years old, and she'd always taken full advantage, but even more so after she'd filled out in all the right places and had started attracting lingering, lusty stares.

"Blanchard," she said with a curt nod as she stepped up to the balcony rail. She always called him by his last name. Never Wayne. Always "Blanchard," as though needing to keep a professional distance from him despite their closeness in other ways.

"Clara."

She frowned down at him, of course having seen the wagon. From her vantage, she could see what was inside, too. At least she could see the blanket.

She returned her gaze to the Rimfire foreman and moved her full lips a little but didn't seem able to form words, an unusual thing for her. Her eyes shone with curiosity and maybe a little—what? Hope?

Hope that the blanket covered the body of her lowdown, dirty, half brother?

"The old man up there?" Blanchard asked, knowing his boss would be this time of the day, knowing she'd likely taken a toddy up to him after his midafternoon nap. He always took his medication with a toddy—hot water, rotgut whiskey, and a couple of spoons of brown sugar.

"What is it, Wayne?" croaked a voice through the open door behind Clara.

Clara's chest tightened a little as she stared mildly, hopefully down at Blanchard. She glanced over her shoulder, toward the open balcony door, and then turned back to the foreman, wrinkling the skin at the bridge of her nose incredulously.

She said, "Blanchard . . . maybe you should . . ."

"What is it, for chrissakes?" came the angrily croaking voice behind her again.

The old man stepped out through the door—a stout bulldog of a man in longhandles and a tattered velvet bathrobe, the robe open to expose his considerable, rounded paunch, the cloth belt hanging free. A thick stogie poked out from one corner of his mouth. His square, granite-like skull was carpeted in thick gray hair that stood up in tufts.

He'd once been a big, forbidding bruin of a man, a man with no yield in him—not one bit—and while there was still no yield in him, and damned little tenderness, the syphilis had shrunk him so that his shoulders poked against the robe like the wings of some large, ancient bird. It had made him shorter by several inches, made him stoop a little, though he'd never been the stooping sort. He'd always been quick to violence, and he still had that air about him. The air of a dog who'd been trained to fight and always looked for it in other dogs. He wielded his cane like that now, swinging it around as though always threatening a strike.

Tom Gyllenwater's face was a mass of red sores—some open and oozing.

He was paying for his whoremongering ways, which had cost him three marriages. He'd been paying for years. The mercury pills and tinctures the doctors had prescribed him were even worse than the disease. Then you added raw opium and whiskey toddies to the mix, and cigars, and you got what Blanchard saw on the balcony above him now. Just looking at the old rancher made Blanchard's cojones rise up taut and shrink to raisins beneath the buckle of his cartridge belt.

That old raging fool up there on the balcony would be paying the devil until he howled himself off into the syphilitic whoremonger's own private, lonely, bitter hell on the deathbed that Blanchard could glimpse behind old Tom Gyllenwater and his angelically lovely daughter, with its accompanying table covered in bottles, and its rumpled quilts and blankets and dented pillows.

The stench was nearly eyewatering way down here.

"What you got, Wayne?" the man croaked over the balcony rail at the Rimfire foreman, through the wreath of cigar smoke wafting around his head.

"It's not good, boss."

Blanchard glanced at Clara. She stared back at him, her expression bland except for the almost black eyes. Devilishness shimmered in her smokily amused gaze.

Blanchard had made a mistake. He should have told the old man in private. But what was he supposed to do—cart Collie's mangled carcass all the way upstairs?

Tom Gyllenwater stared through the wafting smoke at his foreman. His eyes, dark with apprehension, indicated that he, too, knew who was under that blanket. As opposed to his daughter's eyes, Gyllenwater's eyes were cast with dread—the dread of an old man who was about to be shown his dead son. His only son.

"Show me," he wheezed.

"Maybe you'd better come down here an'—"

"I can see him from here. Show me."

"I was just gonna . . ." Blanchard's voice cracked. He hadn't expected that. He hadn't expected to feel sympathy for this tyrannical old weasel. But he did. Even if the son he'd lost was the vermin, Collie.

Blanchard cleared his throat, drew a deep breath. "I was just gonna let you have a look at his face because I knew you'd want to see . . . to be sure."

Gyllenwater's puffy, wasted features blossomed with rage. "Show me the whole cussed thing, hang you, Wayne!"

Clara turned to him. "Pa, are you sure?"

Gyllenwater pounded his cane on the balcony floor. "Pull back the blanket!"

Blanchard and Clara shared an uneasy glance. He arched his brow at her. She hiked a shoulder with a non-committal shrug.

Blanchard wrapped the reins around the brake handle and swung a leg over the seat to step back into the wagon box. He dropped to a knee, looked up at his old, wasted employer, then pulled the blanket back from Collie's face. Gyllenwater's own face, set atop two swollen jowls spiked with gray beard stubble, showed nothing but anger. It turned maybe one or two shades redder as the old man kept his eyes on his dead son.

Gyllenwater said, "Farther."

Blanchard frowned. "What's that?"

Gyllenwater gestured angrily. "Lift the blanket all the way up, dammit, Wayne!"

Blanchard glanced at Clara. Improbably—or probably, depending on how well you knew her—she hooked one corner of her mouth in a wry smile. Blanchard sighed, then stood and pulled the blanket clear of Collie's body, so that the long, lean body lay naked and bloody for his father's inspection.

"Good God!" Old Tom stared down, his mouth open, his eyes wide. "You found him like *that?* Without a stitch *on?*"

"That's how he was killed."

"Where?"

"Madam Delacroix's." Blanchard said it without hesitation. The information that Collie Gyllenwater had frequented parlor houses would not be news to his father. Collie's reputation preceded him. Like father, like son, after all.

Blanchard glanced at Clara again. She gazed down at the mangled carcass, that devilish half-smile remaining on her lips. Her dark brown eyes glittered faintly. Blanchard would be damned if she wasn't enjoying this!

"Shotgunned?" Gyllenwater asked. He had one hand around his cane. He dug the fingers of his other hand into the balcony rail before him.

"Yes."

Gyllenwater switched his eyes to Blanchard and tossed his head to indicate the room behind him. "Get up here." The old buzzard glanced at his daughter and, as though sensing her joy at her worthless brother's demise, said, "You—*out!*"

As Blanchard drew the saddle blanket back over the body, he heard Clara say in a tone that was laughingly meek and obviously manufactured, "I'm so sorry, Pa."

Gyllenwater didn't buy it for a second. "No, you're not. Hell, I'm not sure if I am, and he's my son! Get *out!*"

Blanchard stepped tenderly down from the wagon box. Such a maneuver was not easy for a man of nearly fifty and feeling every year of it, a definite stiffening in his muscles and joints that were a result, no doubt, of having spent most of the past nearly fifty years on the backs of half-wild horses for sometimes longer than the sun was up on any given day. He was tired of his job. He was tired of the saddle, of hard outdoor labor—hot, cold, sometimes wet labor—and of bunkhouse grub.

Now this.

Of course, he'd known it was coming. Collie Gyllenwater had been a dynamite keg sporting a lit fuse since the day he'd dropped from his mother's womb. His mother was long gone. She'd gone back to Illinois years ago. Her son had taken too much after his father for the taste of the regal Belle Holloway. She hadn't been able to stand either one, nor to stand *against* their alliance against her.

As well as the whoremongering.

Clara's mother, the beautiful Sonja, was gone, too. Back to Mexico. The daughter of a man Gyllenwater had once owned a mine with in Chihuahua, she'd been born in Mexico. Delores lived in Durango with her wealthy mother. Clara joined them from time to time, but the two women were too much alike to get along for more than a few weeks at a time. Clara always came back here to be with her father. She was the only one who knew how to handle him. She'd hated Collie but she seemed to genuinely love the old man.

A loner despite her rarified beauty and rustic south-of-the-border charm, Clara liked it here on the ranch because she had plenty of time alone with only her horses. She enjoyed being fawned over by her father and the men he employed. She could take care of herself, Clara could. Even at only twenty-three years old. No one fooled with Clara unless she allowed them to fool with her—including Wayne Blanchard. Only, she needn't worry about him. It was *he* who needed to worry about *her*.

It turned out she liked her men older, pot-bellied, and reeking of horses. Or maybe she just liked how a man the foreman's age could appreciate a girl her age. How he could make her feel after his many years of practice with women older and more experienced than she.

He ordered two men to haul the wagon away and to get to work on a coffin, and then he headed inside and ran into Clara on the front porch. She stepped boldly up to him, threw her arms around his neck, and poked her tongue in his ear.

"Isn't this wonderful?" she said. "That crazy javelina is dead and out of the way."

Blanchard looked around self-consciously.

"Don't worry—no one's watching," Clara assured him, poking her tongue in his other ear. "The old man's too deaf to hear us down here."

Just the same, he peeled her arms from around his neck. "Clara, dear Clara, this isn't good."

"How can it not be good? He only complicated—you know"—she paused then lowered her voice to a whisper—"the will!"

"It would have been fine if anyone else had killed him."

Clara frowned. "What? Who killed him?"

"Federal men."

"What are you talking about—*federal* men? What's federal men?"

From upstairs, the old man bellowed, "Wayne—what the hell are you doing down there? Polishing the silver? That's what Clara's for. Get up here!"

Blanchard sighed and tried to step around Gyllenwater's daughter but she stepped into his path again, smiling friskily up at him. She was like a wild colt sometimes, prancing around, all legs and tail and arched neck, looking high and low for trouble to get into.

"Blanchard," she said, dipping her chin and looking at him impudently from beneath her dark brows. Her eyes were as black as indigo ink. He loved the way she spoke blunt Western English—the English she'd been raised with out here—in her lilting, upper-crust Spanish accent. "I guarantee you this is going to turn out to be a very good thing. So, the old man will have his neck up for a spell. His bloomers in a twist. A couple of raggedy-assed federal men—whoever they are—will die hard deaths. What did they *think* would happen when they crossed Tom Gyllenwater?"

"Wayne!" came the old man's throaty wail.

Keeping his voice low, Blanchard said, "Clara . . ."

Again, he tried to step around her. Again, she flounced into his path, smiling coquettishly up at him. "I am going to make you feel so much better, *mi amor*. Later tonight, I'm going to rub liniment into *every inch* of that worn-out old carcass of yours!"

"Shhh!" Again, he glanced around quickly, nervously.

"Wayne!" came the old man's bray.

"Christ almighty," Blanchard said, giving the girl a none-too-friendly shove out of his way. "You two are gonna be the death of me yet!"

He headed upstairs.

Behind him, Clara laughed and called in a taunting singsong: "Over every *inch* of you!"

Chapter 15

"What the hell were you doin' down there?" Tom Gyllenwater groused as Blanchard entered the old man's bedroom, which doubled as an office. The bed lay before the foreman as he entered the room. The man's oak desk, stacked with years of account books, files, range and stock manuals, and loose papers, lay to the right. Tom Gyllenwater sat in a rocking chair fronting the double doors that led to the balcony.

The room had been nice at one time, with fresh wallpaper and neatly hung photographs and oil paintings, but that was back when there were women here—wives here—to look after things. Now there was a worn shabbiness to the room. To the entire house, in fact. Clara wasn't much of a housekeeper. Gyllenwater hired a Chinese widow gal, who lived in the old summer kitchen behind the house, to cook and do the laundry, but she was so old she could barely keep up with that, even with Clara's minimal help.

The room owned the sour stench of long illness.

"Not polishing the silver," Blanchard said, trying to take shallow breaths against the nasty smell.

He removed his hat and sat in the swivel chair at the

old man's desk, swiveling around to face his longtime employer.

He hiked one boot on the opposite knee and hooked his hat on the arm of the chair. He'd meant the retort to be a joke, but the old man ignored it. He sat with a glass of whiskey in one hand, the stogie in the other hand, leaning forward in the rocker, staring at something on the shabby rug at his horny bare feet. Or maybe at life with his demented son no longer in it, likely weighing his feelings to see how he really felt about it.

Collie had been a problem, no doubt about it. A deadly prankster who'd once killed a nester just for fun. That had led to obvious law problems that Gyllenwater had to work like hell to untangle him from. Still, Collie had been his only son. While the "boy" had been in his mid-thirties, even pushing forty, Gyllenwater had still held out hope that one day he'd come around and be the equal of the ranch. That he'd be able to run it after Gyllenwater was gone.

Now that obviously wasn't going to happen. The old man's main concern at the moment, however, was a practical one.

He looked up at Blanchard, his red-rimmed eyes cold, hard, and mean. Blanchard had never seen eyes as mean as Gyllenwater's could get. Dangerous mean. Soulless mean. Frighteningly mean. *"Who?"*

Blanchard sighed and fiddled with his hat.

"Who, damn you?" the rancher said with menace in his low-pitched voice.

"Boss, we need to talk about that."

"That's what we're doin', Wayne. We're talkin'. A man messes with my son, he messes with me. I can't let it go. I won't let it go." Gyllenwater ground the heel of his hand holding the cigar into the arm of his chair. "Blood for blood, by God. People gotta know that or they'll walk all over you! You learned that in the old country! My Scottish ancestors would be storming the gates by now!"

"This ain't the old country, boss. There's no moat to cross, no castle to attack. Hell, we got the train here now. Yours is a well-established operation. Red Cloud is no longer beatin' his war drum on the other side of the Bayonet Buttes. You no longer have to prove anything to anyone."

"That's a load of crap, Wayne, and you know it. If that town thinks I'm gettin' soft, I'm finished. I've made enemies in town. Enemies all around the county. Successful men don't get successful without makin' enemies. Some bad, some not so bad. Ferguson, for instance. If he gets wind I let the killin' of my boy go, he'll start crowdin' me. We'll lose cattle. Maybe a little at a time, but he'll rebrand 'em and market them as his, and suddenly I'll be out real dollars and, worse than that, I'll have lost the respect of my neighbors."

"Ah, that's just silly talk, bo—"

"Who?"

"Two men you can't kill."

"Any man can be killed."

"Not these two. They're federal."

"Federal?"

Blanchard shrugged and absently kneaded the crease in his hat brim. "Leastways, Kentucky thinks so."

"That old fool's soft in his thinker box. Why would a pair of federals kill my son?"

"They didn't know he was your son, Mr. Gyllenwater.

They just knew he was about to blow a whore's brains all over a wall in Ma Delacroix's place."

"Is she a part of this?" Gyllenwater's face puffed up even more severely, both jowls turning scarlet, the nail-filing stubble standing in stark contrast to the rosy flush. "She knows that, by God, if—"

"Not to my knowledge. They was just tryin' to save a whore is all. Birdie didn't have no part in it, to my knowledge."

"'Tryin' to save a whore is all.' By *killin' my son?*"

"Like I said, they didn't know he was your son."

Gyllenwater rocked back in the rocker and again leveled those cold, mean, deadly eyes on his foreman. "I want them dead, Wayne. You know how to handle it. You've handled it before. You're crafty, savage . . . but *delicate.*" He smiled, his eyes glowing as though from a fierce fire of barely restrained fury burning inside his merciless black heart.

Blanchard laughed despite the dread in his own heavy ticker. "No one's ever accused me of bein' *delicate* before." He waited a few seconds, then returned to the subject, knowing he was treading in shallow water where sharks swim. "If we kill a pair of federals, boss, it'll get back to Denver. We don't want that for obvious reasons."

"Denver?"

"Luther Bledsoe sent 'em."

"Who's Bledsoe?"

"U.S. Marshal for the Western District."

Gyllenwater's thin, gray brows bulged. "Why does that name sound familiar?"

"He was out here twelve years ago. He picked up Calico on federal charges. Friend of Kentucky's from the old days,

I understand. Now he's U.S. marshal. Mucky-muck." He shook his head very slowly and met his boss's cold eyes with a direct look of his own, trying very desperately to convey the gravity of the situation to an old man whose brains were being eaten away by the Cupid's itch. "We don't need the attention of the federals, Mister Gyllenwater."

The old man turned his head to stare off, thinking it over. For nearly a minute, Blanchard thought the old man had bought it. Hope grew in him. But then the old man turned back to him, his eyes as cold and merciless as before.

"Do it, Wayne. Take them out. Spread the word in town that if anyone comes sniffin' around, inquiring about the federals, to play dumb. Make sure they understand that if they don't, I *will* send you and a dozen of my nastiest hard-trails to beat them senseless, to rape their women, murder their children, and burn their stores and houses to the ground!"

He'd punctuated the threat by pointing his half-smoked, cold cigar at the foreman with each hard word and narrowing his mean little eyes. Suddenly, he smiled. It was a death's-head grin. He poked the cold cigar at Blanchard again and said, "They know I'll do it, too. No one will say one word."

He set his drink down, grabbed a bottle off the table beside him, and tossed it to his foreman. "Have a drink."

Blanchard snatched the corked bottle out of the air. He set the bottle on his knee and regarded his boss skeptically. "You sure?"

"Sure, I'm sure. It's rotgut, just like we both like." Again, Gyllenwater grinned.

"I'm not talkin' about the panther piss, an' you know it."

"I know one more thing, Wayne. One of us has gone soft. And it ain't me. Too much easy livin'. Oh, for the days when we'd ride out huntin' cattle rustlers or Injuns, which were, of course, one an' the same. Oh, to do that one more time before I'm planted. No other sport like it!"

Blanchard pried the cork out of the bottle, took a pull, and made a face. "Jesus, that's terrible!"

"Hah! Just how we like it!" Gyllenwater dragged a match across the top of the table and lit his cigar. As he rolled the cigar between his lips as he lit it, the flame leaping, smoke wafting, he said, "Are you covering that girl of mine, you old mossyhorn?"

Blanchard had just taken another pull from the busthead. Now he pulled the bottle down and blew out half the whiskey into the air before him.

"Hah!" the old man roared. "I knew it!"

Blanchard swallowed, coughed, and shook his head. Some of the whiskey threatened to plow up through his nose. His eyes burned. When he was finally able to draw a breath, he turned his watery gaze to his old boss and said, "You gonna shoot me?"

"Nah, hell. I'm glad it's you."

"I'm old enough to be her father. Way old enough."

"That's what she wants. What she's gonna need once I'm gone. Someone to take care of her. She don't get along with her mother. There's a lot I don't care for in Clara's character. She's moody and strong-willed and don't give a good cuss about what anybody thinks about her. Can't get her into a dress. Her cooking skills—well, let's not call it *skill*. She prefers horses over people." Gyllenwater grinned as he puffed the stogie. "But she don't like her ma."

"I just want you to know I didn't start it. I came home

late to my hut and found her there. It was late. I was too damn tired to throw her out."

"Wayne, it would take a far stronger man than you to kick a filly like that out of his mattress sack. Hell, I couldn't kick her out, and I'm her father!" Gyllenwater chuckled and turned the stogie, puffing it pensively. Pride now shone in his eyes. "Takes after her mother that way. Damn hard to throw out of a mattress sack. Only way to shut her up, though, is to—er, never mind!" He snorted a bawdy laugh, brushed a sheepish fist across his nose, and glanced at his foreman. "You gonna marry her?"

"Christ, we're to that point already?"

"You marry her, you understand? My son's dead. I was holdin' out hope that Collie would come around and take over the ranch. Now he's gone, and once I'm planted, which will be within the next year, I have no damn doubt, Clara's gonna have nobody. She's gonna need a man to help her run the Rimfire, and that man is you."

He waved a hand, indicating the bunkhouse. "None of my younger hardtrails has a lick of business sense. They can herd cows, dig ponds, haul hay, dig fence posts, and hang rustlers. But none of them got what it takes to keep Rimfire on its feet. I almost lost her once. I won't lose her again."

"That's why I'd like you to reconsider what you want me to do in town, Mr. Gyllenwater. You almost lost it once. But you got it back. Maybe this time you won't be so lucky."

Gyllenwater scowled, anger rising in him again. "I thought that was settled. By God, Wayne, if you can't do that one job for me, then maybe I'll just reconsider about you and Clara. She needs a bull buff with sharp horns and the stomach to use 'em now an' then. Not some old saddle tramp gone to seed and spookin' at shadows. Red Cloud might not be poundin' the drum on the other side of the Bayonet Buttes, but you know what, Wayne?"

Blanchard swallowed another burning mouthful of the whiskey. "What?"

"From here on in, our troubles are going to get more and more complicated if'n we don't handle 'em straight up and in the old tried-and-true ways. *Times* may be a-changin'." He smiled shrewdly and shook his head. "But *men* don't change a bit. They stay as savage as they ever were. Even the ones in twenty-dollar suits!"

Blanchard replaced the cork in the bottle, pounded it down with the heel of his hand. He sighed, rose from his chair. He walked over and set the bottle down on the old man's table. "All right."

"That's more like it." Gyllenwater nodded, his eyes glinting with the thrill of the prospective kill. "Wish I could ride along. Them were the days!"

"No sport like man-killin'." Blanchard moved to the door, feeling heavy and old and gone to seed. "I'll take care of it."

"I know you will. That's a helluva woman. Careful she don't kill you!"

"Oh, but what a way to go!" Blanchard said as he walked out the door.

He drew the door closed and heard the old man crow out a laugh on the other side.

Blanchard lifted his head to see Clara step out of the shadows, wearing a knowing, lopsided grin. "You boys have a good talk?"

Blanchard looked at her wearily. "You heard?"

She nodded. "What did you expect, really?" Clara kissed

him. Drawing her head away from his, she gave his lower lip a painful but arousing bite.

"Come on downstairs." She smiled alluringly. "I'll make you feel better."

She took his hand and led him to the stairway.

He said, "You two are gonna be the death of me yet!"

"Oh, but what a way to go!"

Chapter 16

The thin, balding gent who owned the gun and ammunition shop in Harveyville set four boxes of revolver and rifle shells and one box of shotgun wads on his scarred counter and said, "That will be six dollars and fifty-five cents." He leaned forward, looked at each of his two customers in turn, jutted his chin, and said in a quiet voice chilled with menace, "And it ain't nowhere near enough bullets to keep you two from bein' turned into human sieves and dumped in shallow graves!"

Slash glanced at Pecos. Pecos arched a brow.

Slash turned to the balding gent who wore a green eyeshade and sleeve garters. "Well, then, just how many bullets *would* be enough to keep us out of shallow graves?"

The balding gent threw up an arm to indicate the well-stocked shelves in his cramped little shop. "I don't have enough bullets in this whole damn place. There ain't enough bullets in this whole town to save you. Mister Gyllenwater has a good twenty, nasty, gun-hung, savage fightin' men on his roll. Always has. They come an' they go, but way back when Red Cloud was still runnin' rough-shod over this county, Gyllenwater got in the habit of hirin' the nastiest, meanest, most gun-savvy cow- and gunhands in all of Nebraska and Dakota Territory put together! He's kept up the tradition to this day. Rustlers, don't ya know. Squatters. Rival ranchers."

Again, the balding gent eyed each customer in turn and leaned forward across the counter, jutting his sharp chin. *"Men who shoot his precious little boy to save a whore!"*

Pecos said to Slash, "I didn't see nothin' so little about Collie Gyllenwater. I should say, not above his waistline, anyways."

He and Slash laughed.

"Go ahead," the thin man said. "Go ahead and laugh. But you ain't gonna be laughin' for long. Hurry up and pay me for that ammo an' get the hell out of here. I don't want either one of you nowhere near me when that horde of hardtrail killers comes gallopin' into Harveyville!"

Slash and Pecos paid for the ammo, then gathered up the boxes and walked out of the shop and onto the boardwalk fronting it just as the balding gent placed the CLOSED sign in his window and snapped the curtain closed behind it.

"He's a right nervous little fellow," Slash said.

"I gotta admit, Slash, he made me a little nerv—"

"Psssttt! Psssttt!"

Both men turned to see a girl in a thin lemon-yellow wrap and a black lace shawl standing in the break between the ammo shop and a ladies' shoe shop. It was late in the day, nearly the supper hour, and the thick shadows of the break contrasting with the bright, severely angled salmon sunlight flooding the boardwalk made her hard to see. She beckoned quickly then stepped deeper into the break, where the purple shadows all but consumed her.

Slash and Pecos each placed a hand over the handles of

their holstered pistols as they walked slowly, tentatively to the mouth of the break. They peered cautiously into the break between the two buildings. The girl stood about ten feet back away from the boardwalk, pressing her back against the wall of the ammo shop. She looked nervously around, obviously worried about being seen.

She was the pretty little blue-eyed blonde whom Collie Gyllenwater would have sent singing to the angels if Slash and Pecos hadn't stepped in and saved her, sending Collie himself off to the angels, instead. Or to the ramrod of the devil's coal-shoveling team, that is.

"Why, Miss Wynona," Slash said. "To what or whom do we owe the—?"

"*Shhh!*" The little blonde beckoned quickly, leaning to one side to see into the street beyond Slash and Pecos. "Come here an' keep your voices down, fer chrissakes! Don't you fellas have any idea what kind of trouble you're in?"

"We just recently started gettin' there," Pecos said.

"How you feelin', honey?" Slash asked the girl, noticing her swollen eyes and split, puffy lips. Collie had really worked her over. "Did you see a sawbones about—"

"Never mind me. What are you two still doing in town? I saw you ride back into Harveyville a few minutes ago. Why on earth did you come back? You need to ride the hell out of here right now!"

"Ah, hell, we're not goin' anywhere," Pecos said.

"Why not?"

"We don't run from trouble," Slash said. "We run *to* trouble!"

Wynona stared up at him, her blue eyes wide in disbelief. "You run *to* trouble, do you?" She gave a caustic laugh. "You two old fellas are not only—"

"Hey, wait a minute," Slash said, giving the girl a pointed look. "Who you callin' old, young lady?"

Again, she just stared up at him in mute disbelief, her mouth half open. She looked at Pecos and then at Slash again. She stepped forward and wrapped her arms around his neck, hugging him tightly.

"Please don't die because of me! You two were right brave, if foolish, to step in to save my life. But you didn't really save it. I'm as good as dead as I'd have been a few hours ago if you two fellas hadn't run to my rescue."

Pecos scowled at her. "What're you talkin' about, honey?"

Wynona turned to him. "You killed Collie on account of me. The way Mister Gyllenwater will see it is I caused Collie's death. He's gonna kill me just as soon as he's finished with you two. Oh, he'll be sneaky about it. He'll likely pay one of his cowhands to slip in a window at Madam Delacroix's some night, slit my throat while I'm asleep, and then skin back out to the ranch without anyone seein'. Marshal Kentucky will know who did it, but he won't be able to prove anything even if he wanted to. Which he won't, you know, on account of that old marshal haulin' that evil old rancher's water all these years!"

Slash and Pecos shared a curious glance.

Before anyone could say anything, Wynona bounded toward Pecos, threw her arms around his neck, and hugged him tightly. "Thank you both!" She pulled away from him, brushed tears from her bruised cheeks, and said, "Please don't die on account of me. I'm not worth it. I'm dead, anyway!"

She turned and ran off down the break, turned left at the rear of the shoe shop, and was gone.

Slash and Pecos stared silently after the girl.

Pecos said under his breath, darkly, "All right, now I'm gettin' even nervouser."

"Ain't a word."

"What?"

"'Nervouser' ain't a word. You'd know that if you'd ever learned to read, you cork-headed stump-squatter."

"What in holy hell does it matter if 'nervouser' is a word or not, at a time like this? You knew what I meant."

"On the off chance we make it through the night alive, I wouldn't want you to use such a word in front of Miss Abigail Langdon. She'll find out sooner or later what an ignoramus you are, but why not make it later as opposed to sooner? After you've gotten the chance to see that long, tall body of hers without a stitch—"

"You're nervouser, too!"

"What? No, I'm not. I was never nervous."

"Yes, you are. That's why you're correctin' my words. You always do that when you're nervous or upset about somethin'. You correct my words—"

"Speech."

"You correct my *speech* or pull some devilish trick like jerk away a chair I'm about to sit down in, to distract yourself about how nervous or upset you are."

"I am rarely, if ever, nervous or upset. Both those things are for damn sissies."

"That's another thing you do when you're nervous or upset. You call me a sissy!"

"You are a sissy. You're a big, ugly sissy. I'm embarrassed to be seen in public with you."

"Damn."

"What?" Slash asked.

"I'm hungry."

"That's because you're nervous. You always eat when you're nervous."

"Will you shut up about that!" Pecos had turned to stare up the darkening main street toward the Copper Nickel Saloon. "What do you say we go over and have a couple drinks to calm my nerves and get us a steak and a pile of beans? If we're gonna die tonight, I'd just as soon do it with a full belly."

"That's the smartest thing you've said all day."

Still carrying their newly purchased ammunition, they walked up the street, which was nearly vacant now as shadows filled it. Most folks were home eating supper or closing up the chickens. Succulent aromas wafted from the stovepipe poking out the Copper Nickel's shake-shingled roof, however, which likely meant supper was being served.

Slash pushed through the batwings and stepped to one side, taking both of his boxes of ammo in one hand and closing his free hand around the grips of his right-side .44. Pecos stepped to the opposite side of the doors and touched his own gun handles. The two former cutthroats had ridden with bounties on their heads for a good many years, so they were always cautious—even when they hadn't killed the prized son of a notoriously vengeance-hungry rancher.

There were eight or nine customers in the place, scattered around five or six tables. None appeared ready to claw iron. There were two cowpunchers in the usual cowpunching garb. The rest appeared to be local shopkeepers. Two doxies sat alone at a table near the stairs, smoking and looking bored while they waited for business. One of the doxies, a pudgy brunette in a cream bustier and torn silk stockings, had been yawning as Slash and Pecos had wandered in. The yawn died a sudden death as the doxie took in the two newcomers who everyone in town, and possibly the entire county by now, knew had punched Collie Gyllenwater's ticket.

The two doxies looked at each other then rose from their table. The brunette stubbed out the cigarette she'd been smoking, then followed the other one away from the table and over to the stairs. She glanced over her shoulder at Slash and Pecos and then followed the other doxie up the stairs.

All other eyes in the room were on the two newcomers.

The doxies' apprehension at sharing the same breathing air with the two men who'd killed Collie Gyllenwater must have been catching. By ones and twos, the customers cleared their throats, slid their chairs back, slugged down their beers or tossed back their whiskies or stubbed out their cigarettes, set their hats on their heads, and bent their legs for the batwings. They stepped cautiously around the two newcomers, regarding them as though they were escaped circus animals—panthers with the blood of the widow's favorite cat on their teeth.

When they all were gone, there was only the owner, Rivers's doll-faced daughter in a too-tight but otherwise nondescript day frock standing in front of the bar, holding a tray loaded with two steaming platters and two cups of smoking coffee. She was barefoot, and a couple locks of blond hair were sweat-pasted to her chubbily pretty ivory cheeks touched with the rose of the supper rush.

Former supper rush, that is.

"Oh, you two are *real* good for business!" she snapped, flaring one nostril of her cute little ivory nose. Even with a slightly swollen and blackened eye, she was cuter than a speckled pup.

Slash lifted his arms to sniff his pits. He glanced at Pecos. "Ain't me. I smell fresh as a Carolina rose."

Pecos shrugged at the girl. "I had a bath just last week."

"I hope you like fried chicken and black-eyed peas," the girl said, striding forward with the steaming tray, slapping her feet down hard on the scarred puncheons. "Them two Alabama lumbermen always order the same thing every night. With boiled greens and pecan pie for dessert." She set the tray on an empty table near Slash and Pecos, straightened, the bodice of her simple frock drawing taut against her lively bosoms, and said, "So here you go." She stuck her small, pale hand out. "You can pay me in advance before someone shoots you from ambush."

"Who would do a lowdown dirty thing like that in Harveyville?" Pecos asked her.

"I heard a couple of men talking about that very thing." Mary Kate Rivers held the tray down against her legs, likely not wanting to interrupt the view of her chest she was obviously so proud of. "One of 'em had a debt he owed to Mister Gyllenwater. Said shootin' you two through a window might be a good way to pay it off. He an' the other man laughed, so I doubt they were serious. I just thought you might want to know that ideas are being tossed around." She snapped her fingers. "That will be one dollar and twenty-five cents."

Slash removed his hat and stepped forward, drawing the meal's succulent aromas deep into his lungs. "That smells good enough to eat in one bite! Pay the girl, Pecos. I spent the last of my jingle on ammo." He set his hat and ammo on the table then kicked out a chair. "Fetch us a bottle of good stuff, will you, honey? If this is my last night on earth, I'm gonna go out roarin'."

"Two beers, too," Pecos added with a grin.

The girl looked at each man in turn, dropped her chin, and pulled her mouth corners down. "Oh, all right. Since it's your last night, an' all."

Chapter 17

Slash unbuttoned his shirt cuffs and rolled his sleeves up his arms. "How come you're not upstairs readin' your schoolbooks?" he asked Mary Kate, then glanced at Pecos and winked. "Your pa said you're too purty to work down here at night."

"Because Pa's in the outhouse. Someone has to serve when he's usin' the privy. He had beans and bacon for lunch, so he'll likely be in there half the night, thumbin' through a wish book while I do all the heavy liftin' around here. Which I always do, anyways, but . . ."

Both men were elbow deep in the feed trough, so to speak, when Mary Kate returned with two frothy beer schooners, two shot glasses, and a labeled bottle of bourbon.

"You two sure seem to have right healthy appetites for dead men," she said as she set a beer schooner in front of Pecos.

Slash indicated Pecos with his fork. "He eats when he's nervous."

"What about you?" the girl asked, setting the whiskey shot down in front of Slash. "Ain't you nervous?"

Around a mouthful of food, Pecos said, "Slash ain't afraid of dyin'. Put him in front of a preacher, though . . . on his *weddin' day*, and it takes six big men to keep him on his feet."

He threw his head back, laughing.

"You married?" Mary Kate asked Slash.

"Just the other day," Slash said, pausing in his chewing to sip his whiskey. "First time."

The girl considered that, staring down at him, pursing her lips and nodding. She reached behind her to turn a chair around, then sank into it and set the tray on her thighs. "Well, then, you best do yourself a favor and ride on out of here while you can still keep that pretty bride from becomin' a widow."

"How do you know she's pretty?"

Mary Kate blinked once, slowly. "You'd have a pretty one."

"Slash don't ride *from* trouble," Pecos said. "He rides *toward* trouble." He chuckled, then ripped off a good chunk of crispy meat from a chicken leg followed by a forkful of gravy-drenched potatoes.

Slash was tugging meat from a juicy thigh. "Besides, I'm right curious."

"About what?" the girl asked.

"How you got that black eye, for starters."

"Pa gave it to me."

"How come?"

"I was foolin' with the wrong man, to his way of thinkin'."

"Which wrong man?"

"Wouldn't you like to know?"

Slash smiled at her. "Why would you mess with the wrong man when you could have your pick of the town?"

Mary Kate gazed back at him, blushing. She shook her hair back from her face, set one bare foot atop the other, and said, "I'll take that as a compliment. But, you see, sometimes I'm attracted to the wrong sort. To Pa's way of thinkin', anyways. Pa don't want me mixin' with just any man. Especially the wrong sort. He says he's savin' me for the right man. A man with money and a future, and some book learnin' wouldn't be so bad, neither."

"That don't seem like such a bad idea to me," Pecos said. "Sometimes purty young ladies make wrong decisions. You know—about the wrong sorta man."

Mary Kate wrinkled her nose, vaguely sheepish, and again some color rose in her cheeks.

She turned to Slash and frowned. "Say, you said you was curious about my eye just for *starters*. What else you curious about?"

"We're curious about what happened to Ned Calico," Pecos said over the chicken wing he held in front of his mouth and the meat that he was chewing. "We was sent here to see about him."

"To *see* about Ned Calico?" said Mary Kate.

"Right," Slash said. "To see about Ned Calico. We were led to believe he might be causin' trouble here in Harveyville. Him and his pards." He turned his head to one side and narrowed a curious eye at the girl. "Seems to me a purty girl like you might attract all sorts . . . includin', possibly, a fellow like Ned Calico. Maybe especially a fellow like Calico—one just let out of prison an' all."

Slash looked at Pecos. "Wouldn't she be one helluva sight for sore eyes?"

Pecos glanced over his chicken wing at Slash, brows beetled with incredulity, apparently wondering about his partner's course of inquiry. Slash shrugged, then glanced at the girl again. "You didn't happen to brush elbows with this Calico fellow—did you, Mary Kate? Was that the fella your pa blackened your eye for you for?"

Mary Kate stared back at Slash, her eyes bright and quick, her plump lips slightly parted, as though she had something to say but was hesitating.

Deciding to follow the trail his partner was bushwhacking, Pecos said, "I haven't seen any prettier girls in town. No, sirree. Just whores. I got a feelin' Slash might be right this one time. I bet a man like Calico would be attracted to a young lady like you. Sweet and purty. Young and pure. Hard workin'. Like a moth to a flame, in fact."

He flashed an admiring smile at the girl.

Mary Kate's cheeks flushed. She looked down at the tray on her lap, deeply thoughtful. She shifted her bare feet beneath her chair, then leaned slightly forward and shook her hair back again though it didn't really need it.

She looked at Pecos and then at Slash. "You two sure do live dangerous-like. *But . . .*" She looked toward the batwings then glanced quickly around the room, as though making sure they were alone. She leaned even farther forward, and, keeping her voice very low and narrowing her eyes, she said, "Ned Calico is all man. I can tell you that firsthand."

She winked and quirked her mouth corners with a devilish smile, eyes twinkling. Those same eyes quickly grew hard and dark and narrow once more. She hardened her jaws as she said, "And neither he nor his friends deserved what this town—"

"Mary Kate!"

She, as well as Slash and Pecos, turned to see her father, the heavy-gutted and walrus-mustached Norman Rivers, step through the curtained doorway flanking the bar. The saloon owner cast a red-faced, hard-jawed glare at his daughter, and dropped a fat Montgomery Ward & Company catalogue on the bar top before him.

"You ain't tellin' tales out of school, now, are ya, Mary Kate?"

The girl returned her father's glowering stare with a hard-eyed one of her own. Her eyes became twin pools of roiling blue fire.

Rivers jerked his arm out in an enraged, commanding gesture. "Get upstairs an' stay there till I tell you to come back down and wash the dishes!"

The girl gained her feet, swept her right arm back, and, screaming with mindless rage, sent the tray spinning toward her father. Rivers gulped, then ducked as the tray went flying through the air to slam into the shelves behind the bar, causing several bottles to smash to the floor.

"*You go to hell!*" Mary Kate screamed, bending forward at the waist.

She swung around and ran up the stairs, her bare feet slapping a staccato rhythm on the steps and then in the ceiling over Slash's and Pecos's heads. A door slammed so hard the entire building quavered.

Rivers glared at the ceiling nearly directly above his red-faced head. "By God, she's got some serious punishment comin', that girl does!"

Slash looked across the table at Pecos.

Pecos stared back at him, slowly raising his hands and shaking his head. "Hold on, now, pard."

"You hold on," Slash growled, shoving his chair back with a jerk and rising to his feet. He picked up his shot glass, tossed back the last of the whiskey in it, set it back down, then set his hat on his head.

He strode slowly toward the bar, Rivers watching him

with a growing apprehension in his eyes. Slash bellied up to the bar, leaned forward, resting his weight on an elbow, and crooked his finger at Rivers. The barman stared at him uncertainly, color rising again in his fleshy face, brows beetling.

He rubbed his fat hands on his apron and said, "Wh-what . . . you want?"

"Come here."

"No."

Louder, Slash said, "Come here."

"You're gonna hurt me."

"It's gonna hurt a lot worse if I have to come back there."

The man drew a breath, his large, lumpy chest expanding and contracting. He made a little face of deep reluctance, then stepped slowly forward, saying, "Look, she's my daughter. I'll raise my daughter however the hell—"

He stopped when Slash reached over the bar, hooked his left hand around the back of the man's neck, and slammed his face down hard on the scarred mahogany. Pecos closed his eyes and winced when he heard the hard, crunching thud of the man's face unceremoniously meeting with the hardwood. That crunch was the man's nose breaking. Had to be.

Pecos sighed and said, "Slash, Slash, Slash . . ."

Rivers screamed as Slash held his face down taut against the bar with his left while drawing one of his Colts with his other hand. Slash pressed the Colt's barrel against the crown of the fat man's nearly bald skull, and clicked the hammer back.

"It ain't nice to smack your daughter around, Rivers. That ain't nice at all. What I feel like doin' right now is blowin' a forty-four caliber hole right down through the middle of your ugly head."

"Slash!" Pecos said.

Ignoring his partner, Slash said, "There ain't no sin in makin' the world a better place!"

"Please!" Rivers wailed. "Don't kill me!"

"You ever gonna lay a hand on the girl again?"

"No!"

"Are you sure?"

"No! Er . . . I mean YES!"

Boots thumped somewhere behind Pecos. Spurs chimed. A man's gravelly voice said casually, "Slash Braddock and the Pecos River Kid."

Slash glanced into the backbar mirror. Town Marshal Kentucky O'Neil had just walked into the saloon. He still wore a good bit of trail dust on his shoulders, hat, and mustache. He stepped forward, letting the batwing doors rattle back into place behind him.

Slash released the barman's head and lowered his Colt. Rivers lifted his head from the bar. His nose was tomato-red. Already, both eyes were starting to swell. Cupping his nose with both hands, he glared at Slash and yelled in a nasal, liquid voice, "You're plumb loco! Never shoulda come here! You're gonna die bloody and I'm gonna dance on your unmarked graves!"

With that, he swung around and pushed through the curtained doorway.

Slash turned from the bar and holstered his six-shooter. Kentucky O'Neil stood in front of the batwings, a cunning smile on his mustached mouth and glittering in his dark blue eyes.

"I thought your faces looked familiar," he said. "Had time to think about it on my little wagon ride. You know the one." He gave a sly wink. "I saw you. Not on the way out there but on the way back. I saw you ridin' around me, headin' cross-country."

Slash shared a sheepish glance with Pecos, who was still sitting at the table, the ruins of his meal on the plate before him.

"That was Slash's fault. It rankles him to have someone else settle his scores. Me, I was just fine with it. I could have sat right here, drinkin' beer an' whiskey."

"Guilty as charged," Slash said, both elbows resting on the bar behind him.

Scowling curiously, O'Neil strolled forward then stopped and hooked his thumbs behind his cartridge belt. "How in holy blazes did a couple of old train robbers end up working for Luther Bledsoe?"

"He hates us—that's how," Pecos said. "It's his way of killin' us slow-like."

"Is that why you're not wearin' badges?"

"Most like," Slash said. "We're very unofficial, Pecos an' me."

"You see," Pecos said, "when you sent that note callin' for 'gun men,' I reckon he sorta thought you wanted his help in an off-the-books sort of fashion."

"I see," O'Neil said, nodding slowly and giving a thoughtful half-smile.

Slash dug in his shirt pocket for his makings sack. "It was you who sent that note—wasn't it, Marshal O'Neil? Or am I mistaken?"

O'Neil flushed a little above his mustache, and his eyes turned hard with sudden anger. "Of course it was. Who else would have sent it? It was signed by me, wasn't it?"

"I don't know your signature," Slash said, carefully

dribbling tobacco onto the wheat paper troughed between the first two fingers of his right hand. He glanced up to say, "You just seemed so surprised when we showed you that letter. It was almost like, well . . . like you didn't write it. That was why you were so surprised to have help ride into town. Help you didn't need. Any longer, anyways."

"For an old outlaw, you think too much," O'Neil said, the hardness remaining in his eyes.

"That's Slash's trouble," Pecos said, and sipped his beer. "Always has been. An added problem is that he ain't much good at it. Still, he does it anyway. Always thinkin'."

"Why don't you two stop thinkin' and ride on out of here before the trouble starts?"

"Gyllenwater kind of trouble?" Slash said.

"You know what kind."

"Maybe that foreman of his will turn old Gyllenwater's horns back around."

"Don't count on it."

"Another one of my problems," Slash said, "is I hate like hell to run with my tail between my legs. Especially when I haven't even robbed a bank or a train or even some lonely backwater drinkin' hole. I just shot some lout who was about to blow a poor doxie's head off."

"That's another one of Slash's problems," Pecos said. "He doesn't like runnin'. If it was up to me, we'd have had supper in Ogallala and be holed up in a nice room at the Platte River Hotel, waitin' on the next train."

"It's not too late," O'Neil said, keeping his hard eyes on Slash. "It will be soon."

"I'd consider pullin' my picket pin," Slash said, firing a match to life on the edge of the bar, "if you'd go ahead and tell me what happened to Ned Calico and those two pards of his. Not knowin' rankles me. I'd find it miserable hard to leave a place not knowin' what I was sent there for in the first place . . . not knowin' if I was leavin' a job unfinished."

"Peculiar turn of conscience for an old renegade," O'Neil said.

"Took the words right out of my mouth!" Pecos agreed.

Chapter 18

Slash smiled at the old lawman through the blue smoke wreathing the air in front of his face. "What *really* happened to Calico, Marshal?"

"I told you," O'Neil said. "He just plumb left. He an' the others apparently got bored with this backwater town an' pulled out."

"Without trouble."

"That's right. Oh, they stomped with their tails up a little, but who wouldn't after twelve years of prison?"

Still smiling, Slash took another drag off his quirley, and said, blowing smoke out his nostrils, "I don't believe you."

"Why not?"

"It don't add up."

"What don't add up?"

"Your concern for a pair of old train robbers," Slash said. He turned the quirley to inspect the coal, then returned his shrewd, incredulous gaze to the marshal. "Why are you so anxious to get us out of town?"

"I don't want the trouble of havin' you here! Not since you've climbed Tom Gyllenwater's hump by killin' his son!" O'Neil's craggy face was red with exasperation. "This is a quiet town. I like to keep it that way. What's so damn suspicious about that?"

Pecos took the last big swig from his beer schooner, belched, and set the glass back down on the table. "Maybe the real reason you're so concerned about a pair of old outlaws is you don't want any *official* federals sniffin' around. Maybe you're afraid, whether we're on or off the books, old Bleed-'Em-So might get suspicious if he don't see us again. Maybe he'll get worried and send men to see about our welfare. And find somethin' you and this town might be tryin' to hide."

Slash whistled, casting his partner an astonished look. "I'll be damned if he ain't smarter than he looks sometimes!"

"Why, thank you, Slash."

"Don't mention it, partner." Slash returned his gaze to O'Neil. "What's more, I don't think you sent that letter. I think someone forged your handwriting, your signature. Someone close to you. Someone who was worried about you. Worried about the town. Worried what would happen if those three cutthroats *stayed* in town." Slash smiled without humor. "That's it—isn't it?"

"Balderdash!" Incensed, O'Neil turned his head and narrowed one shrewd eye at Slash, thrusting his arm and extended right finger straight out from his right shoulder. "Now, look here, Braddock—you don't know what in hell you're talkin' about!"

"Your anger tells me I'm runnin' around the right bush, though." Slash took another, pensive puff from his quirley. "What happened to Ned Calico and the others, Marshal? They dead? Did the town gang up on 'em? Kill 'em? Why not just say so? There's nothin' shameful or unlawful about a town's citizenry rising up to stand together against outlaws. I'm glad they never did it to me, but . . ."

"Yeah, just say so, and we'll be on our way," Pecos said.

O'Neil looked at Pecos. He looked at Slash. Thoughts were moving fast behind his eyes. He didn't say anything for nearly a minute. Then he swallowed, drew a breath, and raised his hands, palms out. He smiled. "All right. I reckon I should've said so right off. I do apologize. That's what happened."

"The citizens revolted?"

"That's right. You see," O'Neil said, taking another deep breath, "I didn't want to implicate anyone. The whole town was scared. Those men are savages. They were here before, so we knew what they were capable of. Hell, I arrested them back then! They were here for revenge." He shook his head. "But I and the good citizens backing me weren't having it."

No one said anything. Slash and Pecos looked at each other. They turned back to the old lawman.

"Makes perfect sense to me!" Pecos said, slapping the table. He grinned at Slash. "Now we can get the hell out of here—right, partner? My curiosity has been satisfied. Ain't yours?"

Slash said to O'Neil, "Where they buried?"

The old lawman frowned. "What's that?"

"Where they buried?"

"Oh . . . hell, I don't know." The marshal tugged on a corner of his mustache. "A coupla fellas hauled 'em outta town. Not sure where."

"Which fellas?"

"Huh?"

"Who all was involved in the, uh, revolt?" Slash blew out a smoke ring and hiked a shoulder. "I'm sure the feds would want a list of names. Maybe an affidavit signed by each. We best dot our I's and cross our T's—make it all official-like."

Pecos slapped the table and turned to his partner, who was casually blowing another smoke ring. "Oh, come on, Slash! That's goin' too far!" He cast his exasperated gaze to O'Neil. "See how he is!"

"Yeah, I see how he is." The dark anger returned to the old marshal's eyes. "I told you—I don't want anyone implicated. You can blame it all on me."

"All right," Slash said, walking slowly over to the table he'd shared with Pecos. A cloud of cigarette smoke followed him. "We'll blame it all on you." He stopped at the table and looked at the marshal. "But who really did it? Just out of curiosity."

O'Neil stared back at him, his features taut, his mouth a straight, thin line across the lower half of his face, mantled by the thick, white soup-strainer mustache. He didn't say anything. Two veins forked in his forehead, and he said with quiet menace, "You've been warned to get out of town! Nothing good can come of you bein' here! If you leave, we'll have peace. We can all go back to the way it was before . . ."

He let his voice trail off. Uncertainty flickered in his gaze.

"Before what?" Pecos probed, sliding his chair back and slowly gaining his feet.

O'Neil didn't respond to that. He stepped up close to Slash, his eyes dark with—what? Fear as much as anger, Slash silently opined.

The marshal's jaws bulged where they hinged, and he said, "If you have any sense at all, you'll leave. That's all I have to say on the matter. *Please . . . just . . . leave!*"

He swung around and made his bandy-legged way back through the batwings and out onto the night-cloaked street. The batwings clattered back into place and then silence settled over the building until a woman's voice said quietly, "He's right. You should leave."

Slash and Pecos turned to see Mary Kate standing halfway down the stairs, half-turned to face them, one hand on the rail. She shook her head. "There's nothin' you can do. Tonight, you'll likely be killed, and it'll just bring more trouble until none of us has anything. Even less than we got, and that ain't much." She nodded slowly. "The old man's right. Go and save yourselves and us in the bargain!"

She swung around and hurried back up the stairs.

Exhausted from the day's chores, which ended with her working sourdough into a nice tight ball that she would let rise overnight then divide into buns at first light, Nancy O'Neil poured a cup of coffee. She added a spoonful of sugar, stirred the steaming black liquid, and wiped sweat from her brows with the hem of her apron.

She blew on the coffee, sipped, and smiled at her young son. Danny sat at the far end of the kitchen table, cyphering out the arithmetic problems she'd laid out for him earlier. He knew he wasn't supposed to, but he used his fingers for the tougher calculations. He kept his left hand hidden away beneath the table, where he didn't think Nancy could see it.

But she could see the hand, all right. She could hear him counting under his breath.

He leaned forward and scratched a number down with the pencil he kept sharp with his pocketknife.

Nancy smiled again. Such a fine, handsome boy with

wavy red hair. A little bit of a sneak, but weren't all boys sneaks? He did have a wild streak. The boy could cover a lot of territory in one day, and it was hard to get him settled down at night with his schoolwork.

Still, weren't all boys like that?

She sipped her coffee again, narrowing her eyes as she scrutinized the boy closely. With obsessive closeness, as though there might be signs on his face or in his hands or the way he moved that might indicate the kind of man he would one day become.

Would he become a good man? Or . . .

She closed her eyes, shook her head. A voice inside her remonstrated her sharply once more: *Will you stop? He has as much of you in him as* . . .

Then, as though he'd been reading her mind, Danny looked up at her suddenly, frowning.

Surprised by his sudden attention on her, when hers had been so intent on him, Nancy said, "What is it, son? What's on your mind?"

"I was just . . . I was just wonderin', Momma . . ."

"About what?"

"Pa."

"Who?" Of course, she'd heard. It had just caught her off guard. It really was as if the boy had been reading her mind.

"Do you think Pa will come around this summer?"

"Why. . . I don't know." Frowning, Nancy rose slowly from her chair. She walked over and sat down at the table, near the boy, and raked her fingers through his thick, wavy red hair. "What makes you ask, son? Have you been thinking about him?"

Again, she castigated herself for the lies she'd told Danny over the years. Of course, there'd had to be lies.

He'd been too young to understand. Now, however, maybe he was approaching the age where he could understand the intricacies of an intimate relationship, however brief. Soon, he'd have to be told.

Not now. No, she couldn't bear to tell him now. Not yet. She'd delay another few months, maybe a year. Still, all the delays . . . and the lies . . . were going to make it that much harder to finally tell him the truth of who his father really was.

"I reckon prospectin' keeps him busy down in Mexico."

"Yes, I'm sure it does."

"An' fightin' Injuns . . . an' bad men . . ."

"Yes, I'm sure there are plenty of both down in Mexico."

Danny studied the tip of his pencil for a time, then returned his questioning gaze to his mother. "Funny he never writes a letter, though, ain't it?"

Nancy feigned a chuckle that belied her heart's quick beat. "Oh, he was never much of a writer, your father."

"I wish I could see a picture of him."

"I'm afraid he was never much of a picture-taker, either."

The boy drew his mouth corners down and nodded. They'd been through it all before. He'd known what her responses to his questions would be even before she'd given them.

Nancy studied him, her heart breaking. She was afraid she'd break down in tears. Her heart continued to beat faster and faster as her mind raced.

Now, she thought. *It's time to end this charade right here and now. The boy should know. He deserves to know the truth. He doesn't deserve to be kept waiting for his adventurer/gold seeker/Indian-fighting father to return from Mexico, for godsakes!*

Besides, she had a feeling that deep down the boy knew they were lies. All lies. So far, he hadn't pushed the matter because he sensed how upset his mother got when he brought up the subject of his father. But as he got older, he would press the matter until Nancy finally had to tell him the truth. The longer she waited, the harder it would be and the bigger fool . . . the bigger liar . . . she would be.

She drew a breath, slid a stray lock of hair from her eye, and placed her hands flat atop the oilcloth table covering. "Danny, son . . ."

He looked up at her, expectant. "Yes, Momma?"

"I have to tell you someth—"

Footsteps sounded in the yard, growing louder as someone approached the house. A boot thudded on the stoop and then the door was pulled open and Nancy's father stepped into the kitchen, doffing his hat with one hand while pulling the door closed behind him with the other.

He was red-faced around his snow-white mustache, and his blue eyes were rheumy. He was breathing hard, as though he'd run a long way, though Nancy didn't think Kentucky O'Neil had it in him anymore to run a single step. Something was wrong. There was usually a playfulness in the old man's eyes, especially when Danny was around.

Now there was only a flat—what?

Apprehension. Fear.

"Hello, Pa," Nancy greeted her father as he hung his jacket on a peg by the door.

Kentucky nodded, attempted a smile at her and Danny, then walked over to the washstand.

Nancy turned to Danny. She'd have to delay their talk for another time. Soon, she promised herself. Very soon.

"Danny, why don't you go up to bed now? Read for

fifteen minutes before you turn down the lamp. Whatever you like."

Danny frowned at her, perplexed, deeply disappointed. "But, Momma, you—"

Firmly but with a sympathetic smile, Nancy said, "Danny, we'll talk later. I promise."

Danny flinched as though something had bit him. He glanced at his grandfather, who had his back to the table as he washed his face and hands, then slid his chair back and, with his math paper and pencil in hand, sighed and left the room. Nancy heard the creaks and thuds overhead as the boy climbed the stairs.

She turned to her father, who stood patting dry his face while staring out the window beside the door.

Nancy rose from her chair and walked over to him, placed a hand on his shoulder. "What is it, Pa? What happened?"

Chapter 19

"Nothin'." Kentucky pressed his lips to his daughter's forehead. "Nothin' for you to worry about, leastways."

He walked over to the cupboard above the wet sink and pulled out a bottle. He grabbed a glass off a shelf, walked over to the table, and splashed a couple fingers of whiskey into the glass.

Watching him with concern, Nancy said, "Yes, it is. It's my doing. It's those two men Marshal Bledsoe sent to town." She lowered her voice with chagrin. "Because I sent him that letter . . ."

Kentucky sat down in his usual place at the opposite end of the table from where Danny had been sitting. He gave Nancy a fleeting half smile. "I don't blame you for that, honey. I don't blame anyone except myself."

"Why would you blame yourself, Pa? I sent the letter, forged your signature." Nancy strode over to the table and sat down at the corner of the table near Kentucky and placed her hand on his wrist. "I got scared and I sent it. I panicked. I wasn't thinking clearly . . . remembering . . ."

She looked down at the table and closed her eyes as though to shut out the stubborn reflections.

Kentucky sipped the whiskey and turned to her with his sympathetic half smile. "You were remembering twelve years ago."

Keeping her eyes closed, chin down, she nodded.

"It would have been all right if the first thing they had not done when they got to town was kill Collie Gyllenwater." Kentucky flinched and shook his head. "That was what lit the fuse."

"I take it you weren't able to convince Gyllenwater . . ."

Kentucky shook his head. "I didn't see Gyllenwater. I ran into Wayne Blanchard. He took the body on back to the headquarters."

"What did Wayne say?"

"He said he'd try to convince the old man to turn his horns in, but you know Gyllenwater. The chances of that happening . . . of not seeking some sort of restitution for the murder of his son . . . well, the chance of that is damned slim."

"Murder? You said he'd been about to kill a girl."

"Oh, it was a justified killing, all right." The weary old lawman took another sip of the whiskey, sloshed it around in his mouth, and swallowed, a whiskey flush rising in his cheeks and glinting in his eyes. "Just the same, Gyllenwater will call it murder. Especially in his current state, hopped up on mercury and raw opium, he'd never call the killing of his son anything except murder. And he'll want a reckoning. A bloody one."

"And Wayne will likely give him one."

Kentucky looked up at her, held her gaze for a moment, then pursed his lips and nodded. "You know Wayne. He will. Wayne's a practical man. He's kept his job all these years by dancing to Old Tom's fiddle. If he hadn't, he'd be long gone. No other man has ridden for Gyllenwater as long as Blanchard has. Wayne knows who butters his bread. He's killed a lot of men, Wayne has. On Old Tom's orders. But he's grown softer with the years." He cast another quick glance at Nancy. "Not as hard as before. More reluctant to kill when it's not absolutely necessary."

Kentucky shook his head as he stared down into his whiskey glass. "Still, Gyllenwater calls the shots. Wayne's not getting any younger, and he knows it. He'd never find another ranch to ramrod. Not this late in life. The Rimfire is his home. Especially in this situation, he'll shoot the shots Tom calls. He might let his toughnuts do the actual *killing*, but he'll come, all right. And he'll make sure old Tom's orders are carried out so he can go back to his warm bed in his cabin there along the creek. He knows it's too late to start over. He'll die at Rimfire."

Kentucky threw back the last of the whiskey.

Nancy studied him, realizing that he'd been speaking as much about himself as about Wayne Blanchard. It was too late for Kentucky O'Neil to start over, too. Harveyville was his last stop. What happened in the next several hours, maybe days, could mean big changes in his life. Not good changes if Gyllenwater did what Gyllenwater always did.

Nancy leaned her head against her father's shoulder. "Oh, God, Pa—I'm so sorry! If only I hadn't sent that letter!"

Kentucky patted her hand. "No, no. This is not your fault. It's Collie Gyllenwater's fault, when you get right down to it. It's my fault, too. I could have told those two former cutthroats riding for Luther the truth about the whole thing. Leastways, part of the truth. I could have said we'd settled the matter right here on our own terms, and that would have been the end of it. But I lied and they knew I was lyin', and now they're damned curious. Just too damned curious. So, they're likely to die tonight."

Kentucky rose and refreshed his drink. He sat back down at the table.

Nancy leaned on her elbows, staring off into space, anxiety and troubling memories a wild horse inside her.

"I was just so worried," she said, her voice barely above a whisper. "I was so worried that when they didn't find what they'd come here for, they'd . . ." She looked at her father through the wavering sheen of tears in her eyes. "I hadn't figured on Gyllenwater. Or . . . Wayne. He nor any of the Rimfire men had shown up in town to handle the matter, so I figured he was going to stay out of it."

Kentucky turned to her, studied her for a time. Her ears warmed a little with self-consciousness as she felt the keenness of her father's probing eyes. Kentucky placed his hand over hers and squeezed it gently. "Tell me something," he said.

She turned to him, frowning, her ears growing warmer. "Anything, Pa. Of course. What is it?"

"I need to know something. I think you need to know it, too. I think it will settle some things in your mind."

"What is it, Pa?"

"You wanted him dead, didn't you? Partly because you were afraid for me. And you were afraid for the boy. Of him seein' who his father was. But partly because he never came over here. He never came over here to see you . . . after all these years. Instead, he stayed over at the Copper Nickel with that younger gal. With Mary Kate."

Nancy stared at her father, stunned. She opened her mouth to speak, but no words came. Only tears came. Tears of loneliness and longing and hating herself for how she felt about the most despicable man she'd ever met.

Tears of horror that her father knew the dark recesses of her mind and heart so well when not even she had been able to so thoroughly plumb those murky depths and put words to what she'd seen there.

She turned from her father's gaze in shame. Tears rolled down her cheeks. Her upper lip quivered. "Yes!" she said. "I thought . . . I thought he'd come!" She sobbed. "I thought he'd come!"

Pecos shoved a shotgun wad into his freshly cleaned and oiled sawed-off's open tube and snapped the loaded gut-shredder closed. "Could be a long night. I'm glad you thought to buy a bottle."

"I always think of everything, don't I? A bottle, most of all."

"You're one humble critter—I'll give you that, Slash."

Slash snorted. He lay on the bed in the dark room at the Longhorn Hotel in Harveyville, nearly directly across the street from Madam Delacroix's. Pecos sat in a badly worn brocade armchair that was angled in front of one of the room's two curtained windows, so he could see along the street to the north, which was likely the direction from which Gyllenwater's men would come, if they came. The Rimfire lay to the southeast.

Both men figured Gyllenwater's men would come. Leastways, they had to be prepared.

Which meant one of them would keep watch while the other got as much sleep as he could before relieving the other. "We could still pull out, you know," Slash said, taking a pull from the bottle he'd bought at the Copper Nickel. The bottle sat on the bedside table, within reach of both men. They didn't bother with glasses. They'd been swapping spit longer than some married couples. Slash was smoking a cigarette, resting his head back against one hooked arm and a lumpy, sour-smelling pillow, staring at the ceiling.

Pecos glanced at him from the chair, his long legs stretched out before him and crossed at the ankles, boots propped on the edge of the windowsill. "I thought you ran *toward* trouble, not away from it."

Slash hiked a shoulder. "I'm married now. I think I forgot that, earlier. I've been married such a short time, only been with her once, that I reckon I'm still wrapping my mind around it."

"How does it feel?"

"How does what feel?"

"Being married!"

"See?" Slash laughed and took a drag off his cigarette. "I still can't get it through my thick head!"

"Answer the question. You were able to share your feelin's with Jay."

"She's purtier'n you."

"Now, that hurts my feelin's!"

"It feels right good. I'm still a little nervous about the whole thing, though. I never used to worry about situations like this. I used to think that if I got shot . . . killed . . . well, hell. No big deal. I didn't have no one waitin' on me in any home. No one to cry and make a fuss and get all lonely and distraught because I wasn't comin' back to them. I reckon there was a freedom in that. But, now . . ." He looked at the coal of his cigarette and peeled a dangling ash from it with his thumbnail, wincing a little at the unexpected burn.

"But, now . . . ?"

"But, now I'm lyin' here wonderin' if this is fair to Jay. Holdin' our ground like this."

"That must be nice."

"What must be nice?"

"Havin' someone who cares if you live or die."

Slash glanced at his partner. "Feelin' sorry for yourself?"

"Yes."

"Oh, I got me a feelin' Miss Langdon would shed a tear or two over your big ugly carcass."

"You're just tryin' to make me feel good."

"She might."

"If we don't pull foot pronto, there's a good chance I may never know what she looks like under those fancy gowns of hers, and that would be a damn shame. Since I been so curious for such a long time!"

They each had a good laugh at that and another drink.

Neither said anything for a good fifteen minutes.

Slash smoked and took infrequent sips from the bottle and stared at the ceiling, thinking about Jay and what their future together might look like if they had one. Pecos sat in the chair, staring out into the dark street where not even a tumbleweed stirred, thinking about Miss Abigail Langdon and what their future together might look like, if they had one.

Slash broke the silence finally with, "You wanna do it?"

Pecos glanced at him. "What? Light a shuck?"

"Yep."

"Yes, I do." Pecos grinned sagely. "But you know neither one of us is gonna do it."

"I know." Slash frowned at the ceiling. "Why is that?"

"It's not who we are, Slash," Pecos said with a sigh and turned back to the window.

* * *

Slash slept only because he was accustomed to forcing sleep on himself in similar situations, when he needed to be fresh afterwards.

He and Pecos switched off sleeping and keeping watch two more times.

At dawn, Slash prodded Pecos awake and said, "Rise an' shine, partner. We got business."

Chapter 20

Slash racked a cartridge into his Winchester's breech and stepped up to one of the room's two windows. Slinging his shotgun over his head and shoulder, Pecos sidled up to the right of Slash's window, curled his index finger over the triggers, and placed his thumb over the rabbit-ear hammers.

He slid the curtain aside with one hand and peered down into the street.

A dozen or so riders were just then galloping up to the hotel, checking their mounts down abruptly, dust lifting in the pink light of early morning to mix with the billowing blue smoke of the town's breakfast fires.

A big man with a mustache sat ahead of the other riders, on a rangy buckskin. Both Slash and Pecos recognized him from the previous day, when he and the three younger men had intercepted Kentucky O'Neil on the old marshal's way out to the Rimfire with Collie Gyllenwater's body. That would be Wayne Blanchard, Gyllenwater's foreman.

Behind the riders still getting their mounts settled in front of the hotel, Slash saw Kentucky O'Neil walking quickly along the boardwalk in the direction of the hotel but remaining on the opposite side of the street. He walked in his bandy-legged, slightly stove-up way, a sporadic hitch in his gait. O'Neil stopped directly across the street from the hotel and stared toward the gang gathered before it with grave interest, the fingers of both hands curled around his cartridge belt.

O'Neil's grandson came running up the street in O'Neil's own path. The old lawman turned, gestured angrily toward the boy, who turned reluctantly and, kicking at imaginary rocks or horse apples, slowly retraced his tracks back along the boardwalks on the opposite side of the street from the hotel.

Meanwhile, the big man lifted his head so that the brim of his black Stetson came up to reveal his broad, mustached, weathered face. He scanned the windows of the rooms on the second story, then lowered his gaze and spoke to someone who must have been standing on the boardwalk fronting the Longhorn.

"What room they in?" he asked.

Slash crouched to open his window. Pecos did the same.

The foreman must have heard the rasp of the sliding wood. He looked up again, frowning uncertainly. Holding the Winchester straight down along his right leg, Slash edged his face up close to the open window and said, "Here."

The foreman tracked the voice to Slash. He glanced toward the window to Slash's right and through which Pecos was now peering while holding the sawed-off in both hands in front of him, a few inches of the double maws poking through the gap between the window and the sash.

The foreman said, "I'm Blanchard, Rimfire foreman."

"I'm listenin'," Slash said.

The man's big face turned red with anger. He narrowed an eye, raised an arm and pointing finger, and swept the arm and accusatory finger from Slash to Pecos and back again, saying, "Now, we can do this the easy way or the hard way. It's up to you!"

Slash glanced at Pecos with a crooked smile, then returned his gaze to the mounted Rimfire foreman. "Always nice to have options."

He actually felt a little relieved. He'd imagined that bullets would have been flying by now and that he and Pecos would have been crawling around the room with glass raining in on them, along with bullets, trying to return fire.

The foreman glowered up at Slash, grinding his heavy jaws. "You both haul your raggedy asses out of here, pronto. Not tomorrow. Not by noon. Not in an hour from now. But now. *Within-the-hour!* Come down an' pad out your bellies and buy some grain for your hosses. Whatever you need. But then you haul your freight. Do you understand what I'm telling you? I've just given you both a new lease on life. One you *do not deserve*, given the man you killed. The son of a very important man! A very important and angry man. So, there you have it. Now, have I made myself crystal clear?"

Slash and Pecos shared a glance of silent conferral. Pecos raised a brow as well as a shoulder, then returned his gaze to the street. Slash returned his gaze to the foreman and said, "You've made yourself crystal clear. We appreciate your candor."

Pecos glanced at Slash, frowning, mouthing the word, "Candor?"

Slash shrugged, then returned his gaze to the street.

The foreman was already wheeling his horse around,

putting spurs to its flanks and galloping back down the street over which the gang's dust was still sifting. The other riders looked around at each other as though in shock. A couple were muttering incredulously, casting glances toward Slash and Pecos and then at the foreman galloping away from them. Finally, they all turned their own mounts and galloped off down the street in the foreman's path, a couple still casting dubious looks over their shoulders at Slash and Pecos.

They were gone as quickly as they'd come.

Shopkeepers in the process of opening their stores stood on boardwalks, staring skeptically after the retreating riders. They'd been expecting trouble but they hadn't gotten it, and they didn't quite know what to make of the lack. Slash didn't blame them. He didn't know what to make of it, either.

He looked directly across the street from the hotel. Kentucky O'Neil was also staring after the riders. When he turned his craggy face toward Slash, Slash would have sworn the man not only looked puzzled but disappointed, as well.

Slash grinned at him and shrugged.

O'Neil glowered back at him and, pointing a finger the way Blanchard had, said, "You heard the man!"

He shot Slash and Pecos a parting warning glance, then turned and ambled back in the direction of his office.

Slash turned from the window. Pecos did, as well, frowning curiously. "What do you make of that?"

"What I make of that is that the Rimfire foreman is between a rock and a hard place."

"Kinda seems that way, don't it?"

"It does." Slash shouldered his rifle and stared off into a corner of the room that hadn't been swept recently.

"He couldn't have been *scared* of us," Pecos said. "I mean, sure, we're mean as hell an' right capable when the chips are down, but—"

"No, it wasn't us he was afraid of. I get the feelin' the Rimfire foreman isn't afraid of much of anything. You heard what Kentucky said about him. I got a feelin' Blanchard's not used to doin' what he did out here just now—*not* throwin' down on somebody—and it gravels him."

"What gravels him about it exactly? I'm a might confused."

"It gravels him to go against orders. And I got me a sneaking suspicion that's just what he done."

Pecos nodded slowly, pulling thoughtfully at his goatee with thumb and forefinger. "It did seem that way, didn't it?"

"Yep."

"Why?"

Slash flicked his finger at his partner. "That there is the question."

Slash set his rifle down, walked over to the washstand, filled the basin with water, rolled up his longhandle sleeves, and dunked his face. He turned his head from side to side, blowing bubbles and combing water through his hair with his fingers.

He lifted his head from the basin, hair dripping, and grabbed a towel. Drying his hair and then his face, scrubbing brusquely with the threadbare towel, he said, "I had a strange dream last night. One that's stuck with me."

Pecos had taken a seat on the edge of the bed and was rolling a quirley. "I get those from time to time." He grinned. "Usually, they're about Miss Langdon."

Slash snorted. "This dream I had . . . well, it wasn't really a dream."

"If it wasn't a dream, what was it?"

"Just a voice, really."

"A voice?"

Slash hung the towel on its peg and shoved his sleeves down to his wrists and turned to his partner. "Just a voice that kept whispering in my ear over an' over again—'Dead men dance.'"

Pecos scowled as he rolled the quirley closed. "Huh?"

Slash walked over to his partner, leaned down, and said in soft but ominous singsong into Pecos's left ear, like a dark lullaby: "'Dead men dance. Dead men dance.' Over and over again, it kept comin', real quiet but odd-like. 'Dead men dance. Dead men dance. Dead men . . .'"

Pecos pulled his head away and scowled up at his partner. "Stop that, now—you're startin' to spook me a little. 'Dead men dance, dead men dance.' You're off your nut!"

"What do you think it means?"

"It means you're off your nut!"

"You heard the man." Slash tossed Pecos his shirt. "Let's go pad out our bellies. Avoiding a lead storm makes me hungry. Besides, I think better when I got my snoot buried in a nice, deep food trough."

He shrugged into his own shirt, grabbed his hat and rifle, and then he and Pecos headed down to the little Bon Ton Café connected to the hotel and run by a diminutive and deferring old Chinese couple and their hulking brute of a son who sported a long braid and mare's tail mustaches and took orders and hustled the food out from the kitchen, moving through the dark little café with all the grace of a bull elk in James J. Hill's private dining car.

The food, however, was good.

They were halfway through their meal before Pecos frowned across the table at Slash and said, "You still thinkin' about that dream—if you can call it a dream?"

"Yeah," Slash said, and forked a bite of eggs and bacon into his mouth.

"You was probably just nervous about possibly dyin' this mornin'. We all dream strange when we're nervous."

"I only get nervous when I get married. Thank God I have that behind me! I'd never want to do it again—I'll guaran-damn-tee you that much!"

"You was so nervous you about made me pee down my own leg!"

They both laughed at that.

Then Slash went back to frowning and studying his food a little too closely as he ate it, not really seeing the food but ruminating again. A seed of something had sprouted in his mind, and over the past several minutes it had been slowly growing. He forked a syrup-soaked bite of buttermilk pancake and ham into his mouth and, chewing, said, "As soon as we finish up here, let's take a ride."

"To Ogallala?"

"No."

"I had a feelin' you were gonna say that. Why not? We avoided a nasty little death by Rimfire firing squad this morning, Slash." Chewing, Pecos shook his head. "I don't think we'll get that lucky a second time."

"Prob'ly not, but let's take a ride anyway."

"All right, but I sure am gonna miss the pleasure of having Miss Langdon warm my blankets of a night."

"You sure know how to put the cart before the donkey, Pecos—I'll give you that!"

They laughed, then finished up and headed out, the next half hour finding them loping their mounts north of town by way of a shaggy two-track wagon trail that hadn't been ridden in a while.

"Kind of lonesome out here, sure enough," Slash said, lifting his gaze from the overlaid prints of shod hooves.

"You feelin' lonely, Slash? You want me to sing ya a song? One a little peppier than the one you got goin' through your head?"

"No, I'm just wonderin' where this trail goes. Don't seem much used these days."

"What I'm wonderin' is what we're doing out here. This trail don't look like it leads to anywhere."

"You don't know that. It might."

"What makes you think so?"

"That song in my head."

"That song in your . . . ?" Pecos let words trail to silence. He shook his head. "Loco. Pure loco. You won't be with Jay a year before you forget how to wipe yourself an' she has to put you in a charity home for wicked former cutthroats with old-timer's disease."

"Shut up an' ride!" Slash said, booting his horse into a hard run. *"Hy-ahh!"*

They galloped for twenty minutes. Then Slash reined up on a low ridge and looked around as Pecos checked his buckskin down beside him. Before them lay a winding creek or river canyon lined with cottonwoods and box elders and shrub thickets.

The creek threaded through the fawn-colored prairie from the northeast to the southwest. The railroad's spur line came down from the north on Slash and Pecos's left, maybe a half mile away. A trestle straddled the canyon to the southwest, and the canyon continued on until it foreshortened off into the misty, sunlit distance under a sky tufted with low, cottony clouds.

Slash studied the rails to his left, then slowly turned

his head to the right, scrutinizing the canyon, frowning, fingering his unshaven chin.

"Where was it now . . . ?"

"Where was what?"

"You remember me mentioning an odd-lookin' tree, when we was ridin' the train through here?"

"No."

"Well, I did."

"That's what we rode out here for? To look at an odd-lookin' tree?"

"Yessir." Slash's gaze suddenly held on a tawny lump of ground poking out of the canyon's gradual slope before him and on his right. "There it is!" he said, pointing. "That's it right there. That odd-lookin' tree sittin' atop a cone-shaped butte!"

He booted his Appaloosa over the lip of the ridge and galloped down the slope carpeted in bromegrass peppered with old and relatively new cow pies as well as deer and antelope scat. He and Pecos galloped down the slope at a gradual northeastern angle and into the crease where the tawny lump rose before him, forming the grassy bluff capped with rocks and a single, wind-gnarled cedar.

A strange fruit appeared to hang from a couple of the cedar's lower, bent branches. Only, as Slash and Pecos gained the top of the rise, nearing the cedar itself, they saw that the tree had not grown fruit, after all. It had been decorated with three dead men hanging from ropes thrown over the two low branches, one on each side of the tree, the ends tied off near the base.

One man hung from the branch on the tree's left side. Two hung from the branch on the tree's right side.

Their boots dangled maybe five feet off the ground, turning slightly this way and that as the slack bodies were nudged by vagrant breezes. The ropes creaked quietly as the bodies twisted and turned.

A big crow sat on the right shoulder of the man on the left side of the tree. Something dangled from its beak. The crow blinked its dark eyes at the unwelcome newcomers then gave an annoyed, "Caw! Caw! Caw!" Whatever hung from its beak tumbled to the ground with a plop.

The carrion-eater spread its wings and flew away in a huff. Slash looked at Pecos. "What'd I tell ya?"

"You was right," Pecos said, "though it pains me to say so for obvious reasons." He squinted up at the tree. "This must be what they call a Panhandle necktie party. I always wondered an' wanted to see one . . . as long as I wasn't the guest of honor, of course!"

The two former cutthroats had a good laugh.

Chapter 21

An hour earlier, Kentucky O'Neil had stood in his office staring out the window, tugging on a corner of his mustache as the two former train-robbing outlaws, Slash Braddock and the Pecos River Kid, rode past him along the main street, from his left to his right. Each man was packing a bedroll, a pair of saddlebags, a canteen, and a scabbarded rifle. The taller of the two, the Pecos River Kid, aka Melvin Baker, had a sawed-off shotgun hanging down his broad back.

They were heading for the countryside—no question about it. The old lawman anxiously bunched his lips. They were riding northeast, too. Not straight north. Ogallala lay straight north. No, they weren't heading back to Denver by way of Ogallala. They were heading northeast, damn their contrary hides.

The nosiest pair of damn owlhoots Kentucky had ever met . . .

He turned his head, tracking the pair until, sure enough, they rode right on past the edge of town and into the rolling prairie, nudging their mounts into dust-raising trots and then lopes. They climbed a distant prairie swell, jounced on over the top of the swell then down, down, down out of sight.

A foot thudded on the boardwalk fronting the marshal's office, making the marshal's heart lurch with a start. The door flew open. Kentucky swung around to face it, automatically closing his hand over the worn walnut grips of the six-shooter holstered on his right hip. He left the smoke wagon in the scabbard when he saw that his visitor was his grandson, Danny, who turned to him wide-eyed, yelling, "Grandpa, Grandpa—why in tarnation did—"

"Good Lord, boy," Kentucky exclaimed, heart racing, "you done about kicked me out with a cold shovel, comin' in here like a Brahma bull boltin' through a chute!"

"Sorry, Grandpa, but what I'm wonderin' is why in hell . . . er, *heck!*—did Wayne Blanchard backwater like that?"

Kentucky drew a calming breath. "I don't know. That's kind of what . . ." Then he caught himself. "But that's a good thing, son. Not a bad thing." He walked over to the door and placed his hands on the boy's shoulders. "You understand that—don't you? Violence is a bad thing. It always is. We need to be glad no one was killed here today."

"Oh, right . . . sure, sure, Grandpa," Danny said, though the disappointment was plain in his light brown eyes. He had a harder time throwing bull around than full-grown men did, Kentucky absently opined. Danny had a harder time throwing it around than his grandfather did.

Christ, what kind of a boy was he and Nancy raising? He'd wanted to see a bloodbath over at the Longhorn this morning, and he was deeply disappointed that he had not seen one.

On the other hand, Kentucky himself had begun to think

it might not have been such a bad thing if old Gyllenwater had turned those two former cut-throats toe-down. He'd had a pretty damned good suspicion those two weren't going to leave here without nosing around and making trouble. Now, he knew that better than ever.

"But why'd he do it, Grandpa?" Danny wanted to know, staring wide-eyed up at his grandfather. "Why'd he turn tail? Everyone knows that ol' Blanchard has killed more than his fair share of—"

"Danny, dammit, Blanchard did not turn tail," Kentucky said, not only annoyed with his grandson's bloodthirstiness but his very presence in his office when the marshal was trying to sort out a problem. A big one. "He was merely doing the right thing by not making trouble. Now, run along, will you . . ."

He turned his attention to the Copper Nickel on the other side of the street and to the west a few yards. "Hold on . . ."

"What is it, Gramps?"

"Do those four mounts tied to the hitch rail out front of the Copper Nickel belong to Ivan Cutter and Luther Sprague an' the two others who ride with 'em? Carter an' the Mex called Blanco?"

If anyone would know, Danny would. The boy kept tabs on everyone coming and going in Harveyville. Sometimes Kentucky was tempted to deputize the kid.

"Let me see." Danny turned to face the open door and the street beyond, sliding his gaze to the Copper Nickel. He glanced back at his grandfather, nodding. "Yep, they sure are." The boy's eyes grew wide again with eager expectation. "You gonna go over and arrest 'em?"

Kentucky frowned. "Why would I do that?"

"'Cause they still haven't paid for the damage they done to Madam Delacroix's place. And I can tell you, the madam's still mighty steamed about havin' to have that new window shipped in all the way from—"

"Damn, boy!" Kentucky scowled down at his grandson in disbelief. He hadn't known that Danny knew about the dustup over at Madam Delacroix's the last time Cutter's and Sprague's market hunters had pulled through Harveyville. But of course Danny would know. Even if it had happened late one night after Danny had been long asleep. Danny knew more about the town than Kentucky himself did.

"What is it, Gramps?"

"Never mind." Kentucky had already turned back to the window. He studied the four horses on which long-barreled Sharps rifles jutted from scabbards. His heart quickening, he chewed his mustache thoughtfully, then turned to Danny again and said, "Danny, do me a favor, would you?"

"You bet, Gramps!"

"Go on over to the Copper Nickel and tell them hunters I'd like to—" Kentucky stopped abruptly as a voice inside his head chastised him severely.

You're actually going to have your grandson summon killers for you?

And you're worried what kind of man the boy will make? What kind of a man are you, Kentucky O'Neil?

"Yeah, Gramps?" Danny asked from the doorway. "Tell them what?"

Kentucky shook his head. He turned from the window and walked to the door, the full flower of deep chagrin showing on his weathered face. "Never mind. You get on over to the post office with that mail before Wilkes tans you over his rain barrel for bein' late."

Danny held out his hands. "What mail? The mail don't come in till day after tomorrow, Gramps."

Kentucky saw that, indeed, the boy did not have a mail bag slung over his shoulder. Racked with annoyance, he said, "Well, go see if Madam Delacroix don't have some wood for you to chop! Get on outta here, boy! Right now! *Git!*"

"All right!" Danny said in exasperation. "I'm goin'! I'm goin'!" As he slouched off down the boardwalk, heading west, he glanced over his shoulder and griped, "Boy, someone sure got up on the wrong side of the bed!"

Kentucky grabbed his hat off a wall peg, set it on his head. He stepped out onto the boardwalk and looked around, pondering, feeling his old ticker increase its pace. It had steadily been beating faster since the idea had occurred to him. His palms were getting slick, and his shirt was sticking to his back.

He looked toward the four horses—two duns, a sorrel, and a palomino—standing at the hitchrack fronting the Copper Nickel.

He hitched up his pants, adjusted his hat, then stepped down into the street. "God, forgive me."

He crossed the street, walked around the horses, and pushed through the batwings into the saloon. The four men he was looking for stood at the bar, leaning forward over their drinks, chinning with Mary Kate. The girl stood behind the bar drying a glass and regarding the four market hunters with a sultry sneer curling one side of her mouth.

"I think you're seventeen," the gang's leader, Ivan Cutter, was just then saying to the girl. He glanced at the man standing to his right. "Don't you think so, Luther? She looks seventeen to me."

"She looks a whole lot older'n that to me," Luther told Mary Kate.

Color rose into Mary Kate's pretty cheeks, and she flounced a little in place as she said, "And just how old do you think I am, then, if'n I ain't seventeen?"

"Hmmm." Luther leaned farther across the bar to look down at the floor behind it. He lifted his chin as he ran his gaze up from the girl's feet until his eyes were lingering on the well-filled bodice of her dress. Kentucky could see where the man's eyes were on the girl, because he could see the faces of all four market hunters in the backbar mirror.

"Me?" Luther said. "I'd say you was—"

"Cutter. Sprague." Kentucky interrupted the conversation.

All four men looked at the marshal in the backbar mirror. The girl turned her head to regard the old man with an annoyed expression as she dried another glass.

"Ah, hell," Cutter said with a grimace. He was horse-faced and bearded; a scar lay above and below his left eye, drawing a pink line through his brow where no hair would grow.

He turned around to face Kentucky. The other three did, then, as well, glowering expressions on their sunburned, unshaven faces. They were dull-witted, savage men who stunk of death. Blood from the game they killed for the railroad stained their ragged trail clothes and lay crusted beneath their fingernails.

"Now, look, Marshal," Cutter said, raising a gloved

hand, palm out in supplication, "about that fifty dollars we owe fer . . ."

"Yeah, about that fifty dollars," Kentucky said, tucking his thumbs behind his cartridge belt. "You want me to see if I can get that debt forgiven?"

The faces of the three hanged men were nearly gone—most of the flesh pecked away by birds. Their bodies were swollen from bloat, and their tongues protruded grotesquely from their mouths. Between the three of them, only one eye remained in its socket but it, too, had nearly been picked away and hung by only a ragged, bloody thread.

Still, it was still relatively easy to distinguish the three corpses, to see that one was medium tall and blond, another short but thickset, downright muscular in the fashion of a bare-knuckle fighter. The third one, hanging beside the thickset man and half-turned to face him, was tall and lanky; a dark brown mustache drooped down over both corners of the dead man's mouth.

He was missing one boot. He must have done the midair two-step right out of it. That sock was half off the badly swollen, bootless foot, revealing most of the man's fish-belly-white heel.

The boot was nowhere around that Slash could see. Some predator, likely a young coyote with a sense of sport, had run off with it, likely teasing the others with its trophy.

The one thing all three dead men had in common was that all three had been shot likely before they'd been hanged. Dried blood showed here and there on each body—leg and arm wounds, mostly, but a couple of shots to the lower torsos of two. Probably not killing shots. At least, not right away. They appeared to have been beaten, too. Beaten after they'd been shot and lay helpless, most likely.

One or two might have been dead before they'd been hanged. The man who'd kicked out of his boot had obviously been alive when he'd been hanged.

"A might whiffy on the lee side!" Slash said, lifting an arm to defend his nose against the putrid odor as he studied the three cadavers.

"You think it's them—Calico, Stockton, an' Wheeler?"

"Yes, I do."

"Now, why is that?"

"Who do you think it is?"

Pecos hiked a shoulder and glanced around. "We're on someone's graze. Could be cattle rustlers." He frowned at his partner. "What're you eyeballin'?"

He turned his head to follow Slash's gaze down the north side of the bluff. Five ancient mud-brick shacks, crumbling in on themselves, sat in a horseshoe of the nearly dry creek that had carved the canyon. The area around the shacks was bare except for tufts of buckbrush and prickly pear. A moldering hitchrack stood outside the largest of the hovels, part of whose brush roof had caved inward to the right of the dark rectangle of the missing front door.

A bird flew out of that dark rectangle and into the sunlight—likely a sparrow or a barn swallow nesting inside.

"What's that?" Pecos said.

"I don't know. Let's have us a look-see. But keep an eye out."

"How come?"

"We left town in broad daylight—for all to see. Might've been followed."

"Mmm," Pecos said, looking around. "And, like you said—mighty lonesome out here. A coupla fellas could disappear without anyone the wiser. Unless, of course . . ."

"Unless, of course, what?"

"Unless ol' Bleed-'Em-So wakes some night in his Denver digs with some voice singin' in his ear about our tragic fates." Pecos licked his lips and sang, *"Slash an' Pecos dance . . . Slash n' Pecos dance . . ."* He chuckled and slapped Slash's arm with his hat.

"Yeah, well, I wouldn't count on him losin' any sleep over it," Slash said. "Or on doin' anything about it."

"Sometimes you're too right, Slash. You're too damn right!"

"Uh-huh."

They nudged their horses down the bluff.

Chapter 22

Slash and Pecos reined their horses up and regarded the adobe brick huts, most of them in ruins, that formed a roughly circular shape around them. Swallows flew in and out of the gaping windows and doors beyond which, in sharp contrast to the bright sunlight outside, lay stygian shadows.

Worn cedar hitchracks stood outside most of the huts.

"What do you suppose this place was?" Pecos asked, looking around. "Military outpost of some kind?"

"Prob'ly somethin' like that. Maybe an old hide-hunter's camp."

"Maybe one before the other."

"Uh-huh."

Slash and Pecos studied the ground.

"Been riders through here," Pecos opined aloud. "Quite a few."

"Uh-huh. A week or two ago. The dirt's been buffed up by a recent rain or two, maybe a little wind. But some of the prints are right clear."

"Some o' them horses was movin' fast," Pecos said,

riding around slowly, leaning out from his saddle to study the ground. "Side-steppin' an' such."

Slash reined his horse over to a small shack on his left. "Let's look around a bit."

"What're we lookin' for?"

"I got no idea."

"We'll know when we find it—that sorta thing?"

"Maybe."

Slash rode around the small shack. There were no prints in the tufts of short, wiry brush surrounding it. Tumbleweeds had blown up against its west side to form a secondary wall nearly as high as the brush roof from which a rusted chimney tilted. Spying nothing that caught his eye, he rode over to the largest of the five buildings and inspected the front and the west side. He could smell pent-up air and wood rot and rodent droppings issuing from the front door and the west window. He reined up at the rear, near a cellar that abutted the rear wall.

One cellar door was open. Overlaid horse tracks lay all around the rear of the building. Many of them were badly scuffed. The brush around the doors was bent and broken.

Slash stuck two fingers in his mouth and whistled.

Hooves thudded and a horse blew and then Pecos trotted his buckskin around the hovel's east side, frowning beneath the brim of his brown Stetson. "What you got?"

"Take a look."

"A cellar." Pecos looked around, scowling, eyes moving quickly through the broken grass and scattered tumbleweeds. His gaze halted on a patch of what appeared to be brown paint staining the grass in several places. Some of the grass was matted beneath the dried blood.

"Well, well . . ." Pecos said.

"Mm-hmm." Slash turned his horse right and forward, then pointed down at the ground before him. "Two cartridge casings. No, three."

"Another over here," Pecos said. "Forty-four Winchester."

The two men sat facing each other from twenty feet behind the building's rear wall and the open cellar. They gazed around pensively then met each other's gazes at the same time.

Pecos said, "Them three tree ornaments were killed here."

"Or I'm a monkey's uncle," Slash said.

"Then they was dragged"—Pecos pointed to a couple of long scuff marks in the dirt and through the prickly pear off to the northwest and in the direction of the knoll the hang tree was on—"over there."

"They were shot, beaten, and dragged to the cedar."

Pecos gave Slash a sidelong, skeptical look. "Why shoot 'em *and* hang 'em?"

"To set an example? Like with rustlers?"

"Well, maybe they are rustlers," Pecos said.

"Could be." Slash studied on it. "Could be whoever killed 'em was angry. I mean, really piss-burned angry. He . . . they . . . ambushed 'em from the buildings around the compound. When they had 'em down, they rode in and beat holy hell out of 'em. Then dragged 'em an' hanged 'em."

"What do you suppose Calico did to cause so much anger?"

"Usually when there's this much anger, there's a woman involved."

"How would you know? Until Jay, you only slept with whores!"

Slash smiled heavy-lidded at his partner. "All right, then, Casanova. You tell me. There a woman involved, or not?"

"Oh, yeah," Pecos said, pursing his lips and nodding slowly.

Slash turned to peer down at the base of the nearest building's rear wall. "What about the cellar?"

Pecos gave Slash a sardonic look. "Maybe they was rustlin' turnips."

Slash spat to one side, drew a heavy breath, adjusted his position in his saddle, and turned to Pecos again. He canted his head toward the ornamental tree on the knoll. "Let's say it's Calico an' them other two cutthroats up there."

"Because it probably is them."

"Right. So, what the hell? Kentucky and a few of his cronies from town tracked Calico's boys out here an' killed 'em. Why should that mean anything to us? Bleed-'Em-So sent us out here to do the same thing. Or at least, to gain the same result. Maybe not shoot them *and* hang them, and beat holy hell out of them, but to get rid of them."

"That there is a bonded fact, Slash."

"They must have had their reasons. We've both met that old marshal. He may have ridden the long coulees in his giddy-up years, but he's no cold-blooded killer."

"Exactly."

"But what about the anger?"

"Yeah—what about that?"

"Still Kentucky?"

"Maybe, maybe not."

Pecos looked around thoughtfully then turned to Slash, scowling. "Why should we care?"

Slash nodded slowly. "Right. All right—I feel better. I think I will be perfectly satisfied to board the next train back to Denver and report to Bleed-'Em-So that the job had been taken care of by the time we got here. He sent us on a wild-goose chase. End of story."

The two men turned their horses and began walking them slowly around the larger of the hovels, retracing their tracks.

"He still better pay us!" Pecos said.

"He sure as hell better or we'll burn down the Federal Building!"

"But only after we pull Miss Langdon out first!"

They had a good laugh at that. As they rode around to the front of the old shack, however, they both stopped laughing abruptly. They reined their horses up and sat their saddles stiffly, staring toward where four horseback riders were riding toward them, angling down from the far rim of the canyon.

The newcomers rode spread out, roughly fifteen feet apart, leaning back in their saddles as their horses took hitching, sometimes faltering steps down the decline, meandering around sage tufts and chokecherry snags. The faces of the four newcomers were shaded by their hat brims, but it was apparent they were staring toward Slash and Pecos. It was also apparent that they were riding toward them with a slow but malicious-seeming deliberateness.

"Hmm," Slash said, "who do you suppose them fellas are?"

"Range riders most likely."

"Think so?"

"Who else?"

"They're riding from the direction of town."

"Doggone it, there you go bein' right again, Slash!"

"Uh-huh."

They continued to sit tensely as the four riders gained the bottom of the canyon and then booted their horses into dust-lifting trots toward Slash and Pecos.

"How do you suppose we should play it, Slash?"

"I don't know. Let's hear 'em out first, maybe . . ."

"Yeah. Maybe."

Slash glanced at Pecos. "If they get iron-slappy, you take the two on the right. I'll take the two on the left."

"Damn, you make it sound easy."

"It was easy . . . a few years ago."

"Yeah, but we're a few years older than we were a few years ago."

"Oh, shut up."

"This ain't no time to make me mad, Slash! You know how I feel about bein' told to shut up!"

"Shut up."

Pecos's nasty retort was stillborn on his lips, for the four newcomers had just halted their horses roughly fifty yards away. They sat their mounts spread out about ten feet apart. They just sat staring, their bearded, sun-burned faces expressionless in the way that snakes are expressionless.

They were not range riders. Range riders were not armed as well as these men were armed. They did not carry heavy, long-barreled rifles in their saddle scabbards, and they didn't wear two pistols and at least two large knives in sheaths on their pistol belts.

No, these men were not range riders. They were either bounty hunters or meat hunters. Probably meat hunters for the railroad running through Ogallala. There was much money to be made in the business of providing meat for the passenger cars. In Slash's experience on the frontier, which was considerable, he'd found little difference between man hunters or game hunters.

Men or animals—it was all the same to them.

These four had that look. They could have been sitting over there staring at two grazing antelope, judging the windage, drift, and distance.

The second man on the left said something while staring straight ahead toward Slash and Pecos. Neither Slash nor Pecos could hear what he said, but they could see his mouth move inside his beard. They didn't move much. He held his mouth and jaws very tight. His eyes were hidden by his hat brim. All four men's were, giving them an added air of malignancy.

As soon as the man finished speaking, all four of them pulled those big, heavy rifles from their saddle scabbards. Slash could hear the sounds of the heavy irons sliding from the oiled leather. Then he heard the squawk of the saddles as all four men dismounted, holding their rifles in one hand until they had both feet on the ground.

Then they took those long shooting irons—Sharps rifles, or Slash had never seen a Big Fifty before—in both hands and raised them chest-high.

"Slash," Pecos said out of the side of his mouth, "remember what you said about never runnin' from trouble but always runnin' *toward* trouble?"

"Yeah," Slash said, his voice tight and tense. "I was full of hot air. *Whip that hoss around an' run for your life, Pecos!*"

Both men did just that as they heard the malevolent clicks of the Sharps' heavy hammers being rocked back.

They ground spurs into their horses' flanks and tore straight out away from the hunters, the buckskin and the Appaloosa seemingly knowing the danger and running like mules with tin cans tied to their tails.

Behind the fleeing riders came the thundering volley of all four rifles at nearly the same time. The reports sounded like giant boulders crashing together, or the peels of near thunder—a horrific, violent, bone-chilling sound. The large-caliber rounds made an eerie humming, like fast-moving birds approaching, approaching, approaching . . . the humming growing louder and louder . . . until the lead screeched past or over both fleeing riders' heads to blow up big gobs of ground before them.

One bullet ripped up an entire sage shrub and tossed it into the air, like flotsam flung up by a raging river current.

"*Damn!*" Pecos said, whipping a horrified look behind him. "Two of those slugs was so close I may not have to shave tomorrow!"

Slash crouched low over his lunging horse's neck, the mane flapping against his cheeks. "I may have to look in a mirror to be sure, but judgin' by the burn I may only have one ear!"

"At least they're single-shots!"

That last word had just left Pecos's lips when the almost supernaturally sinister sound came again—a tooth-gnashingly menacing warbling. The warbling grew louder and louder. It was accompanied by the thunder of the cannonade. Again, the heavy slugs whipped past or over Slash's and Pecos's heads to thump loudly into the prairie around and ahead of them, tearing up pocket-sized chunks of sod.

"They're pretty fast with those single-shots!" Slash

noted aloud as he and Pecos put their lunging horses up the canyon's eastern ridge. As both horses slowed inevitably for the climb, Slash turned to Pecos galloping about thirty feet off his left stirrup and shouted, "Try to zigzag until we've made the top of the ridge!"

Both former cutthroats reined their mounts left, then right, then left again. The only problem with that strategy was that it further slowed the mounts. Also, Slash nearly zigged when he should have zagged and almost got his head cored for his trouble. The prairie rat who'd fired that round had anticipated his move and had led him almost perfectly.

"You all right?" Pecos bellowed.

"Yeah, hell, my head's a little cooler with that hole in my hat!"

Another volley followed but all the bullets chunked into the ground behind them as they rimmed out and booted their horses off across the prairie to the east, trying to put as much distance behind them and the canyon as possible. They'd ridden hard for a good ten more minutes before Slash checked his Appy down and Pecos did the same with his buck. They curveted both horses to gaze back toward the eerie dark line the canyon made in the prairie four hundred yards behind them.

"Think they'll come?" Pecos asked, breathless, his face red with the anxiety of their close brush with having their heads blown off their shoulders.

"Depends on how bad they want to please whoever sent 'em after us," Slash said. "And how much they got paid."

"Or, hell," Pecos said. "Might just be target practice for them."

"Take a look." Slash trotted his Appy over to his partner

and reined the horse sideways so Pecos could see the right side of his head. "How much of that ear is left?"

"Hold your hair back."

Slash swept his hair back behind his right ear with his gloved right hand. "How bad?"

"I'll put it this way," Pecos said. "You maybe should grow your hair a little longer on that side from now on."

"Damn! I just got hitched!"

"Don't worry—that ear is ugly, for sure, but Jay ain't a superficial kinda gal. Ah, hell!"

"What?"

"Look there."

Slash turned his head to follow his partner's wide-eyed stare back toward the canyon. *"Ah, hell!"*

Chapter 23

When Wayne Blanchard had led his Rimfire riders east from the Longhorn Hotel, Blanchard had glimpsed a familiar face on his left. Nancy O'Neil stood on a street corner, the corner of the last side street on the east side of town.

Catching his eye, she stepped forward and said, "Wayne . . ."

He hadn't been able to hear her above the drumming of his own horse's hooves and the hooves of the dozen riders behind him, but he'd read her lips.

An invisible, rusty knife slipped into his belly, and he drew back on his chestnut's reins, halting the mount in the middle of Harveyville's main street. He glanced at his riders regarding him incredulously, and said, "Go on back to the ranch. I'll be along in a minute."

They booted their horses on up the street, a few casting curious glances over their shoulders.

Blanchard blinked against their dust as he returned his gaze to Nancy—a tall, slender woman in a fetching gingham dress. Her rich brown hair was piled atop her head, a small straw hat trimmed with faux flowers pinned to it. She must be in her thirties now. Or was it just thirty?

Still, thirty . . . She was no longer the nubile, young, restless girl of eighteen, a coquettish glint in her warm brown eyes.

My God, the old saw was true. Time did fly. He hadn't seen her in years. At least three. Maybe four. She kept to home with the old man and the boy. He mostly stayed out at the Rimfire. He preferred it out there. He didn't come to town to drink and carouse on the weekends like his men did. Those years were behind him.

After all this time, he hadn't expected that seeing her again would shove that old knife between his ribs and twist it just a little. In fact, he rarely thought of her anymore. At least, not consciously. Only in waking dreams.

Blanchard sat his horse, staring at her, aware that an inscrutable frown ridged his brows beneath the brim of his Stetson. She regarded him expectantly, the skin above the bridge of her nose creased, her lips slightly parted, as though she were wanting to say something.

She moved them again, and again only his name came out. "Wayne . . ."

Blanchard felt a hand shove him toward her side of the street. He resisted it. Too much time had passed. He'd put all of that history with her behind him. And that's where it would remain.

She seemed to read his resolve in her eyes. The light in her eyes changed, darkened. She drew a breath, glanced back in the direction of the Longhorn, and said, "Did you . . . take care of it . . . ?"

"I don't know." Blanchard studied her, found himself giving a sardonic chuckle. "It was you who sent for them, wasn't it? I should have known."

"I was scared, Wayne. I didn't want . . . I didn't want what happened last time to happen again. I was scared!" She paused and added sharply, "You didn't come!"

"Afraid of who?" Blanchard paused, casting her a stony, castigating stare. "Who were you afraid of, Nancy? Of them? Or *you?*" His eyes turned hard as granite; a nostril flared angrily above his thick mustache.

She didn't respond. She only stared up at him, the skin above her nose wrinkling more severely. "I am so sorry, Wayne." She shook her head, a sheen of emotion glinting in her eyes. "I am . . . I am so *sorry!*"

A tear from each eye dribbled down her cheeks.

Rage made untenable by an unmalleable mix of other mystifying emotions burned through Blanchard. He did not want to ask the question that he had held off from asking for twelve long years, but he found the words escaping his lips like lightning-spooked bronco stallions busting through a corral gate. "Is the boy his? Or mine?"

Nancy's eyes widened. More tears flooded them, rolling like rivers down her cheeks. She gave a strangled sob, sniffed, and shook her head. Sobbing, she said, "Because you feel the need to ask that question . . . because it's so important to you . . . makes me not want to tell you, Wayne!"

She lowered her chin and sobbed quietly, tears tumbling from her cheeks to powder the dust at her feet. She looked up at him again, and, sobbing and breathless, barely able to speak, she said, "When you did it . . . you did it for him the *old man*! You didn't do it for *me!*"

He sidled his horse up very close to her and curveted it to glare down at her hard, standing just off his left knee. His jaws bulged with fury. "I did it for me, you damn piece of Harveyville trash!"

He poked the chestnut with his spurs and galloped on up the street into the still-sifting dust of his riders. Feeling that knife in his guts twisting and driving deeper, as though probing for his heart, he followed his men back along the trail southeast of town, loping the seven miles with his jaws locked hard against an onrush of old, bitter memories. He trotted the chestnut through the portal bearing the Rimfire brand and into the yard where his men had reined up. They milled around, waiting for him near the bunkhouse.

They cast each other dubious glances and shuttled those glances to Blanchard, who trotted past them as he headed toward the main house, saying, "Ray has your assignments. I want the C and D herds brought down to Hannaford Creek and I want close tallies on both. If there's been rustling up there, I wanna know about it."

"What the hell was *that* about?"

The sharp-toned query caused Blanchard to jerk back on his reins roughly fifty feet from the house. He turned the chestnut to look back at the men grouped behind him. The speaker had been Thorn Willis—a slender, sinewy-muscled, sharp-faced young man of twenty-five who sat stiff-backed and wild-eyed in the saddle of a fine American cream. Thorn easily grew bored with regular ranch work. He saw himself as a gunslinger, even boasted several notches on the walnut grips of his pearl-gripped, silver-chased Russian that he was always twirling on his finger.

Thorn grew overly excited when Blanchard led him and the other gunnies out after rustlers, or whenever gun trouble of any stripe was involved. He had to be tightly reined in. At such times, Thorn was like a powder keg with a lit fuse. His face would get red, his pale blue eyes overly sharp, and he'd tap that damn Russian with his thumb and forefinger in turn, as though he couldn't wait to pull it and fire the damn thing.

Blanchard thought the firebrand was aptly named. He'd been a thorn in the Rimfire foreman's side since Blanchard had hired him during roundup the previous fall. The foreman had tolerated the kid only because the other men found him charismatic and amusing, and he'd gotten them through the long Panhandle winter without anyone going to town and breaking up a saloon, impregnating a town girl, or killing a whore.

However, Blanchard found him impudent and arrogant; the foreman didn't like it that he tended to rally the other men around him too tightly and against his, Blanchard's, authority. There was a smug, sardonic air about him that most of the others held in check until they saw it in Thorn.

Blanchard had been a foreman for a long time. He'd known many such men as Thorn Willis, and they'd always been double-edged swords. They were good for bunkhouse morale, but sometimes they were *too* good for morale.

Thorn had that hard-jawed, glassy-eyed, openly defiant look about him now. He clenched his jaws so tightly they appeared about to crack. His face was red except for the nubs of his cheeks. Those were floury white.

The fuse of Blanchard's own powder keg had been lit in town, by Nancy O'Neil. He said with a softness that belied his welling fury, "What did you just ask me?"

"I said what in the hell was *that*? Because to me it sure looked like a wasted trip to town. I don't understand it and neither do the others!" Willis glanced at the men flanking him. A boldness grew in their own eyes. A few nodded.

Blanchard turned his own horse full around and trotted back to the group. He reined up in front of Willis and said with a voice as cold as a privy seat in the Panhandle winter,

"The only thing you need to understand is you don't need to understand a damn thing. *Understand?*"

The fire behind Willis's eyes blazed brighter. He narrowed them and flared both nostrils, grinning with his customary arrogance as he said, "You're yaller. You're old an' washed up an' yall—*oufff-achhh!*"

The back of Blanchard's left hand had just delivered a sharp *crack!* to the kid's left cheek. It was followed by a hard thump as Willis struck the ground on his right shoulder and hip. Dust billowed around him, and the horses of the other men started, side-stepping and whickering anxiously.

Blanchard swung down from his saddle much quicker than he'd ever thought possible—at least, quicker than he'd thought possible within the past ten or so years, after having left age forty behind him in a billowing cloud of grave dust. Willis's horse had swung around and run, so Blanchard had free access to the man he'd just slapped into the dirt.

He walked over and, hearing the kid's insolent words echoing inside his head—*"You're yaller. You're old an' washed up an' yaller!"*—he picked him up out of the dust by his shirt collar. The kid blinked, shaking his head to clear the cobwebs, then, focusing his hate-filled eyes on the foreman, hardened his jaws and flared his nostrils. He was about to spew more insults, but Blanchard stopped that nonsense dead in its tracks by tattooing the kid's nose and mouth with his right fist.

He punched him and punched him and punched him again, feeling a strange exhilaration in wiping the impudent smile from the kid's face and eyes. That smile was quickly replaced by fear . . . then terror. After a few more resolute, resounding blows, the face slackened into an expressionless mask, the heavy lids closing down over the arrogant eyes and the head wobbling on slumped shoulders.

Blanchard would have punched him again anyway, if someone hadn't tapped his shoulder from behind, cleared his throat, and said, "Uhh . . . there . . . boss—I think he's done fer."

Blanchard released the kid's shirt.

Willis fell back in the dirt, gurgling deep in his throat, eyes rolling around in their sockets. His face looked like freshly ground beef.

Blanchard stood. "Get him on his horse," he said, turning and walking over to where his own horse stood several feet away. "He's done here."

He grabbed up the reins, shook his right hand, feeling the knuckles begin to swell. The glove was torn; blood oozed through it. He swung up into the leather and rode up to the house, stopping just outside the gate in the picket fence. He glanced up at Gyllenwater's second-floor balcony. The door wasn't open, and the drapes were drawn across it.

Clara stood on the front porch, unusually attired in a flowered skirt and white cotton blouse. Her dark brown hair was pulled back in a mare's tail, and silver hoop rings dangled from her ears. That she'd seen the dustup, if you could call it that, with Willis, was plain in her vaguely incredulous eyes. Both dark brows were severely ridged.

"Blanchard . . ." she said haltingly, sliding her gaze toward the bunkhouse, where several men were hauling the nearly unconscious firebrand onto his horse.

"The old man available, Clara?" the foreman asked the dusky-skinned girl.

She shook her head. "He had a spell last night. Bad fever, strained breathing. I thought he was going to pass."

"You should have told me before I headed for town."

Clara arched a brow. "Would it have made a difference?"

"It might have."

"What happened, Blanchard?" Her aristocratic voice, Spanish-accented, had a dark undertone.

"I'm gettin' old is what happened. Likely yaller an' washed up. You heard it. But I'll be damned if a squirrel like that will tell it to my face."

Clara blinked slowly, drew a deep breath, lifting her chin. "Come inside. I will tend your hand."

"Nah. I need to be alone for a while." The foreman reined his horse around. "I'll be in my cabin. Takin' the rest of the day off. Might go fishin'. Let me know if the old man wakes up."

"Wait, Blanch . . . !" She let the entreaty die on her lips as he put the steel to the chestnut and galloped around the far side of the house.

His own cabin lay back a ways from the house, down a hill and on the far side of a cottonwood and box-elder copse sheathing Whitey's Creek. It was an old trapper's cabin—apparently the trapper had been Whitey himself—that had been here long before Tom Gyllenwater had built the ranch headquarters.

It was a single-roomed, log affair—simple, rustic, time-worn, tight, comfortable, and adequate. Moreover, it was quiet. Blanchard preferred it to the bunkhouse, which he had moved out of six or seven years ago. The older men get, the less willing they become to put up with the crap of younger, more energetic ones whose values greatly differ from their older counterparts.

Gyllenwater's second-in-command, Ray McInally, a tough, stocky, former cavalry sergeant in his late thirties, kept order in the bunkhouse and made sure the lamps were snuffed at nine o'clock every night, that no fights broke out, that all gambling was for matchsticks only, that no girls were smuggled in, and that the men were up at five sharp for breakfast.

Blanchard, who'd always tended the mounts in his own string, tended the chestnut now. He hazed the horse into the hitch-and-rail corral flanking the cabin, with the other five mounts in his own private remuda. He tramped into his cabin, filled a coffeepot from his rain barrel, and set it on the range, adding wood to the still-warm coals in the firebox.

By the time the water had boiled, he'd decided he needed whiskey instead, so he set the pot aside without adding the Arbuckles' he'd already measured out, and dragged an unopened bottle of Old Kentucky down from the shelf it shared with some candles, an old Civil War pistol, rusty tin cups, and mouse droppings. He no longer drank every day. In fact, over the years he'd reduced his imbibing to only on special occasions. He'd torn up enough saloons in his time, busted enough knuckles as well as jaws, and spent enough nights in cold storage, as the saying went, to have learned that he and the firewater did not mix.

Occasionally, however, he grabbed a bottle and drank the whole thing by himself, staggering around in the woods and howling at the moon. Damned refreshing, that. Sometimes a man needed a bender to purge the unnameable but particularly foul crap that tended to build up from time to time in his system and that made him feel old and logy and sad and angry, questioning the man he'd become. The life he'd found himself living. The life he'd already lived.

He filled a grub sack with bread, sausage, and two pickled eggs. He grabbed his fishing pole and his canvas tackle bag, and the bottle, and strolled out to the creek and then up the creek a hundred yards to his favorite fishing hole—a deep, dark, slowly churning pool formed by an old beaver dam. The spring water, issuing from deep underground and miles north of here, was cold even now at high summer.

Blanchard had caught several massive catfish in that pool. A few nights ago, under a full moon, he'd stalked the woods for nightcrawlers. A few live ones still crawled around in a dirt- and moss-filled can.

Blanchard impaled a fat crawler on a hook, tossed it and the cork bobber into the pool, and then sat down on the grassy bank and popped the cork on the bottle that had accumulated several months' worth of dust and grease from his cook range. He drank and fished for a time, catching two small catfish and a bullhead, which he returned to the pool so he could recatch them later when he was more in the mood for cleaning and eating them.

He'd realized after his first sip of the firewater that he was out here to drink, not fish. The fishing was something to do while he drank and tried to forget about twelve years ago.

And about the boy who may or may not be his.

Chapter 24

Clouds rolled in and a gentle rain came down through the cottonwoods and box elders lining the stream and the cool, dark pool on which Blanchard's cork bobber floated, nudged this way and that by the raindrops falling like silver nickels.

He removed his hat, set it down beside him, and tipped his face to the rain. He opened his mouth, stuck out his tongue.

The cool drops felt good on his face. They tasted as sweet as cherries. There had been no rain for a while, and it was nice to see and feel the rain again. He liked the distracting properties of the wetness so much that he drew his hook and bobber in, lay the cane pole on the bank beside the bottle, and kicked out of his boots. He removed his sweaty, dirty socks and then his vest, shirt, pants, and summer-weight longhandles.

He again tipped his face to the gauzy sky from which the rain came, soft and gentle and spiced with the rich, verdant aromas of deep summer. He smiled as he stepped to the edge of the pool, took another step, and dropped over the lip of the bank and into the water.

He plunged straight down, the cold waters closing around him, washing over him. His feet touched the sandy bottom. He sprang off of it with his toes and swam the three or four feet back to the surface, lifting his head above the now churning water, and whipped his hair back away from his eyes. He gave a whoop of pure boyish joy and then kicked around in the pool for several minutes. The water made his right-hand knuckles burn but it was a good, cleansing kind of burn.

Occasionally he glanced around, making sure no one was in the area. He couldn't be seen out here, swimming naked as a jaybird, splashing and kicking and whooping like a damned lunatic.

Of course, he was alone. None of the men from the ranch ever came out here. Even on their days off, none fished. They were young men and did what young men did with free time on their hands—they went to town to slap their greenbacks down on Madam Delacroix's cherry-wood entrance table and to head upstairs for a few minutes of carnal bliss. Blanchard and Gyllenwater used to fish together here on the creek, but the old man was too ill to walk or even to ride out here anymore.

That was all right. Blanchard had come to enjoy his time alone here. The older he got, the more he preferred his own company. He didn't, however, want to die alone. That thought often nagged him, though he would not tol-erate such a worry now. He was alone and happy and un-encumbered here in the pool, and he was half-drunk and having a damned good time acting like a carefree kid again, like he'd once felt back on his family's farm in eastern Texas. Many years ago now. Way back before the Little Misunder-standing Between the States, as some called it. Back when he'd still had a future, though what he'd done with it often

made him sad to think about, and it left him here now at
the Rimfire where he'd been for the past fifteen years, feeling the years tumbling in around him like dirt piled beside
a grave.

He crawled up out of the pool, took a big drink of the
whiskey, then gathered his clothes and fishing pole and
night crawlers and grub sack, which he had not plundered,
having opted for the drink instead. He looped his holstered
Colt and shell belt around his neck and slogged, soaking
wet, the rain hammering down more intensely now, back
toward the cabin.

He'd just brought the dark, wet hovel into sight before
him, sheathed in the big trees and fronted by the creek,
when the aroma of pine smoke peppered his nostrils. He
looked at his chimney pipe and was surprised to see smoke
being ripped away from it by the cool, wet, rain-laced
breeze. He'd been out at the creek for a couple of hours,
so there was no way the smoke was from the small fire
he'd lain in the range for coffee.

Someone was here.

Knowing who it was, he cursed under his breath,
mounted the stoop, tripped the metal latch, and nudged the
door open with a toe. He walked inside, feet dampening
the rough puncheons he'd laid himself, as the shack had
been earthen-floored before he'd renovated it.

"I thought you'd be with the old man," he said, setting
the grub sack on the table and dumping his gear on the
floor. All except his six-shooter. He hung that by the shell
belt from the back of one of the two chairs at his small
eating table.

From the bed came a muffled groan.

He walked over and stared down at the lumpy figure
concealed by his old striped trade blanket and a sheet. She

lay on her side, facing the wall. He could see only her curly dark brown hair, which lay fanned across his pillow.

"Hey," he said, nudging her shoulder through the covers. "Clara, did the old man wake up?"

She rolled toward him with a groan and looked up at him from behind the pretty, mussed locks of her near-black hair. "He passed."

"What?"

"You heard me."

Still dripping, he stared down at her. She looked up at him, her expression inscrutable. She ran her eyes down him, frowned curiously. "My God—what have you been doing, crazy man? You're soaking wet!"

"I went for a swim."

"In this weather?" Her voice was shrill with incredulity, but then she laughed, showing all those splendid white teeth, and looked at him again, this time with love and admiration in her eyes. "Who goes swimming in this weather, Blanchard?"

"I do."

He grabbed a towel off a hook and ran it brusquely through his hair. Clara's declaration of Tom Gyllenwater's death had been like a fist across his jaw. It didn't seem to have hit her nearly as hard, but then she'd been the one nursemaiding the old bull for the past two years toward the door of eternity. She'd been well prepared. Blanchard should have been, too. However, he found himself the opposite. Not so much for Tom's death but for what it implied.

What it meant for him.

"Come to bed with me," she said, reaching for him.

Blanchard tossed the towel on a chair and grabbed the bottle. Suddenly, he was cold; the heat from the stove felt good. He crawled into the bed and drew the covers up, and Clara curved her warm, supple, naked body against his, curving a leg over his, splaying her hand across his chest.

"What happened in town, Blanchard?" she asked. As if to take the sting from the question, she pressed her soft, full lips against his belly.

He gave a soft grunt at the involuntary sensation. "I issued a warning."

She lifted her head a little to look up at him. "A warning?"

"A warning." Blanchard took a drink from the bottle.

"Those weren't your orders, Blanchard."

"Well, the old man's dead now, anyway, so . . ."

Clara lay her cheek down on his chest and fingered the band of fine, dark-brown hair that ran down his chest and over his belly, saying softly, as though she were only musing aloud, "He held the Rimfire in a tight fist. He let nothing go. That is how he held it. I think that is how we have to hold it, too, Blanchard."

"He held it too tight for the times, now at the end." Blanchard took another drink.

She looked up at him again, brows furled with concern. "You saw her, didn't you? In town?"

It was his turn to frown down at Clara, incredulous.

"You saw her." She reached up and pinched his left eyebrow with a vague cajoling. "Your brows are very heavy. Like the sky on a stormy day . . . a day like today."

Blanchard looked away, uncomfortable under this wise, tough girl's scrutiny.

"Did you have words?" she asked him.

"No," he lied. "But I think she sent for the federals."

Clara lifted her head and arched her brows in surprise. *"Why would she do that?"*

"For her father." Blanchard took another sloppy drink from the bottle. "Leastways, that's probably what she told herself. I think she probably did it for herself as much as for him."

"Why didn't she let the old man handle it? Why didn't she let *you* handle it?"

"She'd given up hope."

"She didn't think you'd do what needed to be done, when you've always done so in the past?"

"Not for her."

"You didn't kill Calico for her. Or . . . did you, Blanchard?" Clara's voice was soft and intimate.

When he did not respond, there came to Clara's voice a hard, cold, south-of-the-border chill. "Maybe she thought you would do what you did today, which is *nothing!*"

"Dammit, Clara, sometimes nothing is the best thing to do." He raised the bottle again, but she grabbed it from him and sat up, letting the covers spill down her shoulders, giving him a view of her splendid, dark-skinned body. She raised the bottle to her own mouth and took a healthy pull.

She brushed the back of her hand against her full mouth and gazed down at him through those blazing black eyes that shone in the gray light of the cabin's two windows. Meanwhile, the wind groaned under the cabin's eaves, and the rain pelted the walls. Wet drafts danced among the cabin's smoky shadows.

"Do you want me, Blanchard?" she asked, her voice just above a whisper.

He stared up at her for nearly a minute, then let his eyes drop slowly down her curving, dark figure, all but her legs revealed to him. He felt the old male tug and cursed himself for his weakness.

What man would not want Clara Gyllenwater? What

man could refuse her? Especially one so close to fifty he could feel the cold wind issuing from his own grave. A lonely, eternal one at that . . . and with no children to leave behind him, keeping bits and pieces of him alive . . . so that not every ounce of him would be consigned to that cold, black hole in the ground.

He felt the old chill and the old male tug at the same time. "You know I do, Clara," he said in a raspy wheeze, placing a big, calloused hand against her tender cheek. "You're a rare gift. What I don't understand is what you see in this fat old man."

She drew her head slowly to his and kissed his nose. "When I see you, I don't see a fat old man. I see the toughest bull in the pasture. Look what you did to Thorn. That tinhorn has had that thrashing coming since you hired him. You went out of your way to avoid it. But, when you had to do something about it, you did."

"You don't want someone younger? What about Ray McInally? He's a good man."

She shook her head, smiling at him with admiration and tenderness. "The others are boys. They're weak and they're unproven. They might be able to ride farther than you, dig more fence postholes in an afternoon, stay in the saddle longer, but you could thrash the lot of them two or three at a time. Besides, you command their respect. They might hate you, but they respect you. Now, after what you did to Thorn, more than ever. *Muy hombre!*" She shook her head. "It takes a tough, hard man and one with experience to run Rimfire."

She slid her hand down his belly and beneath the covers, and the smile grew on her lips as a smoky desire smoldered in her eyes. "What do you say, *el toro*? Do you want to start a family with me? Do you want to help me assume control of the Rimfire now that my father is gone? Do you want to spend the rest of your life with me? Given half a chance, *el toro*, I can make you a very happy man till the end of your days."

"I'll die well before you, Clara. We might have ten, fifteen years, if that."

"You'll leave me a couple of big, strapping boys to remember you by, to carry on your name."

"You know I love you, Clara."

"As I love you, Blanchard." She squeezed him, smiling. She removed her hand and gave him a long, thoughtful look before saying, "The trouble in town—it will go away?"

"I don't know."

"And if it does not, it could threaten all that we have."

Inwardly, Blanchard cursed the old man. It had been Gyllenwater's doings—at least his ordering of what had been done—that had caused this mess. Blanchard should not have ridden to town only to do nothing. Now the two federal-sent men would be more curious than ever. And now the old bulldog was dead, leaving Blanchard and Clara to clean it up so that the Rimfire could survive.

Damn Calico for having returned!

Damn Nancy for bringing in the federals!

"Whatever needs to be done," Blanchard said, "will be done."

She arched a mildly admonishing brow. "No more compromises?"

Blanchard shook his head. "No more compromises."

Clara smiled. She placed her hand on him again and lay back against the pillow.

He followed her down.

Chapter 25

Slash stared at the four riders galloping toward him across the fawn prairie, chewing up the sod as though the hounds of hell were hot on their horses' shod hooves.

"We had to know they weren't going to just sit on their heels and sharpen matchsticks," Slash said, reining his Appy round. "Come on!"

"You'd think they'd be considerate enough to give us time to rest our horses!" Pecos said, booting his buckskin into a hard run behind Slash.

"That's the problem with the world—no one has any consideration anymore!" Slash crouched low, holding the Appy's reins loosely in his gloved hands, giving the horse its head.

When they'd galloped maybe a hundred yards, he straightened a little in the saddle and frowned over at Pecos riding nearly even with him, on his right side.

Pecos saw him looking at him. "What is it?"

"This running with our tails between our proverbial legs gravels me somethin' awful. I say if they want a lead swap so bad, let's give 'em one!"

"What're you talkin' about?" Pecos glanced over his

shoulder at the pursuing riders silhouetted against the western horizon. "They're outta range of our rifles!"

"Yeah," Slash said, checking the Appy down. "But they won't be for long!"

He grabbed his Winchester from its boot, fairly leaped out of his saddle, and dropped the reins, effectively ground-tying the Appaloosa.

Pecos reined in his buckskin, saying with a dark fatefulness, "You don't think so, do you?"

"No, I don't!" Smiling with satisfaction, Slash pumped a cartridge into his Yellowboy's action, dropped to a knee, and raised the carbine to his shoulder.

Staring toward the four galloping riders, he frowned suddenly.

"Hah!" Pecos said, still mounted on his buckskin.

Slash scowled toward where their four pursuers stopped pursuing them. The four men checked their own mounts down quickly, pulling back on the reins and jerking their horses' heads sideways. Calmly, they stepped out of their saddles and slid their long Sharps rifles from their saddle scabbards.

"Well, I'll be damned!" Slash said.

"They're still out of range of our rifles," Pecos pointed out, grinning from ear to ear, "but we ain't out of range of theirs! Hah!"

The four pursuers had dropped to their knees and raised their rifles.

Pale smoke puffed around one. There was the orange flash of a hammer dropping on a live round. Then came the eerie whine growing louder and louder until the bullet struck the sod two feet to Slash's right with a resolute thud. The bullet tore up a fist-sized chunk of sod and flung it high. The report followed at nearly the same time that the chunk of sod hit the ground and broke apart.

The other three rifles started puffing smoke and flashing orange flames, and more of those sinister whines stitched the otherwise quiet afternoon air, growing louder and louder.

Pecos said, "You know, Slash—I'm beginnin' to wonder if you ain't as smart as I been givin' you credit for!"

Slash shoved to his feet and swung toward his horse. He'd taken only one lunging stride before a bullet tore into the ground where his left foot had been less than a second before. Slash cursed and lunged into a run, grabbing the reins of his Appy, which was whickering uneasily and sidling away from the thunder of the distant rifles, and shoved the Winchester into his saddle boot. "Yeah, well, the joke's on you, partner," he said, heaving himself into the saddle. "The only time I'm the smartest one in the room is when it's only you an' me in the room! Hah!"

He reined the Appy forward, crouched low over its mane, and put the steel to it.

Pecos had already spurred his buckskin into a lunging run. He glanced back over his shoulder at Slash to yell, "Even on death's doorstep, you got time to devil me, don't ya?"

"It's a nice distraction!"

The thunder stopped and Slash glanced behind to see the four men mounting their horses again.

"Here they come!" he yelled.

"Our only chance is to outrun 'em!" Pecos said. "If they get us in range of them buffalo guns, we're gonna go the way of the buffalo!"

"You know, partner—I'm beginnin' to wonder if you

ain't a might . . . just a *might* . . . smarter than I been thinkin' you are!"

Pecos told him to do something unprintable.

What they needed was high ground, Slash thought as the Appy tore up the sod. If they could get to high ground, they could hold off that pack of kill-happy, Sharps-wielding vultures with their own rifles. The Sharps-wielders could throw lead at them all day, but if Slash and Pecos had adequate cover, they'd only be wasting shots. They could throw lead at them until they ran out of lead, and then Slash and Pecos would win the day.

If they could find a jog of buttes or a prairie dike, say. Even just a hill . . .

The problem was, the prairie all around was nothing but dry brown grass and occasional patches of buckbrush and prickly pear. Occasionally they came to a shallow wash along which chokecherry and hawthorn scrub grew thick, but there was no good cover in sight.

They were still riding hard, angling gradually south, following the grain of the prairie, when the sky turned from cobalt to gunmetal gray. Clouds rolled in and the smell of rain and brimstone stitched the building wind.

"Storm comin'," Pecos said when they stopped atop a low swell of ground to gaze back toward their stalkers.

Slash eyed the four vultures silhouetted atop their horses. They were roughly four hundred yards behind. They'd been keeping steady pace with their quarry, but they appeared to be slowing a little. They were no longer spurring their mounts into hard runs but had eased them back into more leisurely lopes.

"Horses tiring," Slash observed. "So are ours."

"Maybe, when we've all blown out our horses, they'll give up, call it a day."

"Maybe."

Slash turned his face to the wind, felt the dampness of the first raindrops. "We best get moving," he said, reining the Appy around. "We'll be in range of those cannons again in a coupla minutes!"

He put the steel to the Appy, which lunged south in another dogged but wearying lope. A few minutes later, the storm came bounding up on them, roaring like a freight train. Slash and Pecos paused in their flight only long enough to don their oilskin rain slickers. Attired against the downpour, they were off once more, alternating loping their horses and trotting them to keep from killing them.

Every so often, Slash glanced back to see their pursuers behind them, holding a frustrating pace, neither catching up nor falling behind.

Stubborn sidewinders.

Twenty minutes later, through the murk of the slashing rain ahead, Slash saw what appeared to be a town take shape before him. At first, he thought it might be Harveyville. But, no, none of the landmarks around the little settlement looked familiar. Besides, Harveyville was off to the southwest. This was another town—maybe some small honyocker's back-prairie jerkwater.

He and Pecos gained the trail that swept in from the northeast—an old stagecoach and freight trail, most likely—and followed it into the town. As they rode along the trail that was now the settlement's broad main street, Slash swept his gaze from left to right and back again, one hand on the walnut butt of the Colt tied low on his right thigh.

No one was out and about. The storm would have explained that on its own, but no one appeared inside any of the buildings, either. No lamps shone in any of the windows, most of which had been boarded over. Even in the rain, the town had a dusty, bedraggled appearance, the wood-frame and log and mud-brick buildings slouched like ancient men beneath the weight of the years and little to no maintenance. The moldering boardwalks fronting the buildings were piled high with tumbleweeds; brome grew through the cracks between the boards, and pockets of brush and cactus had grown up in the street on both sides of which the paint on shingles and false façades had faded to near unreadability.

"Ghost town," Pecos said above the storm.

"Not quite." Slash nodded toward a building ahead and on the street's right side.

A lamp shone in a window of a two-story building, the first story of which was built of logs, the second story wood frame and clapboard. A false façade jutted high in the gauzy air, announcing WILBUR FULTON'S SALOON in large, green, badly faded letters set against a red background.

Aside from the light in the window, the old saloon looked as abandoned as the rest of the town, but the pattering of an off-key piano ebbed out through the saloon's batwing doors to mix oddly with the rush of the rain and sporadic thunder, indicating the presence of at least one living soul inside.

As Slash and Pecos angled their horses toward the moldering watering hole, a figure climbed out of a chair to the right of the batwings—a small, slender person wearing a spruce-green rain poncho over blue denim overalls. The person stepped down off the batwings and jogged over to the newcomers, half-boots splashing in the mud puddles. Slash saw the boy's pale, fine-featured face and a fringe of blond hair inside the vaguely rectangular-shaped hood drawn up over the kid's head.

"Can I stable your hosses, fellas? Got a nice tight shed behind the saloon. Fifty cents for each, an' believe you me, that's a steal for water, oats, and wild hay this far off the beaten path!"

Slash and Pecos shared a conferring glance. They glanced behind them. Their pursuers hadn't shown yet; there was only the gray curtain of the storm buffeting over the northern prairie. The two men turned to each other again, and Slash said, "I do believe we've come to the end of the trail for the day, pard!"

"Might be more than just the end of the day, but what the hell—I'm thirsty an' so hungry my stomach's been worryin' for several hours now, that my throat's been cut!"

The kid laughed as though it were the first time he'd ever heard the old joke. "That's a good one, mister!" He laughed some more as Slash and Pecos swung down from their saddles. They each tossed him a coin, and the boy gathered up their reins.

The kid watched as both men shucked their rifles from their saddle scabbards, and cast each an uncertain, vaguely cautious glance. Slash racked a round into the action and said, "Best make yourself scarce for a bit, son."

The kid's eyes widened. He turned and hurried into a break off the side of the saloon, between the saloon and a boarded-up harness shop, jerking both mounts along behind him. Slash and Pecos glanced along their back trail. Only the gray murk of the storm there. Their trackers had not yet shown.

They slogged through the ankle-deep mud of the street

and scraped their boots on a hemp mat on the stoop before entering the watering hole, Slash first, Pecos second. In accordance with unwritten custom and old habit, each man stepped quickly to each side of the doorway, so the opening wouldn't backlight him, as the batwings clattered into place behind them, and looked cautiously around.

The rain continued to sluice from their hat brims, making a soft drumming sound on the wooden floor.

The crude pine bar ran along the rear wall, under the dull, glassy stares of several dusty game trophies. A few tables, none occupied, lay between the door and the bar. To the right was the piano, which had continued issuing its off-key tune until Slash and Pecos had pushed through the batwings and the discordant strains of "Sweet Betsy from Pike" had clattered and pattered to silence.

The big man sitting at the piano, who was the only person in the saloon, had turned to face the newcomers, the bench beneath him creaking against his considerable weight. He was a big Indian with a broad, fleshy face and wide-set dark eyes. He wore his long, gray-flecked black hair down his back in a tightly plaited braid. Like the tow-headed boy, he wore a spruce-green poncho.

Slash frowned. "You Wilbur Fulton?"

The Indian shook his head. "Fulton was my stepfather. Long dead. Along with my ma. I'm Sam. Sam Fulton. Don't worry—I'm an apple." He grinned, slitting his eyes affably. "Red on the outside, white on the inside." He rolled a matchstick from one side of his wide mouth to the other and said in a deep, low voice, "Rainy night. Wasn't expectin' business."

Pecos glanced at Slash and said, "Yeah, well, now you might have more than you want. Best make yourself scarce for a few minutes."

The Indian winced. "Men on your trail?"

"Yeah," Slash said.

"All right." The Indian rose from the piano bench. "You want a drink while you wait?"

Slash gave a wry snort. Apparently, the situation was not uncommon here in Wilbur Fulton's Saloon.

"Hell, yeah," said Pecos.

"Take a seat."

Chapter 26

Slash and Pecos walked over to a table in the room's rear right corner, near the piano, and kicked out chairs.

As they removed their rain slickers and draped them over the chair backs, the Indian ambled around behind the bar and grabbed two shot glasses and a bottle. He brought the bottle and the glasses over and set them on the table as Slash and Pecos sat down, their rifles angled across the table before them. The Indian filled each glass and returned the cork to the bottle. He held up the bottle and said, "Want me to leave it?"

"Why not? It's a wet night."

"Sure, sure." The Indian set the bottle on the table, then rubbed his big hands on the bib of his overalls. "You mind payin' in advance?"

Slash and Pecos shared a wry look. "Under the circumstances," Slash said, digging into a trouser pocket for a coin, "totally understandable. Keep the change."

"Just business," the Indian said.

"Yep," Pecos said. "Just business."

The Indian jostled the coin in his hand as he ambled

around the bar and through the door in the wall to the left of the stairs.

Slash stared down at his drink, brows ridged.

"What're you thinkin' about?" Pecos asked him.

"That cellar."

"What about it?"

"I'm wonderin' what was in it."

"You think that's what Ned Calico was killed for?"

"Don't you? Leastways, I got a suspicion it was one of the things."

"Haven't really had a whole lotta time to . . ."

Pecos let his voice trail off as the wet mucking sounds of approaching horses rose in the wet street beyond the batwings.

"Here we go," Slash said and threw back his entire shot, then refilled his glass. As though for security he brushed his hand across the receiver of the carbine resting on the table to his right.

Pecos looked outside, scowling. His Colt rifle lay across a chair to his left. His double-bore rested on the table near his right elbow, between him and Slash. They sat side by side, the table between them, facing the front of the room. Pecos figured the double-bore would be the piece he'd call into action. It was right productive for close-order work, if a bit on the messy side.

As he and Slash watched the shadows move beyond the rain-streaked window, where their four pursuers had reined up in front of the saloon, Pecos said, "I don't know, Slash—what's to stop 'em from shootin' in here from out there?"

"Shoot us through the window, you're thinkin'?"

"Or through the doors. Hell, with them cannons they're carryin', they could blast us through the consarned *wall!*"

Pecos tipped his drink back, downing the entire shot in a single swallow.

"Somethin' tells me they're not the shootin'-through-the-windows-or-walls sorta fellas," Slash opined in a light singsong that belied the cold-steel tension in his shoulders.

"All right," Pecos said with a sigh, rolling his own shoulders as though to loosen them. "I hope you're right."

"Me, too."

Outside, the stalkers had dismounted. Wordlessly, they tied their horses at the hitchrack fronting the saloon. As they slid the hunting rifles from their saddle boots, a short, silhouetted figure moved up to them from the saloon's left side, and Slash and Pecos heard the boy talking.

"Dammit," Slash said tightly, "I told that kid to make himself scarce."

"Well, there's business to be had," Pecos said quietly, with a pensive air. "Kinda hard to pass up business way out here. I don't reckon the Injun or the boy get it all that often."

"I suppose."

Slash was glad when the kid led the four horses off around the saloon's left side. He watched through the rain-streaked window as the four stalkers came together in a brief, quiet conference. They held their rifles down low, one-handed. One of the men stepped up onto the board-walk, his boot heel thudding, the spur *ching*ing softly beneath the low roar of the wind and the rain.

The others followed the first man up onto the boardwalk and then the first man stopped just outside the batwings, peering over them into the saloon. Rain streamed down the crease in his sweat-stained cream Stetson. His eyes were

two dark coals as he stared into the saloon, taking Slash
and Pecos's measure. He blinked once then pushed the
doors open and stepped through them.

He moved to his right, making way for the others, who
followed him into the saloon to form a line in front of the
batwings, facing their quarry.

They were a hard, ragged, savage-looking lot in blood-
stained trousers and waxed tarpaulin ponchos from which
rain dripped to form pools on the floor around their worn,
muddy boots. All four were bearded. Three were hawk-
faced. The heaviest of the four, who stood to the right of
the first man who'd entered the saloon, had a round, moon
face with flat yellow eyes beneath the brim of his sugarloaf
sombrero.

He was the only one of the four who was smiling. He
smiled as though he had a secret he was proud of and
couldn't wait to share. He was also the only one holding
his Sharps rifle in both gloved hands across his chest and
bulging belly. The others held theirs either on one shoulder
or down low along their right legs. The big man looked as
eager to use his buffalo gun as he was to share his secret.

"Howdy," Slash said, smiling. He held up his shot glass.
"Want a drink? Damn good stuff for this far out in the
wild 'n' wooly."

The four men frowned at him then looked at each other
in silent conferral.

The man who'd entered the saloon ahead of the others,
and who was apparently their leader, shrugged a shoulder
and said, "Since you're buyin'."

"I am," Slash said. "You'll have to fetch your own
glasses, though." He hooked a thumb to indicate a pyramid
of shot glasses adorning the bar behind him.

The leader, taller than the others and stony featured, glanced at his three fellow stalkers. "One at a time."

He strode forward, holding his big Sharps straight down along his right leg, and passed Slash and Pecos on his way to the bar. He grabbed a shot glass off the bar, then walked over to the table and filled it from the bottle. He watched Slash and Pecos closely, flicking his flatly probing eyes between them.

He raised the shot glass. "Salute!" He threw back the shot, then slammed the glass down on the table hard. The sound was like that of a pistol shot, echoing around the room. He gave Slash and Pecos each another hard, flat look, then walked back to the front of the room, reassuming his previous position.

As the big, moon-faced man walked past Slash and Pecos's table, he flashed a leering grin. He grabbed his own glass from the bar then came over and, that leering grin in place, filled it from the bottle and tossed it back.

"You were right," he told Slash, raising the glass and winking. "Damn good stuff for this far out in the big empty. I'm right obliged."

"Glad you enjoyed it," Pecos drawled dryly.

The man turned a frigid glare to Pecos and hardened his jaws. "I wasn't talkin' to you. He's the one that offered the drink to the men who's gonna kill him!" He returned his gaze to Slash and smiled ironically. "And I do appreciate it."

Slash cast the man a slit-eyed smile. "How do you know we didn't poison the bottle?"

The big man scowled back at him, eyes widening slightly, and a flush rose in his cheeks. He glanced over his shoulder at the others, all of whom had acquired similar expressions. Especially the group's leader, for obvious reasons. The big man turned back to Slash, his chest rising and falling sharply as his breathing quickened.

Slash glanced at Pecos, who was also grinning, cheeks deeply dimpled. Turning back to the big man, Slash raked out a laugh and pointed a jeering finger at him. "Had you goin'!"

He slapped the table and leaned forward, laughing.

Pecos laughed then, too. Even the other three laughed, directing their laughter at the big man as though only he had been the butt of the joke, though it had been obvious that Slash had put the fear of God . . . or the devil in this case, possibly . . . into all four but into the first man and the big man especially.

The big man's ears turned red as he glared down at Slash.

As the others' laughter dwindled, the big man turned slowly and went back to stand in line again while the other two came over for their own drinks. Neither one said anything, but they kept their hard, none-too-vaguely suspicious gazes on the two men they'd been hunting for the bulk of the day. When the fourth man had gone back to stand in line with the other three, he drew a deep breath.

Like the other three, he raised his rifle up high across his chest, waiting for the dance to begin.

Slash maintained a mild expression. Sure, he was going up against four Sharps rifles, any one of which could carve a hole through him the size of his own clenched fist, but they didn't need to see he was nervous.

"Say," he said, "who in hell sent ya, anyways? Just curious." He gave a knowing half-smile. "Was it Kentucky?"

The stone-faced man who was apparently the group's leader said, "Yep."

"Don't that beat all," Pecos said softly, keeping his own

eyes on the men before him. "He seemed like such a nice fella."

Slash returned the four stalkers' glowering stares. All four squeezed their rifles in their gloved hands. Behind them, rain streaked the windows. Lightning flashed like sizzling witches' fingers in the buckskin-colored clouds. Slash snugged his elbow up taut against his Winchester. Like a coiled diamondback, his hand was ready to strike.

He sensed the tension in his partner, who also held their opponents' gazes.

The only sound was the storm with its distant kettle-drum thunder.

Slash could see a vein throbbing in the forehead of the big, large-gutted man, though the man maintained his devil-may-care grin. Sweat broke out on the side of the leader's face and trickled slowly down toward his jaw, glinting in a brief lightning flash.

He moved in a blur of quick motion, bunching his lips and snapping his Sharps to his shoulder, cocking the heavy hammer back with his right thumb. Instantly, Slash's rifle was in his hands, drawing the hammer back. He leaped out of his chair just as the lead rider's Sharps filled the entire room with an ear-numbingly explosive blast.

As the round punched a fist-sized hole through the back of Slash's chair, punching it over backward, Slash hit the floor on his right shoulder and hip, raised the Winchester up at an angle, and blew the lead rider out the rain-streaked window behind him.

Seeing in the corner of his right eye Pecos leaping away from the table just as two fifty-caliber bullets hammered large holes into it, near where both Pecos and Slash had just been sitting, Slash rolled once more to his right. The thunder of the other three rifles filled his ears, and a jaw-breaker-sized hole appeared in a floorboard inches from his left knee.

More thunder filled the room.

Seeing the big-gutted man flying out through the bat-wings, screaming, Slash knew that Pecos had gone to work with his twelve-gauge.

The two others flung their empty single-shot rifles away and reached, wide-eyed and hang-jawed, for their six-shooters. The only problem was, said hoglegs were hol-stered behind their rain ponchos. Neither one got a single pistol out before Pecos's twelve-gauge picked the left one up off the floor and punched him straight back through what was left of the window after he'd blown the first man through it.

Slash's Winchester crashed once-twice-three times, the empty cartridge casings clinking onto the floor around his boots, blowing the fourth and final Sharps-wielding vul-ture through the window and onto the pile of glass littering the rainy, bloody boardwalk.

Slash lay staring through his wafting powder smoke toward both broken-out windows to the left and right of the batwings, and at the blood-splattered batwings them-selves. To his left and about fifteen feet away, Pecos gained a knee. He turned to Slash and said, "They sure were con-fident in them single-shots."

"Too confident."

"You all right?"

"My arm hurts," Pecos said. "The one I hurt when you slipped my saddle cinch."

Slash gave a wry snort.

"You?" Pecos asked.

Slash took stock of himself, shrugged. "Men old as us

shouldn't roll around on the floor like we just done. It's gonna catch up to us sooner or later. Our bones are brittle."

"You break somethin'?"

"Nah," Slash said, slowly gaining his knees and, wincing with the effort, pushing himself to his feet. "Just thought I'd mention it. Somethin' to consider."

Boots thudded and Slash and Pecos turned to see Sam Fulton walk into the room. He moved past the stairs, looking around, his big face expressionless. He walked up to the front of the room, stopped, and turned his head slowly from left to right, inspecting his broken-out windows.

He turned and scowled angrily at the last two men standing. "Who do I send the bill for them windows?"

Slash and Pecos looked at each other before returning their gazes to the big, incredulous Indian. "Kentucky O'Neil," they both said at the same time.

Chapter 27

The next day, in the late morning, Slash and Pecos checked their mounts down to slow walks as they gained the outskirts of Harveyville. The town fairly glowed in the sunshine blasting brightly out of a cobalt sky that was cloudless and clean-scoured now after yesterday's storm.

The street, however, was still soft and deeply rutted. The two former cutthroats followed a farm wagon toward the heart of town. A man in his sixties wearing an immigrant cap and a woman in a polka-dot dress and white bonnet rode on the driver's seat. Three towheaded little girls sat in the box behind the older people, two leaning against the left side panel, the other against the right one. The girls and the mother kept casting anxious glances behind them at the two middle-aged riders clad in suits and ribbon ties and leading four horses over each of which a dead man lay belly down, ankles bound to wrists under the bellies of the dead men's horses.

Strollers and idlers on both sides of the street stopped or looked up from checkers or cribbage to gawk.

The woman and the girls in the farm wagon appeared

relieved when Slash and Pecos started to angle their horses toward the street's south side, away from the wagon.

Footsteps drummed quickly, and Slash and Pecos jerked their heads hard left to see the marshal's grandson sprinting up the street beside them, glancing at them wide-eyed as he overtook them. He turned and hurried through the door of the town marshal's office when Slash and Pecos were still twenty feet from the hitchrack.

"Grandpa!" came the boy's muffled shout from inside the marshal's office.

He must have lowered his voice, for whatever came next did not permeate the closed door.

"We're right popular in these parts," Pecos drawled.

"I've never felt so welcome anywhere."

As they reined up in front of the marshal's office, the door opened and Kentucky O'Neil stood in the doorway, his Stetson on his gray head, his old Colt strapped around his potbellied waist. The redhead, Danny, stood behind him, craning his neck to look around the old lawman.

O'Neil's grave eyes regarded the riders and their grisly cargo. He kept his head forward as he said, "Stay inside, boy." Then he stepped out onto the stoop and drew the door closed behind him.

Again, he looked at Slash and Pecos and then at the four dead men, and spread his arms a little, trying without success to manufacture a look of genuine surprise. "What's all this?"

Slash tossed his two sets of reins into the mud before the hitchrack. Pecos did likewise.

Leaning forward against his saddle horn, Pecos scowled at the town marshal and said, "You tell us."

"What're you talkin' about?"

"We were dodgin' fifty-caliber balls half the day yesterday on account of you," Slash said.

"I'm afraid I don't understand."

"We've shot men for far less than that trick you pulled, Marshal," Pecos said.

"We'd shoot *you* if you weren't so damned pathetic," Slash added. "That's the only reason we don't shoot you. That and that boy in there who deserves a better man for a grandpa."

Pecos glanced at Slash sharply. Slash saw that his words had cut the old man deep. Suddenly, he wished he'd held back a little. But just a little. The old man had sicced rabid hounds on him and his partner, and they'd come close to accomplishing the errand O'Neil had sent them on. That errand—and no bones about it—had been to murder Slash and Pecos and to leave their bones to the vultures.

Of course, there'd been a chance that the killers had lied about O'Neil having sent them. But not much of a chance. They'd been too confident they'd been about to succeed in their grisly errand.

Why lie to dead men?

Flushed with injury, O'Neil stared at Slash in silent defiance, his jaws hard. He did not say anything. An artery pulsed in his leathery neck.

"We're not leaving here," Slash said, "until we know why you want us dead so bad. Now, we know it's tied up with Ned Calico and those two pards of his. And likely what they found or didn't find in that cellar they were killed around. You come clean on all of it, old man, and we'll leave. Spill it, every detail. Until then, we're gonna continue to make pests of ourselves." Slash raised his hands. "It's up to you. We got all the time in the world."

"In the meantime, we'll be over at the Copper Nickel,"

Pecos said. "My partner an' myself, we like that purty blonde. We like how she talks. She has a nice voice, don't she, Slash?"

"That blonde has a nice everything."

"I like her voice myself," Pecos said, smiling coldly down at the old, glowering lawman. "I do enjoy listening to her talk, and she does seem to enjoy talkin', too."

"Especially about Calico," Slash added.

Pecos pinched his hat brim to the man as he and Slash reined their horses back into the street, leaving the other horses and their lifeless passengers standing in front of the marshal's office. Five minutes later, their entrance into the Copper Nickel was followed closely by a scream. Slash and Pecos both whipped their hands to their six-shooters but left the hoglegs in their holsters. Scowling into the shadows toward the rear of the saloon, they saw that the screamer had been Mary Kate herself.

The girl's scream was followed by a male voice yelling, "*Ow!* Galldang, Mary Kate—you done burned me!"

The girl was backing away from a table near the bar. She held a coffeepot in her hand. One of the two men at the table before her was holding his right hand in his left one and glaring up at the girl, who'd apparently slopped coffee over his hand when she'd seen the two former cut-throats enter the eatery.

She kept her astonished eyes on Slash and Pecos now, backing into the bar, then stopping, crouched slightly forward at the waist, her pretty cheeks ashen. The two men at the table, the girl's only two customers, followed the girl's gaze to the two newcomers standing by the door. Both men, shopkeepers whom Slash and Pecos had seen around town, looked at each other warily, then rose quickly from their chairs, donned their bowler hats, and beat a hasty retreat around Slash and Pecos and out the front door behind them.

"Don't bother sniffin' your pits," Pecos said to Slash. "I'm startin' to think more than our stench precedes us."

"You think?" Slash gave the girl, whose eyes were still riveted on him and Pecos, a mock-affable smile. "Hello there, pretty girl. What's the special?"

"Uh . . ." She drew a breath as though to calm herself and straightened, splaying one hand across her left thigh against which her thin, flowered frock was drawn taut. "Well . . . you're between breakfast and chili."

"Is the chili ready yet?"

"I don't know. I'll have to check. I got biscuits in the oven." Mary Kate did not go check but stood in front of the bar, watching Slash and Pecos skeptically as they slacked into chairs at a table near the room's north wall, near a large, badly faded and dusty oil painting of a slender, scantily clad mulatto woman riding a cream horse through a verdant forest. Lions and tigers and even a monkey stood peering curiously at her from the thick foliage around and behind her.

"All right—we'll be here, honey," Pecos said, tossing his hat onto a chair and sweeping his hand through his hair. "Whooeee—dodgin' them big Sharps bullets sure made us hungry—didn't it, Slash?"

"I'm hungry, and that's a fact," Slash said. "Where's your pa, Mary Kate?"

"Upstairs. He's feelin' poorly. I think it's his nerves. His nerves been jangled ever since you two old desperadoes rode to town." Mary Kate gave a weak, vaguely admiring half smile and a none-too-subtle flirtatious thrust of one hip. Regaining her composure, she shook her blond curls back from her face and raised the coffeepot in her right hand. "Coffee?"

"I'll take a cup," Slash said.

"Me, too," said Pecos.

Mary Kate pulled two cups and two saucers off the bar and carried them over to Slash and Pecos's table and filled them, scrutinizing each former desperado, as she'd called them, curiously. The question seemed to bubble up out of her, no longer able to be restrained once she'd finished filling Pecos's cup: "All right," she said, setting the pot on the table and crossing her arms over her breasts, "how in blue blazes did you two boys get away from Cutter and Sprague an' them big huntin' rifles?"

"Well, you see," Slash said, "those big huntin' rifles weren't invented for short-order work. And they're single-shots."

"They were way too confident," Pecos added. He canted his head to one side and narrowed an eye at Mary Kate. "This Cutter and Sprague, they was bounty hunters?"

"Market hunters, but they were known to hunt men, too, when one with a price on his head rode into their sights."

"Just like you thought, Slash!"

"Who was the other two with 'em?" Slash asked her.

"Blanco and Green."

"Hmm."

"They dead?"

"Uh-huh."

"Boy, you fellas really are bad for business," the girl said, shaking her head slowly, eyes wide. "They were good regulars around here!"

"Like I said, way too confident," Pecos said.

"They underestimated us, I think," Slash said. "Never underestimate a desperado," he told Mary Kate with a wink. "Old or otherwise."

Pecos blew on his coffee, took a tentative sip, and glanced

up at the girl. "Mary Kate," he said, "what'd Ned Calico come back here for after all these years?"

Mary Kate stared down at Pecos, a flush building slowly in her pretty cheeks. She pursed her lips, nodded her head slowly, decisively, and said, "You want to know about Ned Calico? All right." She pulled a chair out from the table and plopped into it, hair dancing on her shoulders. "I'll tell you about Calico!"

"Mary Kate, I'd like a bowl of that delicious chili of yours," said Kentucky O'Neil, suddenly stomping through the front door and scraping the mud from his boots on the rug just inside the saloon.

Mary Kate shot a fiery glare at the old lawman. "Stay out of this, Marshal . . . with all due respect," she quickly added, more softly than the voice she'd started out with. "I got a story to tell, and I'm gonna tell it. Calico loved me. I know you an' the rest of the town don't believe it, but he did, and you—"

"Get upstairs, Mary Kate!" the old man thundered at her, moving toward her red-faced, ridges lining his weather-beaten forehead. "I won't tell you again!"

"I'm tired of being shut down by the men in this town!"

"Get back in the kitchen and stay there till I tell you to come out, or I'll tan your hide. You're not too old!"

"You'd just love that!" the girl accused him, saucily. "You know you would, you dirty old man!"

O'Neil dipped his chin and gave her a cold, hard grin edging toward a leer. "Every slap an' scream."

Mary Kate blinked, her chest rising and falling sharply. A rose-colored flush blossomed in her cheeks and ears. She gave a shrill cry of exasperation then wheeled and stomped barefoot back around the bar and into the kitchen.

The old marshal dragged a chair out from Slash and

Pecos's table with one boot, then sat creakingly down in it, wincing as though the move grieved him greatly.

Slash sipped his coffee and looked at the old lawman. "She's gonna tell that story sooner or later. The quicker we know what's got your drawers in such a twist—"

"She doesn't need to tell it. I'll tell it." O'Neil rested his hands atop the table before him and entwined his red, arthritic fingers. They trembled slightly but not from palsy.

"Well, now," Pecos said with an arched brow.

"Sure, sure—I'll tell it. Then you can make up your own minds about what to do with it—if you get a chance to do anything, that is. Blanchard might have backwatered about the whole Collie Gyllenwater affair, but it won't last."

"What about Calico?" Slash asked, slowly building a quirley. "We found the bodies. We know they were murdered."

"Hanged," Pecos clarified.

"Shot and beaten first." Slash carefully dribbled chopped tobacco onto his creased wheat paper. "What were they lookin' for in that cellar? I'm guessin' loot from that last holdup. Did they bury it out there . . . before they were hauled off to prison?"

"Yes."

"Uh-huh." Slash wetted the edges of the rolling paper and slowly rolled the cylinder closed. "And they were killed for it."

"They didn't find it."

Pecos frowned at the old man. "Then why were they killed?"

O'Neil stared down at his hands, grimly pensive. He sucked his bottom lip under his mustache then drew a deep breath and let it out slowly. He cast each man sharing the table with him a grave, level stare. "Twelve years ago, they hid a hundred thousand dollars in that cellar."

"A hundred thousand," Pecos said in disbelief. "Where'd they find that kind of loot around here?"

"They hit a big railroad payroll. See, the Union Pacific was building a trestle over the South Platte River west of Grand Island. They paid their crews in gold coin back in those days. They happened to stow that payroll gold in the bank in Grand Island—the very same bank that Calico's boys hit. I don't know if they knew about the gold or not. I got a feelin' they didn't. They weren't that smart. Probably just a lucky accident. Well, they rode down this way and hid the gold in that old army outpost cellar before they came into town. But they brought a good bit of the gold to town with 'em . . . started flashing it around. You know—to show what big spenders they were."

"Hmm," Slash said.

"Only, at that time, we didn't know about the buried loot."

"Huh?" Pecos said.

Kentucky said, "After me an' several men I deputized took Calico and his partners down, drunk as skunks, we asked about the rest of the gold. So, of course, did Luther Bledsoe, when he got here. The railroad wanted its money back. Calico said there were three other men in the bunch—three Mexicans. The Mexicans double-crossed the three gringos after the robbery, when they split up to avoid the catch party. The Mexicans ended up absconding with most of the loot, leaving Calico, Stockton, and Wheeler with only ten thousand between the three of them. They had that much in town."

"But that ain't what happened, was it?" Slash said with a knowing smile, drawing smoke from his quirley slowly into his lungs.

"There were three Mexicans. We found that out for sure.

We thought Calico was tellin' the truth when a lawman from over in Wyoming said he'd had a run-in with three Mexicans only a few days after Calico showed up here in Harveyville. They were leading a mule with a packsaddle and stuffed panniers. So, the federal authorities in Colorado and Wyoming Territories organized a posse. The railroad even sent Pinkertons. But those three Mexicans were never found. Everybody figured they somehow made it with the loot down to the border and into Mexico, likely never to be seen or heard from again."

"What really happened?" Pecos asked.

"They were in that cellar," Kentucky said, smiling cagily. "With the rest of the loot. One hundred and ten thousand dollars' worth."

Nodding slowly, Slash took another slow drag off his quirley. "When were they found?"

"When the loot was found, of course. Two of Old Tom's men found it. Came upon it accidentally there in that cellar, which was on open range where those two punchers used to stow bottles of corn liquor to drink during roundup. They rode out there to stow their liquor and smelled the most terrible stench!"

Kentucky made a face and waved his hand in front of his nose. He slapped the table, grinning. "This was only one month after Luther hauled Calico, Stockton, and Wheeler off to Denver."

Slash gazed at the old man with keen interest, eyes hooded, riveted on the old lawman's story. He blew smoke out his nostrils. "Go on."

He had a feeling the story was just starting to get good. He was right.

Chapter 28

"Now, you see, those two cowpunchers had no use for that much gold. There was no question about them keeping it for themselves. The very sight of it frightened holy hell out of them. They told Gyllenwater about it. Old Tom, which was what he was called even twelve years ago, led a pack of his most trusted men, including Wayne Blanchard, out to retrieve the loot."

O'Neil looked up from beneath his brows at Slash and then at Pecos, his tone growing even softer and graver, more secretive but also a little delighted. It was as though he were telling a campfire tale to a spellbound audience—a crackerjack of a tale, no matter how you sliced it, despite its betraying his own weak character. "He kept it, Tom did. Every glittering coin."

Pecos whistled.

Slash nodded. "How did you know?"

"Tom told me," Kentucky said, shrugging. "He trusted me to keep the secret, and I did. I was Tom's man. I've always been Tom's man. Oh, I wouldn't have put it that plainly, bluntly, until today. But, yeah, I've always been Tom's man, all right. The day he put me in this job"—he

brushed his thumb across the badge pinned to his shirt—
"it was understood that I got it so that I would look out for
Old Tom's interests in Harveyville and as much as possible
in the rest of the county. I was happy for the job, even if
it was just thirty bucks a month, and I was happy to do
Tom's bidding. I was not a young man even then, but I was
raising a young daughter alone, and I was running out of
opportunities.

"Yes, I knew about the gold. Soon, the whole town
knew. The story was never told outright, but when Old
Tom, who'd been having cash-flow problems up until about
two weeks after Calico and his pards were hauled off to
Denver, started investing in the town—I mean, making
some big, big investments in Harveyville!—it became
clear to most folks that he had either robbed a bank himself
or had found Calico's gold. This town doubled in size on
Tom's gold. We wouldn't have the spur line without Old
Tom. That's why no one ever mentioned it. At least, not
out loud. No one ever begrudged Old Tom that gold, because he spread it around. We all prospered!"

Kentucky laughed almost deliriously, slapping the table.

Slash and Pecos glanced at each other in silent conferral.

Pecos turned to the old marshal, who stared guiltily
down at the table as though trying to read something that
had been carved into the wood in a foreign tongue. "All
comin' clear to me now," Pecos said. "Calico, he came
back for the gold."

Slowly, Kentucky nodded but kept his gaze on the table.
"He came back for the gold. He and his pards were so confident it would still be where they'd left it, and they'd be
able to go down to Mexico and dance with the señoritas
for the rest of their lives, they stayed here in town nearly a

week. Drinkin' an' dancin' right here an' over at Madam Delacroix's place. Had the whole town on edge, wonderin' what would happen . . ."

"Once they rode out and discovered their cache was no longer where they'd put it," Slash finished for him.

Kentucky nodded.

"And when they went out to retrieve it—what?" Slash asked. "Did you follow 'em out, or did Gyllenwater . . . ?"

"Both. I followed 'em out with four other men. But Old Tom already had men waitin' in those old shacks out at the old cavalry post. Wayne Blanchard . . ."

"Had him a chip on his shoulder, did Wayne?" Slash asked. Mary Kate's snide voice cut through the men's low, conspiratorially pitched conversation like a bayonet blade through flesh. "Tell the man, Marshal! Go ahead, Kentucky. Tell the man about the chip on Wayne's shoulder!"

She was standing behind the bar holding a tray of steaming chili bowls.

"Mary Kate!" O'Neil exclaimed, slapping the table with his open palm.

She cast the old lawman a saucy smile. "Just bringin' your chili, Marshal." She hardened her smile as she walked out from behind the bar and strode barefoot across the puncheons, saying in a cold, jeering, impertinent tone, "The good marshal here had his own dog in the fight— didn't you, Marshal? As did your former weekend deputy, Mister Blanchard."

"Mary Kate," Kentucky said again, keeping his voice pitched low with menace this time, glaring at the girl. His eyes were like polished steel.

Ignoring him, Mary Kate set the tray on the table, then, setting the bowls in front of her customers, she spoke to

Slash and Pecos: "Everyone in town's been wonderin' who the boy belongs to—Blanchard . . . or . . ."

She cast her mocking smile at O'Neil as she set a bowl of chili in front of him, saying, "Well . . . Nancy did seem to take a shine to Calico, didn't she, Marshal? All those years ago when they spent three weeks here in town, throwin' that delicious gold around . . . ?"

She picked up the tray and lay it flat against her bosoms, turning her body but keeping that cold, impudent smile on the old marshal, who sat in his chair looking pale and stricken. "You go ahead and tell the rest, Marshal. I best see about the biscuits!"

When she flounced back into the kitchen, Slash, Pecos, and Kentucky O'Neil sat in awkward silence. The old marshal stared stonily down at his chili. Slash looked from him to Pecos in brief, silent conferral, then raised his brows as he turned back to the lawman. "The boy . . . ? Your grandson . . . ?"

The old man continued to stare down at his chili bowl.

Suddenly, with his right hand, he swept the bowl from the table. It flew fifteen feet, struck another table, throwing chili in every direction, then hit the floor with a crash, and rolled to a stop against the far wall.

"There wasn't nothin' I could do," O'Neil said tightly, staring down at where his chili had been a moment before. "She was sixteen. Mary Kate's age now. Twelve years ago, Nancy was eighteen. A small-town girl. A lonely girl. Never been kissed. Oh, she'd been sparked a few times, but I ran most of the boys off. I wasn't ready to turn her over to other men yet, I reckon. Well, when Calico came to town, he met her right here, where she worked for Rivers. An attractive girl. And, she . . . well, I reckon she saw somethin' in Calico where I only saw devil. Calico had a way with women, you see. Men don't see it, but women do. She fell for him, an' there wasn't a damn thing I could do about it."

Finally, O'Neil looked up and his eyes were clear, though hard and red-rimmed with emotion. "She'd promised her hand to Blanchard, the Rimfire foreman—well, he was only the top hand back in them days. Worked for me on weekends. I approved of Wayne. A good, homespun man, though you wouldn't like to see him mad. An uncompromising rider for Tom Gyllenwater. Still, a good man. It was wrong what she done to him—let herself be seen cavortin' with Calico. Nancy sees it now. Back then—well, it was like he was a snake that had mesmerized her, Calico. She'd been fool enough to believe he was going to take her away and marry her. But then she saw him with another girl—a parlor girl. Heartbroken. I never seen her cry so hard since the day her mother died when she was only seven. My dear Nancy. Purely heartbroken over the outlaw, Ned Calico. And she felt such guilt—still does— over what she'd done to Blanchard!"

O'Neil picked at a callus on the heel of his hand. Suddenly, he looked up at Slash and Pecos and said, "Yeah, the boy's his. Calico's."

"Seems like a good kid to me," Slash said.

"Me, too," added Pecos.

"Well, we'll see what sorta man he shapes up to be." Again, Kentucky picked at the callus for a time, then looked up again. "Now you know. You're all filled in. I'm a thief. The town's a bunch of thieves. Tom Gyllenwater's a thief. His ranch was about to go under due to drought and falling cattle prices twelve years ago. That gold saved him and his daughter and Collie. Still, it didn't belong to us. So . . . what're you going to do about it?"

"I reckon it ain't up to us," Pecos said.

"It's up to Bledsoe," Slash said.

"You'll tell him?"

Slash and Pecos shared another look of silent conferral.

"Ah hell, I don't care anymore," the old marshal said. "Well, I reckon I care about the town and Old Tom. But we've been sittin' on this secret a long time. Secrets are like slivers in the skin. They fester. They cause some men—a man like myself, say, a man who always held himself up as a *good* man—to send wolves out to commit murder in cold blood."

He regarded Slash and Pecos pointedly, then shook his head slowly, his lips set in a straight line beneath his mustache. "That secret's been festerin' for a long time. Maybe it's finally time to pluck it out!"

He planted his bony red fists on the edge of the table and pushed wearily to his feet. He glanced at the chili bowl on the floor, grimaced, and said, "Tell Mary Kate I'm sorry about that mess."

He turned and ambled out of the saloon, muttering to himself, "Damn old fool."

Slash and Pecos watched the batwings clatter into place behind him. Pecos turned to Slash. "What do you think, partner?"

Slash sighed. He looked down at his untouched chili bowl. "I think we'd best tend to this chili before it gets any colder."

They picked up their spoons and went to work.

As they did, Mary Kate stepped out of the kitchen holding an oilcloth-covered tray in front of her. She walked out from around the bar and headed for the batwings. She pushed out onto the stoop, then walked across the street at an angle and mounted the boardwalk fronting the town marshal's office.

She knocked once on the door, then tripped the latch and fumbled the door open. She stepped inside and turned to see Kentucky O'Neil sitting at his desk, hands entwined before him on the blotter. He looked at the girl through his sad, red-rimmed eyes. He looked at the oilcloth-covered tray in her hands then returned his eyes to hers, frowning curiously.

Mary Kate moved into the office. She walked over to the desk and jerked her chin in a silent command. The old marshal removed his hands from the desk, sitting back in his chair, and she set the tray on the desk before him. She removed the oilcloth from the tray, and the aroma from the chili bowl sitting beside two nicely browned biscuits and a small cup of whipped butter and a big wedge of peach cobbler adorned with a liberal dollop of whipped cream, instantly filled the room.

Mary Kate grabbed a water glass from a shelf and set the glass on the tray. She walked around behind O'Neil's desk and opened the bottom drawer on the left side. She pulled out an unlabeled bottle, uncorked it, and poured three fingers of whiskey into the glass. She replaced the cork in the bottle's lip and returned the bottle to the drawer.

O'Neil looked up at her, his gray brows arched like the wings of a bird taking flight. "How on earth did you know I keep a bottle in that drawer?"

"Every man keeps a bottle in that drawer."

Mary Kate leaned down, gave his leathery cheek a tender kiss, then turned and walked back out of the office. She flashed the old man a gentle smile as she reached for the door to pull it closed behind her.

Chapter 29

His conversation with the two former outlaws in the Copper Nickel had left Kentucky without an appetite until Mary Kate had brought the chili.

He wasn't sure if it was the chili itself, accompanied by the still-warm biscuits and the big wedge of pie, or the fact that Mary Kate had brought it to him, possibly as an olive branch of sorts. But as soon as she'd lifted the oilcloth from the tray, hunger bit him like a rattlesnake. He consumed the chili and biscuits in ten minutes, and washed it down with the whiskey.

He filled a cup from the coffeepot he'd kept warm on the stove and leisurely ate the pie with its big spoonful of buttery whipped cream, sipping the coffee as he did. He was in better spirits by the time he'd finished the big, hearty meal. He'd need a nap soon, after packing down all that food, but first he'd take a walk around town to help his food digest.

He tossed back the last of his coffee, rose from his chair, hitched his gun and cartridge belt up higher on his bony hips, and pulled his hat off a peg by the door. He'd just stepped out onto the stoop and set his hat on his head when a carriage came rolling up to the office behind a trotting thoroughbred gelding with a good bit of sweat silvering both withers. He recognized the driver of the carriage— a stylish, red-wheeled, leather-seated chaise—as one of Tom Gyllenwater's men. A trusted older waddy on the Rimfire rolls.

The man halted the thoroughbred near the hitchrack fronting the marshal's office and gave Kentucky a cordial nod and a pinch of his hat brim.

"Howdy, Marshal."

"I'm afraid I don't recall your name," the lawman said, pitching his voice with rote apology. In fact, he didn't know if he'd ever heard the man's handle. Even if he had, there were too many names out at the Gyllenwater spread for him to remember. He only remembered the troublemakers—the ones he customarily had to throw in the cooler for a day or two after a weekend dustup. He didn't believe this man—in his forties and with a pot gut not unlike his own—was one of those.

"I'm Riley Becker, Marshal O'Neil. Miss Clara out at the Rimfire sent me to fetch you. She'd like a private word with you out at headquarters."

"She would?" Kentucky said, frowning. "What about?"

"If you'll forgive me, Marshal, Miss Clara just told me to fetch you. She didn't say why."

"Is it Tom?"

Becker stared at him, and blinked, as though he hadn't heard the question.

"All right, all right," the lawman said, stepping forward.

"Dad, may I go with you?"

Kentucky stopped and turned to see Nancy standing just off the stoop to his right. She wore the patterned cream and brown day dress and tasseled straw hat she usually wore when she came downtown to buy groceries and dry goods and to pick up the mail. A wicker grocery basket was hooked over her arm. At the beginning or end of such trips, she usually stopped by the marshal's office to poke her head in the door and say hi.

That was apparently what she'd been intending to do just now, before Becker had shown up.

"Oh, Nancy . . ." Kentucky said, frowning at her incredulously.

"I'm sorry—I overheard." She flashed a friendly smile at Becker, and said, "It would be all right, wouldn't it, Mister Becker? It's been a long time since I've visited with Clara Gyllenwater." She looked at her father with no small bit of pleading in her eyes. "Since you're riding out there anyway . . ."

Becker said, "It don't make no never mind to me, Miss O'Neil. My orders is to fetch the marshal. Miss Gyllenwater didn't order me *not* to bring anyone else along with him."

He flashed Nancy a smile, hiking a shoulder. O'Neil could tell that the man wouldn't mind having Nancy's company in the chaise one bit. She was far easier on the eyes than Kentucky was.

The old lawman studied his daughter suspiciously. She flushed a little under his gaze. That bit about her wish to visit with Clara Gyllenwater had been hogwash. The two women had never been anything more than acquaintances who irregularly greeted each other with a nod and a smile in church on Sunday or on the streets of Harveyville. They had nothing in common, and they were seven years apart in age, which was quite a gap to folks in their twenties and thirties.

No, it wasn't Clara Gyllenwater whom Nancy wished to see. The person she really wanted to see was Wayne Blanchard. That much was obvious by the beseeching her father recognized in her wide, light brown eyes. It was almost a desperation, which made it impossible for him to refuse her, though he wished like hell he could.

She wanted to make amends for the past, but while she was thirty years old, she was not yet old enough to know that the passage of years often made making amends nothing more than a yearning that could never be satisfied. It would torture the hell out of her if she let it.

"Oh, for goodness' sakes," Kentucky said, extending his hand to the young woman.

"Wonderful! It's such a beautiful day after the rain!"

Kentucky gave a caustic grunt as he helped her into the chaise, then sat beside her on the carriage's rear, quilted leather seat. He patted the seat's leather arm and said, "It was nice of Miss Gyllenwater to send such a stylish rig." He leaned toward his daughter and added in a voice lowered in mock secrecy, "Or she thinks I'm just too old to sit a horse anymore."

Nancy and Riley Becker chuckled as Becker released the brake and reined the thoroughbred into the street and then full around to head back in the direction from which he'd come. "I best warn you, Marshal, ma'am—the trail's a little muddy after the storm. Might get some mud thrown at you."

"That's all right," Nancy said, holding her straw hat on her head. "A little mud never hurt anyone!"

She glanced at her father and flashed a grateful smile. The smile had been meant to make him feel good. It did not. It made him feel sad, wondering how long she'd wanted to talk to Blanchard. Had she been pining to do so for the past twelve years? Or was it merely a recent whim? Possibly fueled by her having spoken to him briefly on the street the other day, which Kentucky had witnessed when, striding back to his office from the hotel, he'd cast his gaze up Patterson Avenue and seen the two together, talking in the sifting dust of Blanchard's riders.

It had been a short discussion and, judging by the set of her shoulders as Blanchard had ridden away, it hadn't ended happily. At least, not to Nancy's satisfaction.

What had she wanted from the Rimfire foreman, nearly twenty years her senior? Did she still hold a candle for him?

As they rode along in the sunny countryside still damp from the storm, the warm air as clean as the cool, drier air of early fall, O'Neil silently castigated himself for never having brought up the subject of Wayne Blanchard with Nancy. It had been only a half-conscious decision on his part. He'd thought that bringing him up would bring up the entire mess regarding Ned Calico, and that was a subject neither one of them wanted to think about, much less discuss.

Especially when his own daughter had been so deeply involved in an unflattering way that the whole town had known about. *Still knew about*, of course. Those citizens who hadn't lived in Harveyville at that time certainly knew about it now. It was one of those secrets a town buries only so deep—just deep enough that they can dig it up and share it in whispered, insinuating tones over late-night conversations or card games or in the boudoirs of Madam Delacroix's parlor girls.

The stigma of Nancy's having fallen for Ned Calico

didn't seem to bother Nancy herself. She still walked to the business district once a week for groceries, or twice a week if the need arose. She went to church with her son and Kentucky, and she hung around afterwards for coffee and cake and to chat with the other parishioners in good-natured albeit superficial ways.

But she had few friends.

No. She had *no* friends among the women of Harveyville. And in the twelve years since Danny was born, she'd had no gentlemen callers. She was a pretty woman, still youthful and firm-bodied—relatively untouched by the ravages of age. There could be only one reason no man had shown an interest in her—aside from the occasional, sidelong, admiring glance as she went about her business downtown, that was.

The town knew about her and Calico during her troubles, and it had marked her as unacceptable. Her life consisted of her father, her son, and the house they shared. That was all. She was too young for her world to have become that small. But it was.

All because of a mistake she'd made long ago.

But that's all it took.

What on earth could she possibly want to talk to Blanchard about after all this time?

Kentucky hoped she wasn't holding out hope that Wayne would ever forgive her for what she'd done. He really hoped she didn't think that was possible. She may have gotten to know Blanchard in the ways a woman can know a man, but Kentucky knew Blanchard the way a man can know a man. The ugly side, too. Wayne Blanchard was not the kind of man who could forgive a woman for having betrayed him so deeply. O'Neil thought that his daughter had gotten off lucky that Blanchard had not gotten tanked

up and ridden to town in a full rage, and killed them all—
Nancy, Kentucky, and the boy.

And burned the house to the ground.

That was the man Wayne Blanchard was. The old-style
Westerner clad in a hide of pride no bullet could pierce.
That said, he wouldn't harm Nancy now, at this late date.
If he'd wanted to do that, he'd had twelve years to do it.
Even that notion made the old lawman sad in its way. It
told him how much Blanchard had loved his daughter.
Maybe he still did, despite never being able to forgive her.

Kentucky hoped Nancy knew that much. He didn't want
to see her further hurt. Life had tossed her around badly
enough. He'd have liked to bring the subject up with her
now. At least, he wanted to think he could have done that
against any previous ability to do so. But now he had the
excuse of Riley Becker's presence not to. So, he crossed
his arms over his chest, sat back in the comfortable seat,
tipped his face to the sun, and forced himself to enjoy the
jostling ride with the warm breeze rife with the smell of
summer-cured grass and stitched with the musical piping
of meadowlarks.

"Here we are, Dad."

He hadn't realized he'd fallen asleep until Nancy's voice
plucked him out of a doze.

He nudged his hat brim back up on his forehead just as
the wagon passed beneath the crossbar of the Rimfire
portal. The yard was quiet, not unusual for this time of the
day. Most of the men would be out on the range, working
the cattle and tending other chores. One was splitting wood
beside the cook shack, but he was the only one around.
Except for Clara Gyllenwater, O'Neil saw now as Becker
pulled the chaise up in front of the house.

The pretty young woman with dazzling chocolate eyes

and matching hair stood just inside the gate of the white picket fence ringing the Gyllenwater house. She wore black denim jeans, a purple blouse with puffy sleeves, and a short, fawnskin vest. Turquoise earrings dangled along her fine jaws, matching the turquoise of the buttons on the vest. The colors she wore contrasted and accentuated her dark olive skin, smooth as varnished walnut. Clara didn't appear to have a lick of her father in her— at least, not in her physical appearance. None of that ogre Tom Gyllenwater peeked out from that heart-shaped face with its fine, delicate nose and warm, intelligent eyes.

Kentucky had seen the girl's mother only a few times. The mercurial Delores hadn't hung around the Rimfire long, even during the few years she and Tom had been married. But that's whom this lovely creature took after, all right. No sign of Tom . . . until you got to know her, Kentucky knew.

On the other hand, Kentucky didn't think you ever really got to know Clara Gyllenwater. She wouldn't allow anyone that close. Only when you'd been in her company a few times did it become apparent that at her demanding, manipulative, uncompromising core she was Tom Gyllenwater through and through. It was just that her ripe female beauty and finishing school manners hid it from plain sight.

"Hello, Clara," Kentucky said as the wagon lurched to a stop. He removed his hat and gave a friendly wave.

"Greetings," Clara said with a cool smile. Her brown-eyed gaze flashed to Nancy. There was a chill in her eyes, as well.

Kentucky climbed out of the chaise and walked around to Nancy's side of the carriage just as Nancy opened the door. He extended his hand to his daughter, who took it and let him help her to the ground.

Nancy turned to the still coolly-smiling Clara and said, "I hope you don't mind, Clara. It was such a pretty day, I insisted on riding along."

Clara did not respond but slid her gaze to Becker, who remained in the carriage awaiting orders. Crisply, Clara said, "Switch the horse and wait with the carriage."

As Becker nodded, then moved to unhitch the thoroughbred, Nancy glanced at her father, who returned the look with a shrug in his eyes and an arch of his brows.

As Becker led the horse away, Clara turned to the lawman and said, again coolly, "I didn't call you out here on a social visit." She pointedly did not look at Nancy.

"I had a feeling you didn't," O'Neil said with some chagrin. "Nancy, perhaps you should—"

"The foreman's in his cabin," Clara said, turning to Nancy and blinking once, slowly.

Nancy flushed.

"We don't stand on formalities here, Miss O'Neil," Clara said, sliding a thick wing of her hair back with the back of her hand. "Feel free to call on him unattended. I'm sure you have much to discuss."

She glanced at Kentucky, and then it was the marshal's turn to flush. No, the old ogre of Tom Gyllenwater did not lie too far from the surface of this queen-like Spanish personage standing before him and his daughter now.

Nancy's own tone was steely now as she said, "Miss Gyllenwater, you've no reason to take that tone with me. If you don't want me here . . . if you see me as a threat— well, then—"

"His private quarters are down the slope behind the main house. In the woods along the creek. I hope you don't mind a little walk. There's no way to get a carriage through the trees."

Nancy glanced from her father to Clara Gyllenwater, and narrowed her eyes and hardened her jaws. "No. No, I don't mind a little walk at all."

"I'll warn you, he's in no condition for visitors. That said, I'll leave the decision up to you."

She's in love with him, O'Neil thought, regarding Clara incredulously, pointedly. The marshal would be damned if Blanchard hadn't gotten another young one to fall for him. Tom Gyllenwater's handsome daughter, no less! The thought must have occurred to Nancy now, as well, because it was plain in the look she gave her father, flushing again and stepping back, then turning and walking stiffly away.

Clara softened her tone as she turned to O'Neil again. "Come in." She tripped the latch and opened the gate. "I have cake and coffee . . . and news."

Chapter 30

Nancy made her way carefully down the slope behind the house, not wanting to slip and fall on the ground still damp in places from the previous day's rain. She didn't want to give Clara the satisfaction of witnessing the indignity if Gyllenwater's daughter were watching her from one of the big house's rear windows, which she probably wasn't. Still, Nancy felt uncomfortably self-conscious, which aggravated the anger that Clara's steely welcome had provoked in her.

She followed a twisting path through the trees and came to the cabin that, as Clara had said, sat along a creek. Trees and brush cast a dark pall over the cabin despite the bright sunshine. There was moss on the shake-shingled roof, and several large, badly rusted tin tubs hung from pegs in the log walls.

Nancy stopped within twenty feet of the cabin and called softly so as not to overly startle the man inside. "Wayne?"

No response but the whisper of the breeze and the gurgling of the creek flanking the cabin.

"Wayne, it's Nancy," she called, louder.

Still no response. Nancy strode forward, approaching the small, roofed front stoop on which stood a washstand and a cracked mirror hanging from a nail in an awning support post. She stopped before the stoop, placed one foot on the first of the three wooden steps, and placed her hand on a support post to her left. She peered through the half-open door, trying to probe the murky shadows within.

"Wayne, it's—"

"What the hell are you doing here?"

She saw him then, sitting at a table just beyond the door, facing her from the table's far side.

"Wayne, I—"

She stopped when he abruptly slid his chair back and pushed to his feet. A tin coffee cup and nearly empty bottle sat on the table, near a stack of playing cards and an ashtray. He held a long, black cheroot in his right hand. He slipped it into his left hand, then picked up the cup with his right hand and strode toward the door. He walked uncertainly, scuffing his boot heels across the floor's scarred puncheons. The neck thong of his hat jounced beneath his chin.

As he approached her, Nancy felt deep lines of incredulity and concern cut across her forehead. He looked like hell. He looked puffy and sweaty, and to his untrimmed mustache clung bits of tobacco from his half-smoked cheroot. His eyes were red-rimmed and rheumy. Drunk in the early afternoon!

He leaned against the door frame and glared at her—a look that made her heart shrivel and nearly caused her to cry. "What the hell are you doing here?" he asked again. "No one comes out here. This is my own private cabin!"

"I'm sorry," Nancy said, splaying her hand across her

bosoms, sucking back a sob. "Miss Gyllenwater seemed to think it all right."

"She knows you're out here?"

"Well . . . yes. I mean, Wayne . . . I didn't come alone, if that's what you're thinking. She sent a chaise for my father. I happened to be in town at the time and . . . well, it's such a nice day"—she threw up her arms as though to indicate the pretty afternoon around them—"I thought I would ride along."

Blanchard cocked his head to one side and narrowed a castigating eye. "You rode out here because it's such a damn fine day?"

His anger seemed to suck the air from her lungs. He gave her no quarter. She had trouble drawing a breath. When she finally did, she let it out on a sob she couldn't suppress, then raised her hand to her mouth, biting her knuckle to try to quell her suddenly untethered emotions.

"I'm sorry!"

"I can't believe Clara would send you out here." Blanchard glanced suspiciously back in the direction of the house.

"Why?" Nancy said through another sob.

Blanchard looked at her again but didn't say anything.

Nancy looked back at him, composing herself. She lowered her hand from her mouth, drew a calming breath, and said, "Are you two . . . ?"

"Never mind."

It figured, Nancy vaguely thought. He was the kind of man who attracted younger women. Handsome but tough. Surly, arrogant, and commanding. Some young women, like Nancy herself, were attracted to those qualities in men because they inspired certainty and respect as well as admiration. They offered security. Younger men had yet to find their footing in life. They stumbled around and preened like unbroken colts, offering no security at all. Its opposite, in fact.

Nancy remembered the gentleness of Blanchard's hands on her body; she yearned for that sure touch again.

On the heels of that realization, she sucked another sharp breath. She'd kept it a secret from herself until now, but she'd come out here to get him back.

She shook her head as though to dislodge the thought, tucked her hair back behind her ear, and said, "Why aren't you working?" She didn't mention the drink in his hand. That it was whiskey was obvious.

"I'm taking a few days off."

"To get drunk?"

Blanchard scowled at her. "I don't answer to you, Nancy."

"Because of what happened in town? Do you actually *feel bad* for not murdering those two men Bledsoe sent?"

"No." Blanchard shook his head and took a puff from his cheroot. Exhaling smoke, he said, "That's why I'm drinking." He smiled but there was no humor in it. "Besides, Old Tom's dead. He'd want me to have a few in his honor." He raised the cup and drank from it.

Nancy looked up at him, stunned. "That must be why Clara called for my father."

"I suppose. And a few other things, most likely."

"What other things?"

"She's fixing to take the bull by the horns, so to speak. She's gonna send a message that just because Old Tom's dead, nothing has changed out here at Rimfire."

Nancy studied the ground, pondering the implication of what she'd just been told. She looked up at Blanchard again and felt a chill spread across the back of her neck. "Are you saying she's going to . . ."

"I don't know what she's up to. I committed an unpardonable sin when I didn't kill those two federals, so I really don't know." Blanchard took another sip of the whiskey. "But I can guess. Now, if you'll forgive me, I was just getting started."

He smiled again without mirth and started to turn away.

Nancy stopped him with: "Wayne?"

He turned back to her with a severe grimace.

"Why did you kill Calico?"

He stared back at her, not saying anything.

Nancy said, "Was it for Old Tom . . . or for you?"

"What do you care? You're the one who wrote Bledsoe. You obviously wanted him dead."

"Answer the question."

"You'll never know," Blanchard snarled through a mocking smile.

He turned away, stepped back into the cabin, and drew the door closed with the toe of his boot.

Clara already had two slices of coffee cake sitting on the table in the Gyllenwater house's large but spartanly furnished dining room.

"I baked it myself, so I make no promises that it's even edible," she said as she poured coffee into Kentucky's china cup, which sat on a matching saucer with a delicate spoon bearing the Gyllenwater Rimfire brand. She indicated a china creamer residing near three white candles poking up from brass holders in the middle of the table. "Please, help yourself to cream. It's fresh."

"No, thanks—I take it black."

When she'd poured some cream into her own cup, she stirred it slowly and cast her inscrutable, chocolate-eyed gaze to Kentucky sitting directly across the long table from her. The table harked back to the years when more than two or three people dined at it. Long ago, Gyllenwater had a capable male cook and housekeeper who cooked for the men, who dined here with the family after being summoned by an iron triangle which, the old lawman had noted on his way into the house, still hung over the porch. When Gyllenwater's payroll had grown beyond four or five hands, that tradition ended and behind the bunkhouse a cook shack was built and supplied with its own cook and triangle.

O'Neil knew this because at one time, before he'd grown too stove-up for regular horseback rides, he used to ride out here to dine with friends from time to time, for he and Tom Gyllenwater had been close. He'd thought they'd been close friends, but now he was beginning to doubt that. To Tom, they'd probably just had a close working relationship—one that benefited Tom himself but not Kentucky all that much.

Kentucky hadn't been out here in years, and the large, sparsely furnished but well-kept house reminded him of better times.

Or at least of younger years.

"My father has passed."

Clara's words froze Kentucky's fork, with which he'd just impaled a bite of coffee cake, three inches from his open mouth. Closing his mouth and lowering the fork back down to his plate, he scowled across the table at the young woman, who regarded him without expression, as though she'd commented on the weather or something else just as innocuous.

He studied her in shock. But, then, he supposed he should have guessed Tom's passing had been the reason she'd sent for him. Kentucky had thought . . . or hoped . . . that maybe Tom had asked to see him one more time. In fact, the lawman had felt sure that that was the reason he was here.

"When . . . ?"

"This morning."

Kentucky hesitated, studying the tablecloth as though searching for the right words. "Clara, I'm . . . so sorry . . . for your loss. So very sorry."

"Thank you, Marshal. However, it did not come as a shock. Old Tom has been failing for some time. His sickness well, it's probably the ugliest thing a man can die of."

Clara's eyes blazed in sudden anger, and Kentucky felt himself tighten in his chair. Back when Gyllenwater had first come down with the Cupid's itch, Clara had ridden into town and threatened to cut the throat of the whore who'd passed the disease to her father. She likely would have, too, if Madam Delacroix hadn't only a few days earlier shipped the girl off to Omaha.

"But he is gone now, and that is a blessing."

"Yes . . . I suppose so." The old lawman's heart sputtered in genuine sadness. Tom had been a hard, uncompromising man. He was no man to have for an enemy. Old Tom had not been his enemy. Maybe he hadn't really been his friend, but Kentucky had considered him a friend. Friends, especially at Kentucky's age, with time so limited and so many memories to look back on, were hard to lose.

He studied the young woman sitting across the table from him. She'd lost her brother and her father within a few days of each other, but if she felt even as sad as Kentucky felt, she was doing a good job of concealing it. Her eyes were clear and emotionless. They were all business, in fact, which was a little off-putting for Kentucky, under the circumstances. It left him bewildered and wondering if informing him of her father's death was the only thing Clara had called him out here for.

He didn't have long to ponder the question.

They ate their cake and drank their coffee slowly, talking little and only about the preparations of the body and the funeral arrangements.

When they had each finished their cake, however, Clara was quick to get down to brass tacks. She refilled Kentucky's coffee cup and then her own and placed her arms on the table, leaning forward, casting the old lawman a disquietingly commanding look.

"My father is now gone," she said matter-of-factly. "And I am sorry to say that his passing has required me, who now has full control of Rimfire and all of my father's other business interests, to make a few other changes, as well."

Chapter 31

Fifteen minutes later, Clara stood at the parlor window as Kentucky O'Neil and his daughter climbed aboard the chaise. Father and daughter each had a decidedly crestfallen expression, their shoulders slumped. Their moods seemed to affect even the driver, Riley Becker, who studied them uncertainly then glanced curiously toward the house.

Finally, when his two passengers were seated, Becker climbed into the driver's seat, released the brake, and shook the reins over the back of the white-socked bay in the traces. As the horse pulled the carriage ahead, the old marshal cast a grim, fleeting look toward the parlor window, as though he were aware of Clara's eyes on him. His eyes met hers through the glass an instant before he snapped his head back forward, and the carriage jounced off across the ranch yard.

Footsteps sounded on the carpeted floor behind Clara.

She turned as Thorn Willis entered the parlor, his flat-crowned white Stetson in his hands. His nose and eyes were badly swollen and black, but a dull, devilish smile shimmered in them, anyway. The mirth pulled at the young man's thin-lipped mouth.

Willis plopped casually into a chair near the door, tossed his hat in the air and caught it, his bold eyes on Clara.

"What are you smiling about?" she asked the firebrand.

"I do believe you enjoyed that."

"Yes? Well, you're wrong," she said, flaring her nostrils at the man. "Doing what I just did gave me no joy. Kentucky O'Neil was a good friend of my father's for many years. I was merely doing what had to be done. Some things have to be done if one is to survive in these changing times."

"Out with the old and in with the new?" Again, Thorn tossed his hat in the air and caught it, his smile broadening, flashing in his swollen, painful-looking eyes.

"Don't be glib."

"I don't know what that means, Miss Clara."

She chuckled. "No, you wouldn't. But then, I have not hired you back for your brains."

He smiled again and tapped his thumb against the pearl-gripped revolver holstered on his right thigh.

"When do you want it done?" he asked.

"Tonight. The next train leaves tomorrow. I don't want them on it. Let it not be said that any man killed a Gyllenwater—even the most worthless of Gyllenwaters—and lived to crow about it. If that were to happen, I'd have wolves baying on my doorstep all the time!"

"Too bad Blanchard don't see it that way."

Clara walked slowly toward the young firebrand. She thrust her shoulders back so that the fabric of her purple blouse drew taut against the twin cones of her breasts. "If you do this well, if the other men work well under you, you can come back permanently . . . and replace Blanchard."

"I like the sound of that." Willis kicked out both his

long, slender legs clad in wash-worn denims, and gained his feet as gracefully as a cat just waking from a nap. He practically leaped out of the chair. He stood over her, gazing down at her, his eyes brashly roaming. "Tell me, Miss Clara"—he lifted a hand to slide a lock of her hair back behind her shoulder—"what else do I get?"

She answered his question with a hard slap to his face, mindless of the battering it had taken from Blanchard's fist. The young man grunted as the force of her blow whipped his head sideways and back. Instantly, his cheek turned crimson. He looked at her, startled, injured.

"Just like a boy," Clara hissed. "Counting your chickens before they're hatched! Leave here, boy, do what you've been instructed to do in the way you've been instructed to do it, and then . . . and *only then* . . . will you be treated like a man!"

After devouring a big steak and a hearty portion of pinto beans and corn, Pecos dropped his fork on his plate in the little Bon Ton Café and, stretching, said, "It's been a long day. I think I'm gonna go over to that little bathhouse I seen by the creek—the one we seen that was run by an old Sioux couple—and have a soak before bedtime. I might even go over to Madam Delacroix's and get my ashes hauled."

Slash scowled at him across the table. He chewed his last bite of antelope stew, swallowed, and said, "You can't go gettin' your ashes hauled."

"Why can't I?"

"Because I can't."

"Hah! Just because you done locked yourself out of the game, don't mean I have, Slash."

"Well . . . think about Miss Langdon."

"Me an' Miss Abigail haven't even held hands yet. Hell, we ain't even been out together yet. No sweet little nothings have we yet whispered in each other's ears. No, no." Pecos wagged his head. "You can't use Miss Langdon to further that argument, Slash."

"Well, dammit, it's just not fair. You'd make me go upstairs . . . alone . . . and lie there . . . alone . . . while you, uh . . . got your ashes hauled?"

"Yes, I certain-sure would." Pecos chuckled. He placed a fifty-cent piece on the table, grabbed his hat and shotgun, slid his chair back, and rose to his full six-feet-four, grinning mockingly down at his partner.

"Damn you, Pecos, this is one of the lowest things you've ever done to me!"

"No, not by a long shot." Pecos turned to start for the door but stopped when Kentucky O'Neil entered the café from the lobby of the Longhorn Hotel.

"Where you goin'?" the old man asked.

He appeared in a particularly surly mood. Surly and something else. Possibly anxious, even desperate. His craggy cheeks were not the deep red-leather color they usually were, in stark contrast to his snow-white mustache. They were pasty and drawn more than usual, as though the old gent were coming down with something.

"He's off to get his ashes hauled, the scoundrel," Slash said, pouting. He leaned forward, elbows on the table, building a quirley.

"No, he's not," Kentucky said, looking up at Pecos commandingly, which registered a little comical since he was a whole head shorter than the tallest of the two former cutthroats. "Sit down."

"How come?"

"Sit down!" Kentucky snarled up at Pecos.

He looked over to where the big, hulking son of the Chinese couple who ran the place was playing with a little kitten on the counter, most of his other customers having finished their suppers and vacated the premises, casting dubious glances at Slash and Pecos as they had.

"Kong," Kentucky said, "bring me a beer in a big schooner. And a shot of whiskey."

"Yeah, I'll have the same thing," Slash said.

"No, he won't," the old lawman told Kong. He glanced at the two empty beer glasses and the two empty shot glasses sitting on the table among the other scraps of Slash and Pecos's meals. "You've had enough. You need to stay sober for the duration of your stay in this fair city, which I formerly considered mine, since I was the lawdog here for damn near twenty years!"

He'd added that last with the expression of someone who'd just eaten a whole lemon in one bite.

"Wait," Pecos said, frowning. "*Was* the lawdog here?"

"Yes, I am no more. Kong, leave that damn kitten and fetch my bump an' a beer!"

Kong frowned as though with injury, then left the tiger-striped gray kitten and ambled over to the beer tap, knocking stacked dishes and bottles with his big elbows.

Kentucky turned to Slash and Pecos and said, "I was invited on a little ride out to the Rimfire. Tom Gyllenwater is dead and his lovely daughter, Clara, fired me—practically with the same breath she told me about Old Tom's passing." He chewed his mustache and shook his head. "You know, I once thought that Old Tom didn't have a match in any man or woman. I was wrong. He not only had his match in his daughter, but I think she might even outdo the old thicket-brawlin' mossyhorn!"

"Why'd she fire you?" Slash said, having a little trouble feeling as sorry for the old man as Kentucky apparently felt for himself. Kentucky had tried to have him and Pecos killed, after all. Slash still had a damned sore ear to show for it, too—one that didn't improve his looks any, either.

"She fired me, most likely, because you two are still alive. But, then, I'm old, as well. She wants a younger, meaner, more capable man looking out for her interests here in town."

"Oh, I don't know," Pecos said. "Sending those four market hunters with those Big Fifty rifles after us wasn't the kindest thing I've ever seen a man do. Downright mean an' lowdown, I'd call it."

Kong set the beer and the whiskey on the table in front of Kentucky, then trudged away to clear more tables. "Still graveled about that, are you?"

"We're thin-skinned, don't ya know," Slash quipped, wincing as he probed his torn ear with his hand.

Kentucky took a big sip of his beer, licked the foam from his mustache, and dumped the entire shot into the beer. He watched it froth as he set it back down on the table. "Well, I'm gonna make it up to you. I'm gonna get you both out of town. Right now. Tonight. Pronto!"

Slash and Pecos shared incredulous glances before turning back to the old former marshal. "Huh?" Slash said.

"She's comin' for you tonight. She didn't say it, but I could read it in her eyes. She knows there's a train tomorrow an' that you two old renegades might be on it. She don't want you gettin' off scot-free to crow about killin' her brother, despite how much she always hated that hydrophobic little ferret."

"Hell, we still haven't decided if we was gonna hop that train," Slash said.

"Yeah," Pecos said. "Me? I'm all for it. But Slash don't like leavin' a situation unresolved. He thinks that's what we'd be doin' if we didn't settle up with Rimfire some way."

Kentucky took another big drink of his beer, then turned an exasperated scowl at Slash. "Good God, man—don't you see that the only way this situation gets resolved is by you two gettin' filled so full of lead you'll rattle when you walk!"

Slash chuckled. "Look at you. You damn near did that very thing!"

"I apologized!"

"Aww," Pecos said.

"I never thought I'd stoop that low, but I did. I was tryin' to save more men than just myself. I was trying to save my daughter and Old Tom. I was trying to save the town! But I was wrong to do it, and I'll have to answer for it by an' by. Maybe I can ease my punishment later on by doing the right thing now. Maybe I can look myself in the mirror again, in the bargain."

Slash and Pecos exchanged long, conferring scowls, then Slash turned to Kentucky and said, "You're sure she's heading this way?"

"She'll be sending men this way tonight. Probably late. I'm certain-sure about that. They won't be headed up by Blanchard. He seems to have fallen out of that black widow's favor, too. According to my daughter, he was back getting soused in his cabin."

Kentucky took another deep drink of the beer, as though he thought the Rimfire foreman had the right idea, given the current confluence of circumstances beyond seemingly anyone's control except Clara Gyllenwater's.

"Your daughter went out to see Blanchard?" Pecos asked.

Kentucky looked down at his boilermaker. "Never mind about that."

"You're the one who brought it up," Slash pointed out.

"Like I said, never mind." Kentucky sipped his beer again. Despite him, Slash, and Pecos being the only three in the room at the moment, he kept his voice low but pitched with passion. "Look, you two have to light a shuck out of here. It ain't just you I'm worried about. I'm worried about the town. Innocent people gettin' killed in the cross-fire."

Slash glanced at Pecos. "You know how I hate like hell to run from a problem, but the old-timer might be right."

"I got a feelin' he is, too. Them men who rode in here after Blanchard did this mornin' didn't look none too happy to be leavin' with all their shells in their belt loops."

"We'd best pull our picket pins." Slash slapped the table and rose to his feet. "All right, we can take a hint. Don't ever let it be said that Slash Braddock and the Pecos River Kid ever overstayed their welcome."

"Where you goin'?" Kentucky asked.

"What the hell do you mean—where we goin'?" Pecos laughed. "We're gonna head for Ogalla—"

Kentucky wagged his head dramatically. "They'll track you to Ogallala. Hell, you won't be any safer in Ogallala than you would be here. The sheriff up there is an old friend of Tom's! Besides, the Rimfire riders would figure you'd ride north. You gotta head southwest—cross-country."

"At night?" Pecos said, skeptically. "I've never rode that way even in the light. Isn't there some rough country between here an'—"

"The South Platte, yes." Kentucky drained his beer glass

and tapped the table, urging the two Bledsoe troubleshooters to sit back down. "But you're right—it's rough country. Dry as a bone. Nasty canyons and thickets. Rattlesnake country. And they might track you; gonna be a full-moon night. But I got an idea."

Slash and Pecos cast each other a dubious look.

"There used to be a stage line that ran through there. Most of the stations are long gone, and the trail is grown over or washed out. But I have a couple of old army buddies who once manned one of those stations—the Prickly Pear. It's in the heart of the buttes near the Platte, honestly rugged country an' make no mistake. Between here an' Julesburg. A tough pair of old salts. Got that way by fightin' Red Cloud. Bill Dilloway, also known as Daddy Longlegs, and Casper Dunn will harbor you there for the night. In the morning, or when the coast is clear, you can ride straight to Denver. There's a chance the Rimfire men will track you there, since they're savvy trackers and they know the country, but I'm bettin' they wouldn't do it till daylight."

Slash studied the old man, frowning skeptically. "It ain't that we don't appreciate the help, Kentucky, but Pecos and I will be just fine on our own."

"No, you won't. The Rimfire men know that country like the backs of their hands. Before the spur line came, they used to trail their herds through there to Denver every fall. They'll run you both down, surround you, and that'll be the end of you. You need a hidey-hole to hole up in, and I got just the place!"

"It'll be the end of us and what we have to say to Bledsoe about Ned Calico's loot," Pecos said with a wry smile twisting his lips. "Your problem will be solved."

"It's already solved," the old man said. "After I got back

from the Rimfire, I sent a telegram to Luther in Denver. I wrote the whole thing out from start to finish. Cost me damn near ten dollars and the old fellow runnin' the wire nearly had a heart stroke! I reckon I wanted to come clean for myself and my family. I have to admit that I felt like stickin' a pin in Clara Gyllenwater, too. Treatin' me like that after all the years I harbored the secret about that payroll gold her father stole and raised her and her worthless brother high on the unholy hog!"

Kentucky slapped the table so hard that both Slash and Pecos nearly leaped out of their chairs, reaching for their pistols. "I was merely a swamper to Old Tom. I see that now. We was friends, sure, but I admired him for his money and his pluck. Did he admire me? Nah, nah. If he admired anything about me, it was about how good I covered his tracks in Harveyville and all across the Panhandle, never once alerting the law to his nefarious dealin's with squatters and nesters an' the like—sodbusters and small ranchers with legitimate claims he either scared away, or most often hanged the way he always ordered Blanchard to hang such innocent men—to show others what happens when you cross the Rimfire!"

Slash and Pecos were still marveling at the fact of the old man having sent that telegram to ol' Bleed-'Em-So.

"You do it, fellas. You head to that old stage station in the Bayonet Buttes, along the Platte."

"How are we supposed to find a stage station in them buttes when we've never been that way before? Leastways, not when we was ridin' slow and lookin' around. Probably once or twice with a posse hot on our heels. But then we didn't have much time to enjoy the scenery."

"Not a problem," the old man said. He looked around the room. Kong had cleared all the tables and returned to the kitchen, where he was likely helping his old parents wash the dishes. Still, Kentucky leaned forward over the table and kept his voice down as he said, "My daughter knows the way."

Slash and Pecos exchanged dubious scowls. They turned back to O'Neil and said at the same time: *"Huh?"*

Chapter 32

Again pitching his voice low with secrecy, Kentucky said, "My daughter's gonna guide you through. I'm gonna stay here and misdirect Clara's riders, tell 'em you headed to Ogallala."

He grinned devilishly and winked. His eyes were glassy from drink. "When they've headed north, I'll head out to meet up with you and Nancy in them buttes along the Platte—if I can still sit a saddle for that long a ride, that is. I used to take Nancy hunting out there, and we'd meet up with those two old scudders at the stage station. Daddy Longlegs would play the fiddle and Casper would dance with Nancy."

The old marshal smiled with fond remembering. "She loved those old coots. We haven't seen 'em in a coon's age. They rarely get to town, and I can't ride out to pay reg'lar visits on 'em no more. I'm assumin' they're still out there. Hell, they didn't have nowhere else to go. But it's a dangerous area. Outlaws like to squat in them buttes till their trails cool before moseyin' on to the Rockies. They'll shoot anything that moves. As the old saw goes, keep a finger on your trigger and one eye on your back trail! Still, though, you got a better chance that way than Ogallala."

Pecos gave a caustic snort and said, "We can't let you do that. Your daughter, fer cryin' in the queen's ale? You loco? You don't want her anywhere near us two old cut-throats!"

"Uh, former cutthroats," Slash corrected him. Turning to Kentucky, he said, "But Pecos is right for once in his life. No can do. We'll take our chances heading north."

The old man smiled that fox-that-ate-the-chicken smile again, hooded his eyes, and shook his head. "Too late. It's already been planned. Nancy is riding out there now. Everybody in town knows she likes to take her mare out on late afternoon horseback rides in the country. Nothin' suspicious about her riding out in the afternoon."

Kentucky glanced out the front window into the street being cloaked now with the long shadows of early evening. "Besides," he said, turning back to Slash and Pecos, "might be more dangerous in town for all three of us."

The old man gave Slash and Pecos a direct look, dark with meaning. If the town didn't already know he'd sent that telegram to the chief U.S. marshal in Denver, it would soon. Clara would soon know that Kentucky had betrayed her. Then none of the O'Neils would be safe here in Harveyville. They'd be sitting on a powder keg with a sizzling fuse growing shorter and shorter.

Slash turned to the old lawman, who looked worn-out and weary despite the drink. "Seems to me you're the only one in Harveyville payin' the price for that stolen gold."

"Clara'll pay. Luther will see to that. Once the feds learn that her father stole that gold and used it to build up his ranch . . . then murdered the three ex-cons who done did their time then came back looking for it . . . she'll have to pay every ounce of that gold back to the government. She'll have to sell the Rimfire. That will gravel that little chili pepper catamount no end. *Hah!*"

He slapped his thigh and lifted his boot and slammed it back down with a *bang!*

"I do worry about Blanchard. But Wayne's tough. I'll warn him to pull out before the feds come, take his savings and head to Mexico. Clara, though—she'll rue the day she ever tangled with Kentucky O'Neil!" He guffawed, then, sobering, added with quiet seriousness, "I shouldn't have done what I did. It's time to do the right thing. Nancy . . . well . . . " Kentucky grimaced, shook his head, and rubbed crumbs from the table with his big arthritic hand. "She feels guilty, too. She wants to do the right thing."

Slash and Pecos shared a dubious glance. The old man was off his rocker, obviously. The daughter, too.

Slash turned to the old man. "Listen, Kentucky—if there is any way we can change your mind, let us know *now*."

Kentucky shook his weathered head. "Too late for mind-changin'. Believe me, Kentucky O'Neil don't want to become some romantic old martyr for justice." He thumbed himself several times in the chest, then smiled. "But I'd pay good money to see the look on Clara's face when she learns that I and Nancy helped you two ride clear of her gunnies, and I detailed the whole thing to Luther Bledsoe!"

Again, he slapped his thigh with glee.

He polished off the last of his beer, rubbed his big mustache with the back of his hand. "Get your horses and light a shuck. Ride north four miles. I'll draw you a map showin' where to swing west and meet Nancy."

He reached into a shirt pocket for a scrap of paper and a pencil, touched the pencil to his tongue, and started sketching a map. Slash looked across the table at his partner.

Pecos shrugged and raised his hands in defeat.

In the hazy orange dusk, Slash and Pecos rode slowly across the short-grass prairie, following the thin, meandering line of an old Indian trail.

"I don't like this, Slash," Pecos said. "I don't like this one bit."

"Me neither, but what're we gonna do? The train's done left the station. Uh, so to *speak.*"

"That old man's off his nut."

"True," Slash said, glancing at the slowly receding bayonet blades of orange sunlight spearing across the dark green sky. "But he's got a guilty conscience. He's tryin' to make up for it, and he's doing the only thing he can think of to do."

"Yeah, an' he wants to spit in Clara Gyllenwater's eye," Pecos added with a snort.

"I don't know. Might be a good plan if the old man ain't totally off his nut. His daughter, too." Slash paused, thoughtful. "Let's play it out. Let's give the old man his reckoning. Tomorrow, we'll get him and his daughter to safety in Julesburg, then head on to Denver. Bledsoe will likely send a good dozen bona fide federals to Harveyville pronto, and Clara Gyllenwater's gonna dance to Uncle Sam's fiddle."

"Won't that be fun?"

They continued westward along a shaggy two-track trail that was apparently the old stage road that had connected Harveyville with Julesburg at one time. The spur line had probably rendered the stage line obsolete, as rail lines often did. It wound off across the desert-like terrain of western Nebraska and eastern Colorado hemmed in on the north and south by low hills carpeted in short grass, prickly pear, and cedar. Gradually, those hills as well as the trail ahead were growing darker and darker, but a full moon had started climbing the eastern horizon over Slash's and Pecos's left shoulders, growing brighter as the hills turned dark.

As the two continued riding, trotting their horses along the uncertain trail, the ever-brightening moon cast a ghostly ambience across the broad, broken land before and around the two former cutthroats—a land of dark shadows relieved by an opalescent murk.

Coyotes yammered distantly by ones and twos. Just as distantly, others answered, their eerie voices echoing, further casting a ghostly spell over this vast and haunted landscape. Owls hooted and night birds gave their occasional cries. Sometimes those cries were followed by a rabbit's pinched scream.

On the heels of one such scream, Pecos sucked a sharp breath and grunted softly, "Damn, life is cruel."

Slash chuckled.

"What's funny?"

"It's taken you this long to realize that?"

"No, I just never mentioned it before." Pecos looked around and gave a little shiver. "Spooky out here—ain't it, Slash?"

Slash peered up a low, steep ridge passing close off his left stirrup to see the two small gold spheres of what could be the eyes of a wildcat flash as the animal blinked, staring down at him. The eyes drew back, growing smaller, dimmer, before the cat retreated into the night's darkening shadows.

Grimacing, Slash turned his head back forward and said through a long sigh, "Gotta admit . . ."

When the two riders had followed the trail into a broad basin that appeared to have been cut long ago by some long-defunct stream, or by a former manifestation of the South Platte River, Pecos said, "How much farther?"

Slash pulled from his coat pocket the scrap of notepaper on which Kentucky had hastily penciled a map, and shook it open, holding it up to the gray light of the moon behind. "Shouldn't be much farther. According to the X on Kentucky's map, the daughter should be holed up on a ridge not far ahead. Look for a low ridge with a big tree on it shaped like the cross on a church's belfry."

"I don't see it."

"Then we keep rid—"

A scream cut him off. A woman's agonized wail.

"What the—" Pecos said as he and Slash followed the source of the scream to a low ridge appearing in the murky moonlight ahead of them now, maybe a hundred yards straight beyond them. Sure enough, the ridge was capped by what appeared to be a church cross—a lightning-mangled cottonwood, which Kentucky had sketched on his map.

To the left of the tree was a small, orange glow. That would be the woman's fire marking her position to Slash and Pecos—and possibly, judging by her scream, unwanted company.

A rifle crashed from the same direction as the woman's scream.

Slash glanced at Pecos. *"Let's go!"*

Leaning forward in their saddles, both men put the steel to their mounts.

They let the horses pick their own way along the trail through the darkness. It was careless to ride this hard in the dark in uncertain terrain, but as former owlhoots who'd been on the run from posses on nights very much like this one, Slash and Pecos were accustomed to the danger. So were their horses, both of which had not lived as long as they had without having been gifted with keen night vision and surefootedness.

Another rifle report crashed out through the darkness. Slash and Pecos saw the orange flashes on the face of the steep ridge before them.

More orange flashes appeared at the very top of the ridge, near where the tree stood, though the fire was no longer visible. Within a hundred feet of the ridge's boulder-strewn base, Slash and Pecos checked their mounts down to skidding halts, shucked their rifles from their scabbards, and leaped out of their saddles while their horses curveted.

As Slash pumped a live round into his Yellowboy's action, a man's voice shouted from the top of the ridge, "Help, pards! Help me, pards!" The man sobbed and in a strangled voice, he continued, "The boy . . . *gut-shot* me— the little fork-tailed catamount!"

His voice, though pain-racked, was crystal clear in the dry, quiet night air.

"We're comin', Vernon!" yelled a voice from the side of the ridge. "Hold on, Vernon!"

"Gut-shot me!" Vernon cried again from the top of the ridge. "Kill 'em both but cut the kid's ears off first in front of his momma!" the wounded man bellowed. Then his voice came again, this time shrill with terror: "No! *No, lady, plea—*"

Slash and Pecos had each taken a knee to stare up the rock- and cedar-strewn ridge, getting the lay of the land as

well as a sense of the trouble. Now, as another rifle cracked
sharply atop the ridge, and Vernon gave a very brief wail,
the two former cutthroats shared a satisfied look.

"So much for Vernon," Slash quipped.

"Nancy O'Neil must have the bark on," Pecos observed.

He gazed up the ridge. He could make out three, possibly four shadowy, vaguely man-shaped forms making their
way up the side of the ridge, wending their way around the
boulders, most of which were the size of small wagons. He
and Slash were thinking the same thing—the cutthroats
had sent one of their own into the woman's camp, maybe
from the backside of the ridge, and Vernon had been given
a pill he couldn't digest for his trouble.

Now the others were approaching the crest from below,
occasionally snapping off shots at the woman firing down
at them from above. All three or four attackers appeared
to have made it about halfway up the ridge; they were scattered roughly fifty feet apart. They were moving slowly,
knowing they had no help on the ridge now that Vernon
was shaking hands with ole Beelzebub.

"Let's go!" Slash said.

There was no reason to talk about it. It was obvious
what was happening and what they had to do about it.

Slash ran up the side of the ridge, pumping his arms and
legs, forgetting his age and suppressing the aches in his
hips and knees. He saw Pecos running up to his right then
angling off across the ridge, away from Slash, intending to
box the three attackers in between him and his partner.

Above, rifles cracked. Bullets *pinged* sharply off rocks.

Roughly five minutes after Slash had started up the
ridge from the bottom, a man-shaped figure came into
view ahead of him, moving up through a gap between two
boulders. Slash stopped, raised the Winchester '73 to his

shoulder, and, breathless, yelled softly, "Turn around and face me, you hyena!"

The man gave a startled grunt and turned around. Slash could see his eyes snapping wide, reflecting the opal moonlight angling in from beneath his hat brim. The man started to raise his own rifle, but Slash drilled him through his chest before he could get his Spencer leveled.

"Thank you," Slash bit out as the man fell back against the side of the ridge with a dull thump and a clatter of his fallen rifle. "I do so hate shootin' a man in the back!"

Chapter 33

Pecos didn't mind shooting a man in the back.

Especially a man attacking a woman and a boy.

The man of topic had just stepped out from behind a boulder maybe ten feet ahead of Slash, turned to face the upslope, jacked a fresh round into his rifle's action, and raised the rifle to his shoulder. He angled the barrel up toward the crest of the ridge.

"No, no, no," Pecos said. The last "no" was drowned by the cannon-like blast of the sawed-off twelve-gauge in his hands.

The only sound his target made was that of breaking wind. The sound was nearly lost beneath the echoing thunder of both wads of buckshot that Pecos had triggered into the man's back. The attacker flew straight up the slope, the flaps of his coat flying out to both sides, and for a second he resembled a bird taking flight.

Or trying to.

A half second later, the force of both barrels of double-ought buck smashed him facedown against the gravelly slope between a wagon-sized boulder and a young cottonwood. His hat flew back off his head to bounce off Pecos's right shoulder then drift on down the moon-silvered declivity behind him.

A hundred feet to Pecos's left, Slash had just gained open ground above the field of boulders. Ahead of him and maybe twenty feet to his right, one of the attackers exploded from a wild berry thicket and raced the last ten feet straight up the ridge. He lifted his chin and howled like a coyote, shouting, "Throw the long gun down, little honey, an' let's get to know each other!"

"Never!" the woman screamed.

Slash stopped in time to see a slender figure appear at the lip of the ridge, swinging a long, slender object out in front of her. The swinging thing connected resoundingly with the head of the attacker just as he gained the crest.

"*Ouff!*" the man cried.

He stopped in mid-stride. He stood on one foot for half a second, then turned slowly to his left. He fell back onto the slope and rolled. His rifle rolled with him, smacking him over and over again. With mute fascination, Slash watched the bouncing man and the bouncing rifle in the silvery moonlight. With each brutal assault of the man's own rifle, the man cried, "Ow! Oh! Ahh! *Damn!*"

The attacker and the rifle piled up together at the base of the thicket from which they'd exploded ten seconds earlier.

The man gave an enraged wail and pushed off the ground. Climbing to his feet, he lifted his chin to peer up the slope, and bellowed, "That there only made me *mad!*"

Slash pumped a cartridge into his Winchester's breech and said, "This here's gonna make you dead."

"Huh?" The attacker leaped around to face Slash, crouching.

Slash shot him and watched him tumble back into the thicket and lie still.

Slash turned to the woman. She was a slender silhouette standing atop the ridge fifty feet above him and to his right.

The lightning-mangled, cross-like cottonwood loomed over her, limned in the light of kindling stars in the vast, black vault of the sky beyond it. As she lowered the rifle in her hands, she turned to face Slash.

Moonlight shone in her hair.

Keeping her voice low, she said, "Mr. Baker?"

"No, but close," Slash said, also keeping his voice down in the quiet night. "I'm Braddock. Are there any more of them, Miss O'Neil?"

As if in succinct answer to Slash's question, a shotgun blasted. It was near enough to make the ground beneath Slash's boots tremble and his ears ache.

Pecos followed up the caroming echoes with: "That there should be the end of 'em."

Strained breathing grew in the darkness of the downslope, as did the heavy tread of a big man. A figure took shape in the downslope darkness and then Pecos stepped into the misty moonlight limning the ridge crest, to Slash's right, holding his shotgun on his right shoulder.

"Miss O'Neil?" he asked.

"Yes?"

"Call me Pecos." He canted his head toward his partner. "He's Slash, in case he ain't already told you. He ain't the talkative sort, so I figure he probably hasn't yet."

The woman turned and stepped back away from the lip of the ridge, saying, "Danny, you can come out now."

Slash and Pecos crested the ridge to the left of the crosslike dead cottonwood. The boy stepped out from behind a nest of shrubs wearing a floppy brimmed hat and with a canvas satchel looped over his right shoulder. He held a pistol in his right hand. He held it low along his right leg. It looked huge in the boy's small hand and hanging down along his slender leg.

The woman held her arms out to him, but he stepped around her and walked over to where a man lay near the still-smoldering ashes of the signal fire. Vernon, most likely.

"Danny," Nancy O'Neil said.

The boy stared down at the dead man. He turned his wide-eyed face to his mother and said, "I shot him, didn't I, Ma?" His eyes widened as he gazed at his mother in silent pleading. "Am I . . . am I . . . *bad* . . . ?"

"Oh, God, no, child!" Nancy hurried over to the boy, drew him close to her, and wrapped her arms around him. "You only shot him to save me!" She pressed his face against her chest and looked over him at Slash and Pecos. Jerking her head to indicate the dead man, she said coldly, flaring her nostrils, "I shot him to finish him. He jumped me from out of the darkness. Danny grabbed my revolver and shot him. That's when the others started racing up the ridge, shooting. I realize it was silly to build that signal fire, but Pa said if I kept it low we should be all right."

Slash and Pecos walked up to her, both men scowling incredulously. Slash shook his head. "I don't understand, ma'am. Why are you out here? With the boy, especially? Why are you doing this?"

"It's not for you, if that's what you're worried about, Mr. Braddock." She looked down at the boy whose face she held fast against her stomach, running her hands soothingly through his wavy red hair. "It's for me. An' Pa. An' my son. It's time I did something useful . . . something right," she said. She turned to Slash and Pecos. "I couldn't leave Danny in town. We have few friends there. We'll have fewer after tonight." She paused, studying the ground, and then her voice turned cold and heavy with meaning as she said, "We'll have none at the Rimfire."

Slash turned to Pecos. "Stay here with them," he said. "I'll fetch our horses. We'd best get a move on before those shots draw even more attention."

Pecos nodded.

Slash turned and tramped back down the slope in the darkness.

Kentucky O'Neil sat on a bench outside his office—*former* office, rather—in Harveyville.

He slowly dribbled chopped tobacco from his ancient hide sack onto the Rizla rolling paper troughed between his arthritic thumb and index finger. When he had the right amount of Durham on the paper, he set the bag on the bench beside him and carefully rolled the paper around the tobacco, adjusting the grains from long habit and by feel. He licked the paper's edge, then sealed the cylinder and twisted it so that it made a compact cylinder, only slightly bent.

Also from long habit, he ran the cylinder from left to right beneath his nose, sniffing it, enjoying the smell of the cured tobacco.

He plucked a match from his shirt pocket, dragged his thumbnail over the sulfur tip. He touched the flaring flame to the end of the cigarette, inhaling deeply. He cast the smoking lucifer into the street, crossed his legs, and leaned back against the mud-brick building's front wall to the left of the door, enjoying the evening.

No, he did not enjoy it, he realized after he'd cast his

gaze up and down the broad main avenue a few times. When he'd first stepped out here after boxing up his belongings inside the office, he'd immediately become aware of a pall hanging over the town. It remained here now. The entire main street was nearly entirely in shadow but with the red and lemon rays of the setting sun painting the uppermost portions of peaked roofs and false façades.

It was a pretty evening—that last twenty minutes or so before the sun slipped down beneath the western horizon and the darkness closed over the town like a heavy wool shroud, and stars kindled. Still, a pall in the form of a sickly yellow-green cloud hovered just above the peaked roofs and false façades, muting the otherwise vibrant colors of the sunset. Kentucky had seen that cloying color before.

Several years ago, a cyclone had thundered toward town from the southeast. It had sounded like a giant freight train, or maybe several giant freight trains combined. It had chugged and roared, chugged and roared, the great tan funnel making a beeline for Harveyville, tearing up trees and brush and sod and even some cows and flinging them toward all horizons. All citizens ran for the cover of ditches and root cellars. At the very last moment before it would have roared through the heart of Harveyville, turning the business district into matchsticks, that great malignant, roaring funnel had jerked to the north, razing only one abandoned honyocker's cabin and an empty stable as well as toppling a windmill and defeathering a few chickens at the town's very edge.

About a half hour before the funnel had poked its rotating white head up above the southeastern horizon, the same sickly yellow-green pall as now had hovered low over the town. Everyone had noticed it and had conferred worriedly in small groups, wondering what it meant. Saloons had closed from lack of business, for the generally good citizens of Harveyville had read the totem, so to speak, and gone home to seek comfort and shelter.

That had happened earlier tonight, as well.

Most of the saloons were closed, though it was only around eight thirty and the grog shops and whores' cribs usually remained open until midnight on weeknights and on weekends until the last drunk had crawled on hands and knees through the last set of batwings. Now, the street was empty. The town looked abandoned.

There was a tightness in the air. It was as though a single finger snap could blow the entire town to smithereens.

Kentucky felt the tension even as he tried to relieve it with his cigarette, which he was trying very hard to smoke leisurely, sitting there on his stoop with his legs crossed. He stared toward the western horizon, trying to find some comfort there in the play of colored bayonet blades of last light slowly mingling and changing hues as the lemon-drop of the sun fell deeper and deeper into the prairie.

Movement on the street's far side attracted his eye.

Mary Kate had just stepped out through the batwings of the Copper Nickel Saloon. She was dressed in another of her homespun, thin, tight frocks that left her shoulders bare and revealed more than a little of her creamy cleavage. She was barefoot, of course, against her father's wishes. Even the blond-haired beauty, the prettiest girl in town, hadn't been able to hold on to the Copper Nickel's clientele until much after seven. That was when Kentucky had seen the last two cowhands stride out of the place, peer nervously toward the southeast, in the direction of the Rimfire, then step quickly into their saddles and gallop out of town to the west and the safety of their bunkhouse.

Mary Kate pushed only one of the Copper Nickel's batwings open, grabbing the door and holding it close against her, almost as though she were making love to it. Holding the door like that, like a lover she couldn't bear to part with, she stepped out onto the boardwalk and cast her own incredulous gaze in the direction of the Rimfire.

She stood there for nearly a minute before her eyes flicked toward Kentucky sitting on the stoop of his former office. The two held each other's gazes for a time. Then Mary Kate slid away from the door, holding it with one hand before releasing it as though reluctantly. She crossed her arms over her breasts, stepped down off the boardwalk, and walked across the street toward Kentucky, her bare feet kicking up little puffs of dust around her ankles.

A breeze lifted, blowing from east to west along the street, picking up Mary Kate's dust and blowing it, humming a little against the building faces, like the first yammering of a building, formidable storm. Mary Kate's blond hair danced across her shoulders in the wind.

"Hello, Kentucky," the girl said as she stepped up onto the stoop fronting the old marshal's former office.

"Mary Kate." Kentucky slid to his right, making room on his scarred bench for the girl. "Light 'n' sit a spell."

"Don't mind if I do. There's a bad wind blowin'."

"Yes."

Mary Kate gave her back to the bench, smoothed her dress across the backs of her thighs, and sat down with a deep, world-weary sigh. She and Kentucky sat there for several minutes, Kentucky smoking his cigarette, Mary Kate leaning back against the wall behind her, crossing her long legs and looking around the street as the fading light continued to fill the street and the breaks between buildings with thick, purple shadows.

Finally, she turned to Kentucky, raising her thin bronze brows. "Is it going to be bad?"

Kentucky took a long puff from his quirley. Blowing out the smoke, he said, "It could be. It's been building for a long time."

Mary Kate turned her head forward, drew another deep breath, and let it out slowly. "Too many secrets."

"Yes."

"She doesn't think anything can hurt her, does she? Miss Clara."

"No. She's like her old man that way." Kentucky hardened his jaws and shook his head. "She just doesn't know when to stop."

"This isn't all because of Collie, is it?"

"No. It's all because of twelve years ago. A simple, stupid mistake that simple, stupid men made, believing they were above the law. I believed *I* was above the law, so I covered for it." Kentucky glanced down at the badge still pinned to his shirt.

Wrinkling his nostrils distastefully, he removed the half-dollar's worth of nickeled tin and tossed it into the street. The badge landed with a thud, lifting dust around it. A first, kindling star reflected dully in its face.

"I lied to this town and to the rules and laws that are supposed to govern men's behavior every time I pinned that badge to my shirt—every damn morning for the past twelve years!"

Mary Kate looked at the badge, then turned to the former lawman, anxiety showing in her eyes. "What's going to happen to this town, Kentucky?"

Kentucky looked at her. "You don't need to worry, Mary

Kate. You may have tumbled for the wrong man, but you're innocent of what happened twelve years ago."

Mary Kate frowned thoughtfully as she stared across the street at the Copper Nickel. "I have a feelin' none of us is innocent of what happened twelve years ago."

Kentucky spread his legs and leaned forward, pressed his hands together between them. "I'm deeply sorry, Mary Kate. I wish I could apologize to every man, woman, and child in this town. I should have stopped it."

Mary Kate slid close to him, rested her head on his shoulder. "You're just a man, Kentucky. No better, no worse than the others."

Kentucky smiled. "That's no excuse."

He turned his head suddenly to the east, frowning. At first, he thought what he'd heard was another building wind gust. He pricked his ears, listening intently.

No. That was no wind gust. The drumming gradually growing louder in the east was from a storm of another kind entirely.

He turned to Mary Kate, who had also heard the galloping horses and sat staring anxiously in the direction of their source. "Thanks for the company, child," Kentucky said, patting the girl's hand, offering a reassuring smile. "It's time for you to get inside now, out of harm's way."

Chapter 34

Kentucky felt a faint lessening of the tension drawing the skin taut between his shoulder blades as Mary Kate pushed through the Copper Nickel's batwings, then closed the inside doors over them. She was off the street and safe now from Clara's jackals.

He'd come to like the saucy girl. She reminded him—maybe too much—of another young lady who'd once worked for Mary Kate's father at the Copper Nickel. A young lady who'd made the same mistake that Mary Kate had in letting herself be duped into falling in love with the savage yet charming Ned Calico.

As the drumming grew quickly louder in the east, where the darkness was nearly complete, Kentucky found himself vaguely wondering whom Clara would have leading her killers now that Blanchard had committed the unpardonable sin of disobeying orders.

Her second-in-command—Ray McInally?

Nah. McInally wasn't the killing sort. He was a warm, genial man—sort of an uncle figure to the younger men on the Rimfire rolls. Oh, he'd likely hang rustlers if he had to, but he wouldn't enjoy it and he'd lose sleep over it.

Ray was a range foreman. Blanchard had been both a cowpuncher and a posse leader who'd done whatever the job had entailed, be it stringing Glidden wire or hanging rustlers from cottonwoods or burning nesters out of their cabins.

He didn't like the grislier aspects of his job, but he'd grown up in cattle country, fighting Indians, and he'd acquired a fatalistic attitude about it. Sometimes, killing was as necessary as blasting a new pond with dynamite.

The thunder grew louder until Kentucky could feel the reverberations of the galloping horses in the floorboards beneath his feet. The gang appeared like a low black cloud at the eastern edge of town. That cloud, filled if not with lightning at least with dark portent, grew quickly as it approached the town's center.

Larger and larger it grew until vagrant light winked off bits and bit chains and belt buckles and cartridge belts and off the butt plates of rifles jutting from saddle scabbards. Closer and closer the malignant horde drew to Kentucky sitting on the jailhouse stoop, his boots fairly bouncing with the reverberations rattling the floorboards beneath them.

As the group came roaring through, thundering past the town marshal's office, Kentucky took note of the lead rider. It was hard to make out much about him in the thickening darkness of the main drag. All Kentucky could really see was that he was mounted on a black-and-white pinto and that he was tall and lean and that he wore a white bandage across his nose. The bandage stood out in the darkness beneath his narrow-brimmed cream Stetson.

And then the entire group had passed from the former lawman's right to his left, their wind still buffeting onto

Kentucky's stoop, rife with the smell of horses, man-sweat, gun oil, leather, and sage. Not even a minute later, they were checking their mounts down on the street in front of the Longhorn Hotel one block east of the marshal's office.

Kentucky rose and stepped to the edge of the stoop, gazing up the street toward the Longhorn. In the post-dusk murk against a periwinkle sky, he watched five men dismount quickly and toss their reins to several of the still-mounted riders. Someone, no doubt the lead rider, said something too quietly for Kentucky's old ears to pick it up, but Kentucky had heard the taut, commanding tone. While the mounted riders shucked rifles from saddle scabbards, cocked them, raised them to their shoulders, and aimed toward the hotel's second floor, the five dismounted men shucked their rifles from saddle boots and cocked them loudly.

Again, the lead rider said something too quietly for Kentucky to hear. Then the five filed up onto the Longhorn's stoop. A latch was tripped. The front door was shoved brusquely open, whining a little on its hinges. All five men filed into the Longhorn's lobby, one after another, spurs jangling, until they were all inside. Kentucky could hear the muffled thunder of the men's boots on the Longhorn's stairs.

Despite the occasional breeze, the night was that quiet.

On the dark street in front of the hotel, the other ten or so riders sat their well-trained, statue-still mounts, aiming their rifles toward the hotel's second story.

A breeze came along the street from the east, as though air currents were disrupted by the storm of men who'd thundered in from the same direction. The wind made a shingle chain squawk, a loose shutter tap; it picked up some dust then dropped it with a slight sprinkling sound. It moaned softly, and then it died.

On the heels of the breeze's death, a loud bang sounded from inside the Longhorn. Men shouted loudly, one whooping crazily.

Kentucky had jumped when the door had been kicked in. He jumped again now as rifles blasted amidst the shouting of the Rimfire riders. They must have capped five or six cartridges apiece before they realized the room was empty.

A man shouted angrily. The fusillade dwindled to silence.

Kentucky shook his head gravely as he stared toward the hotel's second story, where he'd seen the orange flashes in the windows. Some of the bullets had blown out the glass in the windows and thumped into the building or buildings opposite the Longhorn.

"Not here!" a man yelled, his voice hoarse with rage, as there rose the thunder of boots once more on the stairs, descending this time.

The lead rider fairly flew out of the Longhorn's open front door. He stood on the stoop, holding his rifle down low in his right hand. *"They're not here!"* His voice cut like a bayonet blade across the silent night, echoing shrilly.

"Well, where in the hell are they?" growled one of the mounted riders, all of whom had lowered their rifles.

The lead rider stood—a tall, lean, ramrod-straight silhouette—at the edge of the stoop. Seething with silent rage. Finally, he snapped his head toward the marshal's office. He stared toward Kentucky for a full half a minute, Kentucky's insides writhing around like sick snakes.

"Wait here." The leader stepped down off the stoop then swung lithely up onto his pinto's back. The man beside him tossed him his reins, and he leaned forward, booting his horse into a hard gallop toward Kentucky. He reined up abruptly ten feet from the stoop, glaring down from over his white bandage at the old former lawman, who stood squeezing an awning support post in his right hand, feeling the sweat ooze from his palm.

"Where'd they go, old man?" he wailed. "Where'd they go?"

Despite his tension, Kentucky suppressed an urge to smile at this little bulldog's exasperation. Thorn Willis. Local troublemaker who'd been busted from the ranks of most of the outfits in the Panhandle. Now he was not only riding for the Rimfire brand, he improbably appeared to be leading the killers' wing of the bunkhouse.

Well, maybe not so improbably, Kentucky revised his estimation. *Not given who runs the show out there now.*

"If you're talkin' about the federal men," Kentucky said, feigning a casual air, "they headed north."

"You know who I'm talkin' about, you old coot! Did you warn 'em? Did you warn 'em I'd be comin'?"

"Nope."

Kentucky shook his head slowly, suppressing another urge to smile. He wasn't lying. He didn't know Thorn Willis would be coming. In fact, it never would have occurred to him that anyone would have put the hydrophobic little sidewinder in command of gun-hung men. Kentucky looked at the kid's broken, bandaged nose—which was swollen up like a snake that had just eaten a gopher—and wondered if that had something to do with this lowdown miscreant's sudden amazing leap to Rimfire stardom.

Or, more specifically, the man who'd smashed it flat for him.

"You sure?" Thorn Willis asked.

"I'm sure."

"If I find out otherwise, it will not go well for you." As if to prove just how unwell it would go for Kentucky, Willis closed his right hand around the grips of the Russian revolver tied down in its black leather holster on his right thigh. He blinked once, slowly, then opened his badly swollen eyes as wide as they would likely go, which wasn't much.

He reined his horse back into the street, put the steel to it, and galloped back over to the Longhorn, yelling, "Come on, dammit—they're headed north!"

He galloped on past his riders, heading west toward the edge of town. They booted their own mounts after him.

When they were gone, Kentucky stood watching their dust sift darkly in the dark street and listening to the rataplan of the wolfpack's hooves turning just beyond town to follow the old stagecoach trail north toward Ogallala. There was a moon quartering up in the southwest. Kentucky hoped it wouldn't shed enough light to show where Braddock and Baker had turned off the main trail to follow the secondary trail to the west and toward the badlands along the South Platte.

His heart fluttering a little, Kentucky stepped down off the stoop. He turned through the break between his former office and the barbershop and walked back to where his horse, a beefy roan, Old Red, stood saddled and waiting for him, tied to a single cottonwood sapling, which was the only thing except prickly pear growing back here. He needed to get moving before Willis and his marauders returned. No telling when that would be. Hard to tell how savvy they were, but Kentucky thought he'd seen a couple of veteran trackers amongst them—Hought Davis and Archie Mantooth. Old Tom had used both former army trackers more than a few times to track rustlers into the badlands along the Platte.

If anyone could sniff out even well-covered tracks, and knew the ways of hunted men, it would be those two.

Kentucky grabbed his reins from the cottonwood. He turned to his horse and reached up to grab the horn but stopped when something very round and hard was pressed against his back, maybe two inches left of his backbone.

"Not so fast, old man," came a throaty female voice from behind him.

There was the flat ratcheting of a gun hammer being drawn back to full cock.

The voice had been faintly accented.

Facing his stirrup, Kentucky stiffened. "Clara, what in blazes . . . ?"

"Raise your hands and turn around—very slowly."

"Don't worry, that's the only way I *can* move anymore." Raising his hands chest high, Kentucky turned to the pretty girl standing before him. She was dressed all in black— black silk blouse, black leather vest glistening in the moonlight, and black leather, flare-cuffed slacks with silver stitching running down the outside of the legs.

Her high black boots were also stitched in silver. She wore her hair in a thick, black mare's tail down her back. Her lustrous black eyes glistened like twin wells in the moonlight beneath the low-canted brim of her short-crowned Stetson.

She held a pearl-gripped .44 Colt, the barrel snugged taut against the former lawman's bulging belly. She parted her lips to show her perfect, pearl-white teeth.

"I followed my men to town," she said, arching a brow. "How else was I to make sure the job was done properly? Only, it wasn't done properly, was it?"

"Depends on what you mean by 'properly,' Clara."

"Don't get smart with me, you old fool!" Clara spat out, flaring a nostril and curling her upper lip with open disdain. Her black eyes were as cold as two drops of frozen molasses. "You double-crossed me, didn't you? You warned the federal men I was coming for them."

Slowly, Kentucky shook his head, glancing down at the cocked Colt between them. His throat was suddenly very dry. "Of course not."

Clara dipped her left index finger and thumb into a pocket of her skin-tight leather pants and withdrew a sheaf of yellow telegraph flimsies. She held them up and said through a poisonous smile, "Right after Willis and the other men left the Rimfire, a man rode out from town to show me these."

She studied Kentucky's eyes, waiting.

Kentucky looked at the flimsies drooping like the tongues of overheated dogs in Clara's left, gloved hand. A cold stone dropped in his belly. They were, of course, the telegraph flimsies the telegrapher, Warner Flagg, had tapped out to Luther Bledsoe in Denver.

"Look familiar?" the girl asked.

Kentucky drew a deep breath, let it out slowly. "Believe it or not, Clara, I felt I was doing you a favor."

Clara's eyes widened, showing all the white around the two black marbles of her irises. "A favor? A favor? Hah! If you call ruining me a favor, then you might as well call this a favor, too, you old fool!" She rammed the Colt deeper into Kentucky's barrel and hardened her jaws as she said, "Die slow, old man! Die like a dog in the stree—"

"Clara!"

The male voice coming from somewhere behind her stopped her. Clara wheeled as Kentucky saw Wayne Blanchard step up out of the darkness and into the moonlight. As Clara thrust her Colt at him, Blanchard closed his hand over it, wedging the webbed skin between his thumb and index finger between the hammer and the frame. He wrenched the gun from the girl's grip as the hammer dropped against his thumb.

"You *devil!*" Clara screamed.

Mildly, Blanchard said, "Clara, I do apologize." He raised his arm and rammed his clenched right fist across the nub of her left cheek with a soft smacking sound.

Clara moaned as her head whipped to one side and her body tumbled back against Kentucky.

Chapter 35

Keeping his voice low so that the woman and the boy, riding double ahead of them along the narrow trail winding between the bulging bellies of steep bluffs, wouldn't overhear, Pecos said, "You know, Slash, we'd be a lot better off, and they would, too, if they'd let us hightail it on our *own*." He canted his head to indicate Nancy and Danny O'Neil riding maybe fifty feet ahead of them. All that Pecos could see of them was the tail of their horse silvered now and then by stray bands of moonlight filtering over the rock and cactus-tufted buttes.

"Keep your voice down!" Slash reprimanded him, slapping Pecos's stout right shoulder with his hat.

"I did!"

"Keep it lower." Slash glanced at his partner riding just off his left stirrup. "Like the old man," he said just above a whisper, "they're tryin' to do the right thing. And savin' our lives seems to them like about the only right thing they can do right now, after twelve years of doin' the bad thing."

"But they might only get themselves killed!"

Slash cast Pecos a severe look. "We're not gonna let that happen, partner." Slash kept his frank gaze on Pecos and shook his head slowly. "She might not think so," he added, canting his head toward the woman and the boy, "but she's innocent in all this. Just as the boy is. She might've tumbled for Calico, but, hell . . ."

"She was young."

"She was Mary Kate." Slash chuckled under his breath. "At that age, boy, I sure tumbled for some nasty women."

"Hell, you tumbled for nasty women your whole life until Jay!"

Slash shot him a hard, threatening look, which Pecos could barely make out in the moonlight.

"Just sayin'," Pecos said, snickering softly.

He looked around as they came to a break in the bluffs and crossed a dry arroyo. They let their horses pick their way up the opposite bank and then Pecos looked around carefully, noting the ruin of a small stone hut—likely a sheepherder's hut—and turned to Slash, frowning. "You know what, Slash? I think we done been through here before."

"You saw the hut?" Slash smiled. "Yeah. Boy, it was a ways back. One of our first jobs together. We hit the bank in Valentine—way up in the Sand Hills. We traveled by night for three days, so we didn't really know where we were goin'. We were just keepin' that catch party led by that crazy, one-eyed deputy sheriff—what was his name?"

"Pinky Norlatchy."

"Pinky Norlatchy!"

"Shhh!" It was the boy. He'd turned to glare back at the two middle-aged former cutthroats riding behind him and his mother. He pressed two fingers to his pooched lips and said, "This is owlhoot country! I'd think you two'd know how to keep quiet on the owlhoot trail if anyone could—bein' a pair of lowdown dirty bank an' train robbers an' all!"

The boy dipped his chin forthrightly, then turned his head forward.

Slash and Pecos flushed under the whip of the boy's lash.

Pecos turned to Slash and said more quietly this time, "Damn, he was a mean one, ol' Pinky."

"One o' them West Texas rebels turned outlaw himself."

"We spent the night by that sheepherder's hut. Nervous and fidgety. And then it rained."

"Nasty night—I'm surprised we stuck with it all those years," Slash said, just above a whisper so as not to incur the boy's wrath again.

Pecos laughed into his hand. Then Slash did, too. The boy tried to cow them with another look, which of course only made them need to laugh all the harder.

Slash and Pecos never could keep their mouths shut. There were quiet owlhoots and there were loud owlhoots, and he supposed he and Pecos were of the latter variety. Even on the run, they'd always chinned like widow ladies over coffee at temperance meetings. Odd how they'd never gotten caught until old Blecd-'Em-So finally tricked them and ran them down in Colorado. That was only a couple of years ago. Bledsoe had tricked Jay, too—into helping Bledsoe trick Slash and Pecos, but she'd only done her part of the trickery because she'd believed she was saving their lives.

Remembering all that, Slash nearly rode up into the woman and the boy before realizing they'd stopped. He sawed back on the Appaloosa's reins. Pecos did, as well. The boy gave them each a skeptical glance as the woman said, "The cabin's straight ahead, along the river."

"I don't see a light," Pecos said.

Slash checked his timepiece. "It's around eleven. That Daddy Longlegs fella and, and"—he turned to Nancy—"who's the other fella?"

"Casper Dunn."

"Maybe they already turned in."

Nancy removed the leather glove from her right hand and stuck two fingers between her lips. She gave three short whistles followed by one long one. She waited a minute or so and then repeated the signal.

Nothing stirred in the moonlit darkness ahead of them. The only sounds were the soft breeze and the cry of a distant night bird. A large cedar stood roughly a hundred feet straight out ahead of the four-person party, bathed in moonlight, its limbs bobbing slightly in the breeze. It concealed the cabin that apparently lay beyond it, so all Slash could see was the moon-bathed limbs of the cedar and the deep shadows beyond it. To each side and behind, steep buttes rose.

"Hmm," Nancy said.

Slash turned to Nancy. "You an' the boy wait here. We'll check it out."

He glanced at Pecos, and the two dismounted, dropping their reins. Slash shucked his Yellowboy repeater and Pecos swung his sawed-off twelve-gauge around in front of him, wrapping his right hand around the neck and curling his index finger through the trigger guard and over the two eyelash triggers.

He and Slash moved forward, walking about ten feet apart and as quietly as possible. Slash strode around the cedar's left side while Pecos moved around its right side. On the other side of the tree, the pair stopped. Now they were roughly twenty feet apart.

They stood very still, staring at the cabin that lay ahead of them, its front wall in deep shadow. It appeared merely a square box with a slightly peaked, shake-shingled roof. Brush had grown up close around it; a window shutter hung at an angle from a window just left of the door. The window itself was a black rectangle.

Slash and Pecos shared a vaguely incredulous glance, both men silently asking the other: "Abandoned?"

Slash shrugged a shoulder. Pecos did, too, and then, holding the Winchester and the shotgun out in front of them, respectively, they continued forward slowly, crouched over their weapons, ready for the slightest sign that they might be walking into a trap.

They walked up to within twenty feet of the cabin and stopped.

They glanced at each other and then Slash said, "Let's check it out. I'll take the window. You take the door."

They moved toward the cabin. Slash bellied up against it and shoved his rifle through the window, taking a quick look around, half expecting a gun flash and a bullet, keeping his index finger drawn taut against the Winchester's trigger. When he saw no immediate threat amidst the cluttered shadows inside the shack, he glanced at Pecos.

Pecos stepped up onto the board platform fronting the door. There was a crunching sound. Slash winced and turned to his partner, scowling. Pecos's left boot had gone through the platform, which was apparently rotten. Pecos cursed quietly, pulled his foot out, then stepped more gingerly onto the platform and poked his shotgun against the door. It must not have been latched, because it rocked open, old dry hinges squawking like red-winged blackbirds and causing Pecos to wince once more.

If anyone on the lurk here didn't already know they had company, they sure as hell did now.

Pecos stepped inside. As he looked around, Slash covered him and looked around, as well. There wasn't much to see. The cabin was obviously abandoned. Only an iron range and a few sticks of dilapidated furniture remained. There was the cloying odor of rot and mouse droppings.

Pecos turned to Slash, still poking the Yellowboy through the window. "Well, well. Nobody home."

"Uh-huh."

"Let's have a look around the back, make sure we're all alone here before we fetch Miss O'Neil an' the boy."

Pecos stepped back outside, again walking gingerly around the edges of the stoop. He and Slash parted company to walk around opposite sides of the cabin to the back. Out here was a privy and a small pile of moldering firewood. To the east was a small stable and corral, also overgrown with grass and brush. Several cottonwood saplings grew inside the corral off the stable.

The South Platte lay beyond the scattered cottonwoods and cedars. It resembled a black gown covered in flashing sequins. Slash and Pecos could smell the green smell of the water, hear it gurgling against the rocky shoreline beneath the soft rumbling of the breeze.

Between the cabin and the trees and the river lay two low mounds marked with a single pale, upright stone— like a grave marker. In fact, as Slash walked up to it, he saw that it was indeed a grave marker, marking the two mounds of the graves.

"Over here," he said, quietly.

Pecos walked over and stood beside Slash, staring down at the stone in which had been crudely, hastily chiseled: PARDS DADDY LONGLEGS AN KASPER DUN. Below the names and in slightly smaller lettering chiseled unevenly into the stone: KILT BY OWLHOOTS, 1883 OR '4. Footsteps sounded behind Slash and Pecos. They turned to see the woman and the boy walking toward them from around the cabin's east side, the woman saying, "No one's here? They must have pulled out after all this time."

"Oh, they done pulled out, all right," Slash said. He canted his head toward the graves.

The woman walked toward them, her brown dress swishing about her legs. She wore a brown leather vest over the dress, and high-topped riding boots. The moon touched the crown of her man's felt hat. Dead leaves and pebbles crunched beneath hers and the boy's boots as they approached.

Nancy O'Neil stopped and looked down at the graves.

The boy pointed to the stone and sounded out the words as he recited them. When he was finished, he looked up at his mother, wide-eyed.

"I'm not surprised," was all she said. She lifted her head to look around cautiously. "In fact, I'm surprised they held out here for as long as they did. There's a saying that very few men grow old in this country." She turned to Slash and Pecos. "There's still the cabin. I looked inside. Not very comfortable, but . . ." She let her words trail off and shrugged.

Slash shook his head. "It's well hidden, which is why those two old salts likely built it here. But there's too much high ground around it. That'll make it hard to defend if Clara Gyllenwater's men come callin'."

"Probably well known, too," Pecos added. "If her pa's men trailed herds through here, they likely holed up here. Especially with good water nearby for the cattle. I doubt there's many more places like it. They might figure we'd hole up here, too."

"Meaning . . . ?"

"It's a trap," Slash told her. "If we play our cards right, we might be able to make it a trap for Clara's men instead of a trap for us. If they come callin', I mean."

"We'd best figure they will," Pecos said to Slash. "Safest bet."

"Right."

"Meaning?" Nancy asked again, with more emphasis this time.

Slash glanced at Pecos, then returned his gaze to the woman. "Why don't you and the boy go inside and start a fire in the range? We'll make it look like we've taken up residence. Only . . ." He looked around at the buttes humping up sharply around the cabin, easily within a hundred yards of it. "We'll really be up in them buttes."

"High ground," Pecos said.

The boy turned to the woman. "Maybe they ain't as old and raggedy-heeled a pair of old former cutthroats as you thought they were, Momma."

Nancy gasped and turned to the boy, lips pursed in castigation.

Slash and Pecos laughed.

Danny turned to the two old former cutthroats, shrugged, and said, "I, uh . . . meant it as a compliment."

Slash laughed again and tousled the boy's hair.

Chapter 36

"You, uh . . . you an' Clara have a fallin' out, didja, Wayne?" Kentucky asked over the girl falling backward and slack in his arms.

"You could say that." Blanchard stepped forward, crouching and grabbing the girl's left hand. He crouched lower and pulled the girl up and over his right shoulder, and straightened. "I came to try to keep her from getting into any more trouble than she—ah, hell, we—are already in."

Kentucky gave a weak half smile and nodded approvingly. "Wasn't sure you had it in you, Wayne."

"To do the right thing?"

"Nah, I knew you had that. I just never knowed you to hit a girl."

Blanchard grimaced. "It hurt me worse than it hurt her. Let's take her inside and turn the key on her, let her cool off for a bit."

"You're gonna throw Clara Gyllenwater in jail?"

Blanchard smiled. "It's something she can tell her grandkids."

"All right, all right."

Kentucky turned and walked in his bandy-legged

fashion around to the front of his former office. Blanchard followed him inside. Kentucky opened one of the cells, and Blanchard carried her into it and eased her down on the single cot, the girl groaning a little and fluttering her eyes but otherwise not regaining consciousness.

Stepping back out of the cell and quietly latching the door, Blanchard said, "She'll come around in a bit. I just tapped her."

Kentucky was lighting a lamp against the office's nearly complete darkness relieved only by the wan light of the moon angling through the front window. "She's gonna be madder'n an old wet hen."

Blanchard stood in front of Clara's cell, frowning curiously at the old former lawman. "Where are the two federals? I rode in ahead of Thorn Willis's bunch to warn 'em. Since they weren't in their room, I figure they either pulled out on their own or you got to 'em first."

Kentucky nodded as he hung the flickering, fly-flecked lamp from a wire hanging down from the room's low ceiling. He canted his head to his right and said, "They headed west. Nancy an' Danny are leadin' 'em out to the cabin of them two old rascals, Daddy Longlegs and Casper Dunn."

Blanchard scowled, his face coloring. "*Nancy?* An' the *boy?* You sent *them* out there?"

Kentucky flinched, and his face slackened with chagrin. "Well, she wanted to do it. She couldn't leave the boy alone in town. And, well, hell, Wayne—it's likely safer out there than it is in town. Clara got word I sent a telegram to Chief Marshal Bledsoe in Denver, detailing the whole blasted thing."

Blanchard scowled, nodding. "I heard." He chewed his mustache, looking around. "You're right—it's probably safer out in the Bayonet Buttes than it would be here, but I still don't like it."

"Davis an' Mantooth?" Kentucky said through another wince.

"Yeah." Again, Blanchard nibbled his mustache anxiously. "They're the best trackers in the territory, and they're ridin' with Willis tonight."

"I seen 'em. I hadn't figured on them two old rattlesnakes ridin' for Clara tonight, dammit! Hell, I done forgot they was even still around!"

Blanchard turned to the door. "I'm gonna ride out there. I'm gonna exchange my blown mount for a fresh one from the livery barn."

"I was headin' that way, too—we'll ride together!"

Blanchard turned back to the old lawman, scowling skeptically.

Kentucky dipped his chin, and his eyes turned grave with determination. "We're ridin' together, Wayne. I got one more ride in these old bones."

Blanchard thought about it, then drew his mouth corners down, nodding. "All right. I'll fetch a fresh mount and be back in a minute."

When he'd gone, Kentucky turned back to Clara. She was moving around on the cot, moaning, waking up. Kentucky walked over to his desk, opened the bottom drawer on the left, removed his bottle, popped the cork, and took a swig. As he took another, Clara's voice said, "You're gonna need more of a bracer than that if you think you're going to go up against my gun hands, old man."

Kentucky lowered the bottle. She was sitting on the edge of the cot now, her feet on the floor. She held her hand over her chin as she worked her jaws. A welt was blossoming on her left cheek.

Angrily, Kentucky pointed the bottle at her. "You're gonna hang, Clara. Don't you realize that, for the love of God? You can't murder federal men! Even a pair of ex-train-robbing cutthroats!"

But then, he thought, suddenly embarrassed by his self-righteous indignation, hadn't he tried the same thing? He was damned lucky he hadn't succeeded.

Clara gave him an impudent look through the bars. "It's my father's way, old man. That's how he managed to hang on out here as long as he did." She rammed her thumb several times into the hollow between her breasts. "By being the biggest, most vicious wolf in the pack!"

Kentucky took another pull from the bottle and stared at her, shaking his head in amazement. "Beautiful. Beautiful . . . savage . . . and stupid," he said quietly. "You're gonna lose everything because you couldn't let a thing go."

"That's my brother you're talking about. That 'thing' I couldn't let go."

"Don't make me laugh, Clara—you hated Collie as much as or more than all the rest of us who ever knew him did!"

"It doesn't matter." Clara looked at the floor now, her expression growing more pensive than severe but just as resolute. "He was my blood. Blood for blood."

"Yeah, sure enough," the old lawman said with a deep, fateful sigh. "There's gonna be more blood, all right. Some of it's gonna be your ow—" He stopped and turned his head to the window, listening. Hoof thuds sounded in the west, growing steadily louder.

Riders coming fast.

Willis and the rest of Clara's kill posse? Kentucky's heart thudded.

* * *

Blanchard led a saddled blue roan out of the livery barn two blocks east of the marshal's office and on the same side of the street. As he curveted the horse to face him, he slid his Henry repeating rifle into the saddle scabbard. He grabbed the horn, then froze when he, too, heard the soft thunder of several galloping riders.

Blanchard turned to gaze west along Harveyville's dark main thoroughfare. His gut tightened when he saw the shadow of maybe half a dozen riders angling toward the marshal's office, from the front window of which a red lantern light slanted out the window and onto the hitchrack fronting the place.

"No, dammit," Blanchard growled as he watched moonlight and lamplight glint off the gun iron the half-dozen riders were wielding. Then, imagining old Kentucky O'Neil and Clara inside, defenseless, he shouted, "No, dammit— stand down, damn you!"

One of the riders milling in front of the marshal's office shouted, *"Here's a message from Thorn Willis, you double-crossin' old rattlesnake!"*

Guns flashed and roared. A window broke with a shriek of shattering glass.

A woman screamed.

"Clara!"

Blanchard hurried into the saddle, turned the horse west, and booted it into an instant hard run. He shucked his Henry from the scabbard, cocked it one-handed, and raised it to his shoulder in both hands. As he did, he stared in dread as the half-dozen riders fired their own rifles through the adobe building's front window and spindly wooden door.

As the blue roan thundered westward, the jostling shadows of the half-dozen riders growing larger before him, their gun reports louder, he triggered the Henry three times quickly, punching two Rimfire riders from their saddles with pinched yelps.

Another man triggered another round through the window, then turned to Blanchard. He had two pistols in his hands. Both flashed and roared.

A bullet burned across Blanchard's left shoulder. He'd caught the slug just as the horse swerved. Holding both the reins and his rifle, the foreman reached for his saddle horn and missed it. He kicked free of the stirrup as he flew sharply right. He and the horse were side by side, two feet apart, for a half-second before the dark street came up to slam the foreman hard about his head and shoulders.

He rolled as the horse lunged back toward him and then across his path and forward, its rear hooves narrowly missing a decisive encounter with his now-hatless head. He rolled twice, heavily, and came up on his right shoulder to see the marshal's office door burst open from the inside. A bandy-legged, silhouetted figure with a high-crowned Stetson raised a rifle to his shoulder.

Flames lapped from the barrel as the Winchester hiccupped loudly in Kentucky's hands.

The man who'd shot Blanchard had been about to deliver two killing shots to the foreman with both the pistols he'd tracked the foreman to the ground with. Kentucky's bullet slammed into the back of Royle Muldoon's head, throwing his head forward, chin down, his hat falling over his saddle horn. When Muldoon's head came up again,

Blanchard saw the dark, fist-sized exit wound just above the man's right eye. It was a fleeting glimpse, because just then Muldoon's buckskin buck-kicked, tossing its dead rider from its saddle, wheeled, and galloped east along the street, trailing its bridle reins.

Kentucky's rifle spoke twice more, and two more Rimfire riders, momentarily distracted by Blanchard's appearance and apparently dumbstruck by their compatriots' unexpected demises, went flying off of their own whinnying, stutter-stepping mounts.

One of the last two riders—Vick Beecham—landed in the dirt only four feet from where Blanchard lay, near a stock trough on the side of the street opposite the marshal's office. Beecham lay cheek down to the ground, looking at Blanchard and rapidly blinking his eyes. He gritted his teeth as he placed one gloved hand against the ground and rose, straightening his arm. In his quivering left hand, he started to bring his Bisley .44 to bear on Blanchard, who was surprised to find that he'd somehow managed to hold on to his Henry.

He heaved himself up to a sitting position, both his legs curled beneath him. Beecham seemed to be having trouble cocking the Bisley, gritting his teeth with the effort, keeping his cold, frightened, angry gaze on the Rimfire foreman. Blanchard slid his Henry toward him, cocked it, aimed at the man's face, and fired.

The bullet plowed through the man's left eye, exiting his skull from the back and puffing up dust in the street. Beecham sucked a sharp breath as the force of the bullet slammed him over on his back where he lay quivering, dying fast.

Blanchard pumped a fresh round into the Henry's action

and held the rifle in one hand out before him, sliding it left to right, ready for another target. Then he counted the fallen, dark shapes of six unmoving men, and depressed the Henry's hammer. He lowered the rifle and leaned back on his elbows, wincing against the burn in his right shoulder. His belly contracted and expanded quickly as he breathed, sweating.

He inspected the oily darkness of blood oozing from the torn seam of his shirt, then looked up to see Kentucky standing over him, holding his Winchester down along his right leg. Kentucky stared down at him grimly.

"You all right?" the old man asked.

Blanchard winced against the bullet's burn; he remembered the scream just after the shooting had started, and his heart thudded with worry. "Clara . . . ?"

Staring down at him, Kentucky pursed his lips and gave his head a single, slow turn from side to side.

The foreman felt all the air rush out of him, all of his blood pool in his belly. "Ah, hell."

"I was tryin' to get her out of the cell when she took one of the first shots."

Blanchard leaned forward, bowing his head nearly to the street. Grief was like an anvil on his shoulders. "Clara . . . Clara . . . Clara . . ." He choked back a sob then, keeping his head bowed close to the street, and raised his left hand.

Kentucky grabbed the hand with both of his and helped the Rimfire foreman to his feet. Blanchard drew a breath and, holding the Henry in one hand, stepped heavily around Kentucky. He walked across the street slowly, stumbling, like a man walking to his own hanging. He mounted the stoop fronting the marshal's office. He stood in the open doorway, head turned slightly to stare at where the girl lay on the floor, half in and half out of the cell Blanchard and Kentucky had put her in.

Kentucky saw the big foreman's broad shoulders slump.

"Dammit, Clara," Blanchard said, and moved slowly inside.

Chapter 37

"What must you think of me, Mister Braddock?"

Slash turned from where he'd been staring down at the cabin from a niche in the rocks strewn about the top of the bluff. He regarded the woman with one brow arched. She sat leaning against a sandstone shelf a few feet below his position, her legs extended before her, ankles crossed. The boy lay curled up against her, on their shared bedroll, his head concealed by his felt hat.

Slash could hear the tired boy breathing deeply, regularly, dead to the world.

The three of them were perched atop a bluff north of the cabin. Pecos had taken a position in a gulch behind the cabin, just beyond where some passing wayfarer had taken the time to bury the two old salts who'd built and lived in the cabin until owlhoots had apparently punched their tickets.

"A fella shouldn't judge," Slash replied. "Especially a fella such as myself."

"Every man . . . and woman . . . judges."

"Be that as it may."

Slash shrugged and turned to gaze down at the cabin, which sat roughly fifty yards from the base of the bluff.

He had a clean view of it from here, no trees in the way. Still, it was a dark, vaguely square smudge in the clearing to the right of the South Platte. Moonlight trimmed the tops of the bluffs and the trees around the cabin, but deep shadows made it only an inky blotch from his vantage. It couldn't be helped. This was the bluff nearest the cabin, and since he and Pecos and the woman were outnumbered fifteen to three, they needed the advantage of the high ground.

"I brought you here for nothing," Nancy O'Neil continued, apparently in the mood for confession. "You walked into a situation you knew nothing about and killed the son of a powerful man."

"And the brother of a powerful sister," Slash drolly pointed out.

"And the brother of a powerful sister." Absently, Nancy stroked the back of the boy curled up beside her, looking down at him with a mother's love.

Suddenly, she looked up at Slash perched on another shelf slightly above her and the boy. "I wanted you to kill him—Calico."

"I know."

"Do you know what my biggest reason was?"

Slash thought he knew but he thought he'd let her say it. She seemed to need to say it—an airing of the soul, so to speak. He stared at her, holding his rifle in the crook of his arm, waiting. She stared back at him, unblinking, her eyes two dark stones in the pale oval of her face.

"He came back here . . . after twelve years, and he . . ." She averted her gaze to the boy again.

"Didn't give you the time of day," Slash finished for her.

She shook her head. "He stayed at the Copper Nickel. The whole town could hear the revelry . . . Mary Kate laughing . . . Three long days of it. I doubt that he thought one time of me."

When she looked up again, the moonlight shimmered in the two dark stones of her eyes. Slash thought he saw her lips tremble before she sucked the top one under the bottom one, composing herself.

"The boy his?" Slash asked, quietly.

She looked down at the sleeping child again and nodded. She sobbed very softly.

"I know it was silly . . . stupid . . . but when he first arrived in Harveyville, I thought he'd come back for me." She shook her head. "Crazy."

Slash gazed down at her, where she hung her head and seemed to be trying with great difficulty to choke back another sob. Finally, he rose from his perch and, walking carefully on the uneven terrain, holding the rifle out to one side for balance, made his way down to her.

He leaned his rifle against the sandstone wall and sat down beside her. He reached over and took her right hand in his. She didn't react to his ministrations at first. Just when he started to think maybe they were unwanted, she turned to him suddenly. Tears shimmered in her eyes, and then she was in his arms, wrapping her own arms around his back, sobbing quietly against his shoulder until he could feel the wetness of tears through his shirt.

"I was . . . so *lonely!*" she cried.

She had a good, long cry. Slash just held her. He felt awkward. He was not in the business of comforting folks. That had always been Pecos's job. But Pecos wasn't here, and if Slash knew anything at all about women—and he wasn't even sure he'd known this until now—he knew when they needed comforting. And this one sure needed comforting now.

He just held her, tried to rock her from time to time, but she mostly just seemed to want him to hold her and let her cry. So he did.

She lifted her head and pulled it back, clumsily brushing tears from her cheeks. "I guess I just wanted to apologize— that's all. For this whole mess. When I called for help, I was desperate. I felt desperate . . . and angry." She shook her head slowly. "I was thinking only about myself. I wasn't considering anyone else at all. I wasn't considering the gold, and what it would mean if . . ."

"All secrets come out sooner or later. Maybe it's good that one came out now. They can be like slivers. The longer they fester . . ."

She nodded, studying her hands.

"Momma . . . ?" The boy's murmur came softly.

Slash and Nancy turned to him. He was sitting up, his hair in his eyes, looking a little desperate. "Momma . . . can I . . . I gotta . . ." He squeezed his crotch.

Nancy glanced at Slash in question.

"Don't go far, boy. Keep us in sight, all right?"

The boy climbed to his feet, slipped into his boots, and walked across the top of the bluff and out through a key-hole of sorts in the rocks littering the crest of it.

"Not far at all, Danny," Nancy said. Then to Slash, she said, "I'm going to keep an eye on him."

"Like I said, not far," he said as she started off after the boy.

Slash returned to his perch, keeping the rifle low so the light of the westering moon wouldn't reflect off the bluing. He looked around at the moonlight and darkness surrounding the cabin. No movement. He looked toward the rear of the small building. Pecos was keeping himself out of sight.

So far, so—

"Slash!"

Automatically, Slash pumped a cartridge into the Yellow-boy's chamber and raised the rifle to his shoulder but held fire. It had been Pecos who'd called his name in a strangled half-yell, half-whisper from out of the darkness of the slope dropping away before him.

"What in tarnation?" Slash said, pressing his cheek up taut against his Winchester's stock.

He heard the scrape of a boot, the rasp of a strained breath. Then he saw a shadow move on the slope below and to his right—a tall figure moving around from behind a privy-sized and -shaped boulder. Pecos kept coming fast, boots sliding on the steep, gravelly inclination, occasionally dropping to a knee before heaving himself up and continuing to climb, holding his sawed-off in his right hand.

Heart thudding, Slash aimed the Winchester down the slope, sliding the barrel back and forth, looking for a target. Pecos wasn't climbing the bluff for the exercise.

When the big man climbed to within six feet of Slash and dropped to a knee, his face showing the strain of the climb, his breathing wheezing harshly in and out of his lungs, he said, "We had it figured wrong."

He grunted and lowered his head, trying to catch his breath.

"*What?*" Slash said. "Get up here, you big lummox!"

He grabbed Pecos's right arm and pulled the big man on up the slope, aiming the Yellowboy with one hand, still waiting for a target. Pecos swung one long leg over a rock at the edge of the butte crest, then the other, then fell to a knee, pulling Slash down beside him.

"What'd we have figured wrong?" Slash wanted to know.

Pecos shook his head. "We figured they'd come the way we came." Again, he shook his head. "They musta swung around us. They're coming across the damn river!" He turned and thrust his arm toward where the river angled like a giant, pearl snake through the darkness to the southwest.

"Ah, hell!"

Pecos looked around, lower jaw hanging. "Where's the woman?" He looked at Slash. "Where's Nancy an' the boy?"

Slash stared, stricken, toward where the two had disappeared. They'd gone down the slope on the side facing the river!

As if to corroborate Slash's sudden flash of unholy terror, the woman screamed.

The boy's voice came next: "Ow—you brigan'! Leave my mother al—"

The sharp crack of a slap cut the boy off. There was a thud as the child hit the ground, groaning.

"*Danny!*" the woman cried. "Leave him alone, damn—" Her voice was cut off as though by a hand clamped over her mouth.

Slash heaved himself to his feet and started scrambling toward the keyhole through which the mother and son had left the top of the bluff.

He stopped when a man yelled, "Slash Braddock! Melvin Baker! You up there, you two old cutthroats?"

Pecos stopped beside Slash, looked at him, his face drawn with anxiety.

"Come on down here, hands empty an' raised—or we'll cut their throats!"

Again, the boy groaned. Then he said, "Ow—damn you!" There was a sharp crack followed by the boy's injured exclamation again: "*Ow!*"

"Stop—don't hurt him!" Nancy cried, breathless from struggling.

"All right, all right!" Slash said, glancing at Pecos again. He set down the Winchester, then raised his hands shoulder high as he made his way through the keyhole and down the short corridor through the rocks until he stood in the open, the chalky bluff dropping away from him.

Pecos walked up to stand beside him, the bigger man's hands also raised.

Ten or so men stood about twenty feet down the slope before them, spread out three or four feet apart. Eight of them had rifles raised to their shoulders and aimed up the slope at sharp angles. The moonlight silhouetted them, shimmering on their hat brims and reflecting off the actions of their aimed rifles and belt buckles and spurs. It was an eerie scene, the ten men regarding Slash and Pecos like nightmare executioners.

Two of those executioners, standing in the middle of the ten-man line, held Nancy and the boy defensively in front of them, bowie knives snugged up to the sides of the mother's and the son's necks. The night breeze made their hat brims bend and their chaps flap around their denim-clad legs. Nancy's hair slid around her face.

As she gazed up the slope toward Slash and Pecos, she lowered her head and sobbed, "I'm sorry! They grabbed us so quickly!"

"What do you have to be sorry about, pretty lady?" said the man holding her and holding his bowie knife against her neck.

It was the tall, thin man with the bandaged nose and

swollen eyes. His teeth shone whitely in his otherwise shadowed face as he said, "You just spent us a lot of time an' trouble's all. An' a lot of cartridge casings. Cartridges can get expensive." He glanced to a man standing on his left. "Robbie, fetch us a coupla ropes." He turned to Slash and Pecos again. Again, he flashed that white smile. "Gonna have us a necktie party. It's a tradition, don't ya know? Never let it be said folks ain't been properly warned what happens when they cross the Rimfire."

Hanging her head, Nancy sobbed again.

"Let 'em go," Slash said tightly.

The man with the bandaged nose said, "Not until you throw your guns down."

Slash shared another dark glance with Pecos. Pecos bunched one cheek up under his eye. That eye twitched a little, nervously.

Nancy continued to sob as Slash gave a heavy sigh and studied the ten men before him and his partner. There were nine now since one had tramped off down the bluff to fetch ropes off one of the horses apparently tied somewhere nearby, though Slash couldn't see them. Slash looked at the woman hanging her head, sobbing, and then he looked at the boy. Danny stood only belly high to the man standing tall above him, holding the glistening blade against the right side of the boy's neck.

Slash couldn't see the expression on the boy's deeply shadowed face against the moonlit sky, but he could sense the fear trembling through every nerve and muscle in the boy's body.

Slash cursed under his breath. Slowly, he slid his twin Colts from their holsters. He looked at them, shining in his hands, and then he tossed them down the slope. They struck with twin thumps and rolled.

Pecos did the same with his own revolver. He unslung the shotgun from his neck and shoulder, tossed that down the slope, as well.

"Let 'em go now," Pecos said.

Bandaged Nose glanced over his shoulder and yelled, "Robbie, where's them ropes?" He turned back to Slash and Pecos and grinned that toothy, specter-like grin that made Slash feel the devil reach up and tickle his toes.

Chapter 38

"Comin'," said the man fetching the ropes. Slash saw him climbing the slope behind the men lined up facing him and Pecos. Slash switched his gaze back to Bandaged Nose then switched it quickly back to the man climbing the slope, carrying a coiled lariat over each shoulder.

Slash frowned. A vague incredulity turned less and less vague and then turned to a strange, almost surreal optimism. His heart thumped, sending lightning through his nerve endings. The man climbing the slope behind the others, thirty feet away now and closing with each lumbering stride, was not the same one who had gone down to fetch the rope. He was considerably thicker and broader, and he walked with his heavy shoulders bowed.

His hat was high-crowned and broad-brimmed. He carried a Winchester in his right hand.

Keeping his eyes on Slash and Pecos, Bandaged Nose said, "Hurry up, dammit, Robbie—Christ, you're wheezin' like an old man!"

A couple of the others snorted laughs.

"Comin', comin'," "Robbie" wheezed out.

"Robbie" looked up the slope at Slash. He raised the rifle, flaring his fingers out from around the neck of the stock. It was a signal wave. Slash glanced quickly at Pecos, who returned the glance with an enervated, hopeful one of his own.

Pecos had caught the signal, as well. As his own body was tensing, preparing for sudden action, he could sense that of his partner preparing, as well.

Bandaged Nose kept grinning up the slope at Slash and Pecos, saying to the man now within ten feet of him, "You an' Roy loop 'em over their necks and give the ends to me."

"Sure, sure," "Robbie" said.

Suddenly, Bandaged Nose turned to face "Robbie." Slash couldn't see his expression, but he knew the man was scowling suspiciously. He was realizing that the man climbing the slope up behind him and now angling to head right toward him, was not Robbie at all. He'd realized it maybe a hair too soon.

Slash looked at Bandaged Nose's hand. He was holding the knife slightly down and away from Nancy's neck as he kept his gaze on the big man angling toward him, within six feet now.

Slash knew instinctively that he had to make the first move, while that knife was away from Nancy's neck and his gaze was on the big man angling toward him and starting to raise his Winchester.

"Pecos—*now!*" Slash leaped forward. So did Pecos.

Slash struck the ground in front of his Colts, grabbed one, and rolled onto his left side, aiming the revolver at Bandaged Nose's belly.

The gun roared.

Bandaged Nose screamed as he dropped the knife and stumbled backward.

Nancy screamed.

"Down, boy!" Pecos bellowed to Slash's right.

Slash saw the big man with the rifle, formerly known as "Robbie," stop behind the man holding the knife on Danny. Blanchard gave a guttural grunt as he swung his rifle in a broad arc, making an eerie whooshing sound. The rear stock slammed with a savage, crunching thud against the head of the man holding the boy. At nearly the same time, Pecos grabbed the boy out of the now-staggering man's grasp, pulled him down to the ground, and rolled over him protectively.

"*Kentucky—go to work!*" Slash heard Blanchard wail as he threw himself into Nancy, driving the woman to the ground and then shielding her with his body in the same way that Pecos shielded the boy.

Slash spied movement across the shoulder of the slope, maybe fifty feet above him and to his right. A man had just run out from a nest of rocks to drop to a knee and raise a rifle to his shoulder.

Slash dropped belly-down as the rifle in Kentucky O'Neil's hands began lapping flames and roaring. Two of the specterlike killers, whipping their heads and rifles around in confounded shock, reluctant to fire lest they should pink one of their own, yelped loudly as Kentucky's first two bullets punched into them and threw them down the slope over Slash's right shoulder.

Slash raised both of his own Colts and went to work on the rifle-wielding men dancing around him now, bringing their own rifles to bear on the rifleman on the slope above them. Pecos's twelve-gauge gut-shredder thundered twice, making the ground rock, and in the corner of his left eye, Slash saw two of the Rimfire men go flying, tossing their rifles toward the stars.

Staying belly down and below Kentucky's firing line, Slash emptied one Colt and grabbed the other. Resting his right elbow on the ground, he clicked the hammer back and raised the revolver but held fire. All five of the other riders were now down, one just then rolling down the slope, groaning, between Slash and Pecos. Pecos lay belly down to Slash's left, his own Colt smoking in his hand as he, too, looked around for another target.

When the man who'd rolled between Slash and Pecos had piled up at the bottom of the slope, unmoving, silence closed over the side of the bluff.

Smoke wafted like fog in the moonlight.

A man lying twenty feet down the slope from Slash rolled onto his back. He pushed up to a sitting position, and Slash saw the white bandage on his nose.

The man shook his head as though to clear it. "No," he said softly, to no one in particular or to maybe death itself. "No . . . no . . ."

He slumped forward then scrambled madly to his feet and, crouched over the slug Slash had punched through his belly, went running and stumbling off down the slope. He tripped, fell, scrambled to his feet again, and continued running at an angle down the decline.

Both Slash and Pecos swung their revolvers to bear on the man.

"No!" Blanchard yelled where he lay on one shoulder beside Nancy, the moonlight shimmering on the revolver in his hand. "Let me have the honors."

Slash and Pecos watched in silence as the big Rimfire

foreman gained his feet. As he did, Nancy rolled onto her side and gazed up at him, incredulous.

"Wayne?" she said with a bewildered air.

As Blanchard began tramping down the slope toward where Bandaged Nose was still running and sort of mewling like a gut-shot dog, Nancy glanced at Slash. Slash could only shrug and then lie there, propped on an elbow and a hip, and watch Blanchard go after the lone living Rimfire man.

Blanchard didn't have to run to catch up to Bandaged Nose. He caught up to him quite easily when his quarry had dropped to a knee again. As the man tried to rise once more, Blanchard pulled him by his shirt collar, swung him toward him, then hammered a left jab straight against his bandaged nose.

Bandaged Nose gave a shrill, girlish cry and fell backwards, rolling.

Blanchard followed him, caught up to him, grabbed him again, and punched the man's face until there was likely nothing left of it and Bandaged Nose lay unmoving.

"Wayne!"

Nancy clambered to her feet and, holding her skirt high above her ankles, ran down the slope at an angle. She slowed as she approached Blanchard. The big foreman turned toward her, stared down at her.

Nancy took another, tentative step toward him. "Wayne . . ."

Blanchard reached forward with both arms. He wrapped both big, bearlike arms around her and drew her toward him until their silhouettes merged into one.

Danny had been lying where Pecos had pulled him to the ground, curled into a tight ball. Now that ball uncurled and the boy quickly gained his feet. He walked quickly down to where Blanchard was embracing his mother. He stopped ten feet away from them.

"Momma?" Slash heard the boy say in the suddenly surreal silence after the battle. "Is Ned Calico my father?"

Blanchard and Nancy had both turned to him.

They stood in silence for nearly a full minute, staring down at him. Then they exchanged a glance. Blanchard dropped to a knee before the boy.

"Nah," he said, placing his hand on the boy's shoulder. "That outlaw ain't your pa, boy." He thumbed himself in the chest. "I am." He glanced up at Nancy, then returned his gaze to the boy. "And it's time for me to start actin' like it."

He drew the boy toward him and hugged him.

Behind him, Nancy sobbed.

"Ah, hell." Slash just then realized that both Pecos and Kentucky O'Neil were standing near where he still lay on a hip and an elbow on the slope. It was Kentucky who'd spoke. "He still loves her after all these years!"

The old man dug out a handkerchief and blew his nose.

Slash rose to his feet and looked up at Pecos. Pecos stood staring down at the big man and the woman and the boy on the slope below them. Blanchard rose and wrapped one arm around Nancy's shoulders, drawing her close to him again. He drew the boy close to him, too.

"Ah, hell." That time, they were Pecos's words. "Ain't that sweet?"

Slash looked up at his partner to see moonlit tears running down the big man's bearded cheeks.

Slash rammed his right elbow into Pecos's ribs.

Pecos yelped and bellowed, crouched forward, holding his sore ribs. "You wicked old devil—why in the hell did you do that? Come back here and take your whippin', Scratch, you black-hearted demon! *You can run but you can't hide!*"

Epilogue
Horns with the Hide!

"So you two scalawags cleaned up the problem in Harveyville, did you?" asked Luther T. "Bleed-'Em-So" Bledsoe eight days later in his small and cluttered office in the Federal Building in Denver. As usual, a cloud of cigar smoke, so thick that his cotton-haired head was at times lost inside it, hovered around him, thickening and lightening and changing shapes like the reflections inside a kaleidoscope.

Pecos pointed to the envelope that Slash had tossed down in front of the chief marshal. "Slash wrote it all out for you on the train down from Cheyenne. Not that there was all that much to write."

"Oh, hell, you know I can't read Slash's chicken scratch," Bledsoe said, exhaling more smoke through his nostrils. "Even when he doesn't write it three sheets to the wind on a jostling train, which is likely never, it looks like the hieroglyphics left behind by some long-defunct race of savages—illiterate savages, at that!" He tipped his ragged head back inside the smoke cloud and laughed with deep enjoyment.

Slash curled a nostril at the old scudder.

When his laughter had dwindled, Bledsoe waved futilely at the smoke billowing around him, and said, "Just tell it to me nice an' plain. We're off the books here, anyway, so go on—spit it out. What happened?"

As it had turned out, the telegram that Kentucky O'Neil had sent to Bledsoe had never made it beyond the key that the Western Union telegrapher in Harveyville had tapped it out on. Having skimmed the message quickly before sending it, and knowing what damage his sending it would have done to the town, the telegrapher had furtively unplugged the key before he began tapping away on it.

In light of the fact that Clara Gyllenwater was now dead and that the Rimfire, having lost Clara and half its men in one night, was now adrift with neither captain nor anchor, the telegrapher had confessed the sin to Kentucky himself the next day after the battle in the buttes along the South Platte.

The way Slash and Pecos saw it, Bledsoe didn't need to know about anything that Kentucky had confessed in his missive. They'd managed to convince Kentucky of that, too.

Slash said, "In a nutshell, Chief, yep, sure enough—Calico was in town with two of his old boys, an' they was runnin' off their leashes, terrorizin' folks an' such. So we beefed him an' the other two. Mission accomplished."

Bledsoe frowned. "Just like that?"

"Sure enough," Pecos said. "It turned out to be just like Marshal O'Neil's letter to you had said it was. He needed help with Calico; we gave it to him. Killed Calico an' vamoosed."

"Hmmm." Bledsoe tapped the edge of his desk and turned to the calendar hanging under the banjo clock on the wall to his left. "Well, how come, if the job was so cut an' dried, it took you two weeks to hustle your raggedy asses back to Denver?"

Slash hiked his left foot atop his right knee, glanced at Pecos, and grinned. Tapping the side of his boot mounted on his knee, he said, "Well, you remember how before we was so rudely interrupted . . . by *you* . . . Missus Slash Braddock and I was headin' off to Cheyenne for our honeymoon?"

Bledsoe scowled. "You didn't!"

Again, Slash grinned. Pecos grinned, too.

"I sent a telegram to Fort Collins, had Jay meet me an' Pecos in Cheyenne to stomp with our tails up for a week, don't ya know. Sorry for the delay, Chief, but we seen no point in delaying the celebration any longer, since our trip back to Fort Collins was gonna take us through Cheyenne anyway!"

He tapped his boot again.

Bledsoe studied him suspiciously, frowning, then slid his gaze to Pecos sitting in the guest chair to Slash's right. "Say, now I think I heard Miss Langdon talkin' in the hall to one of the other secretaries about her taking the train up to Cheyenne last weekend . . ."

Pecos feigned an innocent look, shrugging. "Hmm."

"Yeah, hmm," Bledsoe said, poking his wet stogie back into his mouth and puffing pensively. He removed the stogie from his mouth and pointed the wet end at Pecos as he said, "You don't go despoiling my sacred secretary now, you big galoot. She's right efficient as well as professional and I fear what might become of her if she gets entangled with the likes of you two old ex-cutthroat scalawags!"

Pecos glanced at Slash, smiling sheepishly. "Ah, hell, Chief, don't you worry your pretty head about it. Miss

Langdon's still as pure as the driven snow. I mean, sure, sure, she an' Jay took the train together up to Cheyenne, where they met me an' Slash. But I assure you, it was a chaste celebration . . ."

"Yeah, very chaste," Slash assured the chief marshal. "It was more like a cultural rendezvous amongst appreciators of fine art and food an' drink. Cheyenne has some very nice little restaurants and art museums these days. You wouldn't think so, but it's kinda become the Paris of—"

"Art, huh?" Bledsoe said, scowling at each man in turn, not buying any of it. "You just mind your p's and q's around my secretary. Don't even think about marryin' that girl, Baker, because she ain't one I can replace. Not that she'd consider it." He looked Pecos up and down, chuckling, then laughing and saying, "Nah, nah—I don't have anything to worry about. Hah! Get out of here, you two old desperadoes. I got work to do. Just keep your schedules open, 'cause I'll likely have more trouble for you to iron out . . . off the books . . . in the very near future!"

King Bledsoe dismissed his minions with a wave of his clawlike hands, then leaned forward against his desk, clearing his throat, opening a folder, picking up an ink pen, and getting back to work, puffing the stogie.

Slash and Pecos rose, smiling with satisfaction at each other. The chief marshal had swallowed their version of events hook, line, and sinker, which is exactly what they'd been hoping for. The way they saw it, when a chief marshal hires a pair of lowdown dirty cutthroats to do his dirty work for him, he has to expect to take the horns with the hide. He had to figure they wouldn't always be particularly honest with him.

In this situation, they figured old Bleed-'Em-So wouldn't

have wanted it any other way. All of the mostly guilty parties in the trouble over in Harveyville were now pushing up daisies. Except for the town and Wayne Blanchard, that is. Most of the town wasn't really responsible for what had happened twelve years ago, anyway, though some of the long-time Harveyvillers might have profited by old Tom Gyllenwater's newfound wealth back then. Not that big of a crime in the grand scheme of things.

As for Wayne Blanchard, he might have led up the party that had murdered Ned Calico and his cohorts in relatively cold blood a few weeks ago. But would the world really miss the likes of Calico, Wheeler, and Stockton?

Hell, no!

Besides, the way Slash and Pecos saw it, brazenly donning the hats of judge and jury if not the black robe and opera hat of an executioner, Blanchard had redeemed himself by having thrown in with Kentucky O'Neil to save Slash's and Pecos's raggedy hind ends in the buttes along the South Platte. And to save Nancy O'Neil and Danny, as well.

As well as by making amends with the lonely woman after twelve long years of obviously loving her from a distance. When Slash and Pecos had left on the train the next day after the final dustup for Ogallala, Nancy, Wayne, and Danny were busy making plans for a big, old-fashioned church wedding complete with a town-wide picnic along a creek.

(Slash had had to smile at that. He knew from recent experience that church weddings complete with town-wide picnics along a creek could be a right joyous affair—once a fella got over the initial jitters, that is.)

Last but not least, Kentucky O'Neil was safely

reinstated—on the dubious "authority" of Slash and Pecos, no less—as Harveyville town marshal.

As for what would happen with the now rudderless Rimfire Ranch, Slash and Pecos figured that sorting out that whole mess was above their pay grades. The county and/or Gyllenwater's relatives and ex-wives could hash that out. The two former cutthroats had been content to board that coach car knowing that Harveyville was just a little better, happier, and more peaceful a place than when they'd first arrived

Of course, there were considerably more folks in the ground, snuggling with snakes, but when it came to hiring cutthroats to do jobs off the federal books, well, you had to take the horns with the hide!

Slash and Pecos filed out of Bledsoe's office and into the outer office, where Miss Abigail Langdon was hammering away on a big, black typewriting machine. As Pecos stepped into her sanctuary behind Slash, the pretty Nordic warrior queen turned toward the big galoot, and a pretty peach flush rose in her alabaster cheeks. As for Pecos, Slash could feel the big man's body temperature climb about ten degrees.

"Um . . . Miss Langdon," Pecos said, holding his hat in his hands. "Could I, uh . . . have a word?"

She arched her pretty, red-gold brows and said in her cool, sultry voice, "A *word,* Mister Baker."

"Yes, a *word.*" Pecos glanced at Slash and said, "Miss Langdon and I would like to have a word."

"A *word?*" Slash asked, skeptically.

"You got it—a *word.*" Pecos gave his partner a dismissive wave not unlike the gesture of dismissal they'd just been awarded by their boss.

Slash snorted and opened the door to the hall, saying, "All right—you got it." He wagged an admonishing finger at his partner. "But just a *word*."

As he shoved the door wider and stepped into the hall, he glanced over his shoulder to see Pecos sweeping Miss Langdon out of her chair, into his arms, bending her over backwards and planting his passionate mouth over hers. The pass did not seem unwarranted. Bledsoe's beautiful secretary gave a sudden laugh as she beamed up at her bold accomplice and wrapped her arms around his neck, returning the kiss in kind.

The former Jaycee Breckenridge stood in the hall before Slash, decked out in her finest silk and velvet burnt-orange traveling gown and orange-and-black, plumed picture hat. She floated up to her new husband, her cheeks dimpling enticingly. "What're you chuckling so devilishly about, you cad?"

"Uh . . ." Slash canted his head back toward the door he'd just closed. "Pecos and Miss Langdon are having a word."

"A word?" Jaycee asked, skeptically. "A word like the words they had for two full days and nights in the Territorial Hotel in Cheyenne?"

Slash winked. "Somethin' like that."

He drew his lovely bride to him and kissed her long and with no little passion.

When they drew apart at last, breathless, Slash offered Jay his arm. "Mrs. Braddock, let's get lunch and a drink and book that room at the Larimore for one more night before heading back to Fort Collins. I don't think Pecos is in any bigger hurry to get back to work than I am. What do you say?"

Jay planted a warm, lingering kiss on his cheek and hooked her arm through his. "All I have to say to that is yes, yes, yes, my dear husband, Slash!"

Off they strode—Mr. and Mrs. Braddock, Slash and Jay—through the dark bowels of the Federal Building and out into the warmth and high-country sunshine of a brand-new life together.

Keep reading for more Johnstone action!

A DEATH VALLEY CHRISTMAS

**From William W. and J.A. Johnstone,
the bestselling masters of the American West,
comes a special holiday entry in the Jensen family
saga. This time, they're risking their lives for peace on
earth—and for a piece of hell called Death Valley . . .**

Ace and Chance Jensen usually spend Christmas at the
Sugarloaf Ranch. But this year, the brothers are heading
to Death Valley to claim Chance's prize in a poker game:
the deed to a silver mine. Sure, the mine is probably
dried up and worthless, but what they don't realize is
that half the deed belongs to a ruthless outlaw named
Foxx, a rich vein of silver hasn't been tapped yet, and
another wealthy mine owner is trying to crush the
competition—by killing every miner in the valley . . .

The Jensen boys didn't plan on a Christmas gunfight.
But when they show up at the mine—and learn that a
charity worker is using the silver to fund an orphanage—
Ace and Chance can't help but get into the holiday spirit.
'Tis the season of giving, after all. But instead of gifts,
they're swapping bullets. And instead of Santa Claus,
there's a surprise visitor coming to town.
A man named Luke Jensen—Ace and Chance's
gunslinging father—and he's here
to spread peace and joy.
With a double-barreled dose of holiday cheer—
gunsmoke.

**A JENSEN CHRISTMAS SHOWDOWN
A JOHNSTONE TRADITION**

Look for A DEATH VALLEY CHRISTMAS, on sale now!

France, December 24, 1917

The raucous strains of a French Christmas carol filled the room as the group of a dozen pilots gathered around a wood-burning stove for warmth on this chilly night. The wine they were consuming—a little on the cheap and sour side, but not too bad—warmed them, as well.

No patrols over no-man's-land and enemy territory tonight, they had been told. As long as the Boche stayed on the ground, so would they.

That respite from death was enough of a reason to celebrate, even if tomorrow were not Christmas Day. Casualties had been high in this squadron. They were high in all the flying squadrons.

War, even that fought high in the clean, clear sky, was a dirty business.

On one side of the room, taking their ease in a pair of armchairs, with their legs stretched out in front of them, two men sat and nursed glasses of wine as they watched the ongoing hilarity of their comrades.

One was a compactly built man with a thin mustache.

He wore the uniform of a major in the United States Army Air Service, part of the Allied Expeditionary Forces under the overall command of General John J. Pershing.

The other man was a lieutenant in the same service, younger, more rangily built than his companion, with dark hair and a friendly, open face.

The major reached down to the floor beside him and rubbed the ears of an unlikely creature to be found on a military aerodrome: a half-grown lion cub. A slightly larger second cub lay on the floor next to the lieutenant's chair.

"It's good to see the men enjoying themselves," the major said in a voice with a fairly heavy French accent. "A man should be able to forget about killing . . . and dying . . . at this time of year. At least for one night."

"Reckon that'll be up to the Huns," the lieutenant replied.

His drawl marked him as a man of the American West.

Until recently, both of these men had been part of the already legendary Escadrille N-124, also known as the Lafayette Escadrille, the unit of the French air force manned by volunteer American pilots. The major had been born in France but had spent a lot of time in the United States, even joining the US Army at one point. He had never lost his accent, though.

The lieutenant, like most of the other pilots, had come over here to France partially because he thought it was the right thing to do—and partially out of a thirst for adventure.

Against the odds, both men had survived numerous combat missions against the German fliers and had shot down a number of enemy planes, enough for both of them to be considered aces. Along with the other American pilots, they had been transferred out of the French air force into an American unit a few months earlier, but the danger had continued. If anything, it had intensified. But they had brought with them their courage and skill—and the two lion cubs named Whiskey and Soda, the squadron's mascots.

The major sipped his wine again and said, "Tomorrow it will be back into Death Valley for us, eh, *mon ami?*"

"Probably," the lieutenant agreed. "I've heard rumors the Boche are planning a big push along this part of the line and are set to go any day now. The brass will want us scouting to see if we can pick up any signs of it." He smiled thinly. "And those fellas in their Flying Circus know that and will be waiting for us."

"Death Valley . . ." the major mused. "How many men have we lost there?"

"Six in the past month," the lieutenant answered bleakly. "I expect that's why they gave the name to that swath of no-man's-land."

The major looked over at him. "There's a place out West in America called Death Valley, isn't there? I've heard of it but never been there."

"Oh, sure," the lieutenant said, nodding. "It's in California. Hottest, driest place you ever saw. As bad as the Sahara, I'll bet, although I haven't been there. The Sahara, I mean. I've been to Death Valley. I even camped there with my dad and uncle and cousins. There's an old family story about the place."

"Really?" the major said. "Is it a good story?" He smiled. "Full of cowboys and shooting, like the other stories I've heard you tell?"

The lieutenant laughed. "Sure. My dad and my uncle were right in the middle of it, and it even happened at Christmastime, too."

The major downed the rest of his wine and reached for the bottle that sat on the small table between the armchairs.

"Well, then, let us hear the tale, Lieutenant. Unless you'd rather listen to more of that atrocious singing . . ."

"No, thanks." The lieutenant scratched the ears of the lion cub Whiskey and went on, "It didn't start in Death Valley. My dad and uncle were farther west, in Los Angeles . . ."

Chapter 1

I'll take two cards," Chance Jensen said.

The man directly opposite him at the table smiled as he dealt the cards. "You must have the makings of a pretty good hand."

"We'll find out, won't we?"

Ace Jensen stood a few feet away, with his back to the bar and his elbows resting on the hardwood. The half-empty mug of beer he'd been nursing sat next to his right elbow.

From where he was, he couldn't see his brother's cards. Chance might have the makings of a good hand, as the other man had said—or he might be bluffing.

With Chance, anything was possible.

Ace and Chance were twins, but not identical. Ace was an inch taller, twenty pounds heavier, and had a rumpled thatch of dark hair under his pushed-back hat. Chance's hair was sand colored. He wore a flat-crowned brown hat that went well with his tan suit, white shirt, and brown ribbon tie. Ace preferred range clothes: jeans and a denim jacket over a faded red bib-front shirt.

Both brothers packed guns. Ace carried a Colt .45 on

his right hip, in a well-worn holster. Chance had a Smith & Wesson in a cross-draw rig under his coat.

They had ridden into the California settlement of Los Angeles earlier today. It was a fast-growing community. The railroad had arrived a few years earlier and brought a lot of new businesses with it.

However, this saloon on the old plaza was a throwback to the days when Los Angeles was a sleepy little hamlet that served the needs of the cattle ranchers in the nearby hills and valleys. The bar wasn't crowded. Customers sat at about half the tables. The poker game in which Chance played was the only one going on.

In one corner, an elderly Mexican sat on a stool and strummed a guitar's strings as he played a quiet tune. A few young women in low-cut gowns drifted around the room, delivering drinks and visiting with the customers.

One of those saloon girls came up on Ace's right side and smiled at him.

"Hello, cowboy," she said. "You look like you could use a drink."

Ace tipped his head toward the beer mug beside his elbow. "Got one."

"Well, you could buy one for me," she suggested.

Ace considered that idea. She was a good-looking girl. Not short, not tall. Dark brown hair that spilled over her shoulders and a short distance down her back. Heart-shaped face. Painted cheeks, but Ace got the impression that they would be rosy even without the paint. Her brown eyes were almost as dark as her hair.

The gown she wore was tight enough and cut low enough to draw any healthy young man's interest. Ace was plenty healthy. He knew all he'd be buying for her was a glass of watered-down tea, but he didn't care. Saloon girls had to earn a living, too.

"Sure," he said. He straightened from his casual pose and turned toward her. "What's your name?"

She cocked her head a little to one side. "They call me Trixie."

"Maybe that's what they call you. I asked what your name is."

She caught her lower lip between straight white teeth and hesitated for a second before saying, "It's Myra. Myra Malone."

"Hello, Myra. I'm glad to meet you." He caught the bartender's eye, slid a coin across the hardwood, and nodded toward the girl. "My name's Ace."

"Maybe that's what they *call* you." Her smile seemed more genuine as her words poked at him.

Ace laughed. "Yeah, I reckon I had that coming. My real name is William Jensen, but I've been called Ace since farther back than I can remember. My brother's name is Benjamin, but he's called Chance. That's him at the poker table, in the brown hat."

"Ace and Chance," Myra repeated. "Your mother must have been a gambler."

"No, but a gambling man raised us. Our mother passed away when we were born. We're twins, although you wouldn't know it to look at us."

Myra's smile dropped off her face.

"Oh, I'm sorry," she said. "Not about you being twins, but about . . . I mean . . ."

"It's all right," Ace told her. "I know what you mean. I'm sorry we never got to know her, but you can't miss what you've never had."

"No, I suppose not."

The bartender put the drink he had poured for Myra on the bar in front of her. His hand swooped over the coin Ace had laid down and made it disappear. Myra picked up the glass and raised it to Ace, who lifted his beer mug in response.

"I'm glad to know you, Ace Jensen—" she began.

She stopped short as a man said in a loud voice, "You bluffed me with a hand like *that?*"

He sounded more surprised than angry.

Ace looked around. Whatever was going on, more than likely Chance was involved in it.

Sure enough, Chance had leaned forward in his chair to rake in the pot from the center of the table. It was a good-sized pile of coins and greenbacks. What looked like a folded piece of paper was mixed in with the money.

The man across the table from him stared at Chance for several seconds, then leaned back in his chair, shook his head, and laughed.

"Well played, young man," he said. "I figured you had at least three of a kind."

"I know," Chance said. "That's what I wanted you to think."

Over at the bar, Ace leaned closer to Myra and said, "Do you know the fella my brother bluffed out of that pot?"

"I do," she said, nodding. "His name is Tom Bellamy."

"He's not the sort who's going to get mad and pull a hideout gun or a knife because he got beat, is he?" Ace set his beer down as he asked the question. His hand moved to hover near the butt of the holstered Colt on his hip.

"I don't think so," Myra said. "If your brother bluffed

him and beat him fair and square, I think Tom's more likely to admire that than to get mad."

The way she said the man's name made Ace feel that she was well-acquainted with him. That was a reasonable assumption, since both of them no doubt spent a lot of time in this saloon.

Chance sorted the greenbacks from the pile, squared them up and tapped them on the table to even them out.

Bellamy said, "You're going to give me a chance to win some of that back, aren't you?"

"My brother and I just got into town earlier and haven't had supper yet," Chance replied. He grinned. "There's enough here to buy us some mighty nice steaks."

"There's more than that."

"Yeah, I know." Chance tucked away the folded money inside his coat. He picked up the folded piece of paper. "When you threw this into the pot, you said it's the deed to a silver mine?"

Bellamy's lean, dark face grew solemn. "That's right. It's up in the Panamint Mountains, over on the western edge of Death Valley. Nothing you'd be interested in, kid."

"I don't know about that," Chance mused as he unfolded the deed and studied it. "I've never owned a silver mine."

Ace listened to this conversation with great interest. Chance was right. Neither of the Jensen brothers had ever owned much of anything other than the clothes on their backs, some good guns, and a pair of good horses.

That was all they needed, because they never stayed in one place for very long. They had been born with the urge to drift. It might wear off one of these days, but until it did, they didn't want anything tying them down.

On the other hand . . . *a silver mine* . . . It was hard to turn down an opportunity like that.

Bellamy spread his hands and shrugged.

"If you're sure," he said. "I still think it's only fair that you give me a chance to win back some of what I lost, though."

"Maybe another time."

Chance folded the deed and put it in his coat pocket with the money. He took off his hat and raked the coins into it. Then he stood up, nodded to the men sitting around the table, and said, "Good game, gentlemen. I enjoyed it."

"You should have," one of the men said. "You 'bout cleaned us all out."

"No hard feelin's, though," another man added. "You're good, kid."

"I had a good teacher," Chance said.

He didn't explain that he and Ace had grown up under the care and tutelage of Ennis "Doc" Monday, a professional gambler who had been in love with their mother and had promised her when she was on her deathbed that he would look after the boys. Doc wasn't their father, not by blood, but he had raised them.

Their real father was someone totally different.

Chance carried the hat over to the bar and set it on the hardwood. The coins inside it clinked.

"You reckon you could turn those into bills for me?" he asked the bartender.

"Sure, I suppose so," the man said. He started digging the coins out of the hat.

Chance turned to Myra and smiled. "Well, hello there. I see you've met my brother."

"That's right, Benjamin," she said.

He frowned at Ace. "You told her our real names?"

"I sort of had to," Ace said. "It was only fair." He didn't explain. Instead, he nodded toward the girl. "This is Miss Myra Malone, sometimes known as Trixie."

"Myra is a much prettier and classier name," Chance said as he took her hand. Ace thought for a second Chance was going to kiss the back of it, but he just clasped it instead. "And as such, it suits you much better."

From the corner of his eye, Ace watched the bartender count the coins and then take some greenbacks out of the till. He didn't have any reason to believe the man might try to cheat them, but it never hurt to be careful.

When they had their money, Chance said, "We were about to get some supper. How would you like to join us, Myra?"

She shook her head and sounded genuinely regretful as she said, "I can't. I have to work the rest of the evening. But I recommend that you go along the street a couple of blocks, turn right, and eat at Howell's Café. The food is good, and it's not terribly expensive."

Chance took his hat back from the bartender, put it on, and pinched the brim as he nodded to her. "Much obliged to you for the suggestion," he said. "Maybe we'll see you again."

"I'm here most of the time," she told them.

The brothers walked out of the saloon. The game had resumed at the table, but Tom Bellamy wasn't playing the next hand, Ace noted as they left. He had gotten up and appeared to be headed toward the bar. Myra looked like she was waiting for him.

None of his business what she did, Ace told himself.

"I like Los Angeles so far," Chance said. "Winning a silver mine and meeting a pretty girl in the same evening! What are the odds?"

"Yeah," Ace said. "I reckon this town is just full of luck."

Chapter 2

Howell's Café turned out to be a frame building with a homey atmosphere inside. Delicious aromas floated in the air. Ace and Chance sat at a table with a blue-checked tablecloth. A waitress with blond braids and dimpled, smiling cheeks came over to take their order.

"We'll have two thick steaks with all the trimmings," Chance told her. "And plenty of coffee."

"I'll tell the cook and then bring you your coffee," she promised.

The Jensen brothers took their hats off and set them aside on the table. Ace said, "Let's see the deed to that mine."

"You heard that conversation, did you?"

"I'm in the habit of keeping an eye—and an ear—on you."

Chance scoffed. "That's right. You have to look out for me, don't you, *big brother*? How many minutes older than me are you? Five?"

"That's enough to make me the responsible one."

Chance looked like he might dispute that. Then he shrugged and said, "It's not worth arguing about." He reached inside his coat, took out the folded paper, and tossed it in front of Ace. "I would have showed it to you, anyway."

Ace picked up the deed. He unfolded it and read everything on it, paying close attention to the description of the mine's location.

"Surprise Canyon," he said. "Ever heard of it?"

Chance shook his head. "No, and I hadn't heard of the Panamint Mountains, either. I'd heard of Death Valley but didn't know there were any mountains there. We've never managed to get over into those parts."

"That's one of the intriguing things about this silver mine, isn't it? It's an excuse to go somewhere we haven't been."

Chance leaned back in his chair and grinned. "Yeah, I thought about that. I also thought about the possibility of that mine making us rich. How would you like that, big brother?"

"I'm not sure I'd know what to do with a lot of money if we had it," Ace replied honestly.

"Oh, I'll bet we could figure it out."

They fell silent for a moment as the blond waitress returned with cups, saucers, and a coffeepot. She filled their cups, then said, "The cook's out now, killing a cow for you boys."

"Tell him to make it a good-sized one," Chance joshed back at her. He had never met a woman he couldn't flirt with. "We're growing lads, you know."

She eyed both of them with appreciation and said, "I'm sure you are." She turned and went back to the counter with a little extra added sway to her hips.

"So, about this mine," Ace said as he tapped the paper with his index finger. "The deed's registered in the land recorder's office in Panamint City. We'll have to figure out how to get there. I suppose when we do, whoever runs the place can tell us exactly where to find the mine." He frowned. "Do you know anything about mining for silver?"

Chance smiled, shook his head, and said, "Not a blessed thing."

"But you think it's going to make us rich."

"I think it *might*. That's what I'm hoping, anyway." Chance spread his hands. "How hard can it be? You dig the ore out of the mine and see if there's any silver in it."

Ace had a hunch the actual process would turn out to be a lot more difficult than that. But first things first, and that meant getting to Panamint City.

A short time later, the blonde returned with big platters filled with steaks, potatoes, greens, and huge fluffy biscuits. She fetched a gravy boat from the counter, added more coffee to their cups, and brought bowls of deep-dish apple pie to round out the meal.

As she was about to leave the table again, Ace asked her, "Do you happen to know how to get to Panamint City?"

"Well, a stagecoach runs between here and there a couple of times a week. You could take it."

Chance said, "There must be a good road, then, if the stage uses it."

"Well, there's a road," the waitress said. "I don't know how good it is. I've never traveled over there myself." She shook her head. "Goodness, it's hot enough here in Los Angeles. I've heard stories about Death Valley. It's hard to even imagine how hot it must be. I've heard some old desert rats say that it's the hottest place they've ever been. The hottest this side of Hades!"

"It's probably not that hot in the mountains that run around the valley, though," Ace said.

"Maybe not, but I'm still all right staying here." The young woman laughed. "I never lost anything in Death Valley!"

Neither had he and Chance, Ace thought, but the likelihood was that they were going there, anyway.

The food was good, as Myra had told them it would be. As they ate, Ace said, "What about Luke?"

"What about him?" Chance replied.

"Well, we wrote him that letter and said we might meet him here in Los Angeles for Christmas . . ."

"*You* wrote him a letter and told him that. Anyway, you sent it, what, six months ago and never heard one word back from him."

"More like five months, I'd say. Maybe a little longer."

Chance snorted. "Which doesn't really change a thing. Anyway, I like Luke, but spending Christmas with him versus claiming a silver mine that could make us tycoons . . . I'm not sure that's really much of a choice."

"He *is* our father," Ace pointed out.

"Yeah, and how many years did we get along just fine without knowing that?"

"He didn't know it, either. Even after we met him, he didn't have any more idea we're related than . . . well, than we did!"

Ace spoke the truth. They had been acquainted with Luke Jensen for several years, but other than having the same last name, they hadn't been aware of any connection. In their wanderings, they had met Smoke Jensen, the famous gunfighter and Luke's younger brother, first. They had even joked about the possibility of being related to somebody as well known as Smoke.

The idea that he was actually their uncle had never entered their heads.

Over time, they had gotten to know Smoke pretty well and had spent time at the Sugarloaf, his ranch in Colorado. They had met Luke, as well as Smoke's adopted younger brother, Matt Jensen; and Smoke's mentor, Preacher, the old mountain man. By then, Ace and Chance had been regarded as good friends and honorary members of the family and had always been welcome at the Sugarloaf, whether it was a holiday or not.

Then, almost a year earlier, at the previous Christmas gathering at Smoke's ranch, Doc Monday had shown up, and the truth had come out at last: Ace and Chance *were* members of the family. Back in the Missouri Ozarks, in the days when the Civil War was erupting to tear the country apart, a young Luke Jensen was in love with the local schoolteacher, Lottie Margrabe. Unknown to Luke, when he went off to enlist and fight the Yankees, Lottie was carrying his children—twin sons.

Life had taken a lot of tortuous twists and turns since then. For many years, Smoke had believed that Luke himself was dead, murdered through treachery during the last days of the war, over a shipment of Confederate gold.

For his part, Luke had used the last name Smith and avoided his family, as he had lived the dangerous life of a bounty hunter, a profession that many folks regarded as disreputable and shameful.

In recent years, some of that had changed. Luke had reunited with his family and had started using the name Jensen again. And then, as much of a surprise to him as it was to them, he'd discovered that he was a father and had a pair of tough, strapping, gun-handy sons. And like him,

Ace and Chance had been born to wander, too. None of them were likely to settle down anytime soon.

Because of that, the idea of getting together to celebrate Christmas in Los Angeles this year had been a shot in the dark. With the holiday only three weeks away, Ace and Chance had planned to tarry here until after the first of the year.

But that was before they had found themselves the owners of a silver mine.

Well, legally, *Chance* was the mine's owner, Ace reminded himself, but the brothers had always shared most things. He figured the mine would be the same. Chance hadn't said anything to make him think otherwise.

Chance took a drink of his coffee and went on, "If you want to wait here until after Christmas, just in case Luke shows up, I don't suppose I'll argue with you. But I have to admit, I don't much like the idea of letting that mine just sit there. Somebody else might move in and claim it. We might have a fight on our hands."

"That's true," Ace admitted. He frowned in thought. "Why do you reckon Bellamy is over here in Los Angeles, playing poker in a saloon, if he's got a silver mine in the mountains?"

"I don't have any idea. Maybe he came to buy supplies and left some fellas there to work the mine while he was gone. I didn't think to ask him. I was more concerned with making him think I had good cards in my hand, instead of no two alike and the highest one the nine of hearts!"

"That's what you bluffed him with?"

"Yeah," Chance said with a smile.

"But . . . I was watching. You bet just about everything we had on that hand."

Chance tapped his coat where he had cached the money and the deed. "And it paid off, didn't it?"

"But if he hadn't folded—"

"We'd have done something else. That's the good thing about living the way we do. Every day's a new adventure, isn't it?"

Ace nodded. "You're right about that."

"So . . . are we going to Death Valley?"

"I reckon we are."

Chance picked up his coffee cup, then raised it, as if he were making a toast.

"To becoming silver tycoons."

"Silver tycoons," Ace repeated. He clinked his cup against his brother's.

Connect with Us

Visit us online at
KensingtonBooks.com
to read more from your favorite authors, see books
by series, view reading group guides, and more.

for sneak peeks, chances to win books and prize packs,
and to share your thoughts with other readers.

facebook.com/kensingtonpublishing
twitter.com/kensingtonbooks

Tell us what you think!

To share your thoughts, submit a review,
or sign up for our eNewsletters, please visit:
KensingtonBooks.com/TellUs.